PRAISE FOR THE *EXECUTIVE SERIES*
by Gary Grossman

EXECUTIVE FORCE

"*Executive Force*, which couldn't be more timely, is as harrowing as it is entertaining—a thrilling race against an ingenious plot to fracture the United States from within. And Scott Roarke is just the hero we need!"

—Joseph Finder, *New York Times* best-selling author of *Judgment* and *The Switch*

EXECUTIVE ACTIONS

"*Executive Actions* is the best political thriller I have read in a long, long time—right up there with the very best of David Baldacci. Gary Grossman has written a masterpiece of suspense, powerfully written and filled with wildly imaginative twists. Get ready to lose yourself in a hell of a story."

—Michael Palmer, *New York Times* best-selling author of *Oath of Office*

"Grossman has done lots of research on everything from political infighting to clandestine military operations.... Holds reader interest right up to the inevitable conclusion."

—*Publishers Weekly*

EXECUTIVE TREASON

"Intricate, taut, and completely mesmerizing, Gary Grossman's thriller *Executive Treason* is a hit! Grossman expertly blends together globe-spanning locations, well-researched technology, finely crafted narrative, and intriguing characters to create a virtuoso tale. Highly recommended."

—Dale Brown, *New York Times* best-selling
author of *The Moscow Offensive*

"As topical as tomorrow's Internet blog…fast-paced, with vivid characters and a plot right off the front pages. Surprises you on every page. A winner."

—Larry Bond, *New York Times* best-selling,
author of *Arctic Gambit*

"More chilling than science fiction. Gary Grossman shows how the media itself can become a weapon of mass destruction. You'll never listen to talk radio again without a shiver going down your spine."

—Gary Goldman, Executive Producer of *Minority Report*
and Screenwriter for *Navy SEALs* and *Total Recall*

EXECUTIVE COMMAND

"Moving at break-neck speed, *Executive Command* is nothing short of sensational. Grossman is a master storyteller who sets you up and delivers. Expertly woven and highly researched. *Executive Command* is not just a great book, it's a riveting experience. So well written, I found myself re-reading sentences seeking a double dose of the fine craft."

—W.G. Griffiths, award-winning and best-selling
author of *Methuselah's Pillar*

EXECUTIVE FORCE

GARY GROSSMAN

DIVERSION BOOKS

Also by Gary Grossman

Executive Actions
Executive Treason
Executive Command

Old Earth
Red Hotel
Superman: Serial To Cereal
Saturday Morning TV

Diversion Books
A Division of Diversion Publishing Corp.
443 Park Avenue South, Suite 1004
New York, NY 10016
www.diversionbooks.com

For more information, email info@diversionbooks.com

First Diversion Books edition August 2018.
Paperback ISBN: 978-1-63576-442-0
eBook ISBN: 978-1-63576-441-3

LSIDB/1808

For Roger Cooper
For all that you've done for me
and so many other writers
you nurtured, mentored, launched, and celebrated
during your phenomenal publishing career.
Thank you.

Coincidences take a lot of planning.
—Malcolm Nance's Law
Malcolm Nance, former U.S. Navy Intelligence Officer
Author, expert, media commentator on terrorism

REAL WORLD NEWS

SEPARATISTS WANT TO BREAK CALIFORNIA APART

A new ballot proposal in California will put an unusual question to voters: Do they want California to be split into three separate states? Under the proposal, California would be divided into California, North California, and South California. It's far from the first attempt to divide a state into smaller states. In California alone, separatists have tried to divide the state more than 200 times. Dissenting pockets in many other states have wanted to free themselves from their government.

JUDGE SHOT OUTSIDE OHIO COURTHOUSE

An Ohio judge was shot outside the Jefferson County Courthouse in Steubenville, about forty miles west of Pittsburgh. Police said they believe the assault was a deliberate attack on the judge.

NORTH KOREA'S HIDDEN SUBMARINE THREAT IS ANOTHER WORRY

The chilling thought of North Korea's submarines firing a nuclear ballistic missile isn't as far-fetched as some might think. Pyongyang has made major advances in submarine warfare in recent years and shown a willingness to use its submarines for offensive military actions.

NEW WEAPONS AMERICA SORELY NEEDS

The secret Naval facility in the Damagundam Reserve Forest, India houses an Extremely Low Frequency base station, built as a global hub for submarine communication. India is only the second country to use ELF for communication purposes after Russia. The United States dismantled its facilities in 2004.

PRINCIPAL CHARACTERS

WASHINGTON, D.C.

Morgan Taylor, President, United States
Admiral James Drivas, Director, National Security Agency, NSA
Jonas Jackson Johnson, Vice President, United States
Cpt Penny Walker, U.S. Army Intelligence Officer
Scott Roarke, U.S. Secret Service
Admiral Walter Conn, Chief Of Naval Operations
John Bernie "Bernsie" Bernstein, White House Chief Of Staff
Vinnie D'Angelo, Central Intelligence Agency Operative
Norman Grigoryan, Secretary, Department Of Homeland Security
Joe Poppiti, White House Press Secretary
Eve Goldman, U.S. Attorney General
Dr. Debra Decapo, CIA Psychologist
Bob Huret, Secretary Of State
Duke Patrick, Speaker Of The House, U.S. Congress
Dr. Holt Yates, National Security Advisor
Robert Mulligan, Director, FBI
General Eddie Pollack, Chairman Joint Chiefs
Roy Bessolo, FBI Agent
Katie Kessler, Senior Advisor To Chief Justice
Duane Parsons, FBI Agent
Jack Evans, Director, Central Intelligence Agency
Leopold Browning, Chief Justice, U.S. Supreme Court

UNITED STATES

Lucas Burke, States' Secessionist Activist
Clay Lindstrom, Political Strategist
Josh Collins, Campaign Worker

THE DEMOCRATIC PEOPLE'S REPUBLIC OF KOREA

Jee Gyuen, Teacher
Chin-wah Lee, Navy Computer Programmer

SOUTH PACIFIC

Cdr Nat Segaloff, Captain, USS Chicago

FRANCE

Le Fantôme, Assassin

ISRAEL

Ira Wurlin, Deputy Director, Mossad

RUSSIA

Col. Mikhail Gladkov, FSB, Federal Security Service

PROLOGUE

The boy was more interested in basketball than history, but the history lesson today would stay with him. So would a new friendship forged at the private school.

Snow covered the outdoor court, which he could see from his seat near the second-floor classroom window. It would be months before it would be warm enough to play outside. The Swiss winters were long and cold and most of his lessons that kept him indoors were long and boring. At least he had his basketball games on his PlayStation and his Doors CDs.

His father had sent him to Krieg-Hegler School to gain a greater sense of the world and also get him out of the way.

Three months earlier, on the first day at the prestigious private school, the headmistress had introduced him to the class. The five-foot-nine sixteen-year-old with short-cropped hair, a Chicago Bulls sweatshirt, Nike trainers, and blue jeans took an empty seat between the daughter of a Portuguese diplomat and a Russian boy who belonged to some oil family. He had no interest in either. He immediately began counting the days toward his return home and his real life. There were 274.

He was registered as Chul Yeoung-Su, the son of an ambassador. Neither his name nor his father's position were accurately reported on the application. But the meaning of his name could have provided a hint. Chul, meaning iron. Yeoung-Su for perpetual, eternity.

Chul Yeoung-Su was only a mediocre student, though it wasn't entirely his fault. Classes were conducted in German and English, and he struggled trying to communicate outside his native language. He often looked down at his shoes while talking and fidgeted uncomfortably.

There was little to do in nearby Koniz, so he did little. He was quiet to a fault, though teachers couldn't quite determine if he was shy, homesick, or a slow starter. The basketball court just outside the grey, fortressed building had been his true escape until the weather turned. There he could pretend to be his hero Michael Jordan and win. Winning would be increasingly important to him.

He was actually an adequate player and proud to have an authentic American-made NBA basketball. However, the few athletic friends he had thought he was too short. So more often than not, they picked Chul Yeoung-Su last.

While most students lived in communal rooms, Yeoung-Su lived near his country's embassy in a flat with a private chef, a driver, a tutor, and a bodyguard. Few friends ever came to visit. That's because he had few friends to invite. His father had also warned him not to be drawn into the influence of Westerners.

So, Chul Yeoung-Su bided his time at Liebefeld Steinhölzli, waiting for greater things to come to him and only occasionally feeling awakened by a school lesson.

"My dear Mr. Yeoung-Su," said his sixty-seven-year-old history professor. Like most days, he looked as rumpled and boring as his tweed jacket and brown pants. "Are you with us today?"

"Yes, sir," Chul Yeoung-Su said.

"Then stay with us," Professor Franz Weber aloofly demanded.

The Krieg-Hegler instructor began again for the sake of the disinterested student.

"Presidents and dictators, fair-minded leaders and despots have armies at their command. Planes, ships, and missiles. Nuclear, chemical, and biological weapons. Today's lecture is not about how mighty governments can employ massive shows of force, but how effective they have been firing a single bullet. What is my point, Mr. Chul Yeoung-Su?"

The question engaged Chul Yeoung-Su, but he was slow to raise his hand. Another student, a seventeen-year-old blond American boy, stood. It was his first day as a transfer student. And on his first day, he took a chance getting noticed.

"Professor, an assassin doesn't wear a uniform. He can blend in, plan, stalk, take his time, and affect world history in ways he might not even understand."

"Correct. What relevant examples can you share with Mr. Chul Yeoung-Su?"

He paused while he thought of two. "The assassination of Abraham Lincoln in the United States. Archduke Ferdinand in Austria," he said confidently.

"Names. We are here to understand the depth of actions!"

The teenager abruptly sat down. All he had were topic sentences from elementary and middle school lessons memorized on Army base classrooms from Germany to Japan and South Korea.

"Anyone?" the bearded professor said impatiently.

No one immediately spoke, but the teacher saw that the first student he queried half-heartedly raised his hand.

"Ah Mr. Chul Yeoung-Su, are you ready to participate?"

"Yes, sir." The very word *assassins* had resonated. In fact, he had a keen interest in this aspect of history.

"Assassins have changed governments and launched political movements. But they're also used to maintain stability. To protect people."

"People or a regime, Mr. Chul Yeoung-Su?"

The boy hesitated. "Both? It depends…"

"Sit down," the officious professor said. "This is not a subject where vapid rhetoric will suffice."

"Professor…" Chul defiantly remained standing.

"Two chances to answer sufficiently, Mr. Chul Yeoung-Su, not three!"

The Swiss professor viewed all his students as rich, spoiled, or disinterested. He loathed them almost as much as they did him. Moreover, he preferred to teach front-forward as the expert in the room. *Enough give and take,* he thought.

"Notes, people." Weber said it in English, German, and finally French. Chul Yeoung-Su sat down.

"Ancient history to modern times, the assassin has proven to be an efficient weapon. His bullets brought on World War I and nearly changed the outcome of World War II."

He stared at the American Army brat as he chronicled the 1914 murder of Austro-Hungary's Archduke Franz Ferdinand and his wife

Sophie in Sarajevo, which launched a chain of events that led to an alliance-entangled Europe and to history's most futile war.

"That's the kind of explanation you should have given," he declared.

He bore down on Chul Yeoung-Su when he lectured about a man named Reinhard Heydrich who was shot in 1942 by Czech partisans on the streets of Prague. "Had Heydrich lived, he very may well have succeeded Hitler by fiat, avoided the delusional dictator's tactical errors, commanded the Third Reich, and avoided defeat."

Weber paused only shake to his head. "Is that news to you, Mr. Yeoung-Su? It was in your reading."

"Yes, sir."

"Yes it was news to you, or yes you read it?"

"I read it, sir."

That and more. What Chul Yeoung-Su knew actually might have impressed the professor. From his readings and beyond. Early assassinations. Caesar's slaying in 44 BC. France's King Henry IV in 1610. The last czar of Russia, Nicholas II, in 1918. And particularly important, the 1895 assassination of Empress Myeongseong, Queen of Korea, by Imperial Japanese Army agents. He knew more than the names. He knew the dates and the importance. Some knowledge he had gained by playing a favorite game on his PlayStation. The rest from conversations at home. Even though it was apparent his professor was not interested in listening to him, he tuned into the relevancy of the class.

Engaged now, Chul Yeoung-Su took detailed notes and added a few of his own. In the characters of his native language he wrote *What if?*

"Who knows what would have happened if America's CIA attempts to assassinate Fidel Castro had been successful?" Professor Weber continued. "Clearly, the assassination of President Kennedy changed the course of history, further fueled the Cold War, and reinforced the United States' hatred of the Soviet Union, which contributed to its commitment to the Vietnam War."

More notes, more ideas. More engagement. Suddenly the sixteen-year-old felt like he was inside his PlayStation, creating an unwritten computer program prompted by real history.

The professor explained how the assassination of Abraham Lincoln prevented the president from carrying out his post-Civil War plans to reunite the country. "Something that still has not fully occurred."

"One bullet," he emphasized. "160 years of ongoing tension, inequality, bitterness, and more political assassinations in America."

Yeoung-Su had never heard the professor better. He wrote furiously, underlining every key detail, drawing lines between causes and effects.

"A bullet in the head of Dominican Republic dictator Rafael Trujillo in 1961. Right wing Hindu nationalist Nathuram Vinayak Godse killing Mahatma Gandhi in India in 1948. Did his death also kill a movement that could have led to peaceful change beyond India? Perhaps the only fortunate thing," Weber explained, "was that Godse was a fellow Hindu, not a Muslim. Had it been otherwise, Asia might have been swept into a holy war."

The teacher pointed to governments and presidents, intelligence agencies and lone wolves. The boy wrote more quickly. *The Austro Hungarian Empire, Germany, the CIA, KGB, John Wilkes Booth, Lee Harvey Oswald, Jan Kubis,* and *Gavrilo Princip.* Some remembered, some noted. And the phrase *The Shot Heard Around the World.*

This history was exciting.

Chul Yeoung-Su's hand ached the faster he wrote, but he couldn't, wouldn't stop.

He looked around the room. The American Army brat was equally caught up in the lecture.

"A weapon and a solution," the professor concluded. "A tool that has expanded and contracted borders, built and destroyed allegiances, eliminated and created leaders. A political act and an act of war that, in the hands of the powerful, can change history. The single assassin with a well-aimed bullet, or an army launching a full-fledged attack. Know your history to see what has really made a difference."

The two-hour class ended with Yeoung-Su remaining in his chair and adding to his notes. He didn't even realize that everyone else had moved onto their next classes. He didn't care. Today's history lesson spoke more to him than anything else he had learned in Koniz.

He leaned back in his chair. He closed his notebook and smiled before getting up and offering an uncharacteristic, "Thank you, Professor," to Franz Weber.

In the hallway, he saw the American was waiting to talk.

"Amazing stuff," he said like a true teenager. "You know, my dad's in the army, and when I think about the money the U.S. spends on the military, they could do a lot better with a few more assassins. Take out the problem early."

Yeoung-Su also came from a military family. A point he didn't share with anyone. "But if you dispatch an assassin, you better be ready to defend yourself," the boy replied.

"I guess so."

The two foreign students stood awkwardly. They'd made a connection in a history class. The rest of the school year might not be that bad after all.

"Want to come back to my place? I've got a shelf full of video games."

"We've got classes," the new kid said.

"Fuck school. Let's play."

"Sure," the American replied. "What do you have?"

"Lots of war stuff, basketball, oh, and *Assassins Creed*."

"Great! By the way, we've never really met. My name is Clay." He extended his hand. "Clay Lindstrom. And you're Yeoung-Su. Chul Yeoung-Su," he said smiling. "Weber made that easy to remember."

They shook.

"And as far as I'm concerned, he should stop picking on you."

"Thank you," Chul Yeoung-Su said, happy to meet a kindred spirit.

The two skipped their next classes.

The third and youngest son of his father, the second-born to his father's second mistress, had a new friend. They headed to Chul's off-campus apartment.

Chul Yeoung-Su wasn't used to having real friends, especially American. He was taught not to trust people. That even extended within his own family to his two older brothers. But he and the American bonded that day, perhaps for life, over talk of assassinations.

• • •

Four years at Krieg-Hegler was enough for Chul Yeoung-Su. He returned home to be reschooled in the traditions of his country and the legacy he was to carry forward.

A decade later, his father made a monumental decision. He passed over his eldest sons as immediate heir. When death came to the patriarch, the favored son, his only legitimate child, not the son of a concubine, ascended to lead his family and his nation as Supreme Leader of the Democratic People's Republic of Korea. North Korea.

No longer hiding behind a pseudonym, he quickly eliminated any threats to his reign—by poisons ingested in food, by bullets to the back of the head, and by target practice for his military. One by one, close relatives disappeared.

Within months he bestowed other titles upon himself beyond Supreme Leader: First Chairman of the National Defense Commission, another name for the head of the government; First Secretary of the Workers' Party, which all government officials belong to; Chairman of the Party's Central Military Commission, and Supreme Commander of the Korean People's Army, the top commander of North Korea's 1.2 million member military. The former Chul Yeoung-Su wondered what Professor Franz Weber would think of him now.

PART ONE

CHAPTER 1

PRESENT DAY
FEBRUARY 12
9:15 P.M.
GREAT BARRINGTON, MA

A rifle cartridge is a minute firework comprised of three distinct sections: The primer, the propellant, and the bullet. It's an amazingly simple device in which a small fire starts an even larger one.

It is safe until a finger begins the journey. This part is strictly mechanical. The shooter pulls a gun's trigger back, a spring mechanism acts like a hammer and hits the firing pin, which strikes the primer at the rear of the cartridge. The primer immediately ignites the propellant through a chemical interaction. The propellant burns, quickly generating gas pressure that drives the bullet forward through the gun barrel. In the case of a sniper rifle, the small-scale missile will exit at upwards of 1,840 mph or roughly 2,700 feet per second. Fast. Supersonic fast. Nearly three times the speed of sound.

On its way to the target, the bullet will begin losing horizontal speed due to aerodynamic drag and will slow to subsonic speed rapidly. However, it never loses its inertia, which is derived from its mass. In the hands of an experienced marksman who aims properly, correctly calculates the distance, and adjusts for prevailing weather conditions, the bullet will do what it was designed for.

The bullet leaving the 6.5 Creedmore Bolt-Action Rifle, marketed as "The Long Range King," took a fraction of a second to travel the distance from ground level in the bushes west of the railroad tracks to Lindsay Cocoran's forehead. She was casually walking with her husband up Railroad Street after having a relaxing dinner at Allium Restaurant and Bar. Walking until she wasn't.

The 0.32 ounce, or 140 grain, copper-jacketed lead bullet instantly erased the mayor of Great Barrington's chance to run for the Massachusetts State House, and perhaps even higher office later. There would be no later for the thirty-three-year-old mother of two.

With the exception of the bullet, everything moved in slow motion. Cocoran's husband couldn't process what had happened. Pedestrians nearby froze. Then it occurred to people that a woman had been shot. They ducked not knowing what else to do. Finally, a teenager on the way to the movie theater up the street had the sense to call 911.

Five minutes later police and paramedics arrived, long past the time when the lone gunman packed up, casually walked to his rented van parked on Main Street, and drove south on Route 7 toward Connecticut.

FIFTEEN MINUTES LATER

"Hello, you're on the air," said the evening radio talk host from a nearby Pittsfield AM station.

"Hi, yes, thanks," the voice said haltingly with a slight Boston accent. "The shooting in Great Barrington tonight has me worried."

"What shooting?" Ross Bagley asked. He sat up in his chair in the small studio.

"Right there on Railroad Street. I just heard about it when I tried to park my car to go to a movie. Police wouldn't let me through."

"An active shooter?" Bagley held up both hands to his producer in the control room as if to say, *check it out.*

"I didn't stick around to find out."

"A mass shooting?"

"No, I think just one. But there were a lot of scared people."

"Have they identified the victim?"

Bagley hadn't been in a local breaking news situation like this in years. He was getting excited.

"I heard from a woman who was at dinner…"

"It happened in a restaurant?"

"No, no on the street. But the woman was near where the mayor was sitting."

"What mayor?"

"The mayor of Great Barrington. The one who was shot."

"God, Charlie, call the police down there," Bagley said on-the-air to his producer. "Get me someone." Then he returned to the caller. "Anything else you picked up?"

"Just my own sense about things." The caller paused. "I'd be afraid to get into politics with this going on."

The assassin smiled to himself as he ended the call on his pay-as-you-go phone, soon tossed to the bottom of the Housatonic River. He had just teased things to come. There would be more.

CHAPTER 2

APRIL 21

Take away the telephone lines, satellite dishes, the paved roads, and the simple French farm houses beyond, the hilltop Brittany town of Dinan appeared museum-perfect right down to their medieval foundations. Thatched roofs had survived stormy winters, and brick-and-mortar walls had stood up to the rampages of time and marauding armies.

It was a perfect place to live; an even better place to hide.

The forty-eight-year-old Frenchman, or the man who successfully posed as a forty-eight-year-old, lived quietly and alone. Neighbors considered him polite, if private. He helped locals when needed, but no one could say they actually knew him. He was just *L'homme sur la route*. The man down the road.

For a simple man, leading a simple country life, he was away fairly often. People speculated that he had money and he liked to travel. Since he didn't mix much, others *up the road* only knew he was away because his small, one bedroom house was dark for more than a day. Sometimes for weeks.

The person who visited him the most was the postman. And even then, only a few times a month. One of those days was today.

The Frenchman heard the mail drop through the front door slot. He turned to the sound and saw a single letter. Feeling no urgency, he continued to sip his coffee and watch the 1970 film *Rider on the Rain.* The French-language mystery, directed by René Clément, starred Charles Bronson, dubbed with an even deeper voice than the American action hero's. It had its taut moments, but from the Frenchman's point of view, it was unrealistic.

After he finished his coffee, he found a good place to pause the film. He slowly rose, walked to the door, and bent to retrieve the letter. Like everything, he examined it methodically.

The name and address were typed, not hand written. His name was correct, as were the road, province, and country. The postmark, eleven-days-old, was from Mexico City. There was no return address.

He brought it back to the kitchen table, poured another cup of coffee brewed through his French press, and returned to the movie. An hour later, after Bronson broke a window and smirked at the film's fadeout, the Frenchman inserted a knife into the upper corner of the letter and slid it across with surgical smoothness.

The letter contained one typed paged with names, job titles, and cities. No further explanation. None was needed from this particular client. He'd never met him. If it was even a *him,* though he suspected as much. There weren't very may *hers* who contracted his services.

He accomplished assignments on his own time and in his own way. As soon as he was finished, and his work was independently confirmed, the second of two deposits was transferred to one of his designated international bank accounts.

Showing no expression, the Frenchman picked up his cell phone, pressed a bank app, then the thumbprint prompt. His account came up. It showed a new deposit. The first half of his payment. He had no doubt about collecting the rest.

NINE DAYS LATER
OMAHA, NEBRASKA

"Welcome sir. Are you a Hertz Gold member?"

"No, and not today, please."

"That's okay." the young female car rental agent replied. "You can sign up online whenever you'd like."

The customer at the Omaha, Nebraska, Hertz desk wouldn't. He had just arrived from Chicago through a circuitous route. His travel was always complex. He began the trip three days earlier in Rennes-Bretagne International Airport, forty-two minutes from his home in Dinan, France. Then Frankfort, onto Calgary, Chicago, and Seattle, before his final leg to Nebraska.

"What do you have in a mid-size?" he asked.

The Hertz agent had a four-door white Chevrolet Malibu available. The man, using a Canadian driver's license and a Best Western Rewards credit card, booked it for two weeks with a return in Omaha. However, he had no intention of returning it to the same airport. He would drop it off without checking in at Bismarck, North Dakota, and get another rental under a different name to drive to Billings, Montana, where he'd take another circuitous route, with no rush, to his next destination.

"License?"

The man handed her a New York State license. She examined the picture and looked at him. Blond, wire frame glasses. Medium height.

"Thank you, Mr. …"

"Zwinchowszki."

She didn't even try to repeat it. It was an unusual name she'd never remember or spell correctly. He was from Brooklyn, New York. His birth date had him at thirty-nine. All she was concerned about was whether it was a match. It was; perfect on an authentic looking, completely functional license. She ran the man's Barclay's credit card, issued in the same name.

It would be the last time this Edward Zwinchowszki would produce or swipe either card. So far he'd made the trip under three different identities. He had more to spare.

CHAPTER 3

THE SAME TIME
10:45 AM PT
LOS ANGELES, CA

From his hotel room overlooking Constellation Boulevard, Scott Roarke peered through his Walmart-bought Steiner Predator 10x42 Binoculars. He focused on an Airbus on its final descent into LAX Runway 25-R; the nearer of the two runways south of the airport and parallel to his hotel. South. He could see a man sitting midway in coach looking back at the buildings. The jet was virtually eye level, less than a mile away.

Roarke shook his head and wrote the number five in a journal. Five on a scale of one-to-five. Five was bad. About in line with every other airport, he thought.

He had already run other soft threat scenarios on LAX, from along the beach and up to a mile out to sea. In every airline's baggage claim area and along Lincoln Boulevard adjacent to LAX on the north side. This survey was gutsier. He successfully checked into a hotel with multiple duffle bags that contained a ready to assemble shoulder-fire missile launcher and missile.

Following 9/11, President George Bush had sent teams of agents and a few savvy screenwriters and novelists to test defenses at potential high-risk targets including malls, government buildings, bridges, tunnels, and airports. This was followed up with practice runs, designed to predict and plan what terrorists themselves might try to pull off. Officially, participants were called the Red Team.

The results were not good then and only incrementally better years later under President Morgan Taylor's watch. But Taylor wanted more information. What could a lone wolf accomplish? The job fell on Roarke, who was completely on his own. If he got caught, he had a *get out of jail card*, but that would only help him if he wasn't shot dead on the spot.

In all, America's online telephone directories listed more than 5,300 people with the name *S. Roarke* or *Scott Roarke*. None of the numbers would ring through to this particular Scott Roarke. Nor would he come up in any simple Google search. A computer hacker might find an extract on a retired Army Special Forces LT. S. Roarke, but no record of any mission.

He wasn't ever officially in Mazar-I Sharif, Beijing, Bahrain, or Moscow. He wasn't even where he was today…officially.

Roarke topped off at six feet. He had bright green eyes, dark brown wavy hair, and a slight scar under his chin. His build could best be described as a swimmer's physique—tight stomach and biceps that pushed at the threads. He could apply convincing muscle when necessary or disarm people he met with his open smile. Recently, he'd used his smile to get into places, and used his physicality to get out quickly.

His field work reinforced one basic, terrible truth. *The attacker has the advantage.*

It was the new world paradigm, contrary to classic military field theory. Simple. Almost elegant. On one hand, a terrorist only needed to focus on a small target to inflict anxiety, fear, and death. A car ramming a crowd of people. A school playground. A supermarket. But there were also high value targets. Big ones. Obvious ones that were always attractive to terrorists. Jumbo jets.

The advantage is all his, he thought again. *And airports were basically indefensible.*

Roarke had thirty pages of notes and lots of names he would turn over to Homeland Security. He also had recommendations. Everything from reinforced glass in the hotel windows adjacent to airports to deploying bomb sniffing dogs at all the neighboring hotels and outside each terminal. Dogs would have stopped him today. But instead, he checked in with a missile.

Los Angeles was Roarke's last stop. Since he began the assignment, he'd only been turned away once by security, and even then, he could have penetrated an initial line of defense. That was along the Hudson River as he approached Indian Point Energy Center, a three-unit nuclear power plant just thirty-six miles north of downtown Manhattan. The facility's website sold it as *Safe, Secure, and Vital.* He had his doubts on all three points.

Roarke had boated up the Hudson toward Peekskill at a good thirty-five mph clip in a rented twenty-four-foot Yamaha 242, hugging the shore near Continental Building Products, then slowing within sight of the nuclear power plant. It was the kind of move that might draw attention. It did. A Coast Guard TPSB, an armor-plated thirty-two-foot Transportable Port Security Boat, equipped with two .50 caliber machine guns and anti-swimmer grenades, came up on him fast from the north. The first warning to turn away was a long, loud blast from the vessel's horn. The second from a PA announcement.

Roarke took the cue, politely waved, and steered toward the center of the river. The Coast Guard crew kept an eye on him until he was beyond Lents Cove. Roarke was happy not to be searched. Stored under a bench seat was an M3E1 Super 'Bazooka' Warthog, perfect for urban warfare up to 1,000 feet. He had an ID, but not a real one. Even his get out of jail card wouldn't spare him hours of questioning.

. . .

That day, and every day over the past five years, Scott Roarke served as an agent of the U.S. Secret Service but without the typical schedule or the usual chain of command. He operated with a straight line from a Spartan subterranean White House office to a much more impressive one upstairs.

Roarke had been on research duty for some months since he helped thwart a terrorist plot to poison waters across the country. His leads took him to Europe and ultimately to Ciudad del Este, Paraguay, reputedly the most dangerous city in the Western Hemisphere.

Since then, it had been quiet. Too quiet for the thirty-seven-year-old agent. Anyone else who'd experienced what he had might have relished a break. Even his girlfriend told him he should enjoy the calm. But calm wasn't something that Scott Roarke trusted. *Calm* was what he saw outside the window of the hotel. *Calm* gave an enemy advantage. Roarke blamed his scars on *calm*.

. . .

For the record, Scott Roarke was a salaried government worker in his fifth year, earning close to the top tier of an OF 612 or SF 171 category employee. However, when necessary, Roarke had other accounts he could tap, payable in Drachmas, Yen, Euros, or other national currencies. All were available when he was on the road—which hadn't been recently.

Roarke had been handpicked to serve the White House, shielded by formidable authority. He was hired on faith and experience. It went back to the time Scott Roarke had saved the life of downed Navy CDR Morgan Taylor after a Soviet-designed SAM-16 surface-to-air missile slammed into one of the General Electric F-11 engines aboard Taylor's F/A-18C jet. It was a less than successful mission over Iraq, followed by a harrowing exfiltration managed by Roarke.

Roarke had been secretly inserted as a member of the Defense Intelligence Agency (DIA), the outfit that both analyzes data amassed by the CIA and is dispatched to do some something about it.

The DIA recruits agents no one talks about, including the agents themselves. Accordingly, Roarke's detailed service record remained classified. Because of his training and skills, he was assigned to a unit identified as Defense Humint Service. In spy jargon, "Humint" stands for human intelligence—the kind of data that is collected by operatives on the ground. He collected more than data when the F-18 went down. He collected the man who would later become President of the United States.

Over the course of the next decade, Morgan Taylor rose in the ranks of politics. Immediately after being elected president, he brought Roarke into the Oval Office and rewarded him for saving his life. *Rewarded* often meant putting Roarke in harm's way.

Scott Roarke became President Morgan Taylor's choice for so-called, or more aptly *never discussed*, special assignments. He was given "unique" Secret Service duties that few people knew beyond the CIA, NSA, and FBI chiefs. Taylor classified Roarke's duties under PD16, short for Presidential Directive 1600, an homage to his Pennsylvania Avenue address.

Lucky me, Roarke thought as he packed up at the hotel. *Lucky me*, he thought as he headed to his last stops—a few personal, and a few professional, and very much off the books.

THE OVAL OFFICE
THE SAME TIME

President Morgan Taylor had survived domestic political battles sometimes more demanding than his military service. He lost an election that was rigged to put a Russian sleeper cell candidate in the White House. The spy was killed in a battle under the rotunda minutes before being sworn in. The circumstances of his death were sealed, with the president's hope that they would never see the light of day. In the disorder that followed, the vice president-elect was sworn in as president. His first act was to draft Taylor, from the opposition party, to be his veep, creating havoc within the party, but providing a solid coalition government for the country.

A short while later, the vice president stepped down, which elevated the unelected Morgan Taylor to president again.

As if that wasn't enough, terrorists targeted Air Force One. Taylor's training as a fighter pilot saved his life when he successfully brought the plane down in the Pacific.

He was hailed a hero. The press surely considered him that, but behind Morgan Taylor's public exploits was another hero, the very private Secret Service agent, Scott Roarke.

Taylor, now fifty-six, was a year into his second term and anything but a lame duck. His domestic policy actively focused on rebuilding America's infrastructure, especially after recent terrorist threats to the nation's water supplies. His foreign policy was staunchly defense driven, not a surprise considering his own military background. And on Capitol Hill, he battled opposing Congressional leadership led by his principal rival and obstructionist, Speaker of the House, Duke Patrick.

Patrick wanted Taylor's job. The press knew it, the party knew it. He was a popular Democrat but far from having the temperament or the qualifications of the sitting president. Not that that was always a measure of the job.

The stormy political future was further clouded by concern that Taylor's vice president, also not elected, wasn't likely to engage voters. Jonas Jackson Johnson was a true patriot, a battle-tested four-star general, but all business and little personality. While he could lead the country and successfully represent the United States to the world, he probably wouldn't win the hearts and minds of the voters.

Today, things were relatively quiet by standards of the new normal. *Tomorrow?* The president relied on the intelligence community and its ability to make accurate intelligent assessments.

All of this was front-of-mind as he got the President's Daily Briefing from his Director of National Intelligence, Dr. Holt Yates. Yates culled intel from the CIA, the DIA (Defense Intelligence Agency), the NSA (National Security Agency), and the FBI. The PDB was on Taylor's calendar, every day, 365 days a year, at 0645.

Joining Yates for the early morning meeting were FBI Director Robert Mulligan, CIA Director Jack Evans, and the president's chief of staff, John Bernie Bernstein or *Bernsie* to everyone in the White House.

The president wore his preferred brown turtleneck, khakis, and a Navy flight jacket. Invariably, his Brooks Brothers suits came out later in the day. He looked presidential in both outfits.

Taylor was known for keeping his expressions right at mid-point. Never over the top, never invisible. But his measured manner never reflected any lack of engagement. He was probably the most engaged president in decades, knowledgeable in diplomacy as much as warfare, and conversant in tax law, health care, and climate issues. As ex-military, he supported defense spending with equal concern for domestic programs. Morgan Taylor was a throwback to an old Rockefeller Republican mold, with a Lyndon Johnson Democrat facility for serious arm twisting.

He had a chiseled chin, perfect white teeth, conservative tortoise shell glasses that framed his hazel eyes, and steel gray granite hair that he finally grew longer than service length. To stay at 190 pounds, he exercised daily, and despite the consternation of his doctors and the Secret Service, Morgan Taylor remained current in the cockpit of almost everything the Navy had in the air.

"Best to worst, let's have it," Taylor said beginning the session.

"Russian troops building up in the Baltic," Yates, the former Stanford academician and resident strategist, began. He gave the details of the troop strength.

"What have we heard from Moscow?"

"Publicly nothing. Privately, it was essentially, 'Stay the fuck away.' Conveyed with a smile by an assistant attaché. Knowing it would mean nothing."

"Then forget the back channel. Bring Bob in the loop."

There were a number of Bob's and Robert's in Taylor's government. This Bob was Secretary of State Bob Huret.

"Yes sir."

"More, Holt?"

"Always. China. One of our ocean gliders picked up more mines being deployed around their latest instant Spratly Island. They're dropping them fast. The Navy has left a channel open, but the UUV's (unmanned underwater vehicles) show a lot of activity. They know we know, but they haven't seized this one."

"Yet," the vice president noted. "The *Carl Vinson* is two days out. We could—"

"Do it. Park the carrier battle group at twenty-five nautical miles." The battle group consisted of the carrier, the *USS Carl Vinson*, designated CVN-70, and its support, Carrier Air Wing Seventeen, the Ticonderoga-class cruisers *USS Bunker Hill* (CG-52) and *USS Lake Champlain* (CG-57), and ships of Destroyer Squadron 1, plus nuclear subs that stealthily tag along.

"Tickling the tiger?" the chief of staff asked. Bernsie looked worried.

"In a manner of speaking," the president said. "Borrowing from the parable of 'The Tiger and the Fox.'"

"The what?" Bernsie asked.

Morgan Taylor explained. "A Chinese fable. Once a fox met a terrible and ferocious tiger. The tiger extended his claws, ready to pounce, and enjoy a succulent dinner. But as the tiger prepared to devour him, the sly fox said, 'Dear sir. You must not consider yourself the only king of the beasts. Your courage pales in comparison to mine. So let us walk down the road, with me leading the way. You shall see that men who gaze upon us shall not fear me, for if they did, then I may be your dinner as you intended.'

"The tiger willingly agreed," Taylor continued. "The fox led him. The men saw the tiger in the back and, frightened, ran away. The tiger, not as smart as the fox, thought that indeed the fox had scared the people.

"The fox said, 'So they fled when they saw me. I am the fiercest.' With that, the tiger turned tail acknowledging that the fox was the most formidable."

"But it was a trick," Bernsie replied.

"With potential political rewards."

"And we're the fox," the chief of staff noted.

"Quite so. Let's see how it goes."

Next on the agenda, a valuable ISIS internet intercept, an Afghan smuggling operation using military transports, and the never-ending underwater game in the Pacific, specifically North Korea's increasing emphasis on expanding its *Gorea*-class submarine strength.

Taylor had no fables to cover these issues.

"Status of each, Jack?"

The president now addressed CIA chief Jack Evans. Evans was a spy by desire, from the time he picked the lock to his sister's diary as a kid, to the dangerous clandestine assignments he carried out for the U.S. Out of the field now for some twenty years, he had the job of protecting his assets and their secrets. Since taking the desk job he had gone bald and didn't mind. It made him look all the tougher to his equals in Russia, Israel, and England. It was a toughness he could also back up.

"We're sussing out the information on North Korea's submarine fleet. Small violations. Others we're trying to confirm. CDR Nat Segaloff is on point for us. He commands the *Chicago*."

"Good man," the president said, fully aware of the US Navy commander's distinguished career as a submariner.

"Absolutely, the only problem…" The CIA director continued.

"Yes, Jack?" the president asked with a raised eyebrow.

"The new *Gorea*s haven't been playing by the old rules."

As president and a former Navy commander, Taylor knew the old rules. Mostly underwater tag. But this was different.

"What's changed, Jim?"

His question was for the newly installed NSA Director, Admiral James Drivas.

"We don't know sir," the career officer said. "They could just be trying to spook us. But whatever they're up to, I don't like it."

"Stay on it, Admiral."

"Yes, sir."

Dr. Yates resumed the morning briefing from the intelligence side, coming to no conclusions and no immediate decision points. With the international slate cleared, Morgan Taylor called on FBI Director Robert Mulligan to review domestic issues. Chief among them, reports on busting a domestic terrorist cell in Baltimore, another investigation into money laundering through a Manhattan high rise project, and the seizure of five hundred assault rifles during a routine stop of a semi on Interstate 70 outside of Denver.

"Anything else critical?" President Taylor asked almost sarcastically.

"Not today. There's always tomorrow," Director Mulligan replied.

All in all, there really was no best-to-worse. It all looked bad. A typical day for the government of the United States and President Morgan Taylor.

CHAPTER 4

After dropping off a contraband shoulder-fired missile launcher to the very surprised Alcohol, Tobacco, and Firearms LA Field Division Chief in Glendale, Scott Roarke drove through his old Los Angeles San Fernando Valley neighborhood. This was where he and his father had lived after moving west following his mother's death. This was where his life changed again.

The thirty-minute drive from Glendale to Reseda gave him time to think about the intersects of his past and present. Actually, it was more about being caught in the crosshairs than any intersect.

A young, troubled Scott Roarke was nailed by an LAPD officer in his dreadful attempt to rob a convenience store. The cop spotted him at the exit. The arrest took seconds. He cuffed the teen, loaded him in his squad car, and gave Roarke time to stew. And then a choice: Jail and disappointing his father or getting off the streets and making something of his life.

Roarke wisely chose the latter. The cop enrolled him in a Taekwondo class with a Los Angeles master and later got him involved in a teen police program. Roarke never looked back and never disappointed the officer or his father.

Today he'd pay a respectful visit, pulling weeds from their gravesites and thanking them both for the gifts of life they gave him. After, to lift his spirits, he stopped off at Chablis Food and Wine in Tarzana. The European/American bistro was a favorite haunt and the owner, Saeed, was a long-time friend. Saeed brought Roarke news of his neighborhood. Stories of the old guard leaving or dying. Families moving in. Restaurants that came and went. Private schools popping up. And people actually taking mass transit in Los Angeles.

Scott talked around, rather than about his life, but Saeed suspected where the young Scott Roarke's career had taken him. That's why when they finished, Roarke left with a warm hug and the warning to be careful.

Thirty minutes later, the advice fresh on his mind, Roarke drove to a store in downtown LA. He had a special purchase to make.

CHAPTER 5

YUKTAE-DONG, DEMOCRATIC PEOPLE'S REPUBLIC OF KOREA
EIGHTEEN MONTHS EARLIER

Chin-wah Lee waited. Like he always had to. For things to work. For new software keys. For more quantum encryption tests. For quantum encryption that worked better. For the newest supervisor to learn his fucking job. For that newest supervisor to leave him alone. Everything slowed the process down in the Democratic People's Republic of Korea.

But to a degree, he had seen the process speed up at the secure submarine base where he reported to work daily. There were usually reasons. The reasons usually had to do with the Supreme Leader's fears. Most of the fears had to do with the Americans. So the constant traffic at Yuktae-dong obviously had meaning.

The navy increased security to match America's hacking tactics and ability. It became all the more important with the deployment of missiles in the submarine fleet. Chin-wah Lee knew this. So did the deep cover CIA agent who had identified Lee as a potential mole years earlier.

. . .

Jee Gyuen had a seemingly perfect cover. Party loyalist, country nationalist, and professor of military-bound students who taught lessons according to the Supreme Leader's curriculum. Propaganda. All virtually untrue. Fake news. But students in North Korea were schooled not to question. Yet, sometimes, Jee Gyuen recognized a glimmer of interest; a desire to learn what might be true, beyond the texts and lies.

Jee Gyuen, a thin, bookish thirty-five-year-old teacher, shorter than most, was particularly good at picking up on the cue. That was his training. His specialty. He was one of the best information gatherers for American intelligence in North Korea. And one of the only. But to keep intel flowing, he had to recruit spies. The best were those he could cultivate at an impressionable age. Teaching offered him opportunity. That's how he identified Chin-wah Lee as a potential mole.

It was after class eight years prior. Gyuen overheard Lee boast he could get into a cool government submarine base anytime he wanted.

"Impossible!" demanded a defiant classmate.

"Any time I want. Yuktae-dong. My uncle told me how."

Gyuen listened while putting his lecture notes away. The two students went back and forth, but Lee never really revealed anything. A teenager's crow. Someone wanting to be acknowledged.

Not surprisingly, the conversation turned to girls. But Gyuen thought more of the exchange and more about Chin-wah Lee. The young boy sought adventure. Perhaps one day he might provide a way into someplace secret at a perfect time. That always was his objective. Find a subject, keep him at arms' length, work him; ultimately turn him if he reached a position of responsibility. *The long game.* More than four quarters.

Why Chin-wah Lee? Because a few days later, Gyuen casually learned that Chin-wah Lee had already created a certain fiction about his life. The boy revealed that he didn't really have an uncle. The man he talked about was someone who had once been over for dinner. A work friend of his father's. The relationship was an invention, but Chin-wah Lee was drawn to the intrigue. He'd even written a short story mystery about sneaking into the base. Gyuen offered to read it. Lee gladly gave him the paper. And from a psychological point of view, Gyuen recognized the teen as someone who wanted more. A purpose beyond his state indoctrination.

That year, the next, and those beyond, they met often. Gyuen and Lee became friends. Gyuen never pushed. Too forward. Too dangerous.

So Gyuen watched and waited. "Patience," he had been told by his own handlers at Langley. "Again, the long game."

When it came time for graduation, Gyuen counseled Lee on his college studies, on his military service, even on his love life.

They went to movies and dinners. They double-dated. They talked about the world beyond. They told jokes. Gyuen used jokes like a crowbar to probe. Lee loved to hear them. Most of the time they involved an Englishman, a Frenchman, and a North Korean.

"So, an Englishman, a Frenchman, and a North Korean are having a nice chat."

"Where?" Lee asked. "Not likely in Pyongyang. What Englishman would come here?"

Comments like that reinforced Gyuen's belief that Chin-wah Lee would be approachable some day. *The long game.*

"I don't know. They just meet up. Anyway. They're having a chat. The Englishman says, 'I'm happiest when I'm at home, I'm wearing my wool pants, and I'm sitting in front of the fireplace.'

"The Frenchman, a suave ladies' man, says, 'Oh you English folks are so simple. I feel the happiest when I visit a warm Mediterranean beach with a beautiful blonde, and we're doing what comes naturally.'

"The North Korea then adds, 'In the middle of the night, the secret police come knocking on my door. They're shouting Kang Sung-Mee, you're under arrest! And I say, 'Kang Sung-Mee doesn't live here. He's right next door!' That's when I'm the happiest.'"

Lee laughed. He liked his mentor's jokes. Particularly the political ones. It made him feel he had a kindred spirit, but he never let on. Or at least he didn't think he did.

But Gyuen saw it. He also noted the magazines Lee lingered over at newsstands and those he ignored. He saw how the maturing man differentiated between propaganda and fact but carefully hid his disillusionment.

The long game turned into five more years when the boy, now a man, earned a prestigious job.

"Chin-wah Lee, you must be making your father and the Supreme Leader proud," Gyuen said over coffee one morning.

"Eh," he said half-heartedly.

A promising start, Gyuen thought.

"But look what you've done by applying your studies and contributing to the future of the Democratic People's Republic," he said along party lines. "A true patriot."

"Thank you, Comrade Professor Gyuen," Lee said mockingly.

Gyuen recognized his growing disenchantment.

Soon, Jee Gyuen reasoned. *The next step in the long game.*

. . .

At work, inferior superiors constantly reminded Chin-wah Lee that he had two career routes. Up or down. Up required blind obedience and agreement on all things with those he reported to, creating a further loss of individuality. Down, typically the result of impertinence and public disagreement would invariably lead to loss of career or far worse.

Serve, protect, obey. It was the weekly lecture he and everyone else got. The purpose was to keep citizens submissive, duty bound, and loyal. Lee smiled and nodded and passed every loyalty test in the book.

Chin-wah Lee was a graduate of Kim Il-Sung Military Academy, a post-secondary school founded in 1948 principally to train army officers. His assigned specialty, computers. The machines had no loyalty to the army, navy, or air force. The ones and zeros spoke only computer in any language, and everyone needed them. So at age twenty-six, Chin-wah Lee did what the regime wanted from him. He programmed critical computers, uploaded new software, and worked his way in the right direction—up, to the rank of Security Technician.

The bottom line, which he shared with his mentor one night over dinner, was that he had remarkable access.

Unknowingly, the navy, a division of the North Korean army, had assigned the loyalist to a job completely in keeping with his name. In Korean, Chin-wah meant *ocean depth.* They assigned him to the submarine division.

Lee's first name also had another meaning in Korean. *Truth*. But command also didn't consider that. They should have.

. . .

The Supreme Leader took great pride in the Democratic People's Republic of Korea's Navy, as his exulted father and grandfather had before him. He especially loved the submarine fleet. At least outwardly. And the Supreme Leader instructed the country to love the submarine fleet, too.

For years they mainly operated within fifty kilometers of their borders, in the so-called brown waters. But they pushed further every year. Into the Sea of Japan and now the mid-Pacific. That was exactly why they were on the radar, and more accurately, the sonar of the United States Navy. But the North Korean dictator didn't care.

North Korea was known to have seventy-plus submarines sailing from bases at Yuktae-dong, Sinpo, Mayang-do, and other maintenance ports. The inventory was comprised of former Soviet subs, dating as far back as the 1960s, and some twenty-four newer Chinese vessels, with the rest home built. They carried torpedoes, mines, and missiles. That made them battle ready, deadly, and active weapons of war.

The fleet included twenty-plus Romeo class subs which ran 1,800 tons, forty three hundred-ton Whiskey class vessels, and ten midget and Yono-class subs, plus more. The pluses were the newest subs. *Gorae*-class submarines equipped with Submarine-Launched Ballistic Missiles (SLBMs).

The fleet operated in West and East Coast groups. West to waters between the Korean Peninsula and China. East in the Pacific. Ever deeper and further East from home shores.

When the submarines docked between tours of duty, Chin-wah Lee had unique access to the onboard computers. He would install new programs and scrub drives for any viruses. He'd replace systems with newer ones as they became available, and check for failing hardware. Some of the work was accomplished remotely from his own computer, other times within the subs themselves. He earned the prestigious assignment because of his IT skill and his avowed allegiance. Nonetheless, he always performed his work under the supervision of security officers.

Chin-wah Lee stood five-foot-seven, wore a corporal's uniform, cut his hair to the Supreme Leader's designated style, and wore standard-issue glasses. He looked like every other computer geek staring at his computer screen. He created code, scrubbed systems, and scanned for viruses, the universal enemy of every computer. He was a gatekeeper, aware of the devil in the details.

His life was simple. Work and sleep. He had few friends. No strong female attachments. Only a growing fantasy of a life that could never be. Every day, every single dreary day, he woke up, passed through the security checks, did his duty, went home, and ate a tasteless meal.

That's what the people in the shadows who occasionally followed him saw. That was what made up the mind-numbing reports North Korean domestic spies filled out on him month after month.

But through their incompetence, they missed questioning an important thing. Namely, Lee's longtime friendship with his old school professor.

• • •

"How long have we known one another?" Gyuen asked as they finished dinner at his sparsely-decorated studio apartment.

Chin-wah Lee replied, "Eight, close to nine years,"

"All good?"

"Yes. You've been my teacher and my friend. The best. You know me better than anyone."

"Yes, I believe that's true. And in honor of our friendship, may I tell you another joke?"

"Please. They're all wonderful."

"Ah, but this one carries a little more meaning," Gyuen replied leaning closer.

"Oh?"

"Yes, a parable of sorts."

"Another Englishman, a Frenchman, and a fellow comrade?" Lee asked.

"Of course. However, this time they're at an art museum in Europe looking at a painting of Adam and Eve in the Garden of Eden. This time, Adam's holding an apple. Describing the painting, the Englishman says,

'Adam clearly knows how good that is. He's eager to have a bite, too, and share the rest with Eve. Therefore, I'd argue that Adam and Eve are properly British. So polite and proper. Yes, definitely British.'

"The Frenchman says, 'No, no, no. I disagree. Adam and Eve are walking about entirely naked. There's no question. Adam and Eve are absolutely French!'

"'You're both wrong,' the North Korean argues. 'There's no doubt in my mind. They're from the Democratic People's Republic of Korea. After all, they have no clothes to wear, barely anything to eat, and they still think they're in paradise!'"

Chin-wah Lee laughed and put his hand to his forehead. That's when Jee Gyuen pointedly asked, "So, my friend, do you still think you're in paradise?"

CHAPTER 6

NEBRASKA

The Frenchman always drove at the speed limit. His first stop was a storage facility just off Interstate 29, south of Omaha in Bellevue. He'd been there once before. After this visit, he would never return.

He waited for a pickup truck to leave before he proceeded to a storage unit in the far back corner of the lot. He parked and exited the car, never showing his face to the surveillance camera; a precaution he also took when he signed the rental agreement eight months prior. But just in case, he wore a hoodie, sunglasses, and to avoid leaving any fingerprints, clear plastic gloves.

The Frenchman spent a total of two minutes unlocking the combination lock, retrieving a single duffle bag, replacing the lock with another, and leaving. He got back on I-29, but only for a short distance before cutting over to US 34 and then onto I-80 heading west. Three hours later, he pulled onto Route 44 leading into Kearny, Nebraska.

Enough driving for the day, he thought. *No issues. No obstacles.* The way he liked it.

He passed up the Hampton Inn, La Quinta Inn, Fairfield Inn and Suites, and a Holiday Inn Express for the more egalitarian Motel 6. His choice wasn't based on price. The traveler preferred a motel with a door adjacent to the parking lot, rather than a communal lobby leading to rooms. Although he couldn't always get his way, tonight was important. He had to examine, clean, and oil the contents he had removed from storage. If he found a problem with the package, he would have to divert to an alternate location in South Dakota for a replacement. Either way, he had the time. He always built in time.

WASHINGTON, D.C.
THE SUPREME COURT
THE SAME TIME

Leopold Browning studied the briefs. Endless pages to consider and reject; all requiring jurisprudence and personal forethought. Browning was the most distinguished member of the United States Supreme Court; a venerated and feared Chief Justice, with the record and temperament to back it up.

Decades ago as an Illinois prosecutor, he'd been notorious for gutting opponents who dared blindside him. As a district court judge he would sound the gavel at the first hint of legal theatrics from either side. When he was appointed federal judge, he never allowed attorneys to spell out their own meanings beyond the letter of the law. Now, as the nation's highest justice, Leopard Browning brought all of his experience, his passion, and his love of the Constitution to bear. He had few equals in the country, and at age sixty-eight, he defied anyone lesser to stand before him and argue their case. Those who didn't come prepared surely felt his wrath. Those who stood on solid constitutional ground and knew how to construct a purposeful legal argument earned his respect.

Leopold Browning demanded the same from his immediate staff. His senior staff attorney, a recent appointee, had served as an assistant White House counsel. Before that she was a junior Boston attorney. She earned the big double, then triple jump due to unique circumstances. She was also Scott Roarke's girlfriend.

"Ms. Kessler, if you please."

This was Browning's favored manner of summoning administrative staff, clerks, and even other justices. Medium volume, but enough to be heard an office beyond his secretary.

Katie Kessler typed a response through the internal Gchat system. "Yes, sir. Coming."

Then she decided not to hit send. He hated the system.

Moments later, the thirty-two-year-old, five-foot six-inch lawyer faced the chief justice across from his desk. Katie Kessler was slim, alluring, but equally professional looking. Her curly black hair was shoulder length with a part in her bangs. She had fire-engine red lipstick and taupe eye shadow to complement her eyes.

Justice Browning cleared his throat, as he often did, before beginning. Katie automatically straightened her conservative dark blue suit jacket over her white silk blouse. Not out of nervousness. Browning's formality just encouraged a smart look from smart people.

He didn't rise and barely looked at her. Browning was absorbed in case work spread out on his large mahogany desk. He always favored simple tailored three-piece black suits. Like most days, he was down to the vest, with his jacket properly hung up in his closet. His medium length gray hair added to his distinguished look, punctuated by thin wire-framed glasses.

"Please, Ms. Kessler, sit. You remind me too much of a waitress when you just stand there."

She laughed, but just a little. "Yes, sir."

Katie Kessler had succeeded in cracking Browning's gruff demeanor in a way few others had. For her part in helping expose a sleeper cell spy plot and averting a Constitutional crisis prior to the last inauguration, Kessler earned his trust and an offer of a job, which she didn't immediately take. Now, a year later, she decided the court was the place to be. The Harvard Law School graduate was honored to be working with Browning. She completely respected him, but more than that, Katie Kessler understood him.

"The hairs on the back of my neck are tingling again," he said.

Katie half-smiled. There were no wayward hairs on the back of his clean-shaven neck.

"What do you know about The Declaration of Causes?"

She thought for a moment. "The Declaration of…?"

"'Causes,'" the chief justice interrupted. "Come now, Ms. Kessler. What is the country paying you for?"

She had a basic grasp, but not enough to speak authoritatively. So instead she said, "Apparently today to become an expert on 'The Declaration of Clauses.'"

"Well then, get to it. In detail, with citations."

"Any context to frame it?" she asked.

"Yours to discover, counselor."

Katie Kessler knew she'd have homework for as long as she stayed in law. Now that she was working at the highest levels of the country's court system, it was every night.

Later tonight, she would have no boyfriend issue to deal with. No explaining, *not tonight*. Scott Roarke was out of town. That was okay for now, but there were an increasing number of *Not tonight's*.

Kessler left for her office. Browning returned to the work on his desk, previously used by Chief Justice Earl Warren. It showed signs of wear and worry going back to Warren's landmark decisions outlawing segregation in public schools, the one-man one-vote rules of apportionment, and more. The buffed pen and pencil stab marks on the desk showed the pains Warren went through adjudicating Brown v. Board of Education, Gideon v. Wainwright, and Miranda v. Arizona. Over the years, Browning added to the desk's character and contributed to the stories others would one day read into the dark wood walls directly behind him and to his left.

He knew full well that he was grinding his silver ballpoint pen into the wood while he contemplated a battle ahead. He just didn't see how deep he had already dug.

KEARNEY, NB

The Frenchman unloaded the duffle on the bed. All the parts of the Ruger American Rifle Predator were in mint shape. The barrel was dust free, spotless. The scope would need proper calibration, which he'd do well off road. All in due time.

He had a box of ammunition but counted on one deadly bullet doing the job. There were still logistics to consider when he scouted his next kill zone. However, there was no rush. Rushing led to mistakes. He would drive at his own pace, settle in quietly, and practice. So tonight, the only thing left was dinner. For that, he'd go to the Ruby Tuesday around the corner and settle for one of their chicken dinners and hopefully a passable wine. Before sleep, maybe a few minutes of one of America's late-night TV talk shows. It helped for engaging in mindless conversation with strangers.

GEORGETOWN
11:00 P.M. ET

Katie Kessler hunkered down in her apartment with a salad and a glass of Cocoban pinot noir. She and Roarke kept their own places, yet lived through many dangers together. In Boston and Washington. In the cold waters of the Charles River and on the Capitol steps. They met one another while Roarke was investigating a decades-long conspiracy with deep roots in Soviet Russia and branches into the Middle East. Katie became entangled through the law firm where she worked, helping Roarke and, in turn, becoming entangled in more intimate ways.

She'd been given a job at the White House for her contributions to the president's well-being. However, the Supreme Court called more strongly. And tonight, loudly.

She opened the file she'd begun at her office.

"*The Declaration of Causes*," she whispered as she looked at the first printout. "Tell me what's so damned important about you after 160 years?"

Katie divided the research she brought home into chronological piles. Although virtually every law library was online and accessible on her phone, iPad, laptop and home PC, she still liked holding and highlighting papers. Even at this hour, she figured she'd be working late into the night. Two hours later, when she realized she was fighting to stay awake, she thought about calling Scott. But he'd told her no calls in. He could only call out based on what his boss had him doing.

She hoped he was safe.

LOS ANGELES, CA
THE SAME TIME

Scott Roarke casually walked down Lincoln Boulevard, west of In-N-Out Burger on Sepulveda. The intoxicating smell wafting out of the famed LA hamburger restaurant called to him. But he'd have none of the greasy food tonight. Too easy for dogs to pick up his scent.

He wore a dark reversible jacket and carried a small black bag. Two hundred yards down Lincoln, at a mid-point between two street lights, he ducked and sprinted to the eight-foot high wire fence; a barrier to the runway. Signs warned *No Entry*. His wire cutters suggested otherwise.

Roarke moved quickly. He cut only enough to create a small crawl space that he bent back into shape after clearing.

He was not the first to ever do so at LAX or other American airports. In the past few years, more than 345 incidents were reported at thirty-one airports that handle three-quarters of all U.S. passengers. On average, a breach occurred somewhere every 9.5 days. People committed to getting in the perimeter would scale the barbed wire, sneak through vehicle checkpoints, or ride the conveyer belt back to baggage claim. Usually crazies, but some more dangerous and with lethal intent.

LAX placed fourth on the list of U.S. airports with the most breaches. The top three were San Francisco, Las Vegas, and Philadelphia.

By all accounts, the difficulty wasn't getting in. It was moving quickly enough not to get caught.

Roarke was a sprinter. That helped. He had also chosen a moonless night. That helped more. He had increased his odds by studying the arrival/departure schedule on the north runways at the precise hour. He knew when and where to run. When and where to lay low.

His destination was Terminal 2, home of Delta, Aeromexico, Air Canada, Aer Lingus, and Virgin Atlantic.

Midway across the two hundred-yard expanse, two minutes into his incursion, an airport vehicle with a red-and-blue light bar approached. It drove the circular route and didn't appear to be in any hurry. Still, Roarke hit the ground and laid absolutely flat. A camera might have picked him up, or it was just circling to the south side. He followed the path. It didn't stop at the fence.

Roarke breathed deeply, crouched, and continued low and fast toward the terminals. He'd have to make up the forty seconds he lost, otherwise planes preparing to take off would be on him. That was assuming planes were on time, a variable he couldn't count on. For now, everyone was on schedule, and Roarke believed he hadn't been spotted.

For the rest of the way, he removed his light-weight jacket. Underneath, he wore a knockoff blue TSA shirt, black tie, with an official-looking ID. All bought online. From the jacket pocket, he removed a small fabric backpack, the kind that folded up into virtually nothing. He opened it, put the jacket inside, and pulled the string tight. Attached to the tie was an Air Canada Aeroplan frequent flier member tag and a destination bar code. Now it looked like he was carrying a passenger's actual backpack.

Roarke walked around the Southwest airplanes at the Terminal 1 gates, nodded to a member of the service crew loading an outbound flight, and headed toward the furthermost gate at Terminal 2.

No one showed any concern toward him. But that might quickly change. He saw two LAPD squad cars speed to his original entry point along the parameter road. Most likely they had dogs.

Eleven minutes into his mission, he reached the stairs leading up to a newly commissioned Air Canada Bombardier Commercial CS300 aircraft. Over the noise, he yelled to an Air Canada baggage handler, "Late bag!"

"No problem." The ground crewman even held the door open for Roarke as floodlights went on across the airport illuminating the fence.

He walked up the outside stairs to the jetway, slid by three passengers, and smiled at the middle-aged male flight attendant at the door. "Hey there," he said. "Passenger in 14B forgot a bag. I'll take it back."

"Sure thing. Back there on the right," the flight attendant offered.

"Terrific. I'll just be a second."

Roarke excused himself as he squeezed past people getting their baggage up into the overhead compartment. He even helped one woman in 12C.

At 14B he placed his bag into the storage and nodded to the passenger who had no idea what he was doing.

With that, he walked back to the front of the plane and stopped in the cockpit as the sound of more sirens cut through the night time air.

"Have a good flight, captain," Roarke said.

The Air Canada pilot turned and noted that a TSA officer was addressing him.

"Ah, thanks…" The captain looked at the nametag on his uniform. "…Officer McArdle. Will do."

Roarke had two choices. Voluntarily turn himself in and explain. Or simply walk out the door.

Telling the truth would undoubtedly delay the Air Canada flight for hours as bags were off-loaded and everything was thoroughly checked. Moreover, he expected he'd be grilled while his identity was confirmed, then lectured to exhaustion.

Leaving was far better. Off-sight, he would defuse the situation with a phone call.

Roarke walked to his car, which he had left earlier in the day in the lot adjacent to Terminal 2. There, he changed his shirt, got in, and drove away. Once fully out of LAX, he phoned the White House, spoke to the president, who in turn contacted the Secretary of Homeland Security. Five minutes later, the LAPD got a call to stand down. All was fine. Airport response time was being tested. They'd get a report of the exercise in due course.

This didn't please anyone at LAX. It shouldn't.

Now on his agenda, a cheeseburger, fries, and a milkshake to go at In-N-Out, then back to the hotel. While he satisfied his craving for Los Angeles's best burger, he went through the *LA Times*, starting with the sports pages and working his way back to the news, and finally the Op Ed page. He wished he'd stayed in the sports section.

CHAPTER 7

WASHINGTON, D.C.
TWO DAYS LATER

Katie Kessler welcomed Scott Roarke with a dinner they never finished. He'd been on the road for almost a month, and they were hungry for each other.

After two hours, they made their way back to her dining room table wearing only extra large t-shirts. Neither ever talked about their work over the phone—Roarke for national security reasons, Kessler because of legal confidentiality. When alone, they shared some generalities toeing the line of what they couldn't say, and sometimes crossing it. It was hard not to, considering what they'd been through together in service of the country.

"Looks like you need a bigger place," Roarke said, eyeing the books and pads spread out from her couch to a coffee table to the floor.

"Imagine what two salaries pooled could do," Katie smartly replied, touching on the often avoided discussion.

So far Roarke had resisted moving in. He argued that his life was too dangerous, and he didn't want to expose her to more trouble than he already had. She read his answer as a fear of commitment. Perhaps the only fear she'd ever seen in him.

"Think of what we'd save on leftovers," she joked.

Roarke nodded, as he always did when the cohabitation conversation came up. He also always changed the subject.

"You feeling okay about Browning?" he asked.

"Some days he makes Taylor look like a pussycat. But yes. I really admire him, and he trusts me."

Trust was important to her. That's how she and Roarke survived.

"Of course, half the time he doesn't tell me why he's assigned research," Katie complained.

"So you'll come to your conclusions without prejudice."

"And it works every time."

"Can you talk about it?"

"Like that mattered before." She reached across the table and bit Roarke's ear lightly. As she leaned back she continued talking. "There's no case, but I think I see where he's going. He wants me to understand fundamental history."

"About?"

"*The Declaration of Causes*," she replied.

"The Declaration of what?"

"Causes."

Katie rose, crossed over to her coffee table, and picked out one file.

"It was a pronouncement. The complete wording is *The Declaration of Causes and Necessity of Taking Up Arms.*"

"Sounds historic already," Roarke said.

"Back to 1775 historic."

She read from an abstract.

On this day in 1775, one day after restating their fidelity to King George III and wishing him 'a long and prosperous reign' in the Olive Branch Petition, Congress sets 'forth the causes and necessity of their taking up arms.'

"A call to revolt?" Roarke asked.

"More an affirmation of intent. The Battles of Lexington and Concord had already been fought that April. Now it was do or die, submit again to England's rule or continue on the path toward independence. The Continental Congress convened in May and chose the course of commitment. Seven members were assigned to write the document. Thomas Jefferson's hand was most evident. But it was issued with John Hancock's signature."

"The king ignored it?"

"With Parliament's consent. So Congress's next declaration made it abundantly clear."

"The Declaration of Independence," Roarke noted.

"And the war was on," she added.

"So what's Browning's point?"

"Like always, keep searching. It wasn't so much the first application of *The Declaration of Causes* he wanted me to research."

"Then what?"

"I think it's the second."

MERIDIAN, IDAHO
THE SAME TIME

Lucas Burke called the late-night session to order with the smash of his gavel and a laugh.

"Don't you hate these things?"

The crowd roared, "Yes!"

With that he tossed it over his shoulder. The four hundred-some people who gathered in the large party room at Big Al's on North Eagle Road loved it. Many had heard Burke speak before. This time, Burke needed double the audience space. Next time, Meridian itself would be too small.

Lucas Burke slowly stood and towered over everyone at six-foot-four."

"Now calm down. I didn't break anything."

The men and women, aged eighteen on up, were completely hooked. And Lucas felt it.

His rugged movie star good looks had combined with raw political charisma to create a cult following. Lucas smiled as the crowd laughed at his folksy manner. They needed to feel needed by him. He waved his appreciation. But now it was time to get to work.

"Friends of the New Northwest Front, welcome!"

The greeting brought a full minute of cheering.

Burke took the time to loosen his tie and roll up his sleeves to where his muscles showed. Women gasped.

Lucas Burke was on his way to becoming a political force from Montana, through Idaho, and into the states of Washington, Oregon, and beyond. He was the lead spokesman, the identity, and the poster child of what was becoming a popular grassroots movement. He was virtually unknown two years earlier. Now Burke was galvanizing support by the week and becoming a louder voice in the marketplace of extreme ideas. All convincingly delivered with smile, a chiseled chin, rugged Robert Redford good looks of decades ago, and charm.

"We no longer are united states. We are divided, isolated, and insulated by borders and beliefs. Do we have anything in common with the Commonwealths of Massachusetts, Pennsylvania, or even Kentucky and Virginia."

"No!" the crowd shouted.

"Should we forever continue to state allegiance to states that have nothing to do with us?"

"No!"

"New York, Florida, California, Illinois?"

"No!"

"Delaware and Ohio?"

"No!"

"Our brothers in sisters are in Colorado and New Mexico!"

"Yes!" thundered four hundred voices.

"Arizona and Utah."

"Yes."

"And they will come together just as we have. And we shall come together with them to form an even more perfect union."

This was the fastest Burke had ever whipped up a crowd. He was getting better at it and more people clamored to see him.

"Are you with me? Do I have your support?"

"Yes, yes, yes!"

Burke raised his hands for everyone to stop. They obeyed.

"We have started a movement that will move a nation," he said quietly. "A new nation under God, independent of nonaligned needs, free of direction and intimidation from a capitol building thousands of miles away and its inflated capital that's bought and sold by a walled street that can't see beyond its own greed.

"It's time to come together as friends and family. Time for neighbors to tell naysayers that we've had enough. We want to be left alone. We will do this peacefully and legally. Through our schools, city councilors, and mayors. With the representatives we put in our legislatures. With the governors we elect who will finally, and for all time, represent the real will of the people."

Cheers began to bubble up again, but Burke held them off.

"Of course, we can't succeed overnight. And I sure as shooting can't succeed without you."

Burke was clearly putting himself atop the food chain.

"But together, history will record that we are the founding fathers and mothers of the New Northwest Republic."

Lucas Burke now allowed his minions to cheer, which they did for a full five minutes. After that, he continued to take questions for forty minutes with virtually every answer ending with applause. At the end, Burke's aides got everyone's email addresses, social media handles, and cell phone numbers. In return, they received blue baseball caps with a single symbol stitched in gold thread on the brim. A metal chain broken in half.

WASHINGTON, D.C.
THE SAME TIME

"Actually, second is a misnomer," Katie continued. "There were four more *Declaration of Causes.*"

"When?"

"Remember your history, darling. Who would have wanted to make such a declaration?"

Roarke thought for a moment. He looked at her with uncertainty, but she wasn't going to give up the answer.

"Think," she encouraged.

He ventured a guess; a very educated guess. Realizing that the first declaration had triggered The Revolutionary War, he jumped ahead a century.

"The Civil War?"

"Absolutely. The Declaration of the Immediate Causes Which Induce and Justify the Secession from the Federal Union. The first four states, Georgia, South Carolina, Louisiana, and Texas. The foundation of the Confederacy. Seven others followed."

Now Kessler referred to her own notes.

"Here's what Texas argued. The federal government obstructed its rights by refusing to admit new slave states into the union thus denying the power of expansion. Washington advocated Negro equality, and enlisted the press, the church, and schools against the South in order to destroy the present condition of slaves, and on and on.

"The Texas declaration concluded with a blistering statement. 'We hold as undeniable truths that the governments of the various States and of the Confederacy itself, were established exclusively by the white race, for themselves and their posterity; that the African race had no agency in their establishment; that they were rightfully held and regarded as an inferior and dependent race, and in that condition only could their existence in this country be rendered beneficial or tolerable.'"

She looked up. "It was all so ugly and divisive. The language was similar in other states' declarations. War was inevitable."

Katie gave Roarke the printouts with her highlights in yellow. He read them, sighing deeply.

"I get it." He paused, "But what's Browning's point now?"

"I'm not completely certain, but I think it's this."

She handed him another file.

MERIDIAN, IDAHO

At the front door, Lucas Burke shook the hands of everyone who wanted to connect with him. He received nods of support from those who couldn't wait. An aide kept count. Four-hundred-twelve. All in all, he had scored another rousing victory for the cause and for himself.

Burke was not an Idaho native, but he was a friend to popular causes. He was from Melstone, Montana, just below the center of the state. His family owned a 1,374-acre cattle ranch in Musselshell County. Half of the property had oil. The Burke's had enjoyed power and wealth for generations. Lucas Burke was the first to use it for political gain.

"Thank you for coming," he said to the last of his audience.

"I'm here for you, Mr. Burke," the thirty-five-year-old nurse offered with extra intent.

"I'm afraid you've got it backwards, young lady. I'm here for you."

Burke held her hand a little longer and smiled. "We'll be in touch."

"Wheels up," said a deep voice over his shoulder.

Burke let go. Disappointed.

Burke turned to the command from his chief advisor who pointed to his watch. "We've got one hundred miles tonight."

"I know. But I'm starving, and…" He watched the woman leave.

"And food's in the car," the advisor said, ignoring Burke's obvious desire.

The man at Burke's side was actually more than just an advisor. He was Burke's strategist, marketing chief, advance man, and media coach. At rallies, he hovered almost invisibly in the background. But he was very present in Lucas Burke's ear through an IFB, which people didn't see. During speeches he fed lines as any true political Svengali of the wireless age would.

He also fed Burke praise. He slapped Burke on his back. "Great job tonight. We signed up a ton."

"We did have them," Burke boasted.

"*You* did," was the calculating reply.

The man was two years older than Burke and more experienced. He'd traveled the globe, had moved from school to school whenever his Army officer father was reassigned, and had mastered a few languages. Some considered him an Army brat. He thought he was worldly, especially as he came of age in private school. For college, he went to Philadelphia where he got a degree in business at Temple University. That took him to Washington, first as a K Street lobbyist for a series of international Asia interests, then as vice president for a D.C. opposition research political communications company that advised political candidates. All calculated steps.

His was handsome but had a cruel look about him. It was mostly in his dark brown eyes. He was single, growing a bit paunchy, which actually served his persona. He never drew any attention when he stood next to Lucas Burke. Moreover, he preferred to stay out of the limelight. Right now, he had the best reason in the world. He had a rising cult figure in Lucas Burke and everything was working for Clay Lindstrom—working in a way that had begun in whispers with a friend years ago at a private school in Switzerland.

WASHINGTON, D.C.

Just after midnight, Katie got around to Roarke's trip.

"So sweetheart, what trouble did you get into?"

"Oh, not too much," he said lightly. "I avoided getting stopped while snooping around a nuclear power plant; I successfully carried a shoulder-fired missile launcher into an airport hotel; I left backpacks in LA, Chicago, and Boston subway stations that went untouched for far too long; oh, and I breached security at LAX. Nothing to worry about," he said slyly.

"Maybe when you do it. But Jesus, is it that easy?"

"Unfortunately, it is."

"Anyone know what you were doing?"

"No. That was the idea."

"Scott, you could have been arrested."

"I wasn't."

"Stop that. You know what I mean. You could have been shot."

Roarke took a deep breath and reached over to hold her hand.

"Honey, I'm careful. But the whole idea was to play the part of the lone wolf, hopefully above average. And the worst part is that with the exception of the Indian Point Nuclear Power Plant…"

"Very near my hometown," she interrupted.

"Too close," he continued, "…which I ultimately could have taken. I was able to target airplanes through line-of-sight hotel rooms, from the ocean, and onboard."

"You got onboard?"

"Yes, cutting a fence and breaking into LAX, making my way across the runway, posing as a TSA officer, getting into a plane, and successfully planting a bag in the overhead compartment."

"You put a bomb onboard?" she gasped.

"Not a bomb. A backpack with a jacket in it. I'm sure it had a nice flight to Toronto."

Katie laughed.

"Tomorrow I'll type up my report for the boss. But it's going to be a shocker. Amusement parks, music venues, power grids, oil pipelines, subways in every major city for that matter, and as you well know, water supplies." Roarke continued. "I've seen them all. Chilling. And very little has improved in what…a decade or more?"

"The president must know this already. Did you have to take such chances?

"Yes. It's ammunition to take to Homeland Security, to the Department of Interior, the Justice Department, the FBI, the ATF, and Congress. He'll do it, too. Everything I did proves that the number of potential targets in a free and open society are too great to defend.

"The worst of it is that I got all the background info, floor plans, layouts, and uniforms I needed off the internet," Roarke stated. "Open, unrestricted government websites, Google street images, YouTube videos, even Facebook postings from guards. A terrorist with a modicum of knowledge and savvy can learn almost anything he needs to know to plan an attack on our infrastructure."

"God Almighty," she proclaimed.

"Yup. And you know as well as I do," he added referring their previous exploits, "it's unlikely one thing will bring us to our knees, but if the goal is to create instability—fear of flying, higher gas prices, a stock market crash, shutting down transportation systems—it's all achievable."

Now Katie applied her legal mind.

"Added defenses, more delays, barriers at shopping malls, bags checked at subways. None of those necessarily impede civil rights. They just mean delays. Delays I'd accept."

"And that's what we will have to see," Roarke added. "I'm no statistician, but the equation looks pretty simple. No security improvements equals zero expenditures but a high risk to life. Security improvements equal money spent and lives saved. It's a no brainer."

They talked about the problems and solutions for almost another hour during which time they drained a second bottle of wine. Over the course of the discussion they moved from the dining room table to the couch, to the floor. Now, at 2:25, tired from his travels, but still awake enough to want, he walked his fingers up Katie's leg.

"Okay, okay," he said. "Enough SCOTUS and POTUS for tonight."

"I have a better idea." His fingers found home. "And it almost rhymes."

"Umm," she said softly embracing the obvious idea. "What could that be, Mr. Roarke?"

• • •

Over breakfast they talked about the thing they knew the least. Their schedules. Roarke's belonged to the White House. Katie's to the Supreme Court. The President of the United States and the Chief Justice of the Supreme Court controlled their lives.

"No way to build a life together," she sighed.

"Think we can last it a few more years? 'Til Taylor's out?" Roarke asked. "D'Angelo and I have been talking again."

"You and Vinnie would really do it?"

"We're talking," Roarke replied.

"You'd actually leave the White House behind?"

Roarke leaned across the table and looked into his love's eyes.

"For you, yes."

Katie leaned forward, locked in his gaze.

"How do we do it?"

"Maybe we ratchet it up a notch."

"Maybe we what?"

"Ratchet it up."

"Take it to the next level."

Katie began to get it.

"Mr. Roarke, are you thinking what I'm thinking you're thinking?"

"Depends. What are you thinking?"

"I'm thinking you've picked a really unusual time if you're going to ask me something really important."

Roarke smiled. "This might help."

He removed a small box from his pocket. Just big enough to hold a ring.

CHAPTER 8

THE WHITE HOUSE
THE NEXT AFTERNOON

Louise Swingle called Roarke in his office.

"He'll see you upstairs now."

He was the president. *Now* meant immediately.

"Thanks, Louise. How much time will have I?"

"Fifteen solid. Twenty if you're nice to me."

"I'll need the twenty," he said, completely serious.

Going *upstairs* never rattled Roarke. He always spoke openly with President Morgan Taylor. That was their deal. He also got to call him *Boss*.

"Coffee? You look tired my boy," the president said welcoming Roarke.

Roarke was and Taylor accurately assumed why. He smiled.

"As a matter of fact…"

The president poured a cup. He knew how Roarke liked it. Hot and black.

"Well, you caused quite a stir," Taylor said. "It didn't stop after the first call. The secretary had to handle a shit load of back and forth. Not just with LAPD and the TSA. Your gift to the ATF hasn't stopped giving ulcers to the regional office. Oh, and to that point, you neglected to tell them where you picked up a live Type 91 Kai Manpad."

"Must have been an oversight."

"Truth be told, I'm curious, too."

"It'll be in my report. You'll have it tomorrow. But I'll give you the headlines now."

They sat down across from one another with a coffee table between them. The president sat in his favorite seat, a wooden captain's chair that had belonged to Admiral Halsey. Roarke took the couch. The seating layout allowed for a clear view of the presidential coat of arms stitched into the navy blue carpet. The seal and its meaning never failed to inspire: An eagle holding in his talons an olive branch and a bundle of arrows. Two opposing approaches to handling a crisis. A vivid reminder to the president and everyone who advised him.

Roarke reported more than advised. But he focused on the clutched arrows as he began.

"Okay, Scott. How bad is it?"

"Very."

Roarke reviewed in greater detail what he'd generally explained to Katie. He enumerated names and places. Faults and failures. Then he reminded his boss about an important change in the military paradigm.

"The attacker has the clear advantage. It's the reverse of what you learned at Annapolis and what they teach at West Point and the Air Force Academy. In military terms, the defender must protect large, dispersed ground. Our problem? A terrorist just has to focus on a small target that will deliver high value damage, human or political, social or propagandistic. We've got to protect those definable targets better, and as we learned when our water systems were attacked, we have to get critical tactical intelligence *off* the internet. For God's sake, we couldn't make it any easier!"

Roarke bore down more. "Money, hard decisions, immediate changes. Not just one of the three, boss. All three. Bite the bullet. Americans will get used to the inconveniences. We have no alternative."

President Taylor stood and walked to the window overlooking the

Rose Garden. He stopped precisely where John Kennedy had contemplated the decision to be made over Russian missiles in Cuba. It's where presidents since have considered other weighty measures. Taylor had worn down the spot on the carpet but insisted that White House decorators leave it alone.

"I'll talk with the attorney general and Homeland Security today. It'll be on the agenda," Taylor said.

"Just get it off the goddamned internet."

"Got it, Scott."

Roarke saw the president's annoyance, but he continued.

"If I'm coming up with a hundred ways to penetrate defenses and raise political hell, we damn well better believe there are a thousand more. I don't care if TSA, the ATF or anyone else has a bug up their ass over me. I'm not the problem. Security of America is."

"I said I got it, Scott," the president repeated. "I read the reports every day. I get the briefings. Al-Qaeda, ISIS, domestic terrorists. The Bureau has more than a thousand active probes relating to the Islamic State alone. One thousand suspected terrorists with the resources to monitor only a small fraction. Last year they were stretched to capacity tracking just fifty. Maybe five percent are under twenty-four-hour surveillance. The FBI simply isn't big enough to deal with all the online radicalization. It's reached crisis level inside the FBI."

Roarke knew this and a lot more. He had close friends in the bureau who regularly helped him. From field agents to the FBI's top facial recognition expert.

The president rejoined Roarke at the seating area and returned to a conversational tone. "Scott, we're all worried. And your report is going to make us smarter. We'll work on the internet component with the browsers like we are with Facebook. Most of all, Congress needs to authorize more cash. And you know where the problem is there."

Roarke nodded. Taylor made no attempt to hide his disdain for Speaker of the House Duke Patrick, who continued to fight him on every White House requested appropriation for the FBI and Homeland Security. It was strictly personal.

"So, Scott," the president added, "it's obvious you went a lot further than you needed to make your point. Let's have it. What's really got you so pissed off?"

"Faith."

"Religious?"

"Faith in government." He told Taylor about an article he read in the LA paper. An op ed that considered how, for various reasons, the political climate might be scaring off a generation of rising stars.

CHAPTER 9

SEVEN DAYS LATER
BOISE, ID

C.J. Geller rose from his oak desk flanked by an American flag and the state flag of Idaho. The first term governor, with significantly higher aspirations and a national media glow from spirited appearances on all the cable news channels, had a well-publicized fundraising dinner to attend. He straightened his blue suit, checked his hair in an office mirror, and smiled. It would be a $50,000 night, and he'd be $50,000 closer to creating a Senate campaign war chest. By his personal calculations and those of his closest advisors, he was aiming for eight years in Congress, then four-to-eight as vice president, then a run for the presidency, unless things sped up.

Geller left his office with his chief aide and met up with four members of the Idaho State Police, the governor's principal security detail. They walked down the Capitol steps to a waiting Lincoln stretch limo. The governor and his aide took their seats. The State Police team split in two, driving one patrol car in front of his Lincoln, and one in back. The ride to The Grove Hotel on South Capitol Boulevard was just six blocks, less than ten minutes.

Geller recalled the days as a State Representative when he used to hoof it. Now, when it meant more to him than ever to be on the street to curry votes, the State Police wouldn't allow it. But even in the chilly April air, he kept his window rolled down to wave to pedestrians, many he knew by name.

The limo drove down the center lane on North Sixth Street, under and around U.S. Highway 24, and back to the main entrance of the hotel on South Capitol. The Lincoln driver stopped, waited for the Idaho State Police officers to step out and take up positions, all of which seemed unnecessary to the governor.

. . .

The man from France, now posing as a federal inspector, had settled into position two hours earlier. He'd scouted multiple locations where the governor would pass, walk, or otherwise be exposed. The best was here and now—the fifteenth floor of a high rise where construction had been halted due to an EPA filing—exactly 885.22 yards from where C.J. Geller would exit his car with the sun west of him.

A guard at ground level of the building all but ignored the Frenchman as he approached.

"Afternoon," he said. "Chandler. Inspector."

The Frenchman, for now named Chandler, held a clipboard and yellow pad, *de rigueur* for anyone pretending to have authority. He also carried a large duffle with the state flag and logo on the side. He waved an official looking Idaho State Building Inspector ID.

"You get the call I was coming?" he said keeping his head low, under the brim of his departmental cap.

"Not me. Maybe the last shift," the guard said barely looking up from watching an ESPN documentary on the historic 1977 basketball game between Idaho State and UCLA. Idaho won, which advanced the local team to the Elite Eight.

"Okay then. I'll be a few hours."

The guard waved him through without another word.

Entry was easier than expected. So far, he didn't need to kill anyone. He hoped the distracted guard would remain distracted.

Playing the part expertly, he began a survey on the first floor. He was slow and meticulous in case the guard wanted to check him out. If so, he'd bore him in minutes with silence. If that didn't work, he'd slit his throat.

After reaching the fifth floor, he abandoned his routine and went ten floors higher, which he'd already surveilled two nights earlier. He chose fifteen because unlike the lower enclosed floors, this was still relatively open. And one floor higher compromised his angle.

Chandler slid a storage container toward the window frame. He positioned it so that there'd be just enough room for him to sit facing the window with his back up against the container for support.

Next he removed his sniper rifle from the duffle and loaded a single bullet. He'd tested the weapon in the hills. Range, calibration, and his own aim. All perfect.

• • •

The governor's limo pulled up to The Grove Hotel entrance. The driver, also a State Police officer, exited, circled around the front of the Lincoln and opened the door for Geller. Geller's aide got out from the other side. The rest of the Idaho State Police joined the governor, scanned the area, and told one another everything was okay.

C.J. Geller waved to a small crowd gathered to greet him. *In a few years, this will be thousands,* he thought.

He looked to the right, then forward, and finally to the left; the left where blocks away a gunman held his breath and gently squeezed a trigger.

• • •

The 6.5 Creedmoor bullet took just over a second to travel from barrel to the heart of the governor of Idaho.

Now the clock was ticking against the assassin. He wanted to be street level in three minutes. But as he began to break down the rifle, the building guard stepped onto the floor.

"Hey, what are you doing?"

The man he had casually let in then screwed the barrel back in place and put a cartridge in the chamber.

The guard found out.

• • •

That night, the assassination was the talk of a local radio show with callers wondering if it was safe for anyone to run for office.

CHAPTER 10

WASHINGTON, D.C.
THE SAME TIME

"You wouldn't."

"I would. No, I *will*," Roarke told his drinking companion at St. Arnold's Mussel Bar on Jefferson Place.

It had taken Roarke just under forty minutes to make the 2.9 mile walk from the White House. Most others would need an hour. Not that he was in a rush. It's just how Roarke moved. Quickly, efficiently, and completely aware of his surroundings.

He couldn't believe how many people walked about with their heads in the phones, texting, talking, or reading. Not only did they miss real life around them, but they were also more likely to be in or cause an accident.

In the course of researching how little the average pedestrian was aware of his or her surroundings, and therefore also unaware of potential external threats, he discovered that people's strides were now shorter than decades earlier, meaning it took them longer to get places. The chance of veering off course while walking and texting was more than sixty percent. Getting hit by a car? Forty percent higher than unplugged pedestrians. Bumping into a parking meter or tree? Roarke counted four on today's walk alone. Even worse, looking down, they wouldn't see a terrorist's car or truck bearing down on them until it was too late.

On the occasion he was on the phone, Roarke was usually running toward trouble. His bar mate at St. Arnold's had been with him on some of those runs.

"What will they call us? Consultants?" Roarke asked as he raised his glass of Jim Beam.

"Sure, with an official looking gold emblem on a business card. No address, just a phone number," D'Angelo replied. "Classy."

"No email?"

"Really? Emails, buddy? We'll contact people who need us because we know they'll need us."

"How?"

"Old friends. Favors."

Roarke laughed. Vinnie D'Angelo was right. No emails.

The two men shared a mussel pot. The first. D 'Angelo was drinking a Harp and was ahead of Roarke.

"What's your wife think?"

It was D'Angelo's turn to laugh.

"Considering she doesn't really know everything I do now, she's okay with the idea."

"But consulting could be just as…" Roarke didn't need to add the next word. *Dangerous.*

"There is that," D'Angelo said.

"And the kind of consulting?"

People who moved into the private sector with bona fide intelligence community credentials and high-level references could score big. The work could be limited to analysis or advising. Deeper, a consultant could conduct surveillance or manage subcontractors. Subcontractors were often an antiseptic way of describing mercenaries.

Vinnie D'Angelo had thought about the same things. Like Roarke, he was a utility player who had so far succeeded. He worked for CIA director Jack Evans much the way Roarke *sort of* answered to Morgan Taylor. And like Roarke, there was little on the record except basic bio information. D'Angelo was ex-Army Special Forces.

The CIA operative was a few months shy of his fortieth birthday. He was two inches shorter than Roarke's six-feet, but every bit as fit. As a team, they'd worked in Iraq, Libya, Russia and a few more destinations they wouldn't discuss at the bar. Nor would their aliases come up. They'd long ago buried those identities and the fake passports that came with them.

D'Angelo was especially valuable to Langley because he could pass as Middle Eastern, Hispanic, or Eastern European. That gave him global mobility.

"Our friend from Positano would use us," Roarke said referring to Ira Wurlin, a high-ranking Mossad operative they had met at a dinner in Positano, Italy. "And there's no end to the number of oil companies who need help."

Help often inferred *protection.*

Roarke sipped his drink and motioned the bartender for another pot of mussels.

"But I know you better than you know yourself. You like working for the company, and the frequent flyer miles add up quickly for the family."

"You're right about that, brother," the CIA operative laughed. Just a month ago he'd taken his wife and two kids to Disney World on miles.

Moreover, Roarke also knew how devoted Vinnie D'Angelo was to them. He never allowed his covers to jeopardize family like some undercover DEA and ATF agents had to. Never.

Throughout the conversation, neither Roarke nor D'Angelo used proper names. Not people. Not locations. Not offices. Not the CIA, or the White House. No one needed to know what or whom they were talking about. They were one block from embassy row. Anyone pressed up against the bar could be a spy.

"What about taking some language lessons to break the boredom," D'Angelo said. "That's what I'm doing."

"You already speak Russian, Spanish, Mandarin, and a couple of Arab dialects."

"Yay, but nothing Eastern European. There's money there."

"Great. You learn it and tell me what anyone says."

"*Oczywiście. Będę,*" D'Angelo said.

"What's that mean? Roarke asked.

"Polish. '*Of course I will.*'"

Roarke thought they really could have a go at it. "You're really serious about this business?" he asked.

"Really. More so if you are?" D'Angelo smiled.

Roarke nodded affirmatively.

The CIA agent followed up. "And your sweetie?"

"We're talking again this morning."

"But no time table?"

Now a negative nod. "You're ahead of me by a few years."

"I can wait. But I get nervous when it's too quiet."

Roarke said something under his breath.

"What's that?" D'Angelo asked.

"Calm," he said recalling his Red Team incursions. "Too calm, for too long. You can almost count on something happening."

At that moment, Roarke felt his phone vibrate once. He put his hand over his sports jacket pocket. The cell stopped. Seconds later it began again. A signal.

As Roarke reached for his phone, D'Angelo's rang audibly. They said "Hello," simultaneously and nodded in unison as they got directives.

Each call was quick, summoning them to their respective bosses. They ended their communication at the same time.

"What were you saying about calm?" D'Angelo asked as he put down a fifty.

CHAPTER 11

THE OVAL OFFICE
AN HOUR LATER

"Scott, have a seat."

Roarke nodded to the president and the only other individual in the room, Chief of Staff Bernie Bernstein. For such an urgent call he expected more participants.

"The governor of Idaho's been assassinated."

The president let the declaration settle in.

"When?" Roarke asked.

"An hour ago."

"Professional?"

"By all accounts."

"Hand gun or rifle?"

"Not sure yet. But more likely a rifle shot."

"Christ," Roarke said. Familiar ground for him.

"Geller was looking at a Senate run." The president took his time with the next comment and looked directly at Roarke. "A real rising star."

The Secret Service agent sat up. The phrase hit him hard. *Rising star.*

"I thought that might resonate," Taylor said. "That's why you're here."

The president reviewed what he knew so far from the reports the FBI was assembling from local news, the Idaho State Police, and the governor's office.

"Mulligan is sending out a CIRG team. They're scheduled on a DOJ Gulfstream G550 in an hour."

The Critical Incident Report Group. Sometimes they were specialized SWAT, Hostage Rescue, or Crisis Negotiation Units. At this point, Roarke figured they'd be members of the FBI's lead investigation team. An anti-terrorism investigation team.

"Bessolo?" he asked.

"Bingo," Taylor said. "I want you coordinating with him on ground.

"Rather go it alone, boss."

"Not possible. Play nice. You're on the same team."

"Someone going to tell him that, too?"

"Tell him what?" Bernsie asked.

The president smirked, knowing full well how Roarke and Bessolo had interacted in the recent past.

"We have history," Roarke simply replied.

Roarke's dealings with FBI Agent Roy Bessolo had often been contentious.

"Oil and vinegar," Taylor explained. Then he added with a chuckle, "Even oil and vinegar can flow together."

Actually, Roarke respected Roy Bessolo's investigative prowess, but considered the FBI agent one of the most arrogant law enforcement officers he'd ever had the displeasure to work with. Still, Roarke recognized there was no one better for the job, especially if he had his usual team in tow.

"I want everything he has before I fly out," Roarke stated.

"Done. Your driver will have it for you in the car on your way to Reagan."

"Have them lock down the kill zone for blocks. I want everything on any high rises that a pro would use. Bessolo's probably requested the same thing."

"Bernsie, talk to Director Mulligan."

"Right away," the president's chief advisor stated.

"Go home. Get a few hours' sleep, Scott. Louise will have you out of here early, early morning."

"Nope, I'll leave from here." Roarke always had a rolling suitcase ready in the office. "I can use the time to prepare."

With that, the meeting was over. Roarke just had a call to make.

ROARKE'S OFFICE
MINUTES LATER

"Hey hon, the boss has me traveling again. At four."

"You just got back," Katie responded.

"Something new. You'll hear it on the news."

That was Roarke's cue for Katie not to ask.

"Anything I can do?" she asked.

"Lots," he said lasciviously. "But we'll have to be in the same place for that."

They hung up and Roarke hit his computer. One web search took him to another. Any political enemies Governor Geller might have? Few. Prior credible threats? None. Negative buzz in Idaho print? The usual. Extremist social media chatter? Nothing inflammatory.

C.J. Geller was a political and media darling on the rise. Or at least he had been.

Roarke called up the Google street view of The Grove Hotel and South Capitol Street and virtually drove up and down the street. He went wider to the satellite views. And he made dozens of screen grabs and printed them out.

He drew sight lines from buildings to the target and ruled out all but one building. The mapping took three hours and came back to his initial conclusion.

It was a long gun. A sniper from further away.

Roarke narrowed his thinking to a building where he believed the shot could have originated. He made rough calculations of the distance. Now, even at this hour, he needed to call in some expert help.

"Hello Penny," he said in greeting.

"What? Who? Scott?" answered Captain Penny Walker, his go-to army intelligence contact. Walker was also someone who had known Roarke intimately and understood him, second only to Katie Kessler.

"Sorry, sweetie." He looked at his watch. It was 0225. "It's important."

"Hold on."

He heard Walker excuse herself from her bedmate. Thanks to Roarke's matchmaking, she was now engaged to Duane Parsons, better known on the job as "Touch" for his reputation as the FBI's top facial recognition expert.

"Okay, what do you need?" she asked. "The last time I talked to you at this hour was…"

"I know," Roarke said. "But let's stay on point."

"You're no fun."

"Not quite in a fun mood right now." He explained why and then got to his questions.

"Can you draw up a list of the best shooters in the country? Snipers. Military, retired. Experts at least up to 2,000 yards. And narrow it down to anyone with a grudge. Also, what would be your rifle of choice?"

"Oh, I just press F7 and it'll all come up," she said sarcastically. "Seriously, Scott, I've got to dig deep, cross-reference, and hell, it's a really broad search. Any age parameters?"

"Anyone young enough to have the ability through anyone old enough who can hold a shot steady."

"Oh, that makes it easy."

"Come on, you can do this better than anyone."

"You're right about that. But it's still going to take some time. I mean, I do have other assignments."

"Top priority, Penny. If you need my boss to make a call to some general, consider it done."

"You're going to force me into an early retirement," the thirty-four-year-old career officer said.

"And do what? You live for this."

"Oh man, you've always had my number," she sighed. "Tell me where you want the file."

"I will."

"And I can assume that this has to do with…"

Roarke cut her off. As with Katie, he didn't want to discuss specifics over an open line. "It'll become apparent."

"Roger that."

"Okay and warm up your boyfriend to the idea that I'll be at his door, too."

"You really know how to ruin a good night's sleep."

"Later today, Penny. Top Priority," Roarke repeated.

"I'll send what I have."

Scott Roarke knew she would. She was the best at what she did on and off the books.

CHAPTER 12

THE NEXT MORNING

There was no convenient nonstop commercial flight to Boise, so the president's secretary worked with the Pentagon and the Air Force 11th Wing to get Roarke on a scheduled military transport. He left Joint Base Andrews at 0435. Flying time was fast, under four hours for the 2,048-mile trip. The food service was terrible. A box breakfast. Except for a banana, it was all dry.

Ordinarily the Air Force C-5 Galaxy would have landed at Mountain Home AFB, fifty miles southeast of Boise. When presented the possibility, Roarke insisted they land at the close-in Boise Airport, which had a dual designation as both a civilian and military airport, three miles south of the city.

Roarke was met by a sergeant from the adjacent Gowen Field, home of the Idaho Army National Guard.

"Mr. Roarke, consider me your Uber today. Hop in."

Roarke shook the young enlisted man's hand and read his nametag. "Thank you, Sgt. Patton. I don't suppose you're any relation to the general."

"No, sir. Old family name. Moved out west in the homesteader days.

The closest any of us got to war has been me. I served in Afghanistan."

"Well, I'm sure I'm in good hands." Roarke said. "You know where we're going?"

"A bee line into town. I've got the address. Traffic's a little wild on South Capitol, considering."

The drive was quick. Clearance past State Police, easy. Patton dropped Roarke off one hundred feet shy of an inner area cordoned off by yellow police tape.

Roarke's ID got him further. He saw a familiar profile and immediately approached.

"Hello, Bessolo."

Roy Bessolo did a quarter turn and merely shook his head.

"Been a while, Roy."

"Not long enough," Bessolo boomed. "I suppose this means everything's moved further up the food chain?"

"Yup," Roarke replied good-naturedly. "You know my boss."

"Haven't actually met him."

"Maybe someday I'll get you an invite." He extended his hand. Bessolo shook. Despite the tit for tat, the barrel-chested FBI veteran recognized that Roarke had the real chops and was an able collaborator.

"Good to see you, Scott," Bessolo said breaking the sour mood.

"Likewise. Did you bring the starting lineup?"

"Always," he said referring to Thomas and Shikiar.

Roarke looked around the crime scene. Then he peered down the street at the building he'd identified as the likely spot for the sniper.

"I take it they're down," Roarke pointed to the construction site a half-mile away, "there."

"Well I see you haven't lost your touch. You know, if you ever want to leave your cushy desk job, I'll try you out in the field," Bessolo joked.

Roarke laughed. "I'll keep that in mind. In the meantime, let's hoof it. Is the elevator working? Say to the fifteenth floor?"

"Jesus, "the FBI agent declared. "I've got a fucking leak."

"No, I'm just better than you expected."

THE SUPREME COURT
THE SAME TIME

Katie Kessler woke early and returned to her research. An hour into it she saw the thread. The Revolutionary and Civil Wars were just background. Precedent. Legal grounding.

God, he's sly, she thought referring to the chief justice.

Chief Justice Leopold Browning was indeed sly; a manipulator of the highest order, but a truth seeker and true defender of the Constitution. He demanded nothing less from his staff, and even more from Katie Kessler, one of the most astute legal minds he'd encountered in years. Though he'd never told her as much, the assignments he gave her demonstrated his faith in her.

Man, he got me again.

BOISE, ID
FIFTEEN MINUTES LATER

Beth Thomas, leading Bessolo's field team, appeared exasperated. The FBI veteran, a woman not to mess with, was like a bloodhound. Nothing could take her off the scent. The trouble was, the assassin left no scent, just evidence that he'd been there and one dead rent-a-cop.

"Anything?" Bessolo said as he and Roarke walked off the freight elevator. They put on cloth booties to avoid contaminating the site.

"Whoever did this knew that he'd get away. And he wanted to mock us," Thomas said. "Smudged glove marks on the box he used to lean up against. Some fingerprints, but I guarantee they'll all belong to the builders."

"Footprints?" Roarke asked.

"Sure. Intentional. Right there in the dust. One size ten and one size twelve. He walked in those to throw us off. But this is the spot." She pointed to the box, the window, and the butt impression in the dust.

"So we have an ass print," Bessolo bellowed. "Like we're keeping files on butts now?"

Thomas acknowledged Roarke with a smile.

"Roarke. It's been a while."

"Yup, sorry it's under such circumstances again."

"We're like moths to a goddamned flame," she replied.

He exchanged greetings with Bessolo's other team members and carefully examined the immediate area.

"What about that?" he asked pointing to the floorboard. Something had been put there.

Thomas answered.

"That's where he put the bag with his rifle parts. Close at hand. He assembled it while sitting, made his shot, broke it down, and left."

"Surveillance video?"

"Removed after he killed the guard," Bessolo added. "We're dealing with a real professional."

THE SUPREME COURT
AN HOUR LATER

Katie Kessler pulled her notes together and marched authoritatively into the chief justice's office.

"Ms. Kessler, bright, chipper, and prepared, I hope," Browning said from behind his desk.

"Yes sir," she responded.

Justice Browning could have made it much easier for her. But, she reasoned, where was the lesson in that? Having her determine the issue was better than handing it to her. Now she owned it.

"Coffee?"

"Not just now, thank you."

"Well then…" He gestured for her to take the seat opposite him.

His only directive, research *The Declaration of Causes*. Nothing more. No clues, no dates, no points in history. Yet, she thought she had successfully connected dots between yesterday and today, history and contemporary politics.

Browning raised his left eyebrow. It was his signal to begin. He also noticed something unmistakable. Confidence. He smiled inwardly.

"Mr. Chief Justice, I'll begin with a quote. '*Experience hath shewn, that even under the best forms of government those entrusted with power, have in time, and by slow observations, perverted it into tyranny.'"*

"Thomas Jefferson," Browning cited. "Go on."

She did. She explained the motivation behind Jefferson's quote and how *The Declaration of Causes* was presented as the last chance for King George and the Parliament of England to avoid revolution in the colonies.

Katie read from the declaration, quoting key parts. She paused after three minutes to gather her thoughts.

"I hope that's not all you have!" Browning barked.

"Certainly not, sir. The next time we saw such a declaration issued was when first four, then more Southern states proclaimed their grievances against the Union. As with the colonist's declaration against England, it led to war. The Civil War.

"Now here's where it gets interesting. Congress never declared war. If they had, the United States government would have recognized the Confederate States as a legitimate government."

"And counselor, what difference would that have made?" Browning asked.

"If Congress recognized the Confederacy as a nation, secession couldn't be viewed as an act of treason under the Constitution."

"And…"

"And the U.S. acted to protect the States, not to invade them."

"So far, so good, Ms. Kessler."

She didn't dwell on the compliment. Besides, Katie felt it was just getting good.

"Now, what you really wanted…"

BOISE, ID

"Oh man, the U.S. alone must have trained thousands of snipers. Army, Marines. And then there are the civilian wannabes playing weekend war games. Thousands and thousands. Expand the search worldwide wide and—" Bessolo let the thought linger on the walk back to The Grove Hotel.

"As a matter of fact, I'm digging into just that," Roarke replied.

"How so?"

"I put a friend on it before I left town. Expecting some news soon."

"News? Like a list?"

Roarke nodded.

"Make me a copy, Roarke!"

"You'll get it after I talk with my contact."

Bessolo stopped him on the street. Roarke looked at the FBI agent's hand on his arm and up at Bessolo, who relaxed his grip.

"*After*," Roarke repeated. "Maybe tonight."

THE SUPREME COURT

"*WE THE PEOPLE begin this Declaration of Causes by incorporating the first two paragraphs of the original Declaration of Causes.*"

Browning smiled. Katie didn't see it as she read from her notes.

Continuing to read, "The names of the current violators of our Social Contract are substituted for those of the original Oppressors of the American Colonists, with some further parsing reflecting the manner and the method of our current oppression and enslavement."

She lifted her eyes. "That's from a draft of a modern Declaration of Causes, one of many that have circulated in recent years."

"And what does that have to do with us, counselor?"

"Fringe movements, sir. Fringe separatist groups. They've been growing in size and stature since the 1980s, with a big surge during Obama's presidency. But where these factions were disparate, cash poor, and leaderless early on, they're gaining strength and visibility. They won't get their way, but they're well within reach of becoming significant political disruptors."

The chief justice nodded approvingly. Katie waited for the first of many questions that would really test her research and resolve.

"Who should we be monitoring?"

"Everyone. When it comes to white supremacy groups, The Southern Poverty Law Center is ahead of everyone." She paused. "As you know."

"I want to find out what *you* know, Ms. Kessler. Go on."

"From the thirty-thousand-foot level, there are tremendous regional ideological differences across the country. Religious beliefs, education, the economy, and family all weigh heavily from the Deep South to the Pacific Northwest, from the Midwest to New England. Breaking it down even more micro, Miami/Dade vs. the State of Florida. Los Angeles vs. rural California.

"In 2011, a Republican official in Riverside County called for thirteen other Southern California counties to band together to break off and form a separate California republic.' Another ballot proposal was brought before voters in 2018 to divide California into three states.

"Michigan's Upper Peninsula has its own constituency. A group tried to place a secession bill on a state referendum in the mid-eighties. In the early 1990s, counties in southwest Kansas made noise about seceding from the state to form West Kansas. It died, but not without nine counties claiming they had strong support.

"Staten Island has long talked about secession. In 1993, sixty-five percent of the residents approved a mandate for splitting from New York City, but the state assembly put the kibosh on that idea. It still keeps coming up every few years. Of course, no one has figured out how Staten Island alone could finance police, fire, and community services.

"And that's the main problem with these movements. They can't sustain themselves, so they fizzle out. Ideology, no structure. The legal battle never gets further than the noise level."

Katie stopped and turned over the page on her yellow pad.

"But here's where it gets more interesting. Texas Governor Rick Perry suggested in 2009 that the state might secede from the Union. Although he didn't use the word 'secession,' his statement still recalled the battle cry of the old Republic of Texas.

"More prescient, citizens in the eastern part of Washington State feel they're ignored by the state legislators and Seattle and Olympia. It's conservative vs. liberal Washington. East Washington has more in common with portions of east Oregon and parts of west Idaho. The movement has a name—the New Northwest Republic—and a leader."

"And it's significance?" Browning asked.

"Political power for one, legal battles for another."

"Really, Ms Kessler. Secession from the Union. Hasn't that issue been put to bed?"

"Only in so far as we believe it won't happen. However, given the divisiveness in an already divided national electorate, in time, anger-driven secessionist movements could end up on the front steps of the Supreme Court. Even closer. At your door, sir."

She let her words sink in, then added, "I'll take that coffee now."

THE GROVE HOTEL

Roarke opened the carry-on suitcase on his hotel bed. He had underwear and socks for the week, two polo shirts, jeans, sneakers, a dress shirt, a sports jacket, and his dopp kit. Locked in a metal box, ammunition for his Glock.

Roarke was ready for a shower, but not before checking in with Penny Walker.

"Hi there, how's my favorite?" he asked playfully at the start of the phone call.

"I was never your favorite," CPT Penny Walker replied. "You were waiting to meet your favorite."

"At least I was your best."

"Wrong again, sweetheart. But you picked up more dinners than most. That's why I liked you."

Roarke had to laugh. His relationship with Walker couldn't have survived the intensity they both brought to their affair. That was years ago. What remained was deep friendship, utmost respect and trust, and a valuable inside asset, available 24/7.

"Loved me."

"Liked…a lot."

"Well, like me enough to fill me in. What do you have?"

Roarke grabbed the hotel pad on the desk.

"Two hundred fifty-five names in the system. Marines, Army, Special Forces. Active duty to recent retirees and veterans still likely capable of holding a rifle steady for that kind of shot. Of the two hundred fifty-five, thirty-four are dead."

"Time to update Pentagon files," Roarke interjected.

"No kidding," Walker laughed.

"We've confirmed that forty-seven are currently overseas. Sixty-one more at home."

"We've?"

"Touch pitched in. He crossed-checked FBI data bases. Strictly unofficially."

"Well, I guess he is your best," Roarke joked. "So where's the math leave us?"

"One hundred eleven. Not so good."

"Not at all," Roarke agreed. "How long will it take to clear the list?"

"A few days. The easy part's over.

"But there's another important consideration," Walker warned.

"And that is…?"

"A bigger playing field. It could be international."

Roarke sighed. "A lot bigger. Okay then, keep me posted."

"Will do. Oh, and Touch said if you have any surveillance video he'd pull images for a more complete search."

"Wiped clean. We're checking for anything else. ATMs and the like. But Bessolo is here, too. Don't want to piss him off too much. If they come up with anything, I'll recommend he get it to Touch. Bottom line, we're looking for a pro."

THE SUPREME COURT

"Are we to be concerned?" the chief justice asked.

"We need to watch for a traffic jam," Katie Kessler replied. "A new *Declaration of Causes* might not clear the lowest hurdles, but then again, it might. Especially if there are multiple movements that have state or municipal authorization behind them. Then it could eat up a great deal of judicial time all the way up the ladder."

"Tell me something I don't know," Browning said, making it clear that so far she hadn't dug deep enough.

"All fifty states have petitions to secede in the pipeline."

Browning raised an eyebrow again. She caught the look and doubled down.

"There's paperwork bubbling up through the system spurred on by

Brexit. Alternately titled Vexit or Texit for Vermont and Texas, Calexit or NHexit for California and New Hampshire. They're coming our way. Eventually we'll have to consider whether secession can ever be considered a legal act." For emphasis she added, "Again."

"*Texas v. White*, Ms. Kessler," Browning said pointing her to precedent.

"Yes, sir." She leafed through her pad until she found the decision Browning cited.

"Supreme Court Justice Salmon P. Chase wrote the majority opinion in 1869. It formally struck down the Texas Ordinance of Secession which rendered all acts of secession illegal based on the Articles of Confederation and the Constitution. He wrote, 'The union between Texas and the other states was as complete, as perpetual, and as indissoluble as the union between the original states.'"

"You're aware of Justice Antonin Scalia's opinion in 2006?" he asked

"I am." Without referring to any notes she explained that Scalia maintained the issue of secession was not in the realm of possibility. The United States cannot be party to a lawsuit, and the constitutional basis of the question had been "resolved by the Civil War." "He also wrote that the *Pledge of Allegiance* illustrated the point with the phrase 'one nation indivisible.' But a pledge is just that. It's a pledge, not an oath to defend the Constitution by duly elected state officials."

"So where is the immediate problem?"

"Back to *Texas v. White*. Chase left an opening which contradicts Justice Scalia's learned opinion. Secession could be achieved through 'revolution or the consent of the States.'"

Browning leaned back in his leather chair. Without realizing, he was making another indentation in his desk with his pencil.

Following thirty seconds of contemplation he continued.

"And you actually believe the court could be faced with this, counselor?"

"Sir, more to the point, you assigned me this because *you* considered it possible."

"And because you're good," he declared.

CHAPTER 13

INDEPENDENCE, MO
TWO DAYS LATER

The Frenchman had a real name. A birth name carved into a cemetery monument outside of Nice that hadn't been visited in more than a decade. If anyone with authority had checked, they would have determined that the body buried there was someone completely different. But no one checked. And no one who had known him missed him. Not his parents, his lovers, or the men he had served and fought beside.

The killer gave up everything when he was accused of shooting a Turkish ambassador on the streets of Paris. He easily escaped, collected the kill fee, faked his own death in an Austrian car crash, eliminated his contact, and began his new life leaving little evidence beyond the existence of a phantom killer.

There were records of his assumed exploits in European and American intelligence files. But no agency was certain any particular case could be attributed to one person. Some assassinations had a distinct Russian feel, the handiwork of the FSB. But so many other murders?

It had come down to a simple decision. Whenever there was an unsolved political assassination, investigators put it in the elusive figure's file. It grew larger and larger. So far nothing led anywhere. But along the way, the assassin earned a nickname. French, due to the number of political murders eloquently executed in France. Le Fantôme was born. Or, as the authorities considered, someone was reborn as Le Fantôme.

The Frenchman was reachable through people who knew people who knew people. He took special care when meeting clients, researching everyone who hired him. In turn, those who tried to get too close to him simply out of curiosity regretted it to the end, which came fairly quickly.

Since no one knew him, he could go virtually anywhere under multiple aliases. Work took him to Israel, Australia, the Caribbean, South America, and even Russia. Now, it was the United States. He'd already completed twelve assignments from his present employer, with more challenging ones ahead.

The Frenchman never really cared to learn much about his victims or why they were targeted. But he was told that his American assignment was meant to be highly visible. He clarified the point. The murders were to be highly visible, not him.

In an Independence, Missouri, hotel room, planning his next killing, the assassin repeated a mantra that so far had kept him alive. It wasn't religious or even spiritual. More scientific. Albert Einstein, in fact.

C'est une théorie qui décide ce qui peut être observé.
Translated.
It is a theory that decides what can be observed.

With more targets and more completions came greater possibility for exposure, especially to someone who worked outside the rules as he did. Starting tonight, the Frenchman determined he'd take even extra care.

BOISE, IDAHO

Scott Roarke had worked on multiple theories over the past two days. His best one so far was that there was a disgruntled vet with a marksman rating who wanted to take down a governor. Adding dishonorable discharge as a factor would further focus the search. He was also guided by a lesson he was left with during his training at the U.S. Army Intelligence Center and School in Fort Huachuca, Arizona. "If the facts don't fit the theory, change the facts."

He didn't recall who wrote it. He'd be surprised to find out that his quarry was guided tonight by a different Albert Einstein quote.

INDEPENDENCE, MISSOURI

Missouri Senator Thomas Pleasance accepted the year's top award from the Independence
Chamber of Commerce for his commitment to small businesses. Over the years he'd received many such honors at Stoney Creek Hotel and Conference Center. This one came with votes.

Pleasance proudly held the plaque for photographers and promised it would be the most prominent honor in his office. He was wrong about that.

Pleasance, the state's junior senator to Washington, had Kennedy-good looks, a rural preacher's recall of Bible passages, and ever-increasing national attention. He was, as the local press described him, a true rising star.

But then again, he had always been on an upward track. High school valedictorian, a University of Missouri quarterback with Division I records that still stood, a decorated Marine officer, and now Senate minority whip. Yet Thomas Pleasance had his eye on an even bigger prize.

Heavy rain had moved across the plain. The senator's aide went to get the car while Pleasance waited under the carport with guests from the event.

It was easy for another businessman to blend in and saddle up to the senator for a moment. A moment was all the businessman, with his face turned away from the single closed circuit camera, needed. That and his umbrella.

* * *

The news hit the internet late Saturday night. A duty nurse at St. Mary's Hospital, violating confidentiality, called her boyfriend who, in turn, sent a tweet. A "friend" retweeted it with a hashtag: #senatorthomaspleasance. That amplified the reach nationwide. Although the news stations across Missouri were asleep, the White House was always awake.

Morgan Taylor was alerted by his chief of staff. The president did two things immediately. He had Bernsie reach out to the chief administrator at the hospital, and he personally called Scott Roarke in Boise.

CHAPTER 14

YUKTAE-DONG, DEMOCRATIC PEOPLE'S REPUBLIC OF KOREA
FIFTEEN MONTHS EARLIER

"Good morning."

It wasn't. Every morning was filled with some sort of dread.

Without a reply, the security guard at the submarine base waved Chin-wah Lee through the scanner. It produced the exact same image of the Navy computer geek that it did every day: A broken left wrist fused with a titanium rod and fillings in his teeth.

"See you tomorrow," Lee added, not expecting anything back. He wasn't disappointed.

Lee wasn't allowed to enter the base with a cell phone, wallet, or any portable device—not that he had the disposable income to buy any. Just whatever metals in whatever place were on record. Except he knew a way to get around the scanning. It was above his dental work, on his palate, where he could hide a small USB drive that could produce a huge pain.

* * *

Chin-wah Lee earned a pittance from the Navy. It paid his bills, but it didn't give him what he secretly wanted. Now his mentor, his former teacher, his friend promised him much more. Real money. One hundred thousand American dollars. One hundred thousand that would accrue interest in something called Fidelity Investments.

He looked back on the first contact and how Jee Gyuen worked him for years. Lee's friend was an American agent. He always had been. Now Chin-wah Lee was, too.

The problem with the risks is that he didn't know when it all might come to fruition. Even more uncertain how he would actually escape from the *Democratic*—a word he nearly choked on every time he said it—People's Republic of Korea.

Today, like other days he smuggled in a thumb drive, he wondered whether anything he was doing would make a real difference. And then he worried whether he'd live long enough to experience freedom. Enjoy the money. Travel.

He was also driven by hope. Chin-wah Lee read contraband *National Geographic* magazines. He wanted to see what the world looked like beyond the pages and beyond the government's lies. Travel restrictions and his own job clearances prevented him from leaving. Not just now. Likely forever. And that was assuming the West didn't obliterate his homeland in a first or retaliatory strike. The Supreme Leader's nearly daily proclamations and ever-increasing threats to the West made it all the more unlikely he'd ever have to adjust to another time zone.

Until…

"So, my friend, do you still think you're in paradise?" Jee Gyuen had asked that day many months earlier.

At first Chin-wah Lee laughed. But Gyuen repeated the question.

"Really, do you still think you're in paradise?"

"There is no paradise. Only work and rules, food and sleep. On good days some sex."

"So many of your countrymen think they have paradise here."

Lee sat up. He heard coded words. *Your countrymen…they and think.* Suddenly Gyuen sounded like an outsider.

Jee Gyuen had friendly eyes, the kind that had always encouraged Lee. But in that meeting they had narrowed, revealing another personality.

"If you could go anywhere, where would that be?" Gyuen asked.

The North Korean laughed at the impossible question.

"I'll never be able to go anywhere."

"But if you could?" Gyuen responded.

"Anywhere?"

"Well, first to visit."

"Italy," Lee volunteered quietly. "I'd love to go to Italy. Florence and Venice. Rome, of course. And France. Paris."

"Okay, and where to live?"

This question wasn't just impossible, it was dangerous. Chin-wah Lee looked to his left and right. No one was paying any attention as they walked.

"America," he whispered. "Definitely America. But it could never happen."

"Are you so sure?"

Lee suddenly recognized a change of tone in Gyuen. A tone to match his friend's eyes. He straightened. "I should leave now," he said.

"Please," Gyuen said holding his arm. They stopped. "I didn't mean to make you feel uncomfortable. We're just talking."

Lee studied his companion. He appeared to be a changed man. Stronger than his height suggested. More in control. Aware of his surroundings and what he was saying.

Gyuen saw that he was being scrutinized. He silently counted to five. He had pushed that day. Speeded up the long game. In five seconds his potential recruit would either walk and possibly report the contact, or stay, intrigued; hooked. If Lee remained, Gyuen would have an asset. If he left, he would likely have to eliminate his friend.

Five seconds came and went.

"Chin-wah, I need your help."

That one sentence led to more. They resumed their walk through the streets of Yuktae-dong. America had a new asset.

CHAPTER 15

WASHINGTON, D.C.
PRESENT DAY

Browning's follow up assignment for Katie: Draw up likely actions the judiciary would have to consider.

"Two caveats, Ms. Kessler. The first one: use your White House experience. Predict the legal moves the president would take. Publicly and with Congress. Second, do not *formally* discuss your research with Agent Roarke." He peered over his glasses to underscore his last point. "Do you understand?"

"Yes, sir. Perfectly."

Taking into consideration the way the web of secrets entangled the government, Chief Justice Browning gave her just enough permission to talk to Roarke. Not about the research, but an alert. He shrewdly thought it would be better if both the Judiciary and the White House contemplated the possibilities. Kessler would be his unofficial channel.

BOISE, ID
THE SAME TIME

Roarke and Bessolo sequestered the private dining room at Emilio's in The Grove Hotel. They sat side-by-side at a table for eight. They ordered quickly from the menu, both opting for the Idaho Rainbow Trout and salad. Neither had a cocktail. After the waitress left they turned to shop talk. Roarke reviewed the initial information he'd received from Penny Walker.

"I want to run those names, too," Bessolo said. "Hard copies at my office."

"They'll be there in the morning."

"Any sooner? I've got people waiting."

"I'll see what I can do."

Roarke texted CPT Walker. She quickly replied, *NOT.*

"You'll have it in the AM. That's the best we can do."

"No games, Roarke," the FBI agent said.

"None. My contact has already left. She'd been on it all night."

Roarke then let out an uncharacteristic sigh.

"What's that about?"

"I think we should expand the search. Not just confine it domestically. Too small a universe of subjects."

"Come on. We've got a dead governor, not the president."

"Right. And Russia's hacking and election shenanigans? That doesn't make you more than a little bit curious if there's more to this?"

Bessolo hesitated. "I'm afraid you're right. This isn't the work of just some nut job."

Roarke hoped the food would come quickly because the conversation already had a bad taste.

The thought was interrupted by a call. Roarke answered and listened. Before hanging up he said, "Got it." He rose from his seat and took out a fifty.

"Whoa," Bessolo said. "Where you going?"

"Same place I'm sure you'll be heading," Roarke replied.

"What? Where?"

"Independence."

It didn't mean anything until Bessolo talked to Washington himself.

CHIEF JUSTICE BROWNING'S HOME
GEORGETOWN
EARLY EVENING

"Thank you for coming by, Katie."

The chief justice never called her by her first name in the office. He was less formal at his home.

She kept to protocol.

This was only her second time at his colonial brownstone. The first was the night that she pleaded a case that helped avert a constitutional crisis over the election of Teddy Lodge.

Nothing had changed since her last visit. His collection of classic courtroom movie posters were still up. *Advise and Consent, The Verdict, The Caine Mutiny, The Lincoln Lawyer, Witness for the Prosecution, Anatomy of a Murder, A Man for All Seasons,* and on the lighter side, *My Cousin Vinnie.* It provided a rare glimpse into the personal side of the nation's leading jurist. He loved Hollywood's take on the court, recognizing that it was fundamental to the public's limited grasp of the law.

Some of the posters were signed. Paul Newman to then Federal Circuit Court Judge L. Browning, Mathew McConaughey and Tom Cruise to Chief Justice Browning. He even had Gregory Peck's autograph on *To Kill a Mockingbird* and Henry Fonda's on *12 Angry Men,* though not signed inscribed to Browning.

"I apologize for calling you here, but I will be traveling for a few days, and we need to continue our discussion."

"It's perfectly fine, sir."

"Well then, let's begin. I promise I won't keep you more than an hour."

"An hour will be more than enough. We left me with determining what the Executive branch might do. I have prepared the arguments I would have addressed as White House counsel. They're detailed in a file I'll leave for you. But the greater bullet points basically come down to the following five: One, the military forces at the command of the presidency. A worst case. They would be deployed to a seceding state or states to hold all strategic points and disarm resistance. Assuming that general populations would be more in agreement with fringe groups in support of secession, this would be followed with reaffirmation of the existing state government.

"Two, given the present-day reality, compared with the Civil War era, the White House would count on Americans being more loyal to the country than state. Moreover, military officers have pledged their sworn duty to uphold the Constitution.

"Three, the president would immediately federalize the states' National Guard. Any units that refused would be arrested and charged with treason. That has the terrible ring of execution attached to it.

"Four, the FBI, backed by ATF and the U.S. military, would arrest the secessionists."

Browning listened intently.

"All very determinative."

"All poison bullets, Mr. Chief Justice. It's unlikely it would ever get that far. What Florida retirees really want to give up their Social Security money? What would Oklahomans or Missourians do without FEMA support during tornado season? Or Louisiana or Mississippi when it needed federal hurricane relief?

"On the other hand, Texas might have the wherewithal to support itself as an independent nation. California as well.

"The true bottom line," Katie concluded, "there would be no Civil War. Give it two days, three, maybe a week. But a majority would raise their voices against a splinter minority. It would be over quickly."

"Over for the Executive branch," Browning stated. "The beginning of a long road of law suits for the court."

CHAPTER 16

GLENDIVE, MONTANA
THE SAME TIME

"What kinds of nations fall apart?" Lucas Burke proposed to his supporters at the Glendive Rotary Club.

From the back of the room Clay Lindstrom noted that the crowd hadn't yet found its voice. Burke hadn't worked them up enough. "Come on," he whispered to Burke through the wireless. "Get them going. The shirt! Now the shirt!"

Burke took the cue. "Well, let me tell ya," Burke said colloquially.

He removed his baseball cap and wiped his forehead. Then he loosened his tie, unbuttoned his collar, and rolled up his sleeves. He instantly looked more cowboy; more relatable. Women immediately reacted.

"It all comes down to a bunch of points. Nations don't make it when people's ideology, ethnicity, and economical standing don't square with the government."

A few "Oh yay's" made it up to the stage.

"Well, some of you are beginning to get it," he said lightly.

He earned a few laughs and more affirmation.

"You see," he paused to emphasize the next words, "our beliefs, our heritage, and our wallets unite us. And they separate us from those who seek to govern from far away. Come on. What does Washington know or care about me and you?"

"Nothing!" shouted a man from the third row."

Some fifty more answered as a chorus. "Nothing!"

"You're right, nothing. Ours is an independent heritage, grown in the Old West with rugged individualism."

Lindstrom had Burke adjust that part of the speech depending upon where he was. Here it was the *Old West with rugged individualism.* In New Hampshire speeches he spouted *the colonial spirit founded upon Live Free or Die.* In the South, *the echoes of self-determination can still be heard.*

Lucas Burke always scored when he hit regional secessionist buzz words hard.

"Rugged individualism! Where'd you leave it?" He pointed to a man in the first-row center. "When was the last time you felt it," he nodded to a woman to the side. "Who stole it from you?"

"Washington!" a larger part of the crowd shouted.

Burke put his hat back on but backwards. "I didn't hear you. Who?"

More people responded. "Washington!"

"Who?"

Now the entire room erupted. "Washington. Washington. Washington."

The chant continued.

"What kind of nations fall apart," he shouted over the crowd.

"Ours!"

"What kind?"

"Ours!"

Burke raised his hands high and slowly brought them down to quiet the room.

"Damned straight, ours. The America of today is a country sick with affluenza, technomania, megalomania, e-mania."

The words weren't his or Lindstrom's. They belonged to a retired Duke professor who promoted the creation of The Second Vermont Republic. They worked here in rhythm and impact.

"Washington thinks global. We're local. What do the two have in common?" He held his hand to his ear.

"Nothing."

"Damned straight," he repeated. "The equilibrium proclaimed by the Constitution no longer exists. There is no unifying national interests anymore. There's our interests and theirs. Do they care about ours?"

"No!" the crowd shouted louder than ever.

"Should we care about theirs?"

"No, no, no, no!" The crowded added to the noise by pounding their feet on the ground. They were of one mind; a mob mind, hypnotized by Burke's rhetoric.

"No, no, no, no!" This went on for two minutes before Burke saw Lindstrom's cue. He saw it before Lindstrom spoke in his ear through the wireless.

"Take it home, now," Lindstrom whispered.

Burke's hands came up again, then down. Now quiet.

"Without us, without our interests counting, the United States of America cannot stay united. So, my friends, divided we stand. Divided we succeed."

Lucas Burke would eventually work his way forward into the crowd with a message to take home. He'd offer it up like red meat to the ravenous crowd.

"There's a name for our action. There's a name for our cause. We must be brave. We must be courageous. But know in your heart that we are right. This is the future we choose. Our right. Our destiny. We choose to break the chains."

He took off his hat one more time and looked at the logo.

"We choose to break the chains that bind us to Washington. To be free!"

Burke pointed to the symbol and with a huge windup, he threw his cap out into the audience. Five people jumped for it. A tall trucker won and proudly waved it in the air!

"We choose to establish our own nation!"

"Yes!" screamed the crowd.

"We choose to establish the New Republic of the Northwest!"

"Yes! Yes! Yes!"

And now the message came. A simple thought, a single word that would galvanize this crowd behind Lucas Burke. One word that Clay Lindstrom had inserted into Burke's speech. One word that was part of a larger, overarching plan intended to cost the country time, energy, money, and faith.

Burke took his microphone and walked forward.

"My friends, on this day, this very day, we choose to…" He had them all now and held them with the pause. Then it he said. "Secede!"

The crowd turned the call to action into a boisterous chant.

"Secede, secede, secede!"

Burke let it ring out. It only grew as an aide came out with a cardboard box filled with logo hats. He tossed them one by one, joining in the chant.

Fifteen minutes later, he was at the door shaking hands while staffers collected phone numbers and email addresses, and sold more hats.

• • •

Burke took the first leg of the night's drive to their next stop. He felt particularly energized by the Glendive audience.

"God, the way they erupted. Magnificent!" Burke said with a huge grin. He peered over to Lindstrom in the passenger seat. "We can really do this!"

Lindstrom laughed. "Don't get ahead of yourself, Luke. One step at a time. First, grassroots. The two of us putting miles on and building the base. In another month, you can stretch out in a campaign bus and see yourself on CNN. For now, keep it simple, and let events take on a life of their own."

"Right, right," Burke said, suddenly wondering what events Lindstrom was talking about.

He quickly forgot the point and began thinking of new refrains to work into his speeches.

Regional exceptionalism, economic sovereignty, political pandemic, self-reliance, ideological continental shift.

He wanted to try them out on Lindstrom, but he saw that his advisor, the real leader of the movement, was falling asleep.

CHAPTER 17

INDEPENDENCE, MISSOURI
THE NEXT MORNING

Roarke hadn't even bothered to check on commercial airlines. Thanks to a call from the White House to the Pentagon, to the Secretary of the Air Force, and onto the brigadier general at the 124th Fighter Wing housed at Gowen Field, Roarke climbed up and into an AF VIP Goldstream.

Traveling at 420 mph, the flight to Kansas City International Airport took just over three hours. Roarke landed at 0345. Cabs weren't queued up at that hour, so he ordered an Uber to Centerpoint Medical Center; a thirty-six-minute drive.

After explaining his way past the nurse's station at the Center, Roarke was introduced to Dr. Pooja Anupama, the senior resident on duty. He offered his business card with the Secret Service logo on the left and his name and title on the right, which she barely examined and then handed back.

"A few questions, doctor."

"I'm very busy," she interrupted employing an impatient and inconvenienced tone.

Strike one, Roarke thought.

"About Senator Pleasance."

"I can't talk to the press."

Strike two.

"Perhaps you need to look at my card again." He offered it, but she was disinterested. "I'm investigating—"

"Investigating? You should be speaking with someone in public relations. I have morning rounds. They'll be in at ten."

It was 5:55 a.m. *Strike three.*

"Doctor…" He examined her name ID for impact. "…Anupama, you'll need to find someone else for your rounds. You were on duty last night when Senator Pleasance was admitted?"

"Really, Mr. Roarke, unless you're also a member of the immediate family, I'm prevented from answering patient questions."

"Patient?" Roarke asked. "The patient was a United States—"

"Yes," she interrupted. "But confidentiality…" She stopped short. "I'm sorry. Who exactly are you? The only thing I was told was that someone was coming in from Boise, which doesn't tell me a lot, and I was to meet you and confirm the death of Mr. Pleasance."

"United States Senator Thomas Pleasance."

"Correct, and he died at 11:47 last night."

"Look, doctor, fairly soon the news trucks will be arriving, which I have nothing to do with, and questions will be coming fast. So we have a lot to talk about right now."

"Under whose authority?"

"Under orders from the president of—"

"What was that company on your card?" she coldly asked.

"Company?" Roarke was incredulous, but he had the good sense to turn away as he snickered. A moment later he returned with a look she couldn't misinterpret.

"First of all, Senator Pleasance is no longer a patient. He's dead. You can confirm that?"

"I have."

"Secondly," he said more emphatically, "not so much a company. It's called the government. The United States government. So to your question of authority, I am here on the authority of the president of the United States. In a few hours or less you can expect an FBI agent named Bessolo who won't hesitate arresting you if you give him the same attitude. So let's start over."

He handed his card to her again.

"Please, keep it," he said. "I have more. And I suggest you really read it this time. Oh, and that emblem you're covering up with your thumb means something. My name is Scott Roarke. I'm a United States Secret Service agent."

Dr. Pooja Anupama wisely took a moment to think about the next thing she'd say.

"Agent Roarke, please accept my apology. It's been a long night. We've already been getting calls, and I haven't known what to say."

"I understand. And I'll help you with that."

"Thank you. Give me a moment. I'll have someone cover my rounds. We can talk in the resident's office."

* * *

"All right, here's what we've done," Dr. Anupama began once they were sitting down. "The body is scheduled for a routine autopsy. It will begin," she checked her watch, "in ninety minutes. At that time, we'll examine body fluids and tissues. But having no reason to suspect anything but natural causes—"

"Stop. Senator Thomas Pleasance was in extremely good health. He was physically fit. More importantly, he was a leader in the U.S. Senate. You start with the position that his death was *not* natural, doctor. And nobody touches the body until a team of doctors from the CDC arrive."

He checked his watch. "They'll be here in two hours and fifteen minutes."

"Of course, we can follow procedure and work with your team. But his symptoms were consistent with catastrophic organ failure starting with intestinal bleeding. He checked in complaining of gastrointestinal issues, nausea, and abdominal pain. I immediately put him on an IV for dehydration. Then we discovered the onset of kidney failure."

"Christ almighty," Roarke said under his breath. "That fast?"

"Yes."

His comment wasn't for the sake of sympathy. It was recognition of a very specific condition.

"Did he show any redness in the eyes and skin?"

"Yes, but rest assured, we followed protocol. From my perspective, had he been admitted earlier we could have saved him."

"No, you couldn't have. Think about the symptoms you described. I'm no doctor, but you've described a very specific condition."

Dr. Anupama considered his question. Roarke let her work it out. She came to the answer quicker than she said it. It took thirty seconds before she whispered, "Ricin poisoning?"

LATER

While the CDC doctors from Atlanta performed the autopsy, Roarke went to Pleasance's office to review the senator's schedule for the past week. He asked the grieving chief of staff, an attractive redhead in her late twenties for any occasion that put her boss in close contact with strangers. Liz Mahoney came up with six events. Roarke was most interested in two: A Kansas City television interview four days before his death and a speaking engagement the night prior.

Midway through the conversation, Roy Bessolo showed up.

"Give me a few minutes," Roarke told the staffer. She excused herself.

"Well, better late than never," Roarke joked.

"You could have saved taxpayer's money if you held a seat on your flight."

"My bad."

"From now on we work together, Roarke!"

"You're right. At least I cleared the forest for you at the hospital."

"You did at that."

For the next ten minutes, Roarke brought Bessolo up to speed on what he'd learned. He had more than Bessolo. Now both were eager to get the toxicology tests, though the lead CDC director warned them that it might not be immediately conclusive. They were used to the waiting game.

Roarke called Pleasance's aide back in.

"Take us through all the steps last night," Roarke said to Mahoney.

She had a hard time putting her thoughts together, dabbed her eyes with a tissue. There was no makeup to smear.

"Take your time," Roarke continued.

"It was an award. Senator Pleasance gave a great speech. All off the cuff. No notes, no prompter. He's great at—"

She caught herself.

"We know it's difficult. But you can help us. You were there, Ms. Mahoney. Liz. The best way for you to honor the senator is by helping us."

Bessolo nodded, showing more compassion than Roarke had ever seen.

"Agent Roarke is right," Bessolo added. "You may have a clue to what happened."

"Didn't he just get sick? I mean, he had a heart attack or something?"

"That's what we're looking into," Roarke said. "Everything you remember will be important. It's what Senator Pleasance would expect of you."

Liz Mahoney rewound the evening at the Chamber of Commerce dinner.

"He didn't have any contact with anyone except staff until we got to Stoney Creek Conference Center. And even then, we held him in a side room until it was time to hit the dais and then the dinner table in front."

"Who was there?" Bessolo asked directly. "And do you recall where everyone was seated?"

"Kind of," Mahoney replied. "Here."

She removed a yellow pad from her catch-all purse.

"I can sketch the layout and who sat with the senator."

She narrated as she drew.

"The President of the Chamber was directly to his left. Next to him his wife. Then the chamber VP and his wife. On the other side, three women and one man. The woman was president of the Lions Club, next to her, the Elks president and his wife, and finally a representative from the Veterans of Foreign Wars, another woman." She listed everyone by name. "He knew them all for years. They were friends."

"What about after? Was there anyone in the room not on the guest list," Roarke asked. "Oh, and we want a copy of that list."

"I have it. And no. Between me and George, my assistant, we can vouch for everyone."

Bessolo's mood sharply changed.

"Pardon me, but actually, we don't really know who you and George are."

At first, Roarke was stunned by Bessolo's remark. Then he realized he should have made the same assumption.

"What?" Liz exclaimed. She blurted a series of half sentences. "His staff here. God, what the hell do you think?" Then she took more offense. "Thomas was going all the way."

It was the use of the senator's first name that alerted Roarke to something more.

"Thomas?"

"Yes, the senator," she corrected herself. "We could just feel it. We loved him."

And then Liz Mahoney cried.

Roarke gave her a minute to regain her composure, but he now knew. "And George?" he asked softly.

"Oh, Jesus. He's my brother. Goddamn you both!"

"I'm sorry. One more difficult question, Ms. Mahoney. You and the senator?"

"None of your goddamned business!"

"I'm sorry," he said. "I had to ask."

"My brother warned me. He told me I'd get hurt."

"You're going to be okay. And you can still help us protect the senator's legacy and your memory of him," Roarke offered. "So, anything else you remember?"

"Just that he shook a lot of hands and felt great when he left."

"Did he eat anything?" Bessolo asked.

"No. I'd told the waiters not to even put anything in front of him."

"That seems unusual," Bessolo followed up.

Mahoney lowered her head. "He was waiting to eat. I made him a late-night dinner."

Roarke knew the senator was married with two children. But there was no need to pursue what happened later.

"Okay, I want you to remember what happened when you left the conference center?"

"What do you mean?"

"Was there anyone you didn't know? Anyone who didn't belong?"

"Well, we cleared out ahead of most of the guests. Some were around. But not a lot. Maybe four or five. And while George went to get the senator's car, we all crowded under the overhang in case it started to rain again."

Roarke had a sudden flash. It began with Mahoney's mention of *rain.* His mind instantly connected rain to a historically devious murder weapon. An umbrella.

. . .

Roarke had long known the story of dissident journalist Georgi Markov. Markov was especially critical of the authoritarian Bulgarian leadership while living a presumably safe life in London as a writer for BBC World News Service. But in September 1978, waiting to board a homeward bound bus on Waterloo Bridge, an umbrella-wielding man casually passed him, "accidentally" jabbing Markov in the left thigh. The assailant, later identified as a Bulgarian spy code-named Agent Piccadilly, shot a pellet containing .2mg of ricin into Markov. The act took barely a second. Markov suffered for a year before dying. In the decades since, improvements have vastly increased the turnaround time of the poison.

Ricin works fairly eloquently by getting inside the cells of a person's body, preventing the cells from making proteins. Without proteins, cells die. When cells die, the body begins to shut down and not in a pretty way. Death is especially terrible and will usually occur within thirty-six to forty-eight hours or quicker, as it did with Senator Thomas Pleasance,

.   .   .

"It was raining?" Roarke said.

"Beginning to. More of a drizzle," Liz Mahoney noted.

Roarke stood up and leaned directly into the young woman who had lost her lover.

"Now think about this very seriously, Ms. Mahoney. Close your eyes and picture the scene while you were standing under the portico."

"Okay."

"Did anyone you didn't know walk up to the senator."

She paused to think. Roarke added another element for her to visualize.

"Anyone holding anything?"

Mahoney kept her eyes closed but moved her head as if she were looking around wearing virtual reality goggles. Suddenly she stopped and opened her eyes.

"Yes," she said casting a frightening stare forward. "A man from behind. Just for a moment. Just as George brought the car up."

"And was he holding anything?" Roarke repeated.

"Nothing. Well yes, an umbrella."

"Was it open or closed?" Bessolo cut in.

"Closed."

She remembered more.

"He bumped into Thomas, I mean the senator, and excused himself."

"And then?"

"We got into the car and left. I cooked dinner, and in the middle of the night—" She stopped short. "It was me. It was something I gave him," she cried.

"No, Liz. It wasn't you," Bessolo said.

"I wanted to get him to the hospital, but he didn't want to. I should have…"

Bessolo walked away from Roarke and Mahoney and called Beth Thomas in Boise. Roarke overheard part of the conversation.

"You're coming here." He explained the situation and told his team leader to secure all the CCTV video at the Stoney Creek Hotel and Conference Center. "If anyone asks why, tell them to open their damned inbox. I guarantee you the warrant will be there by the time you arrive."

Meanwhile, Roarke was beginning to get a description of umbrella man through his simple questions and answers. Bessolo would have someone on hand from his team to make an accurate sketch of the suspect, but Roarke was convinced the assassin would look completely different now, nineteen hours after his deadly work.

CHAPTER 18

CENTERPOINT MEDICAL CENTER

The CDC team leader, Dr. Jessica Schwartz, took Roarke aside.

"Two beans from a large grocery store can do it," she explained. "It's actually safer and easier to work with than anthrax or botulinum toxin. Anyone even moderately trained can treat the beans with the right chemicals, also widely available, to extract and purify the protein. The Patent Office took instructions off their website, but there's always the rest of the internet. Detection is still pretty much through the process of elimination. The symptoms lead to the conclusion."

"And once that evaluation is made?"

"Which can be easily missed," Dr. Schwartz continued.

"But if it is made?"

"I'll save you a trip to the CDC website. Our posting says, 'There is no antidote for ricin toxicity.'"

"So he was a dead man walking the moment he was hit with the pellet."

"Not exactly. Had he come right to the hospital, been treated for ingestion, a stomach pump might have prevented the ricin from tracking into the gastrointestinal system. Might have," she repeated for emphasis.

Roarke felt badly for Liz Mahoney. She had tried to get Pleasance out. But, he probably didn't want to be seen with her in public at that hour.

The impact of what Dr. Schwartz explained had far greater implications now. To Roarke's mind, Senator Pleasance's death was clearly a political assassination, though that fact was not going to be made immediately public.

Roy Bessolo impressed that directive upon Dr. Anupama and the St. Mary's Hospital administration, instructing her to make *no* comment.

Roarke started working through another thought. *What do two political assassinations have to do with one another?*

Suddenly he was struck with an epiphany. A frightening thought he couldn't excuse.

What if? he said to himself as he phoned the president.

* * *

"Find out!"

The president's declaration couldn't have been clearer. Roarke had his marching orders, ones he proposed himself.

Since he had called Taylor on an unsecured, open line, he said as little as necessary. But it was enough for the president to offer Roarke all the resources he needed. Roarke turned down additional assistance for now. More people with knowledge could multiply the possibility of leaks. Leaks could accelerate the danger.

"Give me two days and keep the White House kitchen open. If I'm right, then we'll open it up. If I'm wrong, we haven't created a panic."

"Two days, Scott."

"Maybe less."

Roarke took a cab to Kansas City International Airport and began a two-leg flight back to D.C.

Onboard, he got some needed sleep, making up for the last thirty-six hours.

* * *

"Good evening, Agent Roarke," the Marine guard said at the White House West Gate. Even though the officer knew Roarke, it didn't prevent him from checking his current status and ability to enter.

Once cleared, Roarke went straight to his small basement office.

There was already a turkey sandwich on his desk. In the corner, a folding canvas cot. The sandwich won out.

Roarke had one other duty. Call Katie.

"I'm back," he said.

He sensed her displeasure.

"It was busy. Very. It may get busier. I'm holed up at the office. Come on by later. We'll see what we can accomplish on a regulation army cot."

"Oh, back to summer camp. How romantic. Can I call you Bobby?"

"Bobby?"

"Yes, I had a Bobby. I never told you?"

"No. And right now it's too much information," Roarke laughed.

"Oh my, how did you ever get me to admit that?"

"I'm good. But give me some time before I prove it again."

"That serious?" she asked, keeping it cryptic.

"Uh huh."

That was enough for Katie to know, *stop now.*

"I love you," she said, ending the conversation.

"I love you more," he replied with his normal rejoinder. Then he amended it. "I love you most."

. . .

Before Roarke began working, he sent two texts: CPT Penny Walker, letting her know he was back in the office for when she had more. Next was Penny's boyfriend, Touch Parsons who was already working on photo recognition leads based on the suspect sketches that had come out of the descriptions from Senator Pleasance's two staffers.

Now it was time for Scott Roarke to confirm or deny his premise. He began typing key words into multiple search engines. Hightower for magazine stories. Nexus/Lexus for legal cases. Google, Yahoo, and Bing on a more scattershot basis. He hit the *New York Times, Washington Post, LA Times, Chicago Sun Times,* and *USA Today* archives until he realized he was aiming above the playing field.

Boise, Jefferson City. It came to him. *Think smaller.*

Roarke turned to the *Manchester Union Leader,* the *Albany Times Union,* the *Journal Star* in Nebraska, and papers from other state capitals across the country. When he exhausted that list, he went even more local. Hyper local. That's where he found his first clue.

He read from an online edition of the Grand Junction, Colorado *Daily Sentinel*. The paper was founded in 1893 as a staunchly independent paper. Now owned by an out-of-state conglomerate, management still believed in strong local reporting.

Donna McKeel was the reporter of record for a *Daily Sentinel* page-two story five months ago that had initial local traction but eventually worked its way further and further toward the back of the paper before it finally disappeared.

It was exactly the kind of report he was looking for.

Roarke found her easily enough on LinkedIn. He secured her phone number through a two-minute people-finder search on the website Spokeo. He calculated the time difference. *Late, but not too late.* He dialed.

"Hello," a tired woman's voice answered. It was 12:20 a.m. for her. Two hours later for Roarke.

"Hello, is this Ms. McKeel, Donna McKeel?"

"Yes, who's calling?"

"I'm sorry to phone you so late, but it's important. I'm calling from Washington about a story you wrote last winter. A few stories in fact. You reported a suspicious death of a school committee woman."

He hoped *important* and *Washington* would get enough of a rise from the reporter to start talking. It didn't.

"Excuse me, but who is this?" she asked.

"I'm a special investigator for the Secret Service. My name is Scott Roarke."

"And I'm the Queen of England," she responded.

Roarke laughed. "I get your apprehension, Ms. McKeel. Not surprising at all. I'll tell you what. I'll hang up. You look up the main White House number. Dial it and ask the operator for me. Again, it's Roarke. Scott Roarke." He spelled it out. "It's late here, but I'm at my desk."

With that, he politely hung up without another word and began counting backwards from sixty. His phone rang on nine. It was one of the overnight White House operators.

"Yes, thank you. Put her through."

The phone clicked. He was back on with the reporter.

"Hello, Ms. McKeel."

"Hello again, Agent Roarke."

"I'm very glad you called back. Under a minute, I must add."

"I like a challenge," she replied.

"And that's what I sensed from your reporting. You wrote about a gastrointestinal death. Martha Connelly, a member of the Mesa County Board of Education. But you considered it suspicious. In your first report. Then I didn't see that followed up."

"Right. They cut that part of the story after the first article."

"Why?"

"My editor. No evidence I could back up. He said it was speculative and conspiratorial. That I was too close to the story. Maybe he was right to edit me. But I don't think he was right about letting the story fade away."

Roarke followed up her comment with another inevitable, "Why?"

"First of all, Martha was my sister-in-law, and I can assure you she was perfectly healthy. Does someone with no history of stomach issues suddenly come down with a life-threatening illness she'd never been diagnosed with?"

"Sometimes," Roarke replied. He read through her online stories. "But you reported congenital heart failure as the cause of death?"

"That's what made her heart stop. Not what made her sick. It was liver failure. Quick and fatal over two days."

Roarke wrote liver failure on his notepad and circled it three times.

"Did the hospital conduct an autopsy?

"No," McKeel replied.

"It wouldn't have helped," he said under his breath.

"What?"

Roarke stared at a blank wall ahead of him. He had an idea. He removed a pack of three-by-five cards from his desk and wrote Martha Connelly's name, elected position, and city. He did the same for Governor Geller and Senator Pleasance.

The reporter was soon aware that Roarke hadn't responded.

"Agent Roarke? Are you still there?"

"Yes. I'm sorry. Is there anything else you can add?"

"I think that's it," she said. "But what can you tell me? It's not every day a member of the president's Secret Service calls up a small town reporter to chat about a story that's been killed. It's your turn, Agent Roarke."

""Don't read more into this than there is. I'm just trying to understand things. Same as you."

"Right," she said, stretching the word out.

"You've got my number if you think of anything else."

"And you've got mine if you want to give me a scoop."

• • •

Done in Missouri, the Frenchman checked in late to a Super 8 motel outside of Spartanburg, South Carolina. He noted the placement of the surveillance camera and tipped his cowboy hat downward. Cash saved him from wasting a one-use credit card. He signed the ledger with his left hand, not his right. If anyone cared to ask, he was merely a weary traveler with a Texas drawl, in town for a poker game. But the young man at the desk didn't ask. He was barely awake enough to hand over the key.

Once in the room, the assassin unloaded his suitcase filled with materials he'd recovered from a nearby storage facility—all the elements needed to make a very loud statement for his client.

• • •

Roarke made another discovery. This one on *BerkshireRecord.net*, the online edition of the Great Barrington, Massachusetts, newspaper. It was a simple follow-up story that linked back to three other reports from two months earlier. He scanned the extracts. One subheading in particular caught his attention: *Police Still Confounded with the Shooting Death of Mayor. No new details. FBI to be called.*

Two hours later, in addition to fatalities in Boise, Independence, and Great Barrington, Roarke had found six other disturbing deaths. He put the names, titles, and locations of the deceased, not all confirmed as murder victims, on three-by-five cards. As he tacked the last one on a fabric wall installed for just this purpose, Roarke's office phone rang. The White House operator announced the caller.

"A Ms. McKeel for you. From Grand Junction, Colorado."

"Thank you," he said, not really expecting such a quick call back. "I'll take it."

"Agent Roarke, I thought of something," the reporter began. "I don't know if it means much. It's probably nothing, but it's kept me awake since we talked."

"Go on, please."

"You ever listen to talk radio?" she asked.

"Yes."

"There's usually a lot of conspiracy talk, but sometimes you can get the pulse of what people are thinking. True or not. Like letters to the editors."

"And?"

"Someone started ranting on a local station. More chimed in."

"About?"

"Martha's death. Apparently it started that night. A caller suspected it was a political thing."

"What kind of political thing?" Roarke asked.

"Come on, Mr. Roarke. An assassination. That Martha Connolly was assassinated. It's been going on for a while now. More than that, locals are wondering who would ever want to run for office."

. . .

Roarke thanked McKeel. She'd done the right thing. Later, he'd call the radio station himself and see if he could get airchecks.

He made a notation on the card with the Colorado school committeewoman's name; then he pulled up the Great Barrington website again and read a letter to the editor that he'd skipped over. In short it was written by a local who wondered whether, in this political climate, it was safe to hold public office.

Two separate cities. One thought. These were the kinds of signs Roarke paid attention to.

He checked the time. 0430. *What the hell.* Might as well ask Bessolo.

"Bessolo, it's Roarke," he said to the very awake FBI agent.

"You're burning the candle at both ends."

"Sounds like you are, too, brother."

"Oh, we're brothers now?" Bessolo barked.

"Brothers of a different mother," Roarke laughed.

"The only relationship we have is that you're a real Mother!"

"With a question," Roarke continued.

"It's your dime."

"Ours," Roarke responded. "Got anything on an investigation into the murder of a Great Barrington mayor."

"Where?"

"Great Barrington, Massachusetts. Massachusetts/New York State boarder. Near Hudson, N.Y. You remember Hudson?"

"Oh, yeah," Bessolo said. "It was where we bumped into one another investigating the death of Senator Teddy Lodge's wife more than a year ago."

"Me personally? Nothing," Bessolo responded with interest.

"Then you should."

"Why?"

"Someone at the bureau's probably got it. Trust me, you'll want to take it over."

"Christ, Roarke. Three assassinations?"

"More than three. Possibly six that I've found. And that's just in a few hours. Random, but strategic. Elected officials. So far, only covered by local news. If anyone links the senator's death—"

"Which some hot shot will," Bessolo interrupted.

"I'm afraid that's already happening."

Roarke told him about the letter to the Great Barrington editor and the talk radio chatter in Grand Junction.

"Love to hear some of that," Bessolo said.

"Me, too. But I want to do it quietly."

"You sure?" the FBI agent asked. "I've got a buddy at the FCC. He'll make a routine request."

"No, don't. These talk radio guys love yelling fire whether or not there's anything burning.

"I'll take care of it. Besides, I want to find out if there's the same kind of on-air talk in other cities," Roarke added.

"Okay. In the meantime, I'll check out this Barrington thing."

"Great Barrington," Roarke said as he reviewed another article on the newspaper's website. "And the *thing* is the assassination of a mayor."

"How'd you say the mayor was killed?"

"I didn't. But it was a rifle."

Roarke heard Bessolo exhale. "Like Boise?"

"Wouldn't that be interesting to find out? And, as a matter of fact—" Roarke suddenly stopped short when he noticed a phrase in the online Great Barrington newspaper.

"What?" Bessolo asked.

"A phrase in the *Berkshire Record*."

"Which says?"

Roarke read it twice himself then answered. "It described the mayor as a local politico who could go far."

"So?"

"A rising star, Bessolo. Just like Geller in Idaho and Pleasance in Missouri. Stay by your phone. I'll get back to you."

Roarke hung up and added new names to his internet searches.

. . .

By breakfast Roarke had connected with two other reporters. One, a Richmond, Kentucky *Register* writer about the shooting death of the city commissioner. Another from Shreveport, Louisiana, where a mayor had died when his car, as *The Times* story reported, "had inexplicably exploded."

"How would they have rated the victims' political future, and what's the buzz about them on talk radio?"

"Oh, the usual rumors," Richmond writer Cynthia Sherwood volunteered. "Up and comer. Young with potential. And, this is Kentucky. So the usual conspiracy theories."

"And what do you think?"

"Well, we reported it as a robbery."

"I asked what you think."

"Nothing that I can report factually," Sherwood said.

Roarke had the same questions for the Shreveport writer.

"Crazy stuff," *Times* reporter Mitchell Jordan offered. "Makes you wonder."

"And do you wonder? You reported it as 'inexplicably exploded.'"

"Not my phrase. My editor's. I'm still digging. Real shame, though. The mayor had a brilliant future."

"You feel there's more to it?"

"Never seen a car spontaneously explode except in the movies. Have you?" the writer asked.

Roarke had but didn't comment. He thanked the Shreveport reporter and put two more cards on the wall.

• • •

"Got a quick response, Roarke. Not what we'd hoped," Bessolo said.

"Oh man, what is it?"

"No match between Boise and Great Barrington. Both sniper rifles, but not the same one."

"Damn. There goes one theory."

"Well, not completely," Bessolo added. "Different markings. But both recovered rounds were 6.5mm. What's that tell you?"

"The guy is trained, smart, and he's fucking with us."

"Which is why I want to move this up a notch and look at it through MOSAIC glasses," Bessolo declared.

Roarke immediately agreed.

MOSAIC was a threat assessment system developed in the early 1980s to identify and hopefully evaluate and intercept threats against public officials and figures as well as dangers facing judicial officers, and others.

The method was developed by a private security firm, Gavin de Becker and Associates, and refined by Walt Riser of Indiana University and the Los Angeles Police Department's Threat Management Unit. That's where Roarke had first learned about it through his mentor, the LAPD officer who rescued him from the streets.

Today, it's a computer-assisted program used by the United States Capitol Police for threats against members of Congress. Police agencies around the country also employ MOSAIC to protect governors, corporations, and universities.

Its principal purpose is to force investigators to consider a myriad of factors in a potential situation, by analyzing thousands of threats. The computer program creates mosaics culled from comprehensive questions and answers inputted over time. Results are expressed on a scale of one to ten. Once queried, MOSAIC produces a written report.

"But MOSAIC won't point us to an individual," Roarke noted.

"Right, but it may help us determine where, when, and how he'll strike. Like *Minority Report*, which can be effective, unless…"

Roarke filled in the *unless.*

"Unless our perp makes sure there's no pattern to his strikes. He's a smart fucker, and he's fucking with more than just the two of us."

At that moment, the reports of the talk radio chatter came back to him. And with that, a new thought.

* * *

The Frenchman woke up with the morning sun slicing through the slits in the curtains. He rolled over and without looking at the clock, accurately guessed the time. 0642. He stretched his legs in the bed he'd never sleep in again, in the motel he'd never remember, but in the city that wouldn't forget him.

He hit the bathroom quickly then returned to the bedroom for one hundred crunches and an equal number of pushups. Through the routine, he prioritized his day. A shower, a new persona, a trip downtown, and some bodywork on a Ford Explorer.

THE OVAL OFFICE
LATER

"You look terrible," President Morgan Taylor stated when Scott Roarke came in. It was beginning to be his regular welcome.

"Haven't gotten much sleep. Maybe tonight. Assuming I can fall asleep. I have a lot on my mind."

"And it's about to be dumped into mine."

"You bet. I don't know what else you have scheduled, but I need a good fifteen minutes listening time and another fifteen to start planning."

The president served Roarke coffee and ordered a sandwich for the two of them, saying, "I think I better have something solid in my stomach for this."

Before Roarke started in with what he'd found, he asked the president a question. "You know the Leonard Cohen song *Anthem?*"

"Yes, why?"

"He's got a profound lyric that's always called out to me. Especially now."

"Oh?" Taylor wondered.

"This one line. '*There is a crack in everything, that's how the light gets in.*'"

Taylor nodded.

"I've been looking for a crack, boss. I may have found one. And with it some light."

CHAPTER 19

NORTH KOREA

The dictator was in one of his fourteen opulent residences. Many of the homes were hundreds of miles from the capital, Pyongyang. They were heavily fortified and protected by ever-improved security devices. Each retreat, sometimes used only a night at a time, was constructed to hide most comings and goings from U.S. spy satellites. Visitors often arrived through underground train lines. Depending upon the Supreme Leader's disposition any given moment, leaving alive was never a guarantee.

He lived in secrecy but moved constantly. Wherever he traveled and slept, he had the people, the food, the tools, and all the toys he needed to rule and play. Today, he was at Anju, his home in South Pyongan Province. A senior officer from the Reconnaissance General Bureau waited while the ruler gorged on pizza and played the latest edition of *NBA Showdown*. The officer had been summoned to report on an operation that few people knew about. After two hours, the spy was admitted to the living room by a uniformed guard, a major in the People's Army.

"Supreme Leader, exalted president, I have the latest reports."

The operative focused on saying only the right things. He unlocked a brown leather attaché case, which had already been checked for weapons, removed two folders, and handed them to the president.

"Sir, you will be most pleased." *An instant mistake.*

"I will tell you how I feel, you won't," he declared.

"Of course."

The agent stood at attention while the young president leafed through copies of American newspapers and screen grabs of U.S. news accounts. He appeared impatient and eager to return to his PlayStation. But the RGB officer, who just turned forty and hoped to make forty-one, remained quiet.

"Tell me what this means!" the dictator demanded impatiently.

"Sir, I have translation pages, they're—"

"Just tell me!"

The officer described the findings. Extracts from newspaper reports from various unpronounceable United States cities.

"This is all you've found?" He slammed his fist on the table.

"We are constantly refining our searches. I will make certain we have more."

"You absolutely will! This is insufficient, and I am displeased."

The president glanced at his guard. Displeased made the major step forward.

"Do it!"

"Yes, sir. Thank you, Supreme Leader.

The dictator returned to his PlayStation.

An hour later, the North Korean officer screamed at his own staff and threatened two with death. He breathed with a sigh of relief when their work delivered reports from somewhere named Boise.

CHAPTER 20

SAO PAULO, BRAZIL
TEN MONTHS EARLIER

The assassin had only one meeting with his contact. The time and date had been set three times through cryptic internet messages. The Frenchman didn't show up for the first two—at a fruit stand in the municipal market and a cafeteria inside Mosterio De Sao Bento. Not that he wasn't there. The contact had no idea that each time he was being watched at the rendezvous points or that he was followed back to his hotel.

The third location was an out-of-the way bench at Ibirapuera Park. The Frenchman got there first and left his contact a note indicating that the location had changed and where he should go. Also on the note, explicit instructions to leave his cell phone on the bench and not communicate with anyone on his way. An "or else" was implied.

The contact scanned the area. From where he was sitting the only people he could see were two lovers and a woman knitting.

The woman wasn't a woman. The Frenchman watched his contact as he fidgeted. He had the look of someone who wanted to be in control and was pissed that he couldn't be. He was out of his element. Not the Number One, but maybe the Number Two that Number One trusted. Or a non-number who knew very little other than that he was to establish contact. It wouldn't matter…unless it mattered.

The Frenchman sized him up, adding to his earlier impressions. *Mid-to-late thirties. Asian. Not Japanese. Maybe Chinese or Korean. But North or South? Ten pounds overweight and trying to hide it under a loose fitting suit. Or another possibility for the loose suit? To hide a gun.*

The contact left. Soon after, the Frenchman, sitting on a bench diagonally opposite, put the knitting down and casually walked away.

The new location was a dive bar on *Rua Clodomiro Amazonas*. They'd get there long before the nighttime crowd piled in. Moreover, the daytime locals were mostly old drunks.

"Desculpe-me, é este lugar está ocupado?" the Frenchman asked in perfect, but slurred Portuguese.

The man at the bar didn't understand.

"Ah? *Español?*"

"No," he said.

"El Americano?"

"Yes." It was a lie. His accent gave him away.

Korean. Still the question, *North or South?*

"Good. Good. Then may I join you?" he said in intentionally halting English.

"Actually, I'm waiting for a friend."

The man turned around to check the door. It allowed the Frenchman to whisper in his ear in perfect English.

"You're no more American than I am Brazilian. You wanted to meet? I'm here with a gun pointed at you."

The man stiffened, slowly turned back, and felt the barrel at his side.

The Frenchman was now dressed in jeans and t-shirt with the emblem of the national soccer team. He had shoulder-length hair pulled into a ponytail and sticking out of a baseball cap. Altogether, he looked like he belonged. The Korean didn't.

"Why here?" he asked.'

"I like their *Leblon Cachaça.* Order two. I'll be at the table in the corner."

The Frenchman gave him a name. "Call me *Victor.*" It was something he thought he could pronounce. "I'll call you," he thought for a moment, "Mr. Jones. And as far as I can tell, you're merely my contact. You work for someone. And to be sure, I'll figure out who. In the meantime, if I feel you're lying to me anytime during our conversation, you're dead. If you hesitate answering, you're dead. If your eyes shift too much to my thinking, you're dead. And trust me, if I kill you here and now, nobody will care."

The Korean nodded nervously and ordered the drinks. This gave the Frenchman more time to study him. *No gun after all. Just a functionary fulfilling a duty. A functionary, with some military rank.*

Mr. Jones brought the two glasses of clear fruity liquor to the table. "Cheers," he proposed.

"Too soon for a toast."

The Frenchman took on a more threatening tone. "This will be the only time we will ever meet. Any additional communication will be through an address. You'll get it when I am ready."

"A question," Mr. Jones proposed.

"I don't like questions. In fact, I'm not big on conversation."

"I would just like to know why you didn't make the other locations."

"I did. Each time, observing, then following you. It's how I conduct business. I've been in your hotel room. I've looked through everything you have and put it all back as neatly as you had. To proper military regulations."

Mr. Jones winced at the correct assessment. "Thank you."

The Frenchman did not explain that he also copied the contract's phone sim card while he was showering. The 1mg thick card that's in all cellular phones stores phone numbers, security data, and more information. It didn't have everything on the phone, but it had *enough* data to make it easier to draw accurate conclusions and send multiple addresses and bank routing numbers. More importantly, it was going to be valuable if things ever turned bad.

"Now I have a question."

"Yes?" Mr. Jones replied.

"I like to know who I'm working for."

The Korean looked away. "I'm not at liberty to say."

"And if I were to say, 'That's not acceptable?'"

"Then our conversation will go no further."

"I don't believe that's true. Your superior wanted the best. He *needed* the best. The complications, the challenges, and the importance required me. And there is the cost of doing business."

"We're prepared—"

"How close are *you* to the *we?*"

"It's as if you're speaking directly to him," the Korean said.

The Frenchman tried a quick trick.

"But you're not him. Travel from Pyongyang draws attention. Especially from the Americans."

Mr. Jones blinked. The Frenchman got his answer.

"That's not important."

The Frenchman smiled. He took his index finger and ground his nail into the North Korean's left hand, directly on a vein.

"We'll put a pin in that for now. Perhaps it's a conversation we'll return to." Actually the phone sim card would provide all the immediate answers.

The North Korean got the point. But to make extra certain, the Frenchman slid his gun forward under the table, placing it on the contact's leg. It faced forward in an all too obvious direction.

"While we're getting to know one another, a few more concerns."

"Yes," the Korean nervously replied.

"And please, Mr. Jones. Only declarative answers. And without hesitation. All covered by the time I finish my drink." He took a sip. "Starting with how you found me?"

"Well, I didn't really find you."

That much was true.

"I was told how to leave a message for you. Then wait. There is no direct way to find you. But I work for a very important person who has many international relationships…of all kinds. He made that happen."

Mr. Jones looked down as if he could see through the table.

"Perhaps you could remove your weapon?"

The Frenchman offered a smug smile as he slid back his Glock three inches. He now considered the identity of Mr. Jones's actual employer. *An important person. A Korean. An executive with trans-global relationships.* Then the Frenchman thought deeper. *A man with back channel affiliation, money, position, power. Not Korean. North Korean. A leader. A significant leader.*

"Tell me what *your* Supreme Leader wants," he stated with unnerving effect.

Mr. Jones shuddered; indication enough that the Frenchman was correct. Without speaking he removed an envelope from his jacket pocket, placed it on the table, and patted it twice.

The Frenchman casually retrieved it, all the while aware of his surroundings. Inside, scissor-cut newspaper articles printed from the internet. The articles could have been easily explained away or excused in many ways. To a trained killer, the articles conveyed definite intent.

The stories covered a range of locations. All within the U.S. From local, to regional, to national. All in the United States. Men and women. White, black, Hispanic, Asian. And from what the Frenchman could gather, Christian, Jewish, Muslim, and possibly other denominations.

Once he finished thumbing through the clippings, the Frenchman returned them to the envelope, folded it once, and put it in his front right pants pocket. Collectively the articles told him the job was political.

"Those are the first. There will be more," the North Korean explained.

The Frenchman stared directly in the contact's eyes.

"I have four rules no matter how great the assignment. They are all non-negotiable," he said.

The North Korean nodded.

"I alone have the ability to decide when and how the contracts are completed."

"Agreed."

"No children. Not that I like them. It just seems unnecessary."

"There are none."

"And a related consideration. No one who's pregnant."

"I don't know if we'll have that information.

"If I suspect, then that *will be* the determination."

"Agreed," the North Korean said less enthusiastically. "And the third point?"

"Payment and fees." He took a napkin and wrote down the price per. "It will escalate as I work my way through the assignment." He wrote down the escalation clause. "Payments must be made correctly and promptly. I'll get you payment instructions."

"You don't know how to reach me."

"Actually I do, Mr. Jones." He didn't explain that he had contact information through the man's sim card. He withdrew his gun two more inches away from the contract's crotch.

The assassin didn't follow up on the purpose of the mission, though he envisioned the impact it was likely to have. He also didn't care about anyone's politics. He had none himself. No allegiances. No national anthems to sing. And no taxes to pay.

The Frenchman was a deadly capitalist. A rich deadly capitalist. The envelope in his pocket, and the fee structure he would soon propose to fulfill the job, would give him economic independence for the rest of his life. It seemed doable, but he would have to study the clippings closer. He liked the randomness and the ability to move as he pleased. He anticipated the challenges and dangers ahead, especially once the media and law enforcement caught on. But the Frenchman had a firm belief. As the assassin, he had the advantage. He'd always have the advantage.

"You have a fourth rule?"

"I do. If upon achieving your goal, you or your young exalted boss intend to clean up loose ends—and if a loose end includes eliminating someone who could expose your plan—to put it more bluntly, me—don't. I'm invisible. I don't exist. I can go anywhere. I can be anyone. I think you'll agree, I blend in."

The assassin peered right into the contact's eyes. "Rest assured, I will find and punish you and anyone else involved. And I will not stop there. Obviously, you are important, but not the most important. You report to one powerful individual. I know his name. Despite where he hides in your so-called Democratic People's Republic, I can find him. And if I do, he wouldn't know that I've even been there, no matter how impossible the barriers."

The Frenchman looked for reactions. He got one. The North Korean, a colonel in the Korean People's Army, took a hard, loud swallow. The word *barriers* had hit home.

"Do I make myself clear, Mr. Jones?"

"Perfectly."

"I will convey the terms soon."

"How?"

"You'll know when you get them."

The Frenchman removed his gun and offered the promised toast. A cold, calculated toast.

"To all we consider supreme."

He finished his drink and left.

CHAPTER 21

THE OVAL OFFICE
PRESENT DAY

The president called a follow-up session with Scott Roarke that included Bernie Bernstein, CIA Director Jack Evans, Vice President Jonas Jackson Johnson, and probably the most powerful man in the White House second to the president, the new National Security Advisor, Dr. Holt

Yates, a shrewd strategist cut from the Zbigniew Brzezinksi mold.

Roarke saw them as four skeptics with his orders from his boss to convince them. No small task considering the personalities.

"Agent Roarke has a theory to share. I want you all to listen and consider," the president said in his short set-up.

"Thank you," Roarke said uncomfortably. He hated meetings like these. So he started honestly.

"I'm out of my element leading a discussion. But here goes. The president pays me a modest salary. It covers most of my needs, and I cover most of what he requires from me. All in all, it's a fair deal. He gets the same thing week-to-week whether I'm in the field or in my basement office. If I'm filling out paperwork or cleaning my gun."

He didn't explain why it might need cleaning. They got the point.

"Dr. Yates, we've not really done business together since you joined the team. Vice President Johnson and Bernsie can fill in the blanks. But understand this, and pardon me for being indelicate, but I don't fuck around when I'm onto something. And I'm absolutely convinced I'm onto something."

The National Security Advisor listened but didn't respond. The president had brought him in to replace General Jonas Jackson Johnson, when Johnson, or J3 as he was popularly known, was confirmed as vice president. Yates had served as an Under Secretary of State in a previous administration. Before that, he was a former *something*. Roarke suspected NSA.

"That's very nice, Agent Roarke. You're a tough guy with a superiority complex. A type A who thinks that just because he saved Morgan Taylor's life once—"

"Twice, Dr. Yates. And it's President Taylor."

"I stand corrected on both points." Yates turned to the Commander in Chief. "No offense intended Mr. President."

"No offense taken," Taylor replied.

"But Agent Roarke, according to the president, you have developed a theory that you claim other government agencies have missed. A story about lone wolves and political assassinations. Coincidences. I can't wait to hear it."

"Wolf, not wolves, Dr. Yates. And to quote former navy Intelligence officer Malcolm Nance, 'Coincidence takes a lot of planning.'"

"I know the quote, Agent Roarke."

"Good. I recommend we pay attention to it. We're up against a highly coordinated, expertly executed plan, with special emphasis on *the executed*. Any view less than that would be short sighted."

Roarke looked to the president for affirmation. He didn't get anything back. This was his argument to win.

For a moment, Roarke considered walking out. For a moment. If he stood, the act would be followed by his typed resignation and a call to Vinnie D'Angelo for a sooner-than-expected start to their security company. Had it not been for his loyalty to Taylor, and his instant dislike of the National Security Advisor, he would have. But Roarke was used to making the hard case alone. With his words, with his fists, and sometimes with his Sig Sauer P229 pistol.

As an investigator, the root of any case was always *why, what, when, where, and who*? Figure out the goal, the means to accomplishing that goal, and the intelligence behind it all. Right now he had a theory, but truly no hard evidence. But his theory led him to a conclusion.

"The president's life is in danger."

"All the time," Yates responded.

"Not like this," Roarke argued. "The president, members of Congress, and the Cabinet. They all may be on a long hit list that began at a hyper local level. Do you want to take the chance they're not, Dr. Yates?"

Now Yates looked to the president. He didn't get anything back either. It was his argument to lose.

Roarke continued. "Senator Pleasance—"

"Died from heart failure. Natural causes," Yates demanded.

Roarke smiled. Yates just gave up some of the high ground with his arrogance.

"You should speak with FBI Director Mulligan and his lead agent. He's a real sweetheart," Roarke said. "Or you could give me the courtesy to shut up and listen."

Yates was about to pounce, but the president calmed him down.

"Easy, Dr. Yates. You too, Scott. We're all on the same team."

"All right, Agent Roarke," the NSA chief said. "I'm listening."

Roarke replayed what he had told the president. He covered the deaths of the Idaho governor, the Missouri senator, the Colorado school committeewoman, and the Great Barrington, Massachusetts, mayor.

"Two on-site investigations. Hours of research, gentlemen. And I fear that I've just scratched the surface."

"Meaning?"

"There are more assassinations to uncover and likely more to come."

Yates leaned into his chair, suddenly realizing the power in the room had completely shifted to Roarke.

The Secret Service agent stared at the president's new National Security Advisor Yates slowly smiled. "You are everything the president said you were, Mr. Roarke. And more."

The president laughed. The others joined in. They already knew that.

Yates stood, crossed the Oval Office carpet, and offered his hand.

"It'll be good working with you."

"No more games, Dr. Yates. I don't play well with others."

"Okay, I won't tug on Superman's cape," he said jokingly.

Roarke failed to laugh, however he took Yates's hand.

"But I do need the administration's help."

"What help would that be?" Yates replied.

"One word."

"Yes?"

"It's simple. If you have a problem with it, I have my own resources."

Morgan Taylor smiled inwardly. Roarke was fully capable of going it alone.

"What's the word?" Yates said standing eye-to-eye with Roarke.

"One word, with a long tail." Roarke said. "Cooperation."

Yates exhaled. "Cooperation?"

"Yes."

"Agent Roarke. You've got it," the president's National Security Advisor said. "And the council. And all our resources."

"Central Intelligence is with you, too, Scott. Though unofficially since this is a domestic issue," Director Evans said.

"And I'm not so sure of that," Roarke replied.

Morgan Taylor gave the pointed added consideration and smiled. Roarke had won. He had no doubt it would go any other way.

* * *

As the room began to clear, the president tapped the CIA chief on the shoulder.

"Jack, you hang for a few more minutes."

"Sure, Mr. President." He knew enough not to ask why. Taylor didn't want anyone else in the conversation. That included the president's chief of staff who shot a miffed look for the room.

Once everyone else was gone, Morgan Taylor got to the point.

"What's the status of the National Clandestine Service?"

The CIA Director let out a long, deep breath.

"It doesn't exist."

"Of course it doesn't," Taylor said. "Go on."

The National Clandestine Service was, in its most basic form, a kill squad established to track down and neutralize terrorists. Officially, it never became "fully operational." It hibernated in the deep freeze of America's intelligence darkest places—the CIA's undercover spying branch—ready to be activated, but with an unacceptably high risk of failure or exposure.

Extreme secrecy meant that it was hidden from Congress, senior White House officials, and depending upon how much the temporary inhabitant of the Oval Office wanted to know, even from the president, vice president, and national security advisor.

Government lawyers who had heard about the plans voiced concern that the proposed kill teams violated the law. Nonetheless, the National Clandestine Service has always been only an executive order away from activation. Based on Israeli Mossad's approach to dispatching assassins—quickly, lethally, and without due process—much of the work actually had been implemented through more sterile means: drone attacks.

As one official said after one of the first NCS-type attacks, which took out a top Al Qaeda operative in Yemen, "Why would anyone be shocked or surprised by plans to pursue terrorists overseas? That's part of the CIA's mission."

But the CIA operating on ground in the United States proper is another thing. Or has been, up until now.

"Hypothetically only?" Evans asked.

"Even academically."

"All right, as an academic exercise presented to a law class, an agency training session at the Farm, or in a Congressional testimony, we're able to provide intelligence we've gathered through our sources or through Five Eyes, but we are not in on the…"

Director Evans hesitated.

"The hypothetical," the president implored. "I understand the basics. The agency is not permitted to use a drone to observe a suspect within our borders."

"No, sir, we can't. Army intelligence and the FBI are another thing. Perhaps there's some wiggle room if we're invited by the Pentagon. They've got resources at Fort Sam Houston and the FBI has its eyes. But since no National Clandestine Service officially exists, it's a nonstarter."

"One more question. If we track the assassin to another country…"

"Sir, we've taken out terrorists in Yemen, Afghanistan, Iraq, Syria, and Bin Laden in Pakistan. On ground with U.S. Special Forces and overhead with drones. Invited or not, we've struck with extreme prejudice."

"And what if our trail takes us to a friendly, allied nation?" Morgan Taylor asked.

Evans did not like the question at all.

"Like…"

"England, Canada, France, Spain, Italy. I don't know. A NATO ally."

"Then either we coordinate through their intelligence organizations or the National Clandestine Service makes an unannounced house call. Or we send in someone…"

"Or someone's…" Taylor added, thinking along the same lines as his CIA chief.

"We each have our own."

Neither man uttered the names. But clearly they were D'Angelo and Roarke.

THE CIA
LATER THAT NIGHT

"Thanks for hanging so late, Vincent."

"Of course. What's up?" D'Angelo asked his boss.

"Anything going on that would prevent you from going on the road if I need?"

"No, sir. My calendar's open. Got a heads-up?"

"Not yet." CIA Director Evans replied.

"No intel?"

"Nothing you can't find yourself in the newspaper or from one of your *friends*."

That alone was enough for the CIA operative. *Roarke*.

Jack Evans had given him a deniable "go" to get up to speed. He didn't ask if Roarke's boss had done the same thing. *Of course he had.* They'd been an off-the-books team before. Now they were again.

. . .

"Hey guy, working late?" D'Angelo texted

"Always," Roarke typed.

"Got time for a night cap?"

"Kind of busy, but sure."

"Thnx. Usual place. One hr."

"Perfecto. It'll be fun."

"Yay, fun." D'Angelo ended the conversation.

CHAPTER 22

YUKTAE-DONG SUBMARINE BASE, DEMOCRATIC PEOPLE'S REPUBLIC OF KOREA

Jee Gyuen had nothing for Chin-wah Lee to sign, but the new CIA recruit felt he had nonetheless written his confession in blood.

Jee Gyuen promised the North Korean $100,000 and a free ticket past *Go*. Whenever that might be.

Lee was given materials and instructions. He was smart enough to figure out what it was about.

Smuggle in the USB drives. Insert them in his computer. Upload the program into the submarine computers docked at Yuktae-dong and others that he could communicate with during the course of his daily duties. Any one of those steps could get him arrested.

What worked in his favor was laziness on the part of base security and the fact that every North Korean submarine required more than average maintenance.

The nation's fleet was saddled with problems. First of all, their standards were lower than most world navies. Secondly, while the Supreme Leader boasted that the submarine force was the best in the world, it wasn't. The nation's subs required constant trips to port.

This is where and when Chin-wah Lee could do his damage while his money earned interest in mutual funds through something called Fidelity Investments.

It was a simple job. A mechanical job. Get the latest thumb drive from Gyuen, then upload it.

The easiest part was actually smuggling the drive into his workstation. He affixed it to the roof of his mouth with chewing gum. Since he was a serial gum chewer, even the scent didn't trigger concern from the guards.

However, the North Koreans were experts in cyber warfare offensives. Therefore, they were keenly aware of defenses. Lee's job, with one hundred thousand plus interest accruing in mind, was to introduce autonomous malware into submarine mainframes when the ships were in for port repairs, refurbishment, and updates. For that, he had to wait for just the right time to slip in the USB drive so the worm could slither into hiding at its destination and sleep soundly.

He'd read up on Autonomous Denial of Service (DoS) preinstalled internal systems. Except these weren't preinstalled in the submarines. He was the installer.

He suspected that whatever he installed could be activated somehow with a remote radio transmission. What that activation ultimately meant was something he didn't care to think about. He just knew that onboard malware, once activated, could be used to affect command and control, missile launch systems, disrupt warheads, or worse. A computer virus could defeat life support or send a sub into a deep, hull-crushing dive.

A new sub had docked that morning. Lee had the latest malware on the roof of his mouth. He did what he'd been doing for the past few months, hoping the next meeting with his Jee Gyuen, would come with an escape route.

Lee casually used his body to hide his intent from observers and ever-panning CCTV cameras. Next, he coughed, which naturally brought his right hand to his mouth. At that point he reached in with his thumb, located the drive, slid it forward along his palate, and through his fingers into his fist. Depending upon prying eyes, he would wait for the next step. Today it was a fast insertion into his computer port. It took forty-five long seconds to load the virus onto the newest Whale Class ballistic missile submarine computer. Forty-five seconds where he had to still look busy. It went well. But he wasn't finished. Now he had to export the drive, return it to his mouth, and chew the damn thing up. Fortunately, the Americans had laced it with an artificial flavor that tasted like *Yeot*, a traditional sugary candy.

Three more submarines were due into port over the next two weeks. Two were repeats. And with each trip, he had to do it all over again with the latest program smuggled in.

Chin-wah Lee's nervousness was only balanced by his mathematical computations. He calculated the interest he was earning while he did his bidding as a spy for the CIA. He just hoped he'd live to enjoy the money.

CHAPTER 23

THE FBI FACIAL ANALYSIS, COMPARISON, AND EVALUATION SERVICES UNIT QUANTICO, VIRGINIA THE NEXT MORNING

Duane "Touch" Parsons was the FBI's leading FERET expert. Likely the best in the country. FERET, FacE REcognition Technology, is an ever-improving law enforcement tool. It's also used by America's intelligence community and the military to help identify terrorists' identities from orbiting spy satellites.

The first facial recognition research was semi-automated. Developed in the 1960s, it required administrators to calculate distances and ratios between common reference points on a photograph; a subject's eyes, nose, ears, and mouth. A decade later, programs advanced to consider twenty-one markers from hair color to lip thickness. In 1988, linear algebra was applied, requiring less than one hundred values to map a face. The next major advance came in 1991 when characteristics could be detected in comparative images, enabling real-time matching.

With ten more years of research and constant programming upgrades, the public got a visible understanding of FERET. The technology was utilized at the January 2001 Super Bowl to compare surveillance images from archived mug shots.

Today, FERET is a key tool for law enforcement, from petty crimes to global terrorism, missing persons to large event surveillance, passport fraud to tracking down assassins.

That's what Bessolo and Roarke had in mind with the Missouri sketches. Touch Parsons's job was to see if he could find a match with any state driver's licenses, newspaper photos, or passports. His photograph sources were more than five hundred million deep with another 55,000 photographs added every day.

Touch Parsons relied on PCA, Principal Components Analysis, which reduces images to *eigenfaces*, unrelated components that are stored in ever-expanding databases. He also had other FERET programs including Linear Discriminant Analysis (LDA) and Elastic Bunch Graph Matching (EBGM). Given reasonably clear photographs, controlled indoor lighting, and the current technology, success rate could be measured to more than ninety percent. But, of course, not every image met these standards. That's where someone who had the "touch" could extrapolate more. Parsons could feel what the programs couldn't even see, and he never let a picture lie to him.

Unfortunately, it wasn't going particularly well today. The sketches of the man holding an umbrella from Missouri didn't offer him much to work with. It was drawn from poor recollection. *He had dark hair, but not so dark. Long, but it could have been short. It was definitely a man.*

Well, it could have been a woman in suit and pants. He, or she was average height, unless he was bending over. His eyes were blue. No, maybe green.

So far the sketch matched a quarter of the archives.

THE OVAL OFFICE

The president reconvened the meeting from the previous day. Roarke again held court.

"The fact of the matter is that local newspapers have been dying off," Roarke explained. "And where they've survived, they operate with minimal staffs run by remote senior management. Not everything gets reported. Moreover, not everything that's reported finds life on the internet. So it takes digging."

"So reports of murders don't always get posted?" Bernsie asked. "That seems odd."

"Murders probably. But not all murders are known to be murder. If they're not investigated as suspicious, then the newspaper staff may drop it there. And if there's no evidence otherwise, or no reporter who wants to go beyond the obvious, the story literally dies on the local level like the victim. Unless…"

Bernsie leaned forward.

"…it becomes fodder for talk radio. Then it expands and creates fear."

"Where are you going with this?" J3 asked. His questions always carried the weight of his Army rank and his current job.

"To a reasonable conclusion, Mr. Vice President," Roarke replied. "So far I've identified a county supervisor, a school committeewoman, a member of a board of education, a mayor, a city councilwoman, a select-man, a state representative, a state senator, and of course a governor and a United States senator as possible assassination victims. Increasingly, their deaths have led to more chatter, more coverage, more rumors, and noise to the point that people holding or running for elected office have got to think twice about serving."

"You're using rumor as evidence?" J3 argued. "You've been listening to too much late-night talk radio yourself."

It was bold criticism, but Roarke brushed it off. After all, General Jonas Jackson Johnson, the biggest, toughest officer Roarke had ever met, and the most decorated African American four-star, had the stripes and competence to speak frankly. Prior to being elevated to vice president, he had headed USASOC, American's largest command component of SOCOM, the United States Special Operations Command. The boxy, six-foot-four hero was Morgan Taylor's man. That made the fifty-eight-year-old vice president Scott Roarke's man as well.

"I'll give you names, dates, and places, general. When the president sent me to Boise, I thought we just had a sniper to track down. I started working a Pentagon contact on creating a list."

"Captain Walker?" J3 said more than asked.

Roarke nodded.

"A sniper would be easier to track down. But this guy's got more skills, which makes him harder to find."

"Why?" Bernsie wondered.

"ID'ing a former U.S. military sniper with a gripe would have produced a long list, but we could work our way through it. We are, in fact. Already more than eighty percent there. But an assassin who's also expert with bombs, ricin poisoning, and knowledge of other deadly cocktails should narrow the list domestically. But in a much wider world, it's another story."

Roarke let his statement sink in.

The National Security Advisor shook his head, but not in disagreement.

"Psych ops," Dr. Yates stated.

"What?" asked the chief of staff.

"Psych ops," he repeated. "A program to intentionally dissuade people from running for office. To undermine governance."

"From local, low level elected officials, to higher up, to judges and—"

Roarke suddenly stopped.

"What?" the president asked

"Oh my God! Boss, I need your phone."

"Why?"

"Katie!"

Roarke explained while he dialed.

. . .

"I'm working," Katie whispered in the phone. "Can't really talk."

"Whatever you're doing listen. You heard about Senator Pleasance?"

"Yes. Intestinal issues."

"No. Poisoned. And a governor was shot. Same for a mayor and a judge. All killed. Did you hear me?"

"Yes."

"A judge, Katie."

The president listened as Roarke explained the danger to Katie Kessler. Taylor whispered in his chief of staff's ear. "Get the Director of the U.S. Marshals on the phone."

"I think he's traveling." Bernsie replied.

"I don't care. Get him! And the deputy director of the court police!"

Roarke picked up on the president's order and made his point perfectly clear.

"Katie, security is coming your way. Tell Browning!"

CHAPTER 24

The United States Marshal Service is charged with protecting the federal court. In fact, their authority predated the Secret Service by nearly eighty-five years. The Judiciary Act of 1789 authorized the president to appoint a marshal to serve in each district. Marshals attend district and circuit court sessions and carry out all lawful orders including making arrests and delivering warrants, summonses, and subpoenas. They coordinate protection of judges and prosecutors and watch over people hiding in the Witness Protection Program. An 1867 statute added the U.S. Supreme Court to the jurisdiction.

Though there have been numerous conspiracy theories regarding the natural death of Justice Antonin Scalia at an isolated resort in West Texas, U.S. Marshals have done remarkable work protecting the justices in their care.

Surprisingly, however, the justices exert personal discretion over their security. The U.S. Marshals Service can coordinate travel outside the capital, yet, many of the justices, Scalia included, preferred to take care of details themselves. Following his death, the Marshals issued a simple statement: "USMS detail was declined."

At work, Supreme Court justices are protected by a small force. On their own, justices act like ordinary citizens who shop, eat, and pray, usually without being recognized.

As relatively anonymous individuals, they do face the same dangers everyone does. Accordingly, many have been assault victims. One court justice was attacked by a machete-wielding intruder who invaded his vacation home in the Caribbean. Another was once punched in the face by an assailant who objected to Supreme Court decisions on pornography and school desegregation. A third survived a bullet piercing his living room window.

The fact of the matter is that, while the general public can identify the president, only one in five hundred are likely to pick out a Supreme Court justice.

Case in point, years ago a Supreme Court justice was asked by tourists if he would kindly step aside so they could get a better photograph of the Supreme Court building.

The quest for relative anonymity is underscored by their reluctance to have cameras in the Supreme Court. Collectively, justices have felt that telecasting oral arguments could put them at greater risk by raising their visibility. Moreover, U.S. Marshals also maintain that coverage might feed an individual's twisted political grievance or make it all the easier for a mentally unstable person to find his target.

Nonetheless, in recent years members of the Court have raised their own visibility. Justices have accepted speaking engagements at bar associations and law schools, and they've appeared on television from C-SPAN to *Sesame Street*.

So unlike White House advisors who travel with Secret Service agents and congressional leaders who roam Washington with members of the Capitol Police in tow, Supreme Court justices go it alone. Whether a justice is a new appointee getting grounded, the potential swing vote on a precedent-making case, or the Chief Justice, without their robes, they look like ordinary citizens and act as such. And barring any specific threat, the nine men and women who make up the Supreme Court do not have 24/7 protection despite the fact that through the right sniper scope they could be viewed as high level, high value targets.

CHAPTER 25

SPARTANBURG, SOUTH CAROLINA

Congressman Montgomery left his district office after a phone interview with a student reporter for the Spartanburg High School *Norse News*. Seventeen-year-old Lucy Cutler nervously asked her representative to Congress about his position on climate change, LGBT rights, abortion, and health care. The questions were harder put than those from many local reporters. And it was harder for him to pivot. Every time he tried, Cutler followed up with conflicting quotes from his previous interviews and stump speeches. She felt she nailed him. He thought no one would really read the student newspaper. The congressman should have realized she had a twitter account. But it actually wouldn't matter.

Montgomery got in his Ford Explorer, adjusted his mirrors, tuned his radio to the local talk radio show he often called into, put his foot on the brake, and pressed the ignition button. That's when the bomb under the gas tank exploded.

Later that day Lucy Cutler's interview went viral.

BAKERSFIELD, CALIFORNIA

"Ladies and gentlemen…and I see some youngsters who are going to be voting in a few years…it's so good to be here."

Lucas Burke was welcomed with thunderous applause from his biggest audience yet.

"How's this sound? Bakersfield! The capitol of the New Republic of Southern California!"

The room erupted. It was a new line he was trying out. It worked so well that some nine hundred people were on their feet.

"I like the sound of that, too," he shouted.

WASHINGTON, D.C.

Roarke's phone pinged him with a CNN alert.

There were two postings. One from the Spartanburg *Herald-Journal*, another, a social media posting from a high school student noted by CNN.

Roarke called Roy Bessolo.

"Holy shit, how do you keep up with these things?" the FBI agent asked.

"I read high school newspapers."

"I'll work on updating my subscriptions," Bessolo said.

"It's going to blow," Roarke said. "A governor, a senator, a congressman. Even a high school reporter could piece this together. Mulligan and the White House need to figure out what to say when the press starts calling."

"I'll talk to Mulligan," Bessolo offered.

"I'll do the same with Taylor. The clock's ticking."

• • •

His next call was to Langley.

"Hello," Vinnie D'Angelo answered on the second ring.

"I've got another."

"Christ," the CIA operative replied. "Hadn't heard yet."

"You will. The list is growing. Are you picking up any international chatter?"

"None, but I'll snoop around, unofficially, of course."

"Of course," Roarke replied. He hung up feeling better that D'Angelo was engaged, well beyond unofficial.

• • •

An hour later, a *New York Times* online story appeared that had sampled office holders across the country, asking if they felt threatened. Of the forty respondents, thirty-six replied yes. Twelve were working on their letters of resignation.

CHAPTER 26

THE OVAL OFFICE

"Shit," the president whispered. "Put him through, Louise."

Rather than dodging the call, he knew from experience to take the Speaker of the House head on. Over the years, Duke Patrick had worked against Taylor, in Congress and in the press. On more than one occasion Taylor warned him. More than warned. Threatened the arrogant party leader just short of blackmail. Taylor did have politically explosive files on Patrick, which only marginally kept the Speaker in tow, and even then, not for long. A new crisis, mismanaged, could give Patrick the upper hand, and ultimately a route to the presidency, which he sorely wanted.

"Mr. Speaker," Morgan Taylor said when connected.

"Mr. President, I assume you know why I'm calling."

"Let's be straight with one another, Patrick." The president dropped the formality. "You see an opportunity."

"No, no, no, Mr. President. I'm concerned for the nation. Three serious assassinations, two that affect Congress. And not a word from the White House. I've lost a friend from the great state of South Carolina."

"Montgomery is suddenly your friend? Not according to your last committee meeting."

"We could disagree on budget matters and still be friends," Patrick replied.

"Get to your point, Patrick."

"My point, and a growing sense among the press, is there's an organized effort to kill elected officials. So, on behalf of my colleagues, I want to know the following: One, when you're going to make a statement acknowledging this fact. Two, what you're going to do to stop it."

"I hate to cut you short, but I'm a little busy right now. How about I have you and the House and Senate leadership in for a briefing within twenty-four hours when I have more to report to everyone. At once. All at the same time."

"Just as long as we have that meeting," Duke Patrick said in the most condescending manner. "Twenty-four hours. But I can't promise everyone else will want to wait."

"Use your influence, Mr. Speaker. And your homespun charm."

THE OVAL OFFICE
WHITE HOUSE PRESS BRIEFING ROOM
LATER

The president's press secretary completed his briefing and opened the floor to questions.

"Joe!" "Joe!" "Joe!"

Joe Poppiti scanned the room and decided which of the overlapping voices he'd pick.

"Denise."

He went to CNN political reporter Denise Craft. The hardest interviewer the first.

"Joe, a question and a follow up. You stated that at this moment the White House has no information if the assassinations are related. Really? Three political assassinations in a short period of time and they're not related? It seems hard to believe."

"Denise, for clarity, I didn't say the deaths of Senator Pleasance, Congressman Montgomery, or Governor Geller were unrelated. I said we have no information if they are. We are looking at two assassinations. Moreover, at this time, Congressman Montgomery's death has not been determined to be anything other than natural causes."

"But it could be," Craft interrupted.

Poppiti, the forty-two-year-old former ABC news correspondent and now seasoned White House press secretary rested an elbow on the podium and pointed at Craft, as if scolding her. "Director Mulligan is investigating. He has teams in each of the cities. They're examining evidence, talking with witnesses, and determining if there could be any links."

"So there could be. Montgomery's death could have been murder."

"We're investigating, Denise."

"Define *we*."

"The FBI, local and state police. Is that your follow up?"

"No. Has the White House seriously considered that this could be a wide spread domestic terrorist plot? Secondly, what kind of enhanced security will be deployed for members of Congress, governors, and other elected officials?"

"Again, we're in the first stages of investigation. It would be inappropriate to call this anything beyond what we currently know."

He looked for more hands among press, but Craft shouted over everyone else.

"And if it's a foreign-born plot?"

"Denise, I've told you all I know. The president is conferring with Director Mulligan. As for any potential international aspect, rest assured, the intelligence community will be involved."

He turned to Tom Alger from the *Washington Post*.

"Two part question, Joe. Does the bureau consider this a sophisticated operation? After all, a sniper and a bomb? This seems to be a level well above a lone wolf. Second, the White House must be considering that there's military expertise behind it. Perhaps leading to some sort of coup."

Poppiti scowled. "I only heard one question, Tom. To that, I'll reiterate. This is a fast-moving situation, Tom. We're pursuing all possibilities. On your other point, I have nothing to add."

Poppiti saw Alger's reaction. He realized he'd gone one sentence too far. Hands shot up, but Alger persisted.

"You're not denying the possibility of a home grown military coup?"

The room came to an uncharacteristic quiet as the reporters waited for Joe Poppiti's answer. Poppiti had been Taylor's press secretary for his entire term. He'd kept secrets and tiptoed the narrow line between truth and lies. He never made up answers, and he avoided making headlines of his own.

Now he had to walk back a bad response.

"The White House has absolutely no information or evidence to lead to that conclusion. You shouldn't either, and if I gave that impression it is completely unfounded. Next."

• • •

While Joe Poppiti was wiggling out of a thorny White House thicket of his own creation, the Frenchman stepped out of the shadows on a secluded suburban Bethesda, Maryland, street.

"Excuse me, your honor," he said with smile as he approached the distinguished Federal District Court judge.

Lionel Bonaventure, home early today, was taking his thirteen-year-old terrier for a walk. He was beyond his driveway and wide of his surveillance camera's field of view.

"Yes?"

The smile and friendly voice disarmed him. And the seven-inch commando combat knife cut cleanly into his heart. His agony was short, thanks to the expertise of the assassin, who felt badly making the dog an orphan.

THE OVAL OFFICE
AN HOUR LATER

"Tell me what you're thinking?" the president said, muting the news channels.

Chief of Staff Bernie Bernstein had a hard, thankless job in the West Wing. James Baker, Ronald Reagan's chief of staff, once called it, "The worst job in Washington." Certainly, the chief of staff had walk-in privileges. Anytime day or night. But it was what he walked into that made it so thankless.

Of course, Bernsie knew his role, and it wasn't all theater. The president never wanted him to be a yes man. It wasn't difficult. He was already a bit of a curmudgeon. He came with the knowledge to fulfill the request. Bernsie was a historian, a former newspaper editor, and a university administrator. He brought critical aspects of each career to the job. He did so by asking government officials questions the president might not otherwise ask, but without the pressure of them coming from the Morgan Taylor.

Taylor liked the way this worked. Cabinet members and staffers of all stripes had to defend their often difficult positions and opinions, and worse, back them up with facts. Accordingly, Bernsie had the full authority of the president, as Leon Panetta had in the job under Bill Clinton, to make staff and organizational changes to bring efficiency and discipline to the White House.

This didn't shift the center of power to the chief of staff, although Bernstein was very powerful. It just meant that when anyone sought to gain admittance to the Oval Office, they better be prepared to sell the request to the president's man, whether or not there was ultimate buy-in at the top.

Sometimes he had the job of talking the president into doing something. Sometimes out of it.

"Poppiti had a tough time out there today," Bernsie said.

"I know. I'm thinking of jumping in tomorrow."

"Not a good idea, sir," Bernsie advised.

"I need to establish confidence. The longer I wait, the worst it'll get."

"But—"

Bernstein didn't get to complete the sentence. The president's phone rang. It was Roarke.

"No. Who?" the president asked.

The president wrote down a name and some notes as Roarke explained.

The chief of staff only heard one side of the conversation. It was enough to let him know that another official had been killed.

Taylor shook his head and hung up.

"Roarke. More bad news."

Morgan Taylor explained.

"That settles it. Let Joe know I'll join him at tomorrow's press conference."

"Does Roarke have anything you can use?"

"Nothing. He's still fishing. And the waters keep getting deeper."

Taylor looked at his note. *Bonaventure. Maryland. Stabbed.* He knew the judge, but it wasn't his appointee.

"Get Mulligan and Evans on the phone. Better yet, get them in here."

"What about increasing security," Bernsie said. "Quietly."

"You think that can be done quietly?"

Bernsie rethought his proposal.

"At least let's button down the Capitol, key buildings, and your detail until we know more."

The president agreed. "Make it so."

THE WHITE HOUSE
PRESS SECRETARY OFFICE

The moment Joe Poppiti finished talking on the phone with one reporter, he had another to handle. The questions were the same. His replies were the same.

"Come on." He filled in the reporter's name. "The FBI is already on it." Then he added one version or another of, "So don't rush to judgment."

This was one of those times when Poppiti wished he were asking the questions rather than fielding them.

In mid-sentence with a Fox reporter, his secretary slipped him a note.

Mr. Bernstein. Now.

Poppiti concluded the call, grateful to have an excuse to leave. His aides would take the rest and the list of callbacks would stack up.

"Wolves at the door?" Bernsie's greeting had the tinge of gallows humor.

"Yup and ravenous." Poppiti had a notepad in hand ready to write. "I'll work up a draft for POTUS or is he—"

"You're going to get more than a statement."

Poppiti raised his eyebrow.

"Tomorrow. The man."

"Okay." Poppiti's pencil tip snapped on the pad.

"Any hint what's to come?"

"What's to come or what he'll say?" Bernie responded.

"Right. Two different questions. Okay, first what's to come?"

"Depends. If we have a single killer with a grudge or an attack on the whole goddamned political process."

"And that's unknown?" Poppiti asked.

"Correct."

"And the second question. What he'll say?"

"You'll see it as soon as he writes it."

"Not the writers?"

"Not this time."

• • •

Scott Roarke added another card next to Bonaventure's. Winslow, Arizona. Although at this point, speculative. His online search turned up a two-week-old suspicious death of a Navajo County supervisor. Spencer Hurley had fallen off his fifth floor condo balcony. Odd because of the height of the railing. Odd and extremely difficult. Four feet high.

"Bessolo, we need to talk." Roarke said, catching the FBI at his desk.

"It's becoming a regular thing. I swear I think you're beginning to like me," Bessolo claimed.

"I don't like you, but that doesn't change the fact that I need you."

They agreed on a meeting place on the Washington Mall.

Thirty minutes later, with the sun falling behind trees to the west, Roy Bessolo joined Roarke at the Vietnam War Memorial.

"Well, this is unusually secretive," Bessolo said. "Trying out lessons from your CIA spy friend?"

"Naw. I needed to get out of the basement. Figured you could use the walk, too."

"This isn't quite half way."

"Oh, I'm coming more than half way. Here." Roarke said.

Roarke put a USB drive in the FBI agent's hand.

"What's this?"

"More than you have. More than I can keep track of. And there's way more to uncover."

"How much more?" Bessolo asked.

"You tell me. Look for any pattern or connection. Keep me posted wherever I am?"

"Where are you going, Roarke?"

"Wherever this takes me."

KATIE KESSLER'S APARTMENT
THAT NIGHT

Katie greeted Roarke at the door with a kiss and a concern.

"Well, he's not going for 'round the clock protection. Besides, he has some events coming up."

Roarke didn't follow up on her last point. He was more focused on the immediate danger.

"Jesus. Why so stubborn?"

"That's Leopold Browning's middle name."

"I hope they get that right in his obit," Roarke said completely seriously.

"You know he's not easy to convince. He lives for evidence."

"Maybe, but he works for the American people. He can't do that dead."

Katie shrugged. "Your boss is going to have to make it plainer than I did."

Roarke had another thought; a way to convince Browning.

"I know that look. What, Scott?"

"Nothing," he said deflecting her observation. "And the other judges?"

"Browning said it's up to them individually, as it's always been."

"Not this time."

"Starting when?"

"Tonight. 24/7, including Browning."

"I should call—"

"No need. The marshals are perfectly capable of introducing themselves."

"Who says Washington doesn't work," she mused.

"Top down, my dear. And equally important, no cooking tonight. We're going out to dinner."

"A date Mr. Roarke? It's been a while."

"More like an engagement celebration. You've got an hour to get ready."

She thought for a moment. "I'll just need thirty minutes. Any thoughts on what we can do with the other thirty?"

Roarke didn't need a second prompt. He lifted her purple cotton camisole and undid the drawstring on her yoga pants which slipped to the floor. They also didn't need another room. The hallway was room enough.

* * *

"What's the new normal going to feel like?" Katie asked between bites of their Wolfgang Puck classic tuna tarte amuse-bouche served in sesame and sweet miso cones, the first of the Asia fusion appetizers to arrive.

They sat at a corner window table at The Source, Puck's restaurant at Washington's Newseum. Roarke looked out into the room, noting everyone who sat down or walked by. Katie, wearing a scoop-neck dress, leather jacket, and high heeled boots, only had eyes for Scott.

"I guess the same. No, different. We're engaged, but of course that means…"

"A wedding. Oh, my God, Scott, you're right. A wedding. With guests and family."

Roarke lowered his eyes. His parents were gone. So were most of the people in his early life.

Katie understood his mood. She reached across the table and held his hand.

"You'll have a family, Scott. *We* can have a family. We haven't talked about it, but I'd be ready whenever you are."

"I think my life is too dangerous to talk about that now," he offered.

"But you're going to change that. You said so."

"I did. I will. But not right now."

"I get that. But there will be an *after* right now." She gently caressed his hand with her thumb. "And then we can both step away from all of this."

"You've got the dream job," he shyly added.

"I've got the dream man. I can get another job. I don't want another man."

Roarke wrapped his leg around hers under the table.

"Thank you. I love you."

"I love you."

They only pulled away from each other when the waitress brought their next course to share, Sichuan Peppercorn Crusted Prime Filet Mignon "Au Poivre."

For the next ten minutes they only talked about the food and each other. Smiling, laughing, and leaving their real life worries behind. Then Roarke's cell phone vibrated in his jacket pocket. He looked at the number and instantly knew dinner was over.

"Gotta go?" she asked.

"Yup," he sighed, just as the main course arrived. "Briefing upstairs."

"Thank you," Katie told the waitress. "Sorry, but can you pack it to go? My fiancé's just been called back to the hospital." She looked at Roarke and smiled. "Emergency operation."

"No, you stay," Roarke insisted. "Enjoy."

"Right. An engagement meal alone." Katie turned back to the waitress. "To go. And he'll take the check."

The waitress nodded and left with the food.

"You can't," Roarke said.

"I can and I will. Besides, the more I know, the more I can convince Browning to take precautions seriously."

"We're way past the precaution stage," Roarke said. "On a Defcon ranking, we're at two."

"What's one?"

"Nuclear. Or in our case, taking out your boss or mine."

Roarke shut the conversation off when the boxed dinners and check arrived. While Roarke signed, Katie checked her phone. She had a text from Chief Justice Browning.

I said no marshals!

She showed it to Roarke.

"Play dumb."

She typed a response and hit send:

It's for the best

A one word declarative response followed.

NO!

Katie gave up on arguing with Browning for now. But she returned to her point with Roarke. "I'm coming with you. I still have security clearance." She smiled seductively. "That should qualify me for admission. That and your winning smile with Bernsie. Are we clear?"

"Please, Katie," he pleaded.

"Are *we* clear?"

Roarke exhaled. "Clear."

They left and hailed a cab for the ten-block ride up Pennsylvania Avenue. The trip took four minutes. Checking back into the East Wing, another three minutes principally because Katie wasn't scheduled. The walk to the Oval Office, three more. A whispered conversation with Bernsie in his office, and time for him to talk to the president, four minutes. They were held another minute at Taylor's door and then invited in. Louise Swingle took their food and promised not to eat it.

"See, that wasn't so hard," Katie whispered in his ear. "Just fifteen minutes."

"Katie, so good to see you," the president said warmly. "Sorry for the circumstances and for interrupting your dinner."

Katie sighed. "Duty calls, Mr. President. But it's good to see you again. I'm sorry for crashing the meeting, but I insisted that Scott—"

"Your powers of persuasion are well known around here. But given your job at SCOTUS, I can't really have you join us. Issues down the line. I hope you understand."

She did and she didn't, but Katie answered respectfully.

"Of course. I'll just be outside."

"It might be a while," Taylor replied.

"I'm used to waiting for Scott."

The president laughed and closed the door.

. . .

Roarke joined FBI Director Mulligan, General and Vice President Jonas Jackson Johnson, and Bernie Bernstein in the closed-door meeting with the president.

"Okay, let's begin. Are we any further along figuring out who's the triggerman or where this is coming from?" the president asked.

"No and no," Mulligan said.

"Scott, any more insight?"

"I'm working on it, sir, along with Director Mulligan's chief investigator and my own contacts. But just as you've initiated with the Supreme Court, I recommend the highest level of protection going forward for leaders of the House and Senate, the vice president, all cabinet members, and, you, sir. No published travel plans. Bullet proof vests. No public appearances."

"Okay. I'll go public with some of the measures during tomorrow's press briefing," Taylor said.

"It's going to scare Wall Street," said Bernsie.

"Right. Call the Secretary Ramuno tonight with a heads-up. He should be prepared to get on the horn with the bank houses the moment I step away from the mics."

"Got it."

"Now the president addressed his vice president, one of the toughest men he'd ever met.

"J3, we haven't talked about you."

"I've got eyes in the back of my head, sir."

"You may, but you're tall and you stick out in a crowd. So, I'm pulling you in. No exposure. Zero. None."

"I'll try."

"General, you will. That's an order," the Commander in Chief stated.

"Yes, sir."

"You move into the White House and don't take a step outside. If I'm in the crosshairs, then it'll be up to you to run the whole shebang. Am I clear?"

"Yes, sir."

"We have to get to the bottom of this," Taylor continued. "Bob, I want to know who this fucking phantom is, and I want him stopped. And Scott…"

The word phantom hit Roarke. He focused on a spot on the wall and tuned out.

"Scott," the president repeated.

"Sorry."

"Give me something by tomorrow morning. 0600. I'll keep the kitchen open all night for you."

"Don't need to, boss. Katie's got our takeout. Just needs reheating."

• • •

Walking to his office, Roarke offered a contrite, "Sorry the night didn't turn out to be more romantic. I had wanted it to be an engagement meal. I owe you," Roarke offered.

"You sure do."

• • •

The overnight kitchen staff plated their Wolfgang Puck dinner, which they shared as delightfully as possible in Scott's White House basement office. Katie insisted that they eat before getting to work.

They talked about previous unmentionables: Where and when to get married, who they'd invite, and who might be Best Man and Maid of Honor.

"Or, we can fuck it and fly somewhere exotic and just do it," she added.

That idea actually appealed to Roarke more, and she knew it.

They came to no clear conclusions as they savored their Chili Oil Poached Stripped Bass and Sichuan Peppercorn Crusted Prime New York Strip with accompanying Maryland fried rice, wok roasted summer vegetables, marinated tomato salad, and crispy shallots. Forty minutes later, with full stomachs, Roarke was ready to get to work. But he encouraged Katie to go home. It was past midnight.

"Nope, I'm staying. I've got work to do, too. And if I get tired, there's…" She looked around. "Forgot. You don't even have a couch!"

Roarke laughed. "Budgets."

"I'll pull up at your desk," she said. "Browning has me digging deeper into a secessionist fringe group in anticipation of some likely court action."

"Secessionists like Civil War secessionists?" he asked.

"Yup," Katie said kicking her shoes off. "Groups steadily have been gaining momentum. England had Brexit. France has its own. And here, Vermont, Texas, California, New Hampshire? They're calling them Vexit, Texit, Calexit, and NHexit."

"Where have I been?"

"Defending the United States," she only half joked.

"Wasn't this solved a couple of centuries ago?" he asked.

"Since when does history get in the way with a populist movement? Just because it can't happen, which we're certain it can't, doesn't mean groups on the far left and the far right won't try."

"Crazy."

"Real. And what these groups didn't have before, they've got now."

"Cash?"

"What makes cash come in, sweetie?"

Roarke looked confused.

"Come on. Think," she said encouraging him.

"Someone with snake oil to sell?"

"Give the man a prize. There is a group. And they've got a face to match the cause. A smooth talking charismatic figure I've read about who's gone from *a nobody* to *a somebody* in a short time. Now he's filling halls. The only thing missing is some fuse to light. When that happens, he'll be on Fox and MSNBC, Breitbart, Sinclair stations, you name it. Everyone will want him."

"I had no idea," Roarke admitted. "And he's a real rain maker?"

"Yup. Where the movement was splintered and sucking air before, they're catering roast beef dinners now. Cash is definitely piling up. And followers. Into the hundreds of thousands. Maybe more."

"Son of a gun. I had no idea."

"Staggering in this day and age. But, it just goes to show, you have your battles. I have mine. So…"

She stood.

"You know what?"

"What?"

"Suddenly, the idea of no couch with or without you isn't appealing after all. See ya."

She picked up her heels. Roarke laughed.

"Oh, and save some energy for tomorrow, honey. As you said, you owe me!"

They kissed passionately. Katie looked at her ring and smiled broadly.

"You did good, Scott."

Only after she left, Roarke realized he hadn't asked the name of the secessionist movement front guy. *Probably doesn't matter much anyway,* he thought.

CHAPTER 27

WHITE HOUSE PRESS ROOM
THE NEXT MORNING

"I have a brief statement to make, and then I'll take questions."

The president stood before a microphone and cameras in the White House briefing room.

"As Americans, there are definite freedoms that we hold dear. Free speech, equal rights, the right to vote, the right to assemble, freedom of religion, and the right to bear arms. Having these Constitutional rights, basic to our democratic republic, doesn't guarantee there won't be powers, foreign and domestic, that seek to weaken or wage determined assaults on them.

"Today, I'm reviewing possible attacks on another basic right. The right for any man or woman of legal age to run for and hold public office. It was guaranteed in the Fourteenth Amendment. That legal age was amended in the Twenty-Sixth Amendment of the Constitution. Serving in government is a constitutionally given right, and taking that right away is a Federal crime.

"Rest assured, if an offensive against this right is in fact underway, I will not let any stone go unturned across the nation. I will pursue anyone who is responsible to the ends of the Earth. And I promise we will locate, arrest, and then prosecute and punish any perpetrator or perpetrators who have conspired, with deadly intent, against the very workings of our representative process.

"I cannot confirm that a coordinated plot exists. I can tell you that we are acting as if one does."

Morgan Taylor stopped.

"Questions?"

The questions began with a flurry of shout-outs. Taylor selected a CNN reporter first.

ROARKE'S OFFICE
THE SAME TIME

Roarke had spread out photographs and blueprints of the Supreme Court building's original construction. He found them on the internet. Also readily available, a document containing seven regulations governing the Supreme Court Building and grounds prescribed by the U.S. Marshal, and pubic information on the Threat Assessment Unit. His main concerns? Hours open to the public (9:00 a.m.. to 4:30 p.m.), decorum (no noise disturbances allowed), the size and construction of protestors' signs (a quarter-inch thick, no larger than four-feet by four-feet, cardboard, poster board, or cloth), dogs on the property (allowed, but on a leash not to exceed four feet in length), and prohibition of demonstrations.

There was also a regulation covering firearms, explosives, incendiary devices, dangerous weapons, and other substances that could pose a danger. The rules were obvious. Not allowed. Unlawful. Banned.

Having never had real contact with the Supreme Court Police, Roarke wondered how good they were. Not only did the justices' safety depend on them, as far as he was concerned, so did Katie's.

Roarke was tired. Katie was right. He needed a couch. But as he began to doze at his desk, he came up with a plan. He decided to test the defenses. In a few days he'd conduct a solo Red Team incursion on the Supreme Court building.

THE PRESS ROOM

"We're coordinating with local and state police," Taylor said in response to a question about grassroots-level protection. "Director Mulligan is holding conference calls literally by the hour with agencies across the country. From school committees on up."

Next, the president recognized a *Dallas Morning News* reporter, John Walsh.

"John…"

"Is it fair to say, Mr. President, that so far, no murders have been stopped? Every attempt has been successful?"

"We're examining every imaginable case. At this moment, we don't know what might have thwarted or otherwise interrupted. As your reporting has suggested, they appear random. Occurring in broad daylight, after dinners, on city streets, getting in or leaving cars."

"Next. Yes, Besty?"

Betsy Sawyer, the Fox White House political reporter asked, "Has the White House stopped publishing your schedule in light of the circumstances? We haven't seen anything for today or tomorrow. Is that intentional because of the potential threats? And, will you, the vice president, or any cabinet members be seeking safer quarters?"

Morgan Taylor stood tall at the podium. He wore a blue tie with a blue striped shirt. Brooks Brothers like all his others. Simple yet authoritative. He was a war survivor, though much of his story had never been publicly told. Once a warrior, he was always a warrior, a former combat pilot, and a president who wasn't afraid, at least for himself.

"Betsy, the White House must be regarded as safe. Protected and safe. And this is where I work. I'm not going anywhere. As for other members of the administration, it's work as usual, with one caveat. The Secret Service is on high alert."

"Mr. President!" Shouts came from a dozen reporters. Taylor chose *Boston Globe* White House correspondent, Jim Jablanski.

"Thank you, Mr. President. Two questions. You just suggested there could be more than one assassin. What is the FBI telling you? Second, what would you do if a foreign government is responsible?"

TULSA, OKLAHOMA
THE SAME TIME

The Frenchman finished toweling after a long, hot shower. He stood naked front and center before the television set watching CNN's live coverage of the president's press conference. This question interested him.

As the president dodged the questions, the assassin looked at himself in the mirror. His travels and lack of exercise had loaded a few pounds around his mid-section. Not so much that it slowed him down. At least so far. But he took the visual cue as immediate order. He dropped down and counted off one hundred pushups, followed by one hundred crunches. While he exercised, he thought. Thinking always helped him stay ahead of any pursuers. He knew he had more now than ever.

THE PRESS ROOM
THE SAME TIME

"The FBI doesn't limit its thinking. So as for the number of subjects, they'll follow every lead where it takes them."

Taylor hadn't lied. But he didn't really say anything either. Basically because he had no idea. He moved to the second question.

"As for your second question, of course America's intelligence departments are working with global networks. It would be imprudent to speculate anything beyond that."

The president smiled, offered a typical thank you and a wave, and exited. He didn't take a deep breath until he was clear of the room.

OVAL OFFICE
AN HOUR LATER

"Scott. No one can know."

"I got it, boss."

"It's already been tried, and no one's succeeded.

"Not by someone who has a personal reason," Roarke stated. "Not by me."

"You have to take yourself out of it personally."

"Yeah, right."

Taylor wasn't going to win that part of the argument.

"Look, my goal is to breach and strike. We're both worried enough that you want me in. I saw your look, and I believe I can do it. If I can then…"

Roarke didn't finish the answer. Neither did the president.

"Okay, so let me do my job and hope that some good comes out of it."

"Live weapons, Scott."

"They should be."

"You won't be safe."

"Nothing is safe."

Morgan Taylor nodded. *Nothing was safe. Not completely.*

"Okay, then let's talk about how you're going to break into the Supreme Court with the goal to kill the Chief Justice."

MSNBC
THAT NIGHT

The guest was a former CIA operative, now retired, and author of an insider's book on black operations. Whether Keith Niver was the ex-spy's real name or just the name he used as an author was unknown. But his information was accurate and chilling.

"Whoever's out there isn't working from written instructions. He's a self-planner and very, very good at what he does."

"Wait. One person, not more?"

"Of course it's one person," the former operative postulated. "Strategically far easier. More efficient from a killing perspective."

"Then shouldn't that be the focus of the investigation?" the host noted. "The way to make an arrest."

Niver smiled. "Arrest? He's not the kind of man anyone arrests."

"Meaning?"

"He's smoke."

"Someone you know?" the host asked lightly.

"He's a bit of a lot of people. Experienced in stealth killing. Day or night. It doesn't matter. You wouldn't see him coming or leaving. He can attack from a distance or kill close up. When it comes to poisons, he's got any number ways of delivering dozens of them. Fast or slow. Intended to be discovered or not. Thallium or the mycotoxin T-2. Maybe even radioactive Polonium."

"Where's he from?"

"If he's American, Perth Amboy, New Jersey; Tampa, Florida; Nome, Alaska. I don't know. You pick it, Uncle Sam's trained them. But who says he's American?"

"Back to the question for the president. Possibly a foreign assassin?" the anchor asked.

The ex-agent answered the question with a question. "Well wouldn't that be interesting? Then we'd have to ask how and why."

"Do the types of victims, assuming they are related, tell you anything?"

"Yes. I wouldn't want to be holding a public office right now."

Niver was being interviewed remotely from Mesa, Arizona. He wore a plaid shirt and sat in front of a desert background in the KPNX-TV newsroom. His wavy blond hair made him look more like a rancher than a former CIA field operative. However, his eyes gave him away. They were intense; intense enough to suggest he was capable of doing great bodily harm to victims.

"Are assassins willing to die?"

"Good question. And the answer is no. If they are, the act is described as *lost*. They never want to be in that kind of situation. The object is to escape, to be *safe*. The object is to live to kill another day, or live off the spoils. Never to fall into enemy hands. The best way to survive is by concealing the fact that the subject was a victim of an assassination. But in this case, the whole object appears to be the opposite. And that's what's got me completely confused."

ROARKE'S WHITE HOUSE OFFICE
THE SAME TIME

Roarke decided to work out the details on his own. The less the president knew, the better. Even more importantly, he wouldn't tell Katie anything.

For the sake of the Supreme Court Police, he would go in unarmed. But he'd be prepared other ways.

MSNBC
MINUTES LATER

"Forget what you see in the movies or on TV," the former CIA-turned-author explained.

"It's possible to kill with bare hands, but few people are really capable. Even those trained in martial arts will use brute physical force only as an alternative. Much simpler are things you'd find in the kitchen, the workshop, a garage, or even the living room. A knife, a hammer, screw driver, wrench, lamp stand, or fire poker. Rope works, of course, but you have to have physical advantage to use it.

"Abdominal wounds used to be enough to lead to death, but today medical treatment gives the edge to the victim. Cutting the jugular or carotid blood vessels on both sides of the windpipe is more effective, as is severing the spinal cord in the cervical region. A knife or an axe work well under the circumstances, but the results are bloody and more likely to leave clues. Clues are bad.

"Maybe the most efficient way is to make someone take an unintended step off a cliff. Stairwells aren't as good, but an elevator shaft will usually do the trick. Falling into water off a bridge can't guarantee death unless it's high enough and the victim can't swim.

"A fall from a train. A shove in front of a truck. Not bad. Timing is key.

"Then, as I mentioned before, there are drugs. Arsenic, strychnine, and morphine. All proven in the field."

"So many ways," the host added.

"I haven't even mentioned blunt weapons. Useful when directed to the temple, behind the ear, the lower portion of the skull, or for that matter, any portion at the upper skull. And then there are guns."

Niver described various bolt-action long-range rifles. "Perfect to pick off guarded officials and public figures from a distance." Then he outlined scenarios where handguns were preferable, and why, when, and where bombs were the perfect choice.

"Sounds like terrorism to me," the host interjected. "Domestic or foreign. He's a terrorist."

"Consider the distinction between the purpose and the person. The power behind this is employing political terror. The instrument being used is not political. I believe he's a well-paid assassin."

"You're that certain?"

"Of course not. I'm just sound bites on your show," Keith Niver said. "Ask America's law enforcement. But I will tell you what I really think."

The host was seen in a stacked two-camera box shot with the ex-spy. He offered an encouraging, "Yes."

"He wanted police and the public to find out. He wanted you to find out. You and the rest of the press. He wanted people like me on the air speculating.

"You're tools. And now I'm one, too. By being interviewed, I'm likely contributing to whatever plan there is. So in the interest of national security, I suggest we bring this to an end."

Niver removed his microphone and walked off the set. It was a chilling moment of live TV that would go viral.

ROARKE'S OFFICE

Vinnie D'Angelo called from the CIA.

"Roarke, what office records the news channels off-air?"

"The press office. Poppiti's. Why?"

"You're going to want to see something."

CHAPTER 28

DALLAS, TEXAS
THE NEXT MORNING

The Frenchman caught the front page of the *Washington Post* at a Hudson News stand after deplaning at Dallas. He bought a copy, which served two purposes. It brought him up to speed with reports that were breaking, and it helped shield his face.

Multiple headlines covered different aspects of the story. Local accounts from Boise, Bakersfield, Fresno, and Spartanburg, with two line mentions from other cities including Great Barrington.

He didn't see anything that even hinted that the FBI had a lead. But the story did speak to the greater good. The *good*, as he defined it.

The New Definition of the Bullet Voting
By Don Nuendel
Political Writer

Historically, bullet voting has been a common way of choosing a single political candidate when voters can also select more candidates to rank on a ballot. In this way, voters who don't want to hurt their favorite candidate by also marking anyone else, virtually narrow the field. It can help specific candidates running for city councilor, school committee, a judgeship, or other categories rise to the top where voters are able to elect more than one official.

But today, there is a new form of bullet voting. In the wrong hands, it's a cheap way to influence an election whether local, regional, state, or national. Cheap in terms of the cost of a round; a bullet.

A single shot from a handgun costs about $0.33. A round from a sniper rifle is a little more expensive. Depending upon the gun, anywhere from a $1.25 to $1.45. Surely, inexpensive ways to cast a deciding vote on the political process.

Of course, there are other charges when you consider all the expenses: airfare from place-to-place, local car rentals, hotels, clothing changes, and, of course, the fee associated with the job.

The job being the final vote, which takes a political figure out of the election process permanently.

The assassin or assassins engaged in such bullet voting not only chase voters away from their voting booths, American political figures are increasingly in fear of their lives. And many, from California to Washington, D.C., are altogether quitting.

The article jumped to page two and went into detail. It was accompanied by three other enterprise reports and an editorial.

The Frenchman tucked the newspaper under his arm and took the airport shuttle from American Airlines to United and onto the Caribbean for a few days' rest. There, he'd exercise and make certain his bank accounts were up to date.

CHAPTER 29

ARLINGTON, VIRGINIA
2200 HOURS

General Jonas Jackson Johnson only partially accepted the president's order. He stopped commuting from his home in Virginia and finally moved into Number One Observatory Circle, the official Washington residence of the nation's vice president.

That's where he received his first visitor.

The Secret Service agent waved the Speaker of the House forward to a parking space in front of the 1893 residence.

"Thank you for seeing me, Mr. Vice President," Duke Patrick said when greeted at the front door. The general wore jeans, a t-shirt, and shoes without socks. It was a look Patrick had never seen from the usually put together retired four-star.

"I take it it's important," J3 said. Then he added a completely intended political barb, "To you."

"To the country," the Speaker replied.

"Well then, we know the country's business has no hours. Come in."

The vice president led Patrick into his study off the main hallway.

"May I offer you a drink? A port perhaps."

Patrick's reputation around the Beltway was that he could belt more than a few at any hour. 10:00 p.m. was as good a time as any.

"Thanks. A Scotch."

J3 laughed to himself.

"With a splash."

J3 poured two fingers of Jack, holding his better stock for friends. He added a little water.

"Now, what brings you around, Mr. Speaker?"

Duke Patrick took a sip and sat on the couch offered by J3. The general fixed a drink for himself, an eighteen-year port, but did not turn to the congressman as Patrick began to answer.

"Completely confidentially, general."

"I suppose it depends upon what you have to say."

"America's security," Patrick said.

The general swiftly turned and locked onto the Speaker's gaze. "That is a matter for a whole host of people to decide, chief among them the president."

"Yes, it is, general, except if the president is not fulfilling his duties. Many of my colleagues believe he isn't."

Jonas Jackson Johnson internalized the criticism but showed no expression. He sat in a high back leather chair and swirled his own drink. He used the act to frame his response properly.

"Particularly you?"

"In the past week, my staff has recorded twenty-three threats against me. So bluntly, yes."

"You've passed those on."

"Yes! To the Capitol Police, the FBI, my hometown and state police. They don't know where to begin. Multiply the threats against me by the members of Congress and elected officials all across the country. I'll help you with the number. It's incalculable."

J3 nodded. The fact was indisputable. But, he wondered, *Why was Patrick really here?* He decided to take a conciliatory tone.

"We're working on it, Duke. And of course, most of the threats probably aren't credible."

Patrick's eyes bulged. "Tell that to hundreds, no thousands of elected officials who are afraid to go outside. Hell, the *Post* had an article today about resignations all over the place. Soon we won't be able to do any governmental work on any level. We're in recess and I doubt I can get anyone back. We've cancelled committee meetings, stopped going to restaurants. Hell, I won't even be seen on the street. Coming here even scared me. We have bills that can't be passed. A deficit vote due to come up in a week. And—"

"I assume you're coming to your point," the general stated.

"Yes. Leadership."

The vice president put his drink down, a signal he was willing to listen to more.

"The president has not assured Congress, let alone the entire country, that enough is being done. Or for that matter, anything at all."

"And you want me to do exactly what?"

Duke Patrick drew on his drink, then put it on the coffee table in front of the vice president.

"You've managed crises. You've led our forces in battle. Not once, but multiple times. You've commanded, general. To the country's point of view, Morgan Taylor has not."

"Congressman, you should be talking to your colleagues in the House. If you're considering impeachment, there are procedures."

"Your word, not mine. But that means getting the Senate back in session. I can't see us reaching a quorum."

Patrick paused for the line he had practiced all day and conspired with other members of his inner circle.

"There are other ways. They're codified. The Twenty-Fifth Amendment, Mr. Vice President. You could get a majority of the cabinet to vote to remove Morgan Taylor. You, general, can lawfully become president and get us out of this mess."

PART TWO

CHAPTER 30

YUKTAE-DONG SUBMARINE BASE, DEMOCRATIC PEOPLE'S REPUBLIC OF KOREA

Chin-wah Lee lived on the base. On the good side he had three somewhat balanced meals a day and limited expenses for his limited disposable income.

The bad side? Actually plural, bad sides. The base was on an island. As a result, it took additional effort to break free and stroll the streets of Yuktae-dong, the third largest city in the country. But at least once every ten days he had to find a way to meet up with Jee Gyuen.

Lee vowed not to take any unnecessary chances in a country where you were guilty, whether or not proven. And he was guilty.

Gyuen gave him tips on how to check for tails. That alone made him more nervous, but he got better with practice.

At its simplest, spy craft was best with grooves cut into trees, innocent looking chalk marks on a wall, or a book out of alphabetical order on a shelf. Nothing electronic. Nothing in print. An innocuous signal to make a pickup.

Those weren't their means. They had no established pattern or a fixed routine. It was always two friends meeting. Former teacher and former student. They saw one another at restaurants, in the park, or at a movie. Completely in the open. Gyuen transferred the package—the USB drive—with a handshake or a hug.

After months of carrying out his assignment flawlessly, Lee finally asked how Gyuen got the drives.

"You don't need to know. You don't want to know."

One answer protected the CIA agent, the other, the North Korean. But Lee figured that smuggling the USB drive and getting them to Gyuen might be the weak link in the operation.

The drive was little more than cardboard thick and no bigger than a good-sized thumb nail. Jee Gyuen retrieved them from a street vender, an especially well-fed deep cover agent, selling *injo gogi bap*, artificial meat rice. Each drive was wrapped in the paper. If anyone approached, Jee could quickly chew it.

Gyuen visited the vender at least once a week, never on the same day, and not always leaving with a drive. Sometimes he just grabbed a bottle of *Ryongjin*, North Korea's version of a cola that comes flat. So far he'd successfully received and handed over twenty-six drives, which had infected, by his own calculations, much of the entire North Korean fleet with something he didn't even fully understand.

Years ago, Jee Gyuen's own mentor at the CIA had told him the same words he'd passed along to Lee. "You don't need to know. I don't want to know."

CHAPTER 31

WASHINGTON, D.C.
FOUR DAYS LATER

Every week the Coca-Cola delivery truck rolled up to the loading dock at the Supreme Court. The cafeteria went through more than 2,600 bottles of Coke, Diet Coke, Coke Zero, and other company products every week.

Between 6:00 a.m. and 8:00 a.m. the trucks came and went with regularity. Mondays were the busiest, but delivery occurred on a rolling basis all week long.

As with any bureaucracy, the busier things got, the more likely security would excuse incomplete paperwork and trade higher security for faster efficiency.

"Hey, didn't we see you guys Monday?" the loading dock clerk asked when the delivery truck rolled up.

"Yup," the uniformed driver said. "New order. Got it this morning."

"Wait, where's Brokaw?"

"Off Wednesdays. Got my papers here."

Three more trucks pulled in behind the Coke delivery truck for their mid-week deliveries. One partially blocked traffic.

The driver flashed his lanyard ID and took time with the order. The truck in the road honked.

"Need me to pull up?"

"In a sec."

The driver handed over his clipboard. It was stacked with delivery orders. The security officer barely looked at it.

"Damn busy this morning," the driver noted.

"Too busy." The Supreme Court guard handed the clipboard back. "Go ahead. How long?"

"I'll try to turn it around in twenty."

"Christ, okay." The clerk waved the truck forward and tried to deal with the backup.

Scott Roarke smiled. Procuring the truck wasn't all that difficult. People were more likely to okay something out of the ordinary than to take the time to check. Even in Washington, D.C. So once again, the right uniform, the correct looking identification, and a complaining *I don't know, I'm just following orders* attitude worked.

Fully inside the loading dock, Roarke exited the truck, opened the back, and proceeded to off-load cases of soda onto a dolly. At a second checkpoint, this one with a member of the Supreme Court Police, he made small talk to cover the fact that his name was not on the list. But having gotten the name *Brokaw* from the loading dock hand, he mentioned it, which seemed to give him the authority that he knew the regular driver.

"I'll be back and forth a few times."

"No problem," the officer said.

Of course there was. Scott Roarke had just breached security at the United States Supreme Court.

He delivered the first load of bottles to the kitchen off the court cafeteria. He knew just where to go because he'd been there with Katie. Performing this completely normal routine, he returned to his truck, and reloaded the cart for a second time. On his third trip inside, he left the dolly at the refrigerator, took one box, balanced it on his left shoulder and pushed open the kitchen door to the dining area.

No one questioned him.

Roarke walked through the cafeteria, which was as basic as any government building might be. White walls and wood chairs and tables too close together for lawyers or justices to have really private discussions. The only distinctive qualities were the glass chandeliers and blue carpet inlaid with gold emblems of the court.

Roarke continued without drawing any attention. Just another deliveryman moving with purpose.

Some staffers were taking coffee and snacks to their offices. A few sat for breakfast. But generally, it was quiet.

Roarke was familiar with the layout of the 1935 building from previous visits, but today he relied on internet downloaded schematics to avoid guarded areas. The first floor was no problem. He could have placed the box in any open office and probably even gotten an assistant or secretary to sign for the delivery. But he pushed further. His goal was to reach the second floor of the four-story Corinthian building without using the two main spiral staircases. He found the back stairway and although cameras would be on him, he kept his face away from the lenses.

Visitor security was actually tight, which is why he didn't enter through the main visitor entrance located at the plaza level. The main door at the top of the thirty-six marble steps was off limits since 2010. Once inside, guests were required to pass through metal detectors. But not necessarily for those with the right looking credentials making deliveries.

On the second floor, he avoided the main courtroom and The Great Hall, lined with Spanish ivory-vein marble. His goal was further down the hall.

He passed a few clerks and smiled. One even joked, "Particularly unsweetened for Browning."

Roarke laughed.

Twenty more steps and he entered the chief justice's outer office. The secretary hadn't arrived yet. He opened another door and helped himself into an office just short of Browning's. Roarke heard someone entering. He quickly opened the next door and stood five feet away from the stone-cold face of the Chief Justice of the Supreme Court, the Honorable Leopold Browning.

"What? I didn't order any—"

Roarke lowered the box and turned straight on.

"I know you didn't, Mr. Chief Justice, but I'm here to make a point."

He put the box on the jurist's oak desk.

"Agent…" Browning began.

Before he could get the name out, Katie Kessler entered, file folders in hand. It took a moment and then she gasped, "Scott!"

The loud declaration was followed by Browning bellowing, "Roarke!"

"Hi and sorry."

"What are you doing?" Katie exclaimed as she stared at his uniform.

"As I started telling Justice Browning. I'm here to make a point."

"Make it," the chief justice barked.

"I broached your security. Quite easily."

"You couldn't have. We have—"

"Trust him, sir," Katie offered. "If Scott said he did, he surely did."

"Some falsified paperwork on a clip board, a handmade ID, a rented uniform and truck, and a few friendly nods. Here I am, with this box, which could have been a bomb. Or a gun hidden among cans of soda. And if I got in, then anyone equally adept can do the same."

"Impossible!" Browning continued to claim.

Katie took an entirely different tact. "Scott, you could have been shot!"

"Very possible and yes," Roarke said answering both. "Now may I use your phone?"

Browning nodded blankly, still trying to process what Roarke had accomplished.

"…and Katie," he continued, "maybe you should let security know. They're probably going to want to escort me out."

Katie wanted to launch into Roarke, but he held up a finger as he dialed the White House and got the operator.

"Roarke for POTUS," he said, adding his ID number and code word.

CHAPTER 32

KATIE KESSLER'S APARTMENT
THAT NIGHT

"You made your point."

"Sorry, Katie." Roarke could see how unhappy she was. He brought Chinese takeout as a peace offering. But he felt it was going to take more than sweet talking and moo shu to get back in good graces. So he decided on tough love.

"It was too important not to."

"Important enough for you to have gotten shot by someone following protocol, or by a rookie who was just scared?"

She helped him unpack the food but avoided eye contact.

"Yes. Because if I could, he could too. And if I could get face-to-face with Browning in his chamber, then neither he, nor any of the other justices, or for that matter you, can be considered safe."

She stopped and looked up at him. Her slow nod and half smile was sign enough that she understood. It also had the look of love.

"You are one crazy agent," she said, throwing a veggie roll at him.

"Crazy in love with you."

"Well then, no more stunts like that. You'll just have to find other ways to convince me to go along with you."

Roarke smiled seductively and teased, "Should I start now or after dinner?"

"After! I'm famished!"

With their dinner of Moo Shu Pork, General Tang's Chicken, Slippery Shrimp, and Hot and Sour Soup behind them, they closed out by opening their fortune cookies. Rarely did they make any personal sense. And almost never did they contain real fortunes. The real fun was always adding the phrase "in bed" at the end of each. However, Roarke's fortune tonight snapped him back to his job and the likely danger ahead.

Your future requires taking most careful steps.

A phone call ten minutes later reinforced the advice even more.

FBI LABS
NINETY MINUTES LATER

"Are you sure?" Roarke asked Touch Parsons.

"Hell no. Neither is Penny, but it's more than we had."

The FBI computer expert had been working with his girlfriend, CPT Penny Walker, adding and subtracting facial markers, applying predictive qualities, and basically trying to paint a picture of a subject that fit into the *maybe, might,* or *could be* bin.

"Got pictures?"

"Twenty-seven," Walker said as she joined them at Parsons's computer station.

"Hi, Penny."

"Hi stupid," she replied. Walker was always teasing Roarke for breaking up with her, even in front of Parsons.

"Twenty-seven solid leads. That's better than 27,000."

"By a factor of…" Parsons began to calculate.

"Spare me," Roarke said. "Who's looking good?"

"All things considered?" Penny began.

"All things."

"I like nine in particular. I'm checking on their most recent whereabouts. The ones that stand out will be those who aren't where they're supposed to be. The ones I can't find."

"And?"

"And, Jesus, Roarke, this is the nuts and bolts stuff. It takes time."

"Hon, we don't have time."

Parsons typed a command. The nine composites appeared on screen with names and aliases and countries of origin. All had a similar look, though eyes and noses varied. None of them looked familiar, but that didn't surprise him.

The subjects came from a variety of countries. Surprisingly, only two were Americans, the first group they had collectively considered.

Three were English, former SAS officers. One German. A Romanian, a Frenchman, and a Chechnyan. Roarke scanned the names.

"They're all alive?"

"Presumably alive and well," Penny replied. "And up until recently, rumored to be working in the danger zone. Last known jobs, bodyguards, extreme fighters, mercenaries. Except for the Chechnyan and the French guy. Nothing recent on either of them."

"Remember Richard Cooper?" Roarke asked. He referred to the assassin who had worked with a Middle Eastern benefactor to get Congressman Teddy Lodge elected president.

"Of course. Dead thanks to you."

"Missing in action," Roarke replied. His body wasn't recovered after he fell off the Friendship Bridge spanning the Paraná River between Ciudad del Este, Paraguay and Foz do Iguaçu, Brazil. Everyone presumed he drowned downstream. I'm not so sure."

"You actually think he's alive?" Penny Walker asked.

"I'm just saying put him on the list along with one of his best talents."

"Killing?"

"Blending in."

"Right," Parsons noted. "A real chameleon. Okay, consider him added."

"And cross-reference which of your *possibles* have mastered any American dialects. That takes training just like hand-to-hand. If he got it somewhere, there should be a record. Find the record, we'll be closer to finding the man."

"Got it," Parsons said swiveling back in his chair.

"God, you're still good," Penny sighed.

CHAPTER 33

RADIO STUDIO
LOS ANGELES

The opening theme, recognizable across the nation, began at the top of the hour. 10:00 p.m. Pacific, 1:00 a.m. Eastern. More than six hundred stations carried *Coast to Coast AM* in the U.S., Canada, Mexico, and Guam. More than three million people listened each week. People tuned in for news, conspiracies, mysteries, and truth they believed they couldn't get elsewhere. It was natural for the show to book Lucas Burke, a true political rising star.

Burke was scheduled for the second hour. The first featured a regular guest, author/investigator Robert Greene. A burr in the saddle of government agencies.

Greene, a young man who claimed his only way of growing older was to keep his own whereabouts secret, called to discuss the expanding controversy: Is an assassin hell bent on killing American political figures. And who is he?

"Robert, welcome back," the venerable host said. "Are you safe?"

"Thanks, George. I'm fine. Happy to talk with you again."

"As our listeners know, you've gotten more files released through the Freedom of Information Act than anyone. From papers on secret government projects and experiments to extraterrestrial activity. But tonight, we're down-to-earth. You heard President Morgan Taylor's press conference?"

"Sure did."

"He all but warned us we're under attack. Political assassinations without apparent rhyme or reason."

"There's always reason," Greene stated. "John Wilkes Booth, Lee Harvey Oswald. There's always reason."

"And now, what? Ten? Twelve in the past few months?" the host added.

Greene added four more that he suspected.

"So who is he?"

"He?"

"The assassin. Who's the assassin?"

Greene audibly laughed over the phone.

"I can tell you two people who know," Greene said.

"Who?"

"The assassin himself and the person he's working for."

"You don't think he's on his own?"

"Absolutely not. There's too much at play here and too much money that has to be spent to make it all work. There's travel, meals, typical business expenses."

"Some business," the host observed.

"An assassin has to earn a living."

"Can we follow the money?"

"I suspect that's one thing American intelligence is trying to do," Greene hinted.

"And another?"

"Whether he's leaving any other tracks. According to my sources, so far none."

The host was intrigued. His listeners—truckers, insomniacs, and devoted fans—were hooked.

"What kind of scale would you put this on. From one to ten?"

"Conspiratorially, George, it's a ten."

"Are there other scales?"

"Sure. There's the chilling effect on American politics, the ability for elected officials to conduct the people's business. And the X Factor," Greene said knowingly.

"The X Factor?"

"Yes. The fear it instills in elected officials, their families, and the people who work with them. On those scales, also a ten."

BAR
WASHINGTON, D.C.

"Any closer to a decision?" Roarke asked D'Angelo.

"On hold right now, considering." D'Angelo casually scanned the bar. No one appeared to be taking particular notice of them. "How about you?"

"Same."

"Putting any miles on?" Roarke asked.

"About to."

"Any place you can send a postcard from?"

ON THE RADIO

"Domestic terrorism or off-shore?" the radio host asked.

"It's meant to feel local, but I'm not so sure. The copycat threats don't make it any easier for the Feds."

"Are there a lot?"

"Yup. And it's typical. Mostly phone calls. Some on the internet. Few who actually follow through."

"And what about evidence. Have your sources told you anything?"

"Nothing yet. But you can be sure they're examining ballistics, fingerprints, DNA traces, and CCTV camera footage."

The host changed it up. He went to an area that opened up a larger conversation.

"Who goes into this kind of work?"

FBI LABS
QUANTICO, VIRGINIA
THE SAME TIME

When Touch Parsons worked late, he liked to have the radio on. Tonight, he found his favorite late-night program particularly interesting and especially coincidental. *Coast to Coast AM* was exploring precisely what he had in front of him. The radio show painted a psychological picture. Parsons was burning through the night with a visual one.

The show always covered fascinating stories, but rarely ones that seemed to connect so completely with his computer command and function buttons.

Fascinating, he thought as he continued to refine his work.

ON THE RADIO

"An assassin is a trained killer. So who trains people to kill?" Greene rhetorically asked.

"The military."

"Correct," Greene continued. "But there's also organized crime. And career mercenaries."

"So we're seeing the work of a highly skilled talent."

"Talent is right. I'll walk you through the categories, based on a Birmingham City University study.

"It starts with a relative beginner. Well, not a complete beginner. Let's call him the *novice*. Someone who's relatively new to the killing game; someone who might have earned his stripes in the underworld. The mob.

"Next up, the dilettante. This is a *cleanskin*."

"A what?"

"It's spy talk. A *cleanskin* is a person who might not have a criminal record or not yet be on law enforcement's radar. He's accepting con-tracts, but so far he's invisible, without identifiable traits. He's prepared to kill for money and like the novice, is more likely to trip up sooner than later."

"Still deadly."

"Very," Greene replied. "The next category is the *journeyman*. To put it bluntly, this is a guy—"

"Or a woman."

"Yes, and I'll get to that, who is experienced in multiple death arts and kills without malice. Likely a James Bond gone bad. A Russian FSB killer. A rouge ex-CIA agent."

"Got it. So the *journeyman* is at the very top of the paid killers list?" the host asked.

"Well, no. We've got one better. The *master*. And this is who I believe is out there. Defined by Birmingham City University, he's a killer whose identity is unknown."

"Dangerous."

"And smart. Invisible with money and identities to burn."

The show broke for a commercial.

NASHUA, NEW HAMPSHIRE
THE SAME TIME

Lucas Burke and his political advisor Clay Lindstrom were listening to the broadcast in a New Hampshire motel room. Burke was grazing through a box of Kentucky Fried Chicken and getting excited. Lindstrom sipped a black coffee.

"This is great shit. It plays right to our base," Burke boasted. "Can't wait to follow up when—"

"No. Don't go there. Not for a second. If he brings it up, pivot. Say you found it interesting, use it as evidence that the country is broken. Then shift to our talking points. The more you keep talking, the less he'll ask you. You'll be able to go from one segment to the next. Before you know it, two hours will be over."

"If I miss anything?"

"I'll give you notes."

Lindstrom was prepared with a yellow pad.

"Okay, but I guess I couldn't ask for a better lead-in."

"Not at all," Lindstrom said. Robert Greene was an absolutely perfect lead-in to two hours with Lucas Burke. Perfect, considering Clay Lindstrom was the one who proposed it to the radio show's producer.

ON THE RADIO

"We're back with writer, researcher, investigator Robert Greene," the radio host continued. "And we're talking about what it takes to be an assassin. So who decides to do this? Walk us through the major traits? Can we spot a skilled assassin on the street?"

"Great questions. Starting with who. They're cunning and clever. Steps ahead of the authorities and miles ahead of you and me. They'll take risks and be duplicitous, but not look like they're trying to trick anyone. They're guided by a lack of conscience. No remorse or regret, but they still may have a code of ethics."

"Like what?"

"Here I have to differentiate between terrorists and paid assassins. A terrorist is willing to take his own life, bomb an airplane, kill civilians, even children. An international assassin is determined to stay alive, enjoy the money he's earned, and live a long life."

"And you think we're talking about that second kind, not a terrorist?"

"Yes. The fact that there haven't been any political pronouncements in the wake of his killing spree says that he's strategically focused. His work is designed for deep emotional impact. It's not the work of a fundamentalist."

"Okay, so we won't recognize him in a crowd, but he must have a fatal flaw. Something that would tip people off."

Greene took a deep, audible breath over the phone. "I know you'd love to hear that's the case, like in a movie, but it's unlikely. He doesn't get nervous or flustered in stressful situations. He operates completely detached from any human quotient; without remorse. It's likely he doesn't even view his target as a person. He'll show no tendencies toward violent behavior, though that's his stock and trade. He's totally at ease lying and can completely compartmentalize feelings. And if there's any common denominator, it's that…"

FBI LABS

Parsons, now completely caught up in the broadcast, took notes. The conversation was making him think beyond the 1's and 0's that his mainframe computed. Robert Greene was giving him human parameters. He underlined some items and crossed out others. He felt that beyond the millions of others listening in bed, driving across country, or working the night shift somewhere, the conspiracy researcher was speaking directly to him.

ON THE RADIO

"…he likely lives alone."

"He'd surely make a good guest. Love to find out what someone makes in this line of work," George wondered. Without realizing it, he had just reduced an assassin's job to an everyday vocation.

"So, Robert, what's a master assassin get for a typical hit? Ten thousand? More?"

"He's got to earn his way up. Before hitting the top of the pay scale, a novice might get a few hundred dollars. A dilettante or journeyman more, maybe upwards of $25,000. But a master, on the scope of what we're seeing? He's probably on a sliding scale. Maybe starting at fifty thousand and going sky high."

The host speculated how much the assassin could have earned so far. "A million?"

"More. With economic elevators in the deal, he could be at one hundred-plus per kill. Well over two or three million in the bank. Real money. Of course, it depends on how many."

"Who's got that kind of money to burn?"

"They're all over the place. From corporate billionaires to foreign governments. Figures in the shadows to people in the news."

"Do they fit any profile?"

"In this case, not necessarily beyond creating political turmoil."

"Back to the assassin. What about his manner? Does he take chances?"

"No. Assassins are professionals. This guy is at the top of his game. He's more likely to murder when his target is strolling about or shopping in public. That way he can minimize risk of detection. The chaos he creates in a moment allows him to disappear from the scene with the instrument of death. The rifle, the poisoned umbrella, the knife. Whatever.

"Moreover, local law enforcement isn't equipped or experienced in capturing professional assassins."

"Why is that, Robert?"

"Because they blend in. They don't look like someone who's about to commit a murder. They're not acting irrationally. They don't draw attention to themselves. Nor do they draw pleasure or excitement. It's not a high. They're not distracted by feelings. The killers who mess up are the ones who make mistakes. The novices or dilettantes. They talk to others about their accomplishments. They want to be known as tough guys."

"Or women," the host reiterated.

"Yes. And they'll leave forensic evidence behind. But not this guy."

The host repeated his point. "Or woman. I want to discuss whether women get into the assassination business when we come back."

The broadcast went to a commercial for an online food company that specialized in emergency supplies that could be stored for forty years.

NASHUA, NEW HAMPSHIRE

"Man, this is interesting," Burke said. "Sure love to talk about it."

"No!" Clay Lindstrom demanded. "Stay on point."

"Hell, the base will eat it up. This whole political thing can help us. I can just—"

"No!" the handler repeated more forcefully.

"Jesus, Clay. Calm down. You'll wake up everyone down the row."

"I am calm." Lindstrom was anything but calm.

"I just think there's a natural way—"

Lindstrom cut him off. "There's *no* way. Stay on point or I call and cancel right now."

"Okay, okay," said the darling of the secessionist movement. "You're the boss."

Lindstrom smiled and thought, *Yes, I am.* Then he realized, he really wasn't.

ON THE RADIO

"We're back with Robert Greene." The *Coast to Coast AM* host was well into the first hour of his four-hour program. He reiterated Greene's credits and moved to the question that he'd brought up before the commercial break. "Could the assassin be a woman?"

"Could be, but likely, no."

"Why not? Couldn't the killer be like Angelina Jolie in, what was that movie?"

"*Salt.*"

"Right, or *La Femme Nikita?*'"

"I suppose it would be interesting, but a man is still going to move about more easily. Hide in plain sight. A woman could certainly pull the trigger, but more people take notice of a woman in public. And many of the hits have been made in public."

"But there was Mata Hari," the host proposed.

"Right. Possibly the greatest woman spy in the twentieth century. Reportedly responsible for delivering Allied military secrets to the Germans during World War I, resulting in the deaths of nearly fifty thousand French soldiers. But a spy, not a trigger-pulling assassin.

"Most other women in the field, pretty much the same thing. Idoia Lope Riano, nicknamed La Tigresa…"

"Sounds sexual."

"She was," Greene continued. "Legendarily so. She was a leading commando in the campaign for Basque Independence from Spain in the 1980s. Said to have seduced policemen before shooting them."

"A hit-woman."

"In her case, yes," Greene stated. "Then there was Brigitte Mohnhaupt—a member of a West German Communist militant organization in the 1960s and '70s. She and her colleagues from the Red Army Faction attacked Germans, killing upwards of thirty. Mohnhaupt was considered the most evil and dangerous woman in West Germany."

"And another killer. You get my point," the host said.

"I do, but she was captured. Sentenced to life but released on probation after twenty-four years. For that matter, La Tigresa was sentenced to more than fifteen hundred years in prison. And things didn't turn out so well for Mata Hari. She was executed by the French in 1917."

"I get it. Not so much equal opportunity for women in this field. But they're still out there, trained or unwitting pawns. Like the two women in Malaysia involved in the ssassination of the North Korean ruler's half-brother?" the host asked.

"Yes. Nasty family business."

"So the bottom line, Robert?"

"Women are in the business, but based on the level of experience, planning, and talent it takes to execute and disappear, I still say investigators are searching for a man."

FBI LABS

"Absolutely," Touch Parsons said aloud. "No way it's a woman." But the conversation did help him apply some new parameters to his search. All psychological, which in time, could help him create a better picture of the assassin.

WASHINGTON, D.C.

Katie Kessler had the radio on but was listening to a cool jazz FM station while she worked through problems. She came to realize that the secessionist groundswell across the country wasn't just political. The movement was fueled by emotion, tapping into identity, frustration, and a growing sense of independence.

Texans' passion spoke loudly, but petitioners couldn't turn their signatures into action. The legislature had to buy in, which they didn't. Moreover, there was a bigger problem. *Texas v. White*, an 1869 Supreme Court case. The historic ruling affirmed that the United States was an "indestructible union." Federal judges noted that the Founding Fathers "enshrined the right to change our national government through the power of the ballot—a right that generations of Americans have fought to secure for all. But they did not provide the right to walk away from it."

Meanwhile, proponents in California continually put statewide referendum on the ballot. The vote comes up every few years only to fizzle out. Nonetheless, it was now Katie Kessler's job to determine if any attempt anywhere could survive. Her research argued no. But expensive lawyers in support of secession could still clog the system in long legal battles. That made it her problem.

"Thanks so much, Browning," she said aloud as if her boss was present. With that, she dug deeper. Had she been listening to the late-night talk show, she might have realized there was more urgency to the problem.

CHAPTER 34

ON THE RADIO

"Lucas Burke. It's a pleasure to have you on. What part of the nation do we find you in tonight?" the *Coast to Coast AM* host asked.

"Thanks, George. I'm in Nashua, New Hampshire. We're talking up NHexit."

Burke enthusiastically explained the status of the New Hampshire exit plan. He called it another historic movement, though in reality it was doomed. But his message was always positive and upbeat, just as Clay Lindstrom instructed.

"Well, you're certainly the visible face and for us tonight the audible voice behind this sweeping movement," the host added, "so let's start unpacking everything."

"I'm all yours," Burke said. His voice warmly invited the nationwide radio audience to listen just as followers did at his local meetings.

"How many so far, Lucas? There's NHexit in New Hampshire, Calexit in California…. "

Burke picked up the sing-a-long and added the other states. He listed twenty. He could have rattled off groups in all fifty.

Clay Lindstrom slipped a note under him. *Doing great.*

"But you're not actually running for any office?" the host asked.

"No. I'm just a guy out there reminding people who we are and what's gotten in the way of our liberties. It'll be up to others to take it to the next step."

"To be the presidents of any number of separate countries if the secessionist votes stand the constitutional test?"

"That's the idea," Burke said.

"I'm no lawyer, but it seems like you've got an uphill battle, Lucas. I mean countries without armies or social services. Have you really thought this through?"

"It doesn't mean everyone who wants to exit will make it, but some will. The Republic of California will. The Northwest Front or the New Republic of the Northwest will. Enough former states to ensure success. Texas would seem obvious, but it's harder because of their legislative approach. But we've got a strong movement right here in New Hampshire and next door in Vermont."

"Where does it leave the U.S.? The last time states seceded, there was war. The Civil War."

"Absolutely right, but today it's completely different. Peaceful. We're allies with many of the same interests, yet we have ideological divides. They're not racial. This is not about slavery. We're not turning the clock back. Our followers come from all socio-economic and religious backgrounds."

Clay Lindstrom was pleased. He had prepared, no trained, Burke well. He'd groomed him from a series of local radio station interviews and town hall meetings to this national forum reaching millions.

Lucas Burke had been the perfect empty vessel: Charismatic, bold, a mesmerizing speaker, but not smart enough to understand what he had gotten himself into. He was a tool and didn't know it.

"And there's nothing you want out of this, Lucas?"

"I want to see regional needs respected through favorable trade agreements with the United States for the benefit of all parties. I want to see individual rights honored in a way that works for the good of the people. And, I never want to see our new free men and women have to participate in Washington's endless desire to pursue international wars."

"What about the funding that areas now receive from Washington. Upkeep of Interstate Highways? All the federal jobs, from airports to harbors? Law enforcement? FEMA? The National Guard? America, as it presently stands, relies on the dollar and tax money going back to states."

"Taxes will remain in the region rather than feeding the Washington initiatives," Burke replied. "And those states that have no income tax?"

Burke hesitated. Lindstrom, who was listening over the air on a delay, missed his pause.

"That's a great question," he said while thinking. "There are many things to consider. Taxes on goods and services, imports, gasoline, and point of purchase items. Much to work out. But nothing impossible. That's not to say everything will be easy. It won't. But it'll get better."

Burke ignored the other questions with pose, and then eased into his best stump speech arguments. Lindstrom listened, relieved.

. . .

In addition to being on terrestrial radio, *Coast to Coast AM* was global on the internet through paid subscriptions. That's how the North Korean dictator listened live in his Pyongyang office. His interpreter worked hard to give him an immediate and faithful translation. There were some nuances he didn't understand and others he screamed at. Mostly he gloated. The conversation seemed to be going his way. Great the first hour. Not so, when the host began taking calls in hour two.

. . .

"Hi George. Calling in from New York. Very interesting guests tonight."

The host acknowledged the compliment.

"I'd like to find out if Mr. Burke has ever read the book *Brave New World?*"

"No, I haven't," Lucas said.

"Or *A Handmaid's Tale?*"

"Saw the show," he said cheerfully.

"What about *We* or *Lord of the Flies* or *Animal Farm?*"

"Well, yes, *Lord of the Flies* and *Animal Farm*. When I was a kid, but—"

"They're all good," the caller argued. "Novels where citizens are transfixed by happy slogans and false promises. Whole populations that buy into transformative narratives that ultimately result in societies that deprive individuals of freedom."

Lindstrom, worried that Burke would get into a pissing match, gave a cut sign. Burke flagged him off.

"You said you're from New York?" Burke asked.

"Yes."

"New York City?"

"Yes."

Burke laughed, but not in a mean way. "Then we can agree on something."

"What's that?"

"New York won't be following anytime soon."

He didn't stop to allow the caller a response.

"And if I remember right, in *Lord of the Flies*, power is all about gaining territory through violence and domination. Authority comes with fear and punishment. Kids land on an island with no understanding of responsibility and governing. They create a society that's based on dominance and it is disastrous. That's the opposite of our movements. We will not be islands unto ourselves. Not autocratic enemies but democratic partners with the United States. Independent, self-determinative. It's not so bad."

The host nodded to his board producer. The caller had enough time, and Lucas Burke held his own.

"Okay, we'll be back with more calls. Stay with us."

CHAPTER 35

YUKTAE-DONG SUBMARINE BASE
NORTH KOREA

Chin-wah Lee knew very little about real life in the United States. Like many people, he privately believed that Pyongyang's jingoistic slogans, single-minded banners, and simplistic songs couldn't be accurate. But after discounting much of what he'd heard all his life, he still couldn't really comprehend the American way.

Jee Gyuen had described supermarkets and shopping centers, the open internet, and free speech. But they were concepts largely without meaning. He could relate to money. With money he could have a bigger apartment, food in his refrigerator, and maybe his own car. The other things? Like rights and privileges? They were imponderables. And yet, he actively worked as traitor in exchange for one day trying it all out.

He passed through security with his tongue pressed up against the roof of his mouth to make sure the USB drive stayed in place. Chin-wah Lee was searched, scanned and x-rayed. His mouth was not a cavity they ever probed. Sometimes there were others. Less humiliating for him than a woman who had to clear through.

"Never rush," Gyuen told him. So he never did. "Never look nervous." He always smiled.

"Never look suspicious." Chin-wah Lee was friendly and cooperative. "Insert the small thumb drive casually into your computer, and load it into the submarine's command root drive. It will do the rest itself: Finding a nesting place, wiping its own footprints, and erasing history of your upload. Then just as casually, remove it, put it back in your mouth, and chew. Not the best flavor in the world. Not the worst either."

Lee waited more than three hours to plant the latest malware. He used his body to obscure the high camera that covered the room. He opened a five-inch binder and leaned it against the key board to block a mid-level camera. All quite normal. With a move he'd practiced until it was smooth and indiscernible, he dislodged the drive from his hard palate, removed the adhesive strip, and inserted the USB memory stick into his computer port. Next he used his cursor to open the proper drive and hit enter. He counted to thirty. He was told it would take twenty seconds, but many of the regime's computers were slow. So thirty it was again today. Then with equally fluid moves, he exported the drive, held his hand up to his mouth and coughed.

He took the rest of the routine slowly. First squirming in his seat and coming square to the computer screen again. He leafed through his notebook for another few minutes before closing it.

"Never rush," Gyuen always reminded him.

He never did. But he prayed this would be over soon.

CHAPTER 36

WASHINGTON, D.C.
THE NEXT MORNING

The walk gave Scott and Katie lots of opportunities. Opportunities to hold hands. Opportunities to kiss at stop lights. Opportunities to read each other's worries.

They'd been able to read each other ever since they'd met in Boston. The only trouble? Time. They never seemed to have enough. So they used walking to catch up on things they didn't get to otherwise. Even in today's summer drizzle.

The concern Roarke saw today was the same concern he'd seen on her in Boston. Research was getting to her.

"Wanna tell me about it?" he asked at the fourth intersection.

"Same old, same old," Katie replied.

"But it's wearing you down. Or is he wearing you down?"

Of course, the *he* was Chief Justice Leopold Browning.

"He, it," she confessed. "The work. It's all the secession stuff. There's a movement in almost every state. And it could bog us down. Vermont and New Hampshire come at it one way. The Northwest another. They're all going hit circuit courts with different arguments. But the one that has me stymied is California. Calexit."

She explained the general *why*; the ballot measure.

"Come on, the court will intervene. They'll strike it down," Roarke said declaratively. When Katie didn't react immediately he added, "Right?"

"It's not that. It's all the background. You don't really know?"

"Know?" he asked looking trouble.

They paused at the intersection of New Hampshire and Pennsylvania Avenues.

"Let's get some coffee," Katie replied.

PYONGYANG, NORTH KOREA
THE SAME TIME

The Supreme Leader added another flag pin to a map on his wall. The red, white, and blue flag. Not America's. The Democratic People's Republic of Korea flag. He now had sixteen locations marked across the United States. There were still gaps, but they were beginning to take the shape he intended. Six of the flags represented locations that hadn't even been reported yet on American news. This frustrated him. He wanted to leak it. Maybe an anonymous tip to a foreign newspaper.

He'd have to give that more thought. There had to be a way. Success depended on creating chaos and fear. It was building, but he was an impatient man. He wished he could contact his old friend.

WASHINGTON, D.C.

Katie spoke just above a whisper in the Starbucks on K Street.

"Russia."

"What about Russia?" Roarke asked.

"Calexit has Russian roots. One of the principal sponsors lives a good deal of time in Russia and there have been numerous reports that some funding comes from Moscow. It takes fucking with America to a whole new visible level. Break California out of the U.S., and one sixth of the world's economy leaves the U.S. A good portion of that goes to defenses."

"But you said it wouldn't really be possible."

"I know that, but even the debate further splinters an already polarized nation."

Roarke hadn't taken a sip of his coffee. He fixed a stare beyond Katie, beyond Starbucks, and beyond Washington.

"Scott," Katie said pulling him back to the conversation. "I know that look."

"What look?"

"That look. Something far off. Out of sight. Something you're trying to see, but it's not quite visible."

"You know me that well?"

"God, I know you better than you know you. So what is it?"

Roarke looked around the restaurant. People were milling about, but nobody was close enough to overhear them.

"Let me ask you," he said softly.

"Go."

"Say you wanted to jump start secessionists across the country, would threatening elected officials help destroy faith in the system. Would killing them create more instability? Especially if Washington couldn't really do much to prevent it?"

"Well, yes," she replied.

He stood abruptly. "Let's go."

Roarke worked through the idea as they walked. Katie listened. That's all Roarke needed for now. They separated at the White House. Katie went onto the Supreme Court. Roarke brought his idea to the president. Katie had a notion of her own, which she took to the chief justice.

THE OVAL OFFICE

Roarke had to wait forty-five minutes before Bernsie could get him in to see the president. He took the time to put some meat on the bone; some convincing evidence for Taylor to consider.

"Got a wild ass notion, boss," Roarke began to explain.

The president let Roarke run through his thinking without comment. When he finished, Taylor went to the phone.

"Bernsie, I know everyone's beginning to feel like yo-yos, but I need you and directors Evans and Mulligan back in. Holt Yates, too. Our boy Roarke has a theory worth hearing."

Roarke smiled.

• • •

The follow-up meeting started promptly. The president had Roarke tee up his hypothetical and supporting arguments.

"That's pretty far out," Mulligan said after Roarke ran through his argument.

"So was a guy named Teddy Lodge, a talk radio announcer named Elliot Strong, and the people poisoning our water supplies until we understood what we were up against." The president was referring to the two recent crises that had threatened his administration and the entire country.

Jack Evans sighed. "Right."

"Let's start with it's *impossible* and try to get the *possible*," National Security Advisor Yates stated. "Agent Roarke, you propose that Russia is behind this. With money to California and perhaps other states. And an assassin working the back roads to light a spark. Just one question for you."

"Yes, sir."

"Why Russia?"

The room went silent. Roarke realized that *because* wasn't going to be good enough. And the fact of the matter, he had nothing better. So he tried past history.

"The Lodge plot. Meddling with elections. Malware."

"And hence the problem," Yates said. "A theory in search of evidence."

CIA director Evans wasn't willing to dismiss it so easily.

"We can quietly float the idea in Moscow, let it get picked up, listen for denials, and gauge the words that are used," Jack Evans suggested. "It might produce something credible. I can talk to our British, French, and German friends."

Bernsie jumped in. "Hell, look at what Brexit's doing to the EU. If Roarke is right, this could be Moscow's biggest play."

The president addressed his FBI director.

"Bob, anything?"

"Nope."

The agency chief was clearly dismissing the idea.

"Okay, then," the president said as he turned to Roarke. "Scott, have any Russia operatives shown up in your search for the assassin?"

"No sir. We're still narrowing the list."

Roarke thought that Vinnie D'Angelo might have some first-hand intelligence, too. He'd circle back to his CIA friend after the meeting and head to the FBI labs at Quantico.

"Well, gentlemen, I wanted you to hear Agent Roarke, whether or not you buy in. So far we have no proof, but what's the old phrase? The absence of evidence is not evidence of absence. Roarke's got a theory to try to prove. And unless anyone's got anything better, we go with this."

Everyone nodded acceptance except director Mulligan who had already cast his vote.

"For now, keep an open mind. I'm going back on TV later today, and I'll make the suggestion that we're expanding our investigation beyond our borders. It might also give me a little political cover with my old friend Duke Patrick. The man doesn't know when to stop. And that's all off the record!"

The session broke up. At the door Taylor held Roarke's arm.

"Scott, find me the bastard."

Roarke nodded realizing it wasn't an idle comment. It was a presidential order.

CHAPTER 37

THE NEXT DAY

No one knew where it started. Grants, New Mexico, with a letter left with the mayor. A tweet to a Portland, Maine, state representative. A note left on the door of a Santa Rosa, California, judge. A message written in chalk on the sidewalk in front of a state assemblywoman's home in Catskill, New York. A phone message recorded on a school committee member's phone in Trenton, New Jersey. These five and twenty-two more. All threats. All serious enough for local police to kick upstairs to state police and the FBI.

Most law enforcement officials considered them little more than copycat threats. Nuisances. After all, so far, the assassin had struck without warning. But that didn't mean the warnings could be ignored.

The New York assemblywoman and the Trenton school official immediately resigned. "Family concerns," they claimed.

Reporters in other regions asked threatened officials if they had thoughts of resigning. The responses ranged from "No comment" to "Hell yes!"

It was all bubbling up fast and not surprisingly the Speaker of the House believed it meant more political capital was falling his way.

THE OVAL OFFICE

"Mr. President, I figure you've been half expecting my call."

"If it's ground we've already covered, Duke, I have nothing more," the president said dismissively.

"It is and right to the point, I'm calling for a Congressional investigation into the assassinations and the escalating crisis. An investigation into your inaction. I'm giving it to the House Judiciary Committee. If you remember your history, they assumed jurisdiction from the old House Committee on Un-American Activities. Seems *awfully* appropriate."

Morgan Taylor ignored the comment and the slight.

"We're drawing up a list now. We're going to call Mulligan and Evans, and quite likely many more. Subpoenas if necessary. Aside from your press conference, we have no idea if you've got a handle on this crisis and—"

"Are you through, Mr. Speaker?"

"I'm actually just beginning."

"Maybe so, but I've warned you. Don't swim in waters you can't stand in. This thing is big and any public display for the sake of the camera and your career runs the risk of tipping whatever individual or…" The president stopped short of saying *nation*. "…individuals are behind this."

Morgan Taylor had ample practice dealing with the egotistical Speaker with visions of grandeur; the grandest, occupying the White House. But every phone call or meeting tested his patience.

"To be clear, are you suggesting the administration will refuse to cooperate with a House investigation?" Duke Patrick asked.

Taylor paused to measure his response. He reasoned Patrick's staffers were listening in, just as Bernie Bernstein was on the White House end.

"So there will be no misinterpretation for you or anyone on the line," Taylor calmly stated, "we are currently conducting a multi-level national and international investigation, working with our Five Eyes partners and beyond. For the sake of national security, we must keep Intel close to the vest. I will brief you and other congressional leaders when the time is appropriate. I will also talk to each and every elected official across the country who has been threatened. Moreover, the White House is working with Director Mulligan on investigating the threats."

"Mr. President, if you're asking me not to proceed…" It was a cold, hard statement, not a question.

Taylor lowered his voice. "I'm *asking* for the Speaker's understanding for all the reasons we don't need to get into." That was code Taylor counted on Duke Patrick understanding. The president had political ammunition that he could have used against Patrick before. It was a not-so veiled threat now.

Patrick gave an audible sigh. A tactical error to make. Realizing it, he backtracked.

"Then give me something, Mr. President. The American people deserve the right to know what you're doing."

"Tell your leadership that the White House considers threats to government officials at any level a most serious crime. Class C and D felonies that carry penalties up to ten years under 18 U.S.C. §875 and §876 among other statutes. When it comes to judges, the FBI will come at it numerous ways, but not with open discussion. If I need to write an Executive Order to create a higher level of protection, I will. Without hesitation. Including for all members of Congress. But my main focus is to find the bastard who's behind the actual murders."

Duke Patrick didn't immediately respond.

"I believe we've come to the end of this discussion," Taylor finally said.

The Speaker cleared his voice. He was still somewhat thrown by Taylor's veiled comment earlier and vowed to follow up with the vice president.

"For now, Mr. President."

"And I have your assurance that you'll postpone any House inquiry?"

"For now, Mr. President."

"Then, have a good afternoon, and my best wishes to everyone listening at your office."

"Same to you, Mr. President."

They hung up simultaneously.

"Well that was pleasant," Bernsie said sarcastically.

"A shot across the bow, Bernsie. The clock is ticking, and he's feeling pressure, too. In the meantime, I want full coordination between the Secret Service and the Capitol Police. Visible and immediate. Leak it. Let it get reported. That will help assuage Patrick, if only temporarily, but it can also work as a deterrent."

Now he was thinking about how vulnerable Roarke had proven the Supreme Court to be.

"I'll get right on it."

"And get me the phone numbers of all the officials threatened. I pulled that promise out of my ass."

CHAPTER 38

It was 3:18:30 p.m. in Pyongyang, and 1:18 a.m. in Pine Bluff, Arkansas. Not too late on a Friday for Congressman Desmond Willoughby to order one last drink at the Hampton Inn and Suites. A very last drink. He'd given a speech earlier, met with constituents, and stopped at the restaurant for a glass of merlot to take to his nonsmoking room.

On his way to the elevator, he bumped into a woman. He almost spilled his glass, but fortunately, she helped steady his drink.

"Thanks," the four-term congressman, chairman of the House Appropriations Committee, said.

The woman smiled, then continued down the hall.

Willoughby took a sip while going up to his fifth-floor room. Inside, he had another. Feeling tired, he finished the wine, turned on CNN, and went to the bathroom where he fell, cracking his head on the sink. He didn't die from the fall, but the next morning, that's what local investigators first thought. An accident. That assumption changed when a smart doctor who had been reading the news ordered an autopsy.

CHAPTER 39

WASHINGTON, D.C.
MEET THE PRESS
TWO DAYS LATER

It began like fireworks in the second segment. The *Meet the Press* host threw out the first question to the panel. He didn't need a follow-up for six minutes.

"Stan Deutsch, you first. Are we getting a taste of our own medicine?"

The fifty-year-old bearded PBS White House political reporter immediately redefined the host's question. "If you're asking if someone, or some country, has an active covert influence campaign going, I'd say *possibly*. If you're asking if we deserve it based on history, then that's another thing. We're not without guilt when it comes to active measures."

"I would avoid using the word guilt," interrupted former under Secretary of State Nelson Ridgewood. He glared at Deutsch over his half-reading glasses. "Yes, the United States has disrupted elections around the world, most in the post-World War II years, but it was principally to contain communism and foster democratic victories."

Now octogenarian presidential historian, biographer, and professor emeritus Colonel Wm. Harrison entered the fray. "America's fingerprints are all over some very dirty dealings. Millions in payoffs to foreign right wing parties when necessary. And when it was better to do the same to extreme leftist regimes, we did that too. Bad business, right down to the elimination of leaders."

"It's a false equivalency," argued Ridgewood. "You can't link the murder of multiple elected officials across the U.S. to covert influence campaigns in backwater nations. I cover that argument thoroughly in my second book. I think it's still in print."

Some on the panel laughed. Not Harrison.

"As do I, Mr. Secretary, with entirely different conclusions. Italy, Iran, and Chile were not backwater nations. Not then, not now. We settled things to our liking by installing autocrats or worse. After World

War II we boosted Italy's centrist Christ Democrats with loads of CIA cash and forged documents that linked communist leaders to sex scandals. In 1973, we toppled, rather violently, Chilean President Salvador Allende. We ousted Iranian Prime Minister Mohammed Mossadegh in fifty-three, replacing him with an authoritarian monarchy favorable to Eisenhower. We aided in unseating Guatemala's left wing president, Jacobo Arbenz, who fought an American corporation, the United Fruit Company. You want more for your next book? I have more," Harrison declared.

"Allende was a socialist," the former White House official noted.

"Without a doubt, yes, a socialist. And what did we do? Through a military coup we installed a man arguably more ruthless, General Augusto Pinochet. And what about Congo's Patrice Lumumba assassination in 1961?"

"The Russians also have a history of over-running nations. With tanks and troops," offered NPR's Washington correspondent Millie Kocan. "From the deepest red of the Red era to Moscow's meddling with the presidential elections."

"Agreed," Deutsch added, reentering the debate. "Together, the two superpowers, the U.S. and Russia, have intervened in up to one hundred seventeen elections around the globe from 1946 to 2000. So if we're looking for guilty parties, we'll find them on both sides. Both countries have had their fingers on the scales in the global balance of power."

"And bringing the question on the table back to the forefront," Kocan continued, "is the United States the target of a covert influence campaign to disrupt the American political system? There is no evidence that it's foreign, but it certainly is having an effect. And though the mainstream press hasn't covered it enough, the rise of grassroots secessionist movements plays into the dissolution of faith."

"They're going nowhere," Deutsch argued.

"Wrong. They'll take victories where they come. Maybe mostly regionally, but eventually someone will find basis to take it well past state houses and into the courts."

"Where they'll lose," the PBS reporter maintained.

"While poisoning an already poisoned system," Kogan replied. "We're in for a very bitter time."

"Let's get a definition of terms," the host proposed. "Covert influence campaign. Colonel Harrison?"

"It comes from the Department of Defense Dictionary of Military and Associated Terms, a publication that defines it as an operation that is so planned and then executed it conceals the identity of the perpetrator or nation sponsors. It permits plausible deniability. It's not to be confused with a clandestine operation where the mission itself is designed to remain hidden. A covert influence campaign is all about visible impact."

"And what kind of tactics are used?"

"Sabotage of a system from disruption of everyday processes to, well, assassination. The elimination by death of those within the system."

"And you're suggesting a rogue operator?"

"Rogue, well-funded, and dangerous."

"Russia?" the host asked directly.

While the panelists traded their speculation, the show producer gave the host a news update through his earpiece. The *Meet the Press* anchor interrupted the discussion with the report.

"Excuse me," he said lowering his voice. "It's just now being reported that Arkansas Republican Congressman Desmond Willoughby died last night in a hotel room less than an hour south of Little Rock. An autopsy has been ordered."

The host shook his head. No one spoke for ten seconds, then everyone jumped in at once.

CHAPTER 40

THAT NIGHT

"This is a dangerous conversation," Vice President Jonas Jackson Johnson told Duke Patrick during their second meeting.

"And we live in extremely dangerous times," the Speaker of the House replied. "Times that need strong leadership. You have to admit, the country's a wreck. Taylor's in, Taylor's out. Taylor's in. And here you are. Number Two in the nation. But the real rub, general, is that you're the born leader, not Taylor. You're an independent. You have allegiance to the nation over any party. Isn't that true?"

J3 wasn't sure where this would end up. "Yes, but what are you getting at Duke?"

"Just that you're qualified to be Commander in Chief. A position you're more than ready to assume. More than anyone since Eisenhower. All you need to do is bring the cabinet with you."

"And I suppose that would put you in line for vice president?"

"I'd be honored to serve with you," the Speaker said as humbly as possible.

"To be completely transparent, you're suggesting, actually you're advocating that we sidestep the electoral process."

"Circumstances dictate, General Johnson. I'm concerned about all public officers. School committeemen become mayors. Mayors become legislators. Legislators become governors. Governors become members of congress and president. But only if they live. We've been losing America's finest. America's future.

"We can take control of the future. That's my point. Something to think about, Mr. Vice President. The future of the United States."

"You make a convincing argument, Mr. Speaker. How about another drink?"

• • •

Morgan Taylor was awakened at 0500 by his chief of staff.

"Mr. President, sir."

"Jesus, just a moment," the president said sliding out of bed and trying not to disturb his wife of thirty years.

He tiptoed away, threw on his white cotton bathrobe sporting the presidential seal, and joined Bernstein in the hallway.

"What now?"

"Des Willoughby. The autopsy came through. Confirmed ricin poisoning."

"Oh God!" Morgan Taylor proclaimed. "I suppose more threats, too?"

"More than simply threats now. Overnight a truck plowed into a

Louisiana mayor's home. A poorly constructed fertilizer bomb was left at the Grand Junction city hall. Packages with white powder delivered to an assessor in Middletown, Rhode Island."

"The guy we're searching for can't be in more than one place at one time," the president said.

"But it could be more than one killer," Bernsie proposed.

Taylor disagreed. "Copycats adding fuel to the fire. Crazies."

"Including Willoughby?"

"No. That's the work of the pro."

Taylor turned to the bathroom with a last comment. "Tell Poppiti I'll join him at the press briefing again this morning."

PYONGYANG, NORTH KOREA

The Supreme Leader beamed as a general briefed him on the news coming out of America. His plan was progressing magnificently. From his point of view, he was effectively sowing the seeds of America's destruction from within—well beyond what he really might ever accomplish with his limited nuclear arsenal. He laughed aloud, recalling that, in large part, he had his Swiss high school history teacher to thank. But, of course, he never would. He only looked forward to celebrating his own victories.

THE WHITE HOUSE PRESS ROOM

"Thank you, Joe," the president said to press secretary Joe Poppiti as he eased up to the microphone.

Morgan Taylor paused and looked around. Local, national, and international reporters sat up. No one appeared relaxed. The still cameras clicked; photographers hoping to have the front-page photograph. It was more likely to come later in his address. They anticipated a strongly worded one.

The president gripped both sides of the podium with the presidential seal emblazoned in full view.

"Ladies and gentlemen," he began without the benefit of notes or teleprompter, "there can be no remaining doubt that America is under attack by a yet undetermined enemy who is systematically and methodically targeting American political figures.

"Never has such an attack been waged on the United States. Never have those who have sworn to uphold the laws of our great nation been under such personal attack. It is anything but random. Accordingly, America's law enforcement and intelligence agencies are focused on discovering the perpetrators and the purpose.

"Although, we have not identified who you are or where you live. Mark my words—that will change."

Morgan Taylor fixed a gaze straight into the center pool camera lens. The camera operator, transfixed, slowly zoomed in.

"To the individuals," he intentionally didn't say governments, "conspiring against the United States of America, I know you're watching. You may even be laughing as we react. But what appears to you to be inactivity from us, is far from it. We have the means to identify you. And as God and the American people are my witness, we will find you and punish you."

At this moment, the photographers had what they thought were their front-page pictures. The print and broadcast reporters were ready to start writing and appearing on TV. But Morgan Taylor was not finished.

"Now to the killer who has proven himself skilled and brutal. I say killer because we believe there is only one doing the work. You've taken advantage of our open and free society. It will not close because of you. Your training will not protect you from our ability to track you down. And when we do, you will be held accountable, with extreme prejudice for what you have done to this great nation of ours. You are a terrorist, and you are in our sights."

Taylor paused before adding another warning.

"And for those who are imitating, threatening, scaring, and perpetrating copycat attacks, we will treat you as the domestic terrorists you are. Read up on the federal penalty. You're not going to like it. We will track you, as well, and bring you to justice. For anyone contemplating doing harm to an elected or appointed official, I put you on notice. Don't even think of it."

There were audible gasps from the press corp. Out of character, surprised, and real.

"As for teeth, I have just signed an Executive Order which authorizes the call-up of National Guard units across the country to protect every city hall, state house, and county seat. Our mayors, representatives, governors, and other elected and appointed officials, from selectmen to senators, school committee members to justices will be safeguarded twenty-four hours a day, seven days a week until this crisis is over.

"And we will get through this."

The president gestured with his right hand.

"I'll take your questions now?"

Simultaneously reporters drowned out one another.

"Mr. President, what country—?"

"How many troops—?"

"Do you suspect—?"

"Does the CIA—?"

"Has anyone been—?"

He pointed to veteran CBS White House reporter Phil Amato.

"Phil."

"Thank you, Mr. President. Is it true that the Cabinet is considering invoking the Twenty-Fifth Amendment to remove you from office for inaction?"

The president quizzically raised an eyebrow and figured the source had to be Duke Patrick, though he didn't say.

"Interesting," Taylor commented. "I wouldn't call what I've just announced as *inaction*."

"And as follow up," Amato continued, "if it is true, will you be making any changes to your cabinet?"

The president pursed his lips and bore down on Amato, for now, the conduit to the Speaker of the House. In the most measured tone he began. "Phil, I am not aware of any internal coup. Accordingly, I am not responding to a threat to my presidency, but a threat to the United States of America as a whole. I have ordered the National Guard to their posts to protect American citizens, not to protect me. There's no surprise meaning behind my executive actions. I will not be making any changes to my cabinet. Your source is wrong."

MINUTES LATER
WHITE HOUSE HALLWAYS

"All right. We do this systematically," the president decided as he walked with Vice President Jonas Jackson Johnson, Attorney General Eve Goldman, and Bernie Bernstein.

"Bernsie, you poll the cabinet."

"Got it."

"I'm sure there's nothing to this, but confirm what I can only assume is Patrick's leak to the press."

"Eve, take me through the decision making process to invoke this clause of the Twenty-Fifth.

"Consider it an alternative route to impeachment," the attorney general explained. "Solving a quote, unquote, 'Presidency Problem.' It starts with the vice president and a majority of the Cabinet notifying Congress that the president, in this case you…"

"No kidding," Taylor said.

"…is unable, or possibly, unwilling to perform the duties of the office" she said.

"Well, that's not the case. What happens next?"

"The president can tell Congress that he is capable, and unless the vice president and the majority of the Cabinet again notify Congress, it's settled, that is unless…"

"I hate that rejoinder," Taylor remarked.

"Yup," Eve Goldman said. "It's usually connected to something dire. In this case, if vice president and the majority of the Cabinet does notify Congress of its decision, the House and Senate must convene and can, by a vote of two-thirds in the affirmative, permanently remove the president, in this case…"

"Right I got it."

Now the president addressed the one man who could speak to the issue.

"J3? Is there something you need to tell me?"

"Mr. President?"

It wasn't quite the response Taylor required. He cocked his head to the side.

"General!"

"Yes sir," J3 replied stiffly.

"Mr. Vice President, have you spoken with any cabinet members about activating the terms of the Twenty-Fifth Amendment, or for the sake of this discussion, has anyone spoken to you?"

The general stood at attention, but didn't reply.

"Eve. Bernsie. Will you give the vice president and me a few minutes," Morgan Taylor quietly declared.

With shocked expressions they slowly walked away. Bernie Bernstein looked back at the president.

"Sir…"

"I'll call you when we're through. The general and I need to talk."

CHAPTER 41

WASHINGTON, D.C.
WASHINGTON MALL
THE SAME TIME

Roarke wondered how many spies walked along the Washington Mall having conversations like he was having with Vinnie D'Angelo. *Hundreds? Thousands? Foreign agents talking to Americans counterparts or recruits, and vice versa? Russian "diplomats" chatting up with members of Congress? Chinese, North Korean, even German, French, and British agents?* Anyone who's worked in the spy trade in the nation's capital has had clandestine and open meetings in the Mall.

Roarke kept the thought to himself, but he was certain D'Angelo had long considered the same thing.

They weren't talking secrets, but they still talked quietly past surveillance cameras. Today's spy craft was to stroll and laugh. But the topic was no laughing matter.

"You really think you'll get anything?" Roarke asked.

"Gotta try," the CIA agent said.

"Long way to go on nothing."

"Well, we have nothing."

"A whole helluva lot of nothing," Roarke sighed. "What do you think about Wurlin?"

"Great minds think alike. Worth a chat about the names that have surfaced, and those that haven't. Planning on seeing him second." D'Angelo slapped Roarke on the back. "Any other ideas?"

"Yeah, let's start our own business and say so long to this shit."

"Counting the days," D'Angelo laughed.

Before parting ways at the Lincoln Memorial, D'Angelo told him to stick by the phone.

"Always, buddy. Always."

CHAPTER 42

Roarke went old school. He requisitioned maps of the U.S. and attached small circular red dot stickers wherever verifiable assassinations had occurred. So far, he had six maps up on the wall. Each with lines drawn with a thick black marker between the dots, but forming different designs. He hoped he'd see a pattern, but he couldn't will any such thing to appear.

One version had four parallel lines across the country. The top line extended from Great Barrington, MA, to Cedar Rapids, SD, to Boise, ID. A middle line from Rohnert Park, CA, north of San Francisco, through Grand Junction, CO, onto Jefferson City, MO, and eventually across to the country to the mid-Atlantic. There were two other parallel lines all the way from Bakersfield, CA on the West Coast to Goldsboro, NC on the East Coast, and another from Anaheim, CA to Charleston, SC.

That was one map.

Another had fairly straight long and short vertical lines between crime scenes. Lines through California, more down and across Idaho to Utah and onto Arizona, and five more relatively parallel heading east. The one that concerned him the most was the line that stretched from Great Barrington, MA, through Trenton, NJ, to Charleston, SC, directly through the nation's capitol. But then so did one of the cross country horizontal lines. Either way, Washington stuck out. So far there hadn't been any assassination in D.C. But *so far* didn't make him feel good at all.

Roarke walked from map to map. The murders themselves provided no hint. The assassin had freely jumped around the country. Money was no concern. Identities either. The FBI had not found any name that showed up in more than a few cities, and even those were every day, unassuming, men and women with no military history, domestic or foreign.

Roarke wondered if they were dealing with a sleeper spy, with no known identity, or someone who had been embedded in the very fabric of American life, only to be awakened to fulfill the assignment. The investigation into Teddy Lodge had proven that was possible. But Roarke felt that this was different.

Back to the maps.

He examined another he'd created with a huge outer circle encompassing the extremes and internal circles defining smaller quadrants. This one looked positively silly. He tore it down.

In three other versions, Roarke tried to spell letters by connecting dots that looked like they might represent an abbreviation. They also proved useless.

No matter how he considered them, confirmed political deaths in Winslow and Scottsdale, AZ bore no relation to those in Albuquerque and Sorocco, NM, Trenton, NJ, Lawton, OK, or any of the other locations, except for the fact that the dead were dead.

"Come on!" he yelled at his work. "Nothing is this random!"

• • •

FBI computers were working on the problem a different way. Bessolo had instructed his team to identify any common denominators from names of the deceased, political affiliations, age, and religion to population factors, gerrymandering demographics, and cult affiliations. But their computers were just as stymied as Scott Roarke using primitive means.

. . .

Roarke put up more maps. Fifteen more, each with alternate ways to connect the dots. Soon, he was engulfed in his own Rand McNally world.

THE SAME TIME

The Frenchman had left Gainesville, Florida, on a Greyhound bus. His latest work would make news while he traveled to Tallahassee. It was a simple hit. A single round through a first-floor window in the Alachua County Administration Building. The County Manager, a sixty-seven-year-old former public defender, had died face down on his desk, not even disturbing the framed photographs of his wife, children, and grandchildren.

According to the assassin's instructions, all committed to memory, only one target remained. He'd work his way north, for a time taking the bus, then a rental car, one local commuter flight, and finally a train, all under different identities.

Now he took much more care. The news reinforced his success, but it also made his work all the more visible. He was no longer working in the dark. People were looking for him. He half-expected someone might be connecting the dots.

PART THREE

CHAPTER 43

NORTH KOREA

Like the day before, and the day before that, and all the days through the past eleven months, Chin-wah Lee tried to appear casual as he approached the submarine base's security system.

The security officer checked the pings the system set off against Lee's on-file profile.

Metal pin in his wrist and teeth fillings.

"Go ahead," he said. Today's guard had no reason to question such a boring thing. He was thinking about the subject, not the metal.

Lee obeyed with hardly a smile. From top to bottom he was correctly uniformed with his haircut to government specifications.As a member of the People's Army, serving in the Navy, he seemed obedient and loyal. And insignificant. These were the traits Lee projected. The traits that protected him.

Another day of living. Another day closer to freedom. Maybe.

Chin-wah Lee took his seat at his station and checked his duty report. The *Yu Gwan-sun*, an eighteen-hundred ton diesel powered submarine had docked four hours prior. It was one of the latest vessels to join the fleet, named for a leader in the March 1 Movement of 1919, which had been a protest against Japan's colonial rule of Korea. Gwan-sun was only seventeen-years-old when she was arrested, imprisoned, and tortured. She died of injuries in an underground Japanese prison cell before her eighteenth birthday.

Chin-wah Lee knew the celebrated story and even felt a certain nationalistic pride. Something he wished he felt more often. But he had irreversibly set his own course. And today he would continue that path. Today was the day for *Yu Gwan-sun* computer upgrades.

Lee had the latest navy programs to install. And one additional plug-in. But today was also a day when superiors supervised him more closely.

Lee waited. He cracked his knuckles and adjusted his seat, which was cheap and never comfortable. *Now?* He checked over his shoulder. *No. Not yet.* He waited longer. He quietly hummed the emotional patriotic song, "Fly High Our Party Flag." He worked on his computer. He waited. Fifteen minutes later his supervisor got bored watching. Lee gave it five more minutes before leaning forward. Then he covered his mouth and coughed. The security supervisor turned back to him. Fortunately, he never saw anything suspicious because he wasn't actually trained to know what to look for.

So like other days, Chin-wah Lee slid the thin USB drive forward across the roof of his mouth, then palmed it. Next, he ignored it, covering schedule work for fifteen minutes, typing and even taking a two-minute stretch break, counting on the disinterested eyes to be all the more disinterested.

At minute eighteen he adjusted his chair position, used his body to block anyone's view, and inserted the American-made thumb drive, translated into Korean code, into the port. He typed in root directions, hit ENTER, and counted slowly, with extra seconds at the end.

At a minute thirty plus six seconds, he exported the drive and ate it.

Disinterested was still disinterested and chatting with another security officer. Now, Chin-wah Lee took his second deep breath of the day.

Lee lacked a full understanding of what he uploaded. Today or any day. He didn't dare do anything more than export it to the submarine's computers. Then again, he didn't know much about the official government programs either: How they gave *Yu Gwan-sun* the ability to track other submarines. American submarines. How they gave the Democratic People's Republic of Korea's submarine captain command and control of his vessel. How he could fire and guide his missiles with truer purpose because Lee pressed ENTER with the legitimate upgrades.

Chin-wah Lee hoped he was doing the right thing. That his altered sense of patriotism might somehow prevent war. That the personal risks he took would spare his homeland and the new nation he sought to live in as a free man.

Lee's handler assured him it would. "You could very well be responsible for saving millions of lives," Jee Gyuen said early into the assignment.

There were many ways to interpret what Gyuen said. Yes, he might save millions, but would he, as a traitor, still somehow cause the death of hundreds, if not thousands of his countrymen?

Gyuen never answered that question.

CHAPTER 44

RUSSIA
THREE DAYS LATER

Vincent D'Angelo was known to Russian FSB agents. But that didn't mean he couldn't get in and out of Russia. He'd done it dozens of times over the past decade. Sometimes disguised on commercial flights, twice on a fishing boat, four times on a train.

This trip was off the grid and off the books to everyone at the agency except the director. D'Angelo went in unarmed and only moderately disguised. He was on his own, led by instinct and the hope that he'd walk away smarter than when he arrived.

The only other person who knew where he was going was Scott Roarke, who neither tried to talk him out of it nor asked who he would meet. But it was clear why D'Angelo was taking it upon his own to go. *Someone* in Russian intelligence might know what *he* didn't. It was time to call in a favor, or have one owed.

Of course, Russia was open to most travelers with a valid visa and passport. Certain names would trigger questions. Certain questions would lead to deportation or arrest. And certain names would mean FSB officials weren't far behind.

D'Angelo didn't have one of those names when he came into the Port of Sevastopol on a Greek tanker. He'd boarded in Roytta, Finland, with falsified German papers that got him through. German was one of his languages. Once through customs, he casually strolled across to a wharf bar with a backpack slung over his shoulder. No one appeared to be following him. After two vodkas and an hour's wait, he took a taxi to the modest Ekonom Uyut Motel on Gidrograficheskaya Street. There he ripped up his German identification, burned it, and removed papers of an Italian businessman sealed in the cover of a novel.

The next day, he left Sevastopol as quietly as he had arrived, now on the twenty-nine-hour, eighteen-minute train to Moscow. Long and exhausting, but safer.

Moscow never worried him. Although he knew the city's streets by heart, he acted like a businessman with some free time on his hands. He asked for restaurant recommendations, directions, and museums hours. He also visited an art dealer he could have done business with had he really been in the business. He wined and dined as if on a limited budget. He explored stores and examined the goods that were available from luxury items at GUM on Okhotny Ryad near Red Square to smaller gifts in boutiques along Tverskaya Street. He talked to a few sales people, and not pretending to be Russian, he struggled with the language through an Italian accent.

D'Angelo avoided the nightclubs and Russian women. Both traps. He always said that the danger of getting photographed and blackmailed by Russians was nothing compared to what his wife would do.

On his third day in Moscow, he got to work; work that took him to an antiquarian bookstore on Trumpet Street. Secondhand Bookseller was one of the oldest specialized bookshops in Moscow. Its shelves were filled with historical books from around the globe, traditional Russian literature, encyclopedias, dictionaries, travel books, engravings, cards, as well as bronze and porcelain crafts.

D'Angelo arrived shortly after the shop opened. He wore wire rim glasses, dressed conservatively, and carried an umbrella for the expected rain.

He politely held the door for a round elderly Russian woman with books she wanted to sell. The proprietor, a sixty-ish-year-old and appropriately bookish-looking man, acknowledged him with a nod and pointed to a large vase where he should place his umbrella. D'Angelo gave a polite two finger salute and proceeded to browse.

Posted handwritten category labels in multiple languages identified what could be found in each aisle. D'Angelo had nowhere in particular to go, so he began with ancient history. Soon, two young men approached him. College students? Maybe not. He listened to their conversation and smiled as they walked by. They were on the hunt for Homer and in their skinny jeans they had no place to conceal a weapon.

D'Angelo rounded a corner and saw two old men in a corner talking. Again a question. *Friends? Maybe not.* After listening to their conversation in Russian about their wives, he reasoned that they probably had been meeting every Saturday for years, starting at the bookstore and ending up at a cafe.

So far, things appeared as they should, though that didn't make D'Angelo relax.

He continued to stroll the aisles, squeezing past patrons and working his way to the film section that included books about Sergei Eisenstein, director of *Battleship Potemkin, Alexander Nevsky, October*, among other post-revolutionary films. He knew them all as a film buff and a CIA operative. He picked out a 1982 English-language book, *Eisenstein at Work* by Jay Leyda and Zina Voynow and perused the photographs, sketches, and notes.

From behind, a man entered the aisle. He was also interested in film books. D'Angelo sensed his approach, leaned in to allow the man to pass while giving a cursory glance. The two men traded eye contact; a fleeting look that didn't say anything.

Mikhail Gladkov wore a dark brown suit, which tightly covered his forty-six-inch barrel chest. He had a crisp white shirt with no tie, a Breitling Chronomat, and brown lace-up shoes with a high polish. His thinning gray hair was carefully combed back. His cheeks were puffy, but not fat. Mikhail Gladkov looked like he had money. More importantly, he had authority. At fifty-two, he was still on the rise at the FSB.

Gladkov meandered for fifteen minutes as he loved to do. D'Angelo did the same, finding another book to purchase on Eisenstein.

Eventually they worked their way to a far corner of the bookstore, where, facing one another, each could also see if anyone came into view in either direction. For now, it was clear.

Ordinarily, such subterfuge wouldn't be necessary. But Mikhail Gladkov was a colonel in Russia's spy agency. His CIA file flagged him as a shrewd intelligence officer and a rare book collector. Surveillance had shown that this was his favorite bookstore which he frequented virtually every Saturday morning.

"Я уверен, что вы предпочитаете английский, мой друг," Gladkov said. "I'm certain you'd prefer English, my friend."

This was not their first clandestine meeting.

"Да," D'Angelo replied. "Yes, thank you."

D'Angelo had no doubts. Gladkov would report his contact with the American spy.

"And who are you today?" the FSB officer asked with a chuckle.

"Oh, an Italian exporter. Who knows who I'll be tomorrow?"

"You don't believe in the telephone? You could have avoided all the cloak and dagger trappings," the Russian added laughing more.

"Where's the fun in that," D'Angelo replied. "Your last visit to Washington was as an oil executive. We had you at Dulles. The driver was ours."

"Well, I shall let the bureau know we have to take better care with our travel plans. Care to share how you slipped in?"

"Rather not," D'Angelo said lightly.

"Perfectly understandable. So, this is no chance meeting. You haven't come strictly to buy." Gladkov examined D'Angelo's choices. "Ah yes, Eisenstein. Very good choices. I forgot you enjoyed his films. I'll have to update your file."

"And you're a Tarantino fan as I recall," the American quipped.

"Especially *Kill Bill.* The dialogue in Two was wonderful. Poetic. Why didn't your Academy Awards nominate David Carradine?"

"Who's to say why Hollywood does what it does?"

"I'd suggest you pay and we talk more about films over coffee, but I fear that's not your intent."

"No, it's not, Colonel."

"Ah, it is business. A trip specifically to see me. A creature of habit at my favorite book seller. Well, while I decide whether to arrest you—"

"Oh, you don't want to do that. You'd have to answer to my wife."

"Ha! How is Barbara?"

"She's fine, thank you. And Sofia?" D'Angelo responded with mutual respect.

"Happy the twins are out of the house. The boys are in Crimea. Just visiting, of course."

"How many years now?"

"Four. There's so much to see."

"Of course." D'Angelo knew exactly what the Gladkov brothers were doing in Crimea. The CIA had a file on them, too.

This was the nature of D'Angelo and Gladkov's relationship. Professional respect, light-hearted sparring, and the ability to sidebar effectively when necessary.

They continued in whispers, making sure they were not being observed.

"We're still talking circuitously, Vincent. What's on your mind? Obviously something important enough for you to avoid detection." He smiled, and then continued completely seriously, "Of course, I shall have to see if I can retrace your steps and correct any insufficiencies on our part."

"Oh, there are many cracks, Mikhail. But next time, I'll just call for one of *your* drivers. You owe me."

Gladkov laughed again. "Are you buying or selling today?"

"I suppose buying."

"Ah, information?"

"Yes."

"That requires some assurance it won't be used for the wrong reasons."

"It won't be," D'Angelo answered. "You're obviously aware of what's happening in America."

"By that, you mean your democracy falling apart?"

"I mean the attacks on elected officials. The assassinations, Mikhail. Innocent local officials, mothers and fathers, up to members of Congress. I haven't heard the news today. You might know. Anyone I'm missing?"

"As a matter of fact, a low-level County Manager, whatever that is, from somewhere in your state of Florida. I believe what you'd term an up and comer."

D'Angelo shook his head and then fixed a cold, hard stare on the Russian.

"Is this the Kremlin's work?"

"I half expected this meeting more than a week ago. No, it's not. This is much too blatant. Too unsavory."

"Congressman Teddy Lodge wasn't?"

"I have no idea what you're talking about," Gladkov dismissed the question with a wave of his hand.

"Of course you don't."

"But it looks like whatever the problem, you neatly cleaned it up. So who's to say? Your issues today are much different."

Vinnie D'Angelo stared right in the spy's eyes. "Not so much. Mikhail, tell me, has anyone you known gone rogue?"

CHAPTER 45

QUANTICO, VA
THE SAME TIME

"Backwards?" was Scott Roarke's question. He was confused by Touch Parsons's approach.

"Yes. We've been looking for a match going forward first. From a description that is a disguise. Well, we won't find him that way. I'm working on developing a picture of what a chameleon might resemble from more of a psych approach," the FBI facial recognition expert proposed.

"Now you've completely lost me."

"Let's create the blank face and look for him." Parsons rolled his chair over to his powerful computer. "Like so."

From clip art, he selected the outline of a body, black lines over the white screen. Nothing more.

"You more than anyone know what an assassin looks like. Start describing him."

A terrible thought struck Roarke. "Does it have to be a *him*?"

"No, but we'll narrow down by percentages. So, describe the guy."

"That I've never met and presumably never seen."

"Right. Go."

"Okay. Starting with height. Special Forces height. Average is five-nine. But they go taller. I'd say six-one with a runner's body. He's gotta be able to move," Roarke said.

"Good." Parsons shortened his silhouetted figure and thinned him out as Roarke watched. "Go on."

"He'll have to fit into middle American life without drawing attention. To infiltrate. So he won't be Middle Eastern, Indian, or even Black. But we knew that."

"Well, not completely. But we'll call him white, not even eastern European, Hispanic, or Asian."

That gave Touch eyes and noises to choose from.

"He's got to look average," Roarke continued. "His features indistinctive. He'd blend in; you wouldn't look at him twice."

Parsons continued to paint on his program like a canvas. Roarke thought of the features of the last assassin he'd dealt with. All average. An actor without a star's face; a killer who could be anyone.

"He'd usually wear street clothes. Not a suit. Too distinctive these days. Nothing flashy. Nothing related to fashion, particularly for his age."

"What's his age?" Parsons asked.

"A killer at his level. Not a newcomer. Go for thirty-five."

That didn't change much, but it was good for Roarke to hear what he was thinking.

"Most of all, wherever he'd go he'd be invisible. Nobody sees the invisible man hiding in plain sight."

"What kind of shoes?"

Roarke pictured Richard Cooper, his last nemesis.

"Most of the time, tie shoes, rubber soles. Sometimes sneakers. Never loafers or anything with leather bottoms. Always rubber soles and heels."

"Glasses?"

"Only for affectation. He's a sharp shooter. Twenty-twenty eyesight. Glasses would get in the way and contacts can lead a path back through prescriptions. The bureau could track that quickly. Besides, if he's any older, he might need reading glasses. Another reason he's midthirties."

"Positive on that age?" Parsons asked to be certain.

Roarke was. Assassins were either retired or dead by the time they were in their midforties. Or they'd lost their edge or squirreled away enough money to go off the grid.

"Yes, I'd peg him at about my age, with hair long enough to change color, slick back or comb to the side."

Parsons worked on the hair and put the character in a shirt and drab sports coat.

"No, no, no," Roarke said. "Make the jacket bigger. It's got to hide a gun. And his pants have to be looser. Nothing to impede his escapes." Roarke paused. "Wait. Take the jacket away for a moment."

An idea hit him.

Parsons saved his work, then eliminated the coat.

"Give him short sleeves and lighter cargo pants."

"Why?"

"Parkour."

"Park what?"

"It's French. Parkour derived from *parcours du combattant*. A training discipline developed in the 1980s that keys on swift quadrupedal movement. Intensive training, particularly in special forces. It gets practitioners from one point to another without assistive equipment. Did you see that great chase scene in *Casino Royale*? The Daniel Craig Bond film?"

"Yes."

"Like the guy he's chasing. He's vaulting, jumping and rolling, running and climbing all over the place. Fast and furious without the cars. That's Parkour.

"The Royal Army trains Parkour. U.S. Navy Seals, Russian Spetsnaz, and *Le Commandement des Opérations Spéciales*—France's Special Operations Command. So do private military services. Academi, Prosegur, GK Sierra, and Erinys International. It's a big part of their program."

Roarke stopped short. He stared at the representation of a man that was purely a creative invention. It wouldn't lead him anywhere. But the discussion gave him something concrete. It came to him in a word he'd heard before. *Phantom.* His quarry was a phantom.

CHAPTER 46

RUSSIA

"There is a ghost. A man who's is equally invisible in the light as he is in the dark."

As they walked, the FSB agent described an assassin he only knew through rumors.

"He enters and exits countries without a digital footprint. He never passes through customs twice the same way, the same place, or with the same identity. He is tall and short. Fat and skinny. Old and young. He speaks more languages than you, Vincent; so many so well he can look like a local in all but Asia. But I have no doubt he'd find a way to disguise himself even there.

"He is a sniper and swordsman. Adept with a knife and a revolver. He knows bombs and willingly yet strategically uses them. He has special affection for poisons and views from high balconies. He uses both with great success.

"He has blue eyes, brown, and green. His hair is brown, black, blond, and gray, when he's not bald. He has tattoos except when he doesn't. He wears Savile Row's best and clothes he finds off thrift shop racks. He's an engaging conversationalist and a silent killer."

The Russian major's description fit no one. It was probably the *no one* D'Angelo sought.

"I wouldn't recognize him," the FSB operative said. "Neither would you. But we both know his work."

"What did he do here," D'Angelo asked.

Gladkov laughed. "Absolutely nothing. Nobody can defeat our most excellent border security."

"Of course," D'Angelo replied. The CIA operative's presence was clear evidence that Russia's borders weren't so excellent. "But you haven't answered my question. Is he one of yours, Mikhail?"

The FSB major grabbed D'Angelo's arm, holding him back from crossing in front of a car.

"Thank you," the American said.

"A professional courtesy," the Russian replied. "But I owe you an answer. Simply put, I wish we had someone as good. The best we had was probably Bohdan Mykolayovych Stashynsky."

D'Angelo was completely familiar with the KGB assassin who took out two Ukranian nationalist leaders, Lev Rebvet and Stepan Bandera, in the late 1950s. But he figured there were others Gladkov wasn't about to mention.

"But you have a sense of who he could be."

The FSB major patted D'Angelo on the back. D'Angelo didn't confuse it for a sign of friendship. It was a signal to cross the street.

"Were you listening, Vincent? I started with the fact that he is a ghost. He leaves only his work; nothing else."

"Who trained him?"

"Could be any number of forces. I have my own ideas. South African, perhaps. The Israelis. Perhaps France."

"The U.S.?" D'Angelo appropriately asked.

"No."

"Why?"

"His tools and his manners. To be more precise, ballistics, types of weapons, types of murders. You Americans, and your friends the British, tend to be both simple and strategic. We have our favorite ways of killing, but we are also focused and highly political. We all have our ghosts, but we work differently. There are systems, reports, and endless bureaucracy. We live for promotions and ribbons. Honor and loyalty. Duty and national pride. He is a man without a country. No ribbons, no loyalty, no duty. He kills for cash with a single goal you and I will never see—a tropical island retirement. That tells me three things. He's still young enough to enthusiastically be in the field. He's well trained and likely disgruntled or disgraced. That put him in the international market. And he's too smart to be approached through normal means."

D'Angelo and Roarke had already come to the same conclusion on the first two points. It was Major Gladkov's third that caught hold. The FSB official noticed his reaction.

"Ah, a see I planted a seed. You have ways to cultivate the notion?"

"Yes, I do."

"Good. Will you do me a favor then?"

D'Angelo expected the quid pro quo.

"Always something for something."

"Always," Gladkov replied.

"What is it?"

"Kill him for us, too. He's getting in the way of our plans."

Gladkov laughed hard as he waved goodbye.

CHAPTER 47

TEL AVIV, ISRAEL
THREE DAYS LATER

Ira Wurlin welcomed D'Angelo at the door to his office with out-stretched arms and a vigorous, "*Shalom Alaichem!*"

"*Alaichem Shalom.*" D'Angelo returned the greeting with equal sincerity. "So good to see you."

"Likewise, my friend." He patted his stomach. "Though I've put a few pounds on since we last met and lost a good deal of my hair." He brushed back what little was there. It was thinner than it might have been had Ira Wurlin not been Number Two in the Mossad, Israel's spy agency.

"You look fine," D'Angelo offered.

"As long as I continue to look ordinary I'll be happy…and alive."

At fifty-three, he appeared unimposing, the kind of man who disappeared in a party of two. He was a blank man in a world of color, and that fit him perfectly for his job.

Work was his life. Long ago it took the place of marriage and fatherhood, and yet he had a big heart for his colleagues, associates, and friends.

"And you? How is your life?" Wurlin asked. "The last we talked you were hinting at retiring."

"Louder hints, but some pressing issues right now."

"Ah, the fragility of democracies these days. We've been following the news."

D'Angelo assumed they were following more than just the news. The Mossad was probably deep into its own research.

"That's why I'm here." D'Angelo nodded over his shoulder to the door.

The Mossad agent didn't need another cue. He pressed a button under his desk. His office door closed, and shades came down over the windows of the nondescript Tel Aviv headquarters.

"Please, sit," Wurlin said. "Business first. Dinner if you have the time."

Dinner would not be in public.

"Thank you. We'll see."

"Ah, we'll see how the conversation goes. That important?"

"Yes," the CIA operative replied.

"Then I will make a difficult conversation easier for you. You need my help," Wurlin said. He removed his frameless progressive glasses and leaned forward. "Am I correct?"

"Quite. Specifically, can you identity the assassin."

"What did Gladkov tell you?"

D'Angelo laughed. "You are a true son of a bitch."

"Just good at what I do," Wurlin said.

"Who was it? The two students in the shop? The shopkeeper? The men talking?"

"Come now, Vincent. I don't tattle. Besides, you made it harder by leaving."

Wurlin took his seat at his utilitarian metal desk.

"Where aren't you?"

Wurlin shrugged. The answer, unsaid, was the Mossad was *everywhere*.

"So, was Major Gladkov helpful?"

"No names. Just a general picture of a guy who's given him grief, too. Gladkov thinks he's a pissed-off ex-pat with special forces training. Smart. Stealth."

"That's all he gave you?"

The question seemed like Wurlin might have more.

"One other thing. Gladkov called him a ghost."

Wurlin considered the point. He rose, picked up a pencil, and walked around his desk, saying nothing.

D'Angelo turned in his chair to watch.

Wurlin tapped his pencil in his left palm and paced. Finally, in front of a photograph of the current president of Israel, he whispered.

"Not a ghost."

D'Angelo purposely didn't reply. He knew Wurlin was just beginning.

CHAPTER 48

ROARKE'S APARTMENT
WASHINGTON, D.C.
THE SAME DAY

Roarke couldn't sleep. He slipped out of bed at 3:20 a.m., put on a Los Angeles Lakers t-shirt and black Jockey shorts. He pulled the covers over his fiancée's exposed body and tiptoed into the living room. He unrolled a three-by-two foot Rand McNally U.S. map he'd brought from his office and spread it out on the floor. Like the maps at work, red dots marked the locations of the verifiable assassinations. This one had no connecting lines. He stepped back trying to see if a new kind of pattern emerged. Nothing.

Roarke looked at his watch and thought *what the fuck*. He punched in the number on his phone. It rang twice.

"Hello," whispered the women on the other end.

"Penny."

"Oh shit. Roarke go to sleep."

"I can't."

"Well I can."

"I need your help, Penny."

"You can need me when the sun's up," CPT Penny Walker responded.

"Please."

"Jesus. You're impossible."

"We both know that."

"All right, asshole. Give me a few minutes. I'll call you back."

While Roarke waited, he looked at the map again. He was missing something. Roarke taped it to the wall. He stood back trying to think like the mind or minds behind the killings. Nothing came to him.

Roarke's phone vibrated.

"Thanks," he said answering quickly.

"What do you need?" Walker asked with none of her usual teasing.

"There's a pattern to all this. But I don't see it."

He explained what he'd been trying to work out with the maps. Twenty-six verifiable targets recorded. All public figures.

"They were killed by someone who either knew their schedules or could retrieve them. Knew where they lived or could find them. Knew their routines or could research them. They were all picked by someone, Penny. Someone who had put thought behind this and had planned it out. I've got to believe it's someone with a map spread out in front of him. Just like I have."

"We've got a smart killer," she acknowledged.

"We do, but he's just the killer. Who's he working for? The answer for finding both is in the maps."

"So what do you want from me?"

"Another set of eyes. Another way of seeing things. Like an assassin would checking out subjects on their computers. You know, some simple computer back door stuff."

"No, no, and no! I'm not going to hack into public official's computers from the Pentagon. No way."

"A few source URLs? Couldn't that lead somewhere?"

"To what? A person? A corporation?"

"Or a government," Roarke said.

Silence on the phone. Penny Walker was thinking.

"No. The only place it'll lead either of us is jail. Guantanamo for me. Leavenworth for you."

"I might be able to get us a pardon," Roarke said lightly.

"There is that. But the answer is still *no*. Really, Scott. I'm sorry. But you need the FBI, FISA warrants, and court orders. That ain't me."

Roarke understood and couldn't argue the point, but he was getting frustrated. He said goodnight, hung up, and stared at the new map again.

The red dots amidst all the city names became a blur, but his eyes moved across the map in search of some logical pattern.

"It's a big country," Katie said from behind.

Roarke turned.

"You're awake? I'm sorry. I should have been quieter."

"Penny?"

"Yup. I thought she might be able to help."

"Sounded like you were crossing the line and asking her to step right over it, too."

"I suppose I was."

"You can't do that, Scott."

"I'm just so stuck."

As she watched him, Roarke reached out and touched the map, tracing the dots across the states.

"I'm missing something, hon. Just not seeing what's there."

Katie put her arm around her fiancé and lovingly rested her head on his shoulder. They stood together in front of the Rand McNally map with no answers coming this night.

* * *

Four hours later, as they began breakfast, Katie casually said, "I'm going on a trip."

Roarke looked up from his plate, concerned. "Oh?" He put down the bagel he was about to bite.

"Some research."

"What kind," Roarke asked.

"The secessionist stuff. Chances are they'll be hitting the courts one way or another soon. Some states will have special elections. Browning agreed I should get a better understanding of the arguments."

Roarke caught the precision of her explanation.

"Excuse me? He *agreed.* That means this was your idea?"

"Well, yes," Katie admitted.

"Where are you going?"

She cleared her throat. Never a good way to instill confidence.

"Missoula, Montana. The headquarters of the guy who's leading the charge."

She sensed his worry.

"Nothing serious. I won't be too long."

"Too long? How long is too long? What if I go with you?"

More worry, she thought. *Real worry.*

"I'm going to volunteer."

Roarke froze. "Spy. You mean you're going to spy. Infiltrate."

"It's field research."

"Right. Infiltrating and spying. And you told me I was getting close to crossing the line? Does Browning know *exactly* what you're planning?"

"It's not like that. It's innocent."

She looked to the left, often, but not always, a sign of lying.

"And they'll know who you are? You'll tell them you work for the Chief Justice of the United States Supreme Court?"

Katie locked on his eyes again.

"If it comes to that, yes."

"Jesus, Katie. You're dealing with a radical splinter organization that wants to break off from the rest of the country. Hell, what would they have called it if you'd gone to Richmond before the Civil War and planted yourself in Lee's house? Spying?"

"It's not like that. They'll never succeed. I'll be gathering an understanding."

"And Browning accepts this as legal?"

"I won't be stealing anything. Just trying to understand their political perspective." She took a deep breath. "Trust me. It's not as if I'm tying in with a band of armed insurgents. They're ideologues who won't see their ideology come to fruition."

Roarke sighed. There was no way he was going to win this argument.

"You'll check in every day?" he asked.

"Yes."

"You'll be careful?"

"Yes."

"You'll know when to leave?"

"Absolutely."

"And if you get into trouble?"

"I'm a lawyer. I'll argue my way out."

It didn't make Roarke feel any better.

CHAPTER 49

"Excuse me, sir, but this area is closed to the public."

The security officer outside a conference room at the Hyatt Regency Hotel Savannah blocked the door; his intentions were undeniably clear. The gloved workman carrying a metal toolbox wasn't going to get through this way.

"I'm sorry, but there's a lighting issue. I've been called in to look at it."

"No one told me. And it's a closed meeting. Strict orders. I don't have a list, and without one, no one goes in."

The electrician considered leaving. But that wasn't in his nature when he had a job to do. He stood head-to-head with the guard, a man about the same height and build. 1.753 meters. Five-feet nine-inches.

"You don't understand," the workman said.

"No, it's you who doesn't understand."

The refrigerator-wide security officer tipped his head to his right side. The electrician didn't need to look down. He'd already seen the gun.

"A Ruger P345 auto. Is that a threat?"

"It's my last warning," the guard declared. He should have wondered how the electrician knew the make and model of the gun.

As the hotel security officer's hand slipped down, the electrician turned slightly, enough for him to hide what he was doing with his body.

In one smooth movement, he brought the toolbox up and slammed it into the guard's stomach. The blow broke two ribs. The guard doubled over, making his chin an easy target against the fast-rising metal box. That sent the officer backwards, but the assailant instantly pivoted and blocked him from falling against the meeting room door.

There was one more thing for him to do. He swung the toolbox wide, and with lethal force, drove it directly into the guard's temple.

When he finished, he pulled the lifeless body away from the door. Next, he opened the toolbox, removed a Springfield Armory XDM Threaded 9mm with a SilencerCo Osprey. He borrowed the security guard's hat, knocked on the door, and opened it a few inches.

"Judge Hardy, one moment please."

The fifty-three-year-old federal circuit court judge excused himself from his meeting. In the hall he politely said, "Yes?"

The assassin raised his gun and smiled.

"Nothing personal."

He squeezed the trigger and left, avoiding the hotel security cameras on the way out just as he had on the way in.

CHAPTER 50

WASHINGTON, D.C.
TWO DAYS LATER

Roarke decided that the vertical line that went through Washington, D.C. was important. The ultimate target. Beyond that, he made no other assumptions. Another day with no real progress.

MISSOULA, MT

Missoula, Montana, had notable political history. Lucas Burke told volunteers at an orientation it was time to make more.

"Missoula residents put the first woman in the U.S. Congress, Jeannette Rankin, and the longest serving senate majority leader, Mike Mansfield.

"It was founded as a trading post while part of Washington Territory in 1860. It could very well become a founding capitol of a new nation. Do you want to be part of it?" Burke asked his latest group.

Enthusiastic nods *yes*.

"First more history. Fort Missoula was established in 1883 to normalize the economy. As a sovereign country, we can create our own economy. In 1893, the city built the state's first university. With your help, the University of Montana can become a national institution, a leading research facility in a new nation.

"Missoula has been a supply route to the west. Now we supply ideas about how things should be. We had a great lumber industry, now gone, but we grow branches of freedom that are extending throughout the west and beyond. We are on the cusp of great changes."

Burke's voice rose as if he were speaking to hundreds, not a group of fifteen recruits.

"And you are the change makers."

He settled down, smiled and gave each volunteer individual eye contact.

"Welcome to the New Northwest Front. One of many unaffiliated nations you can help pioneer."

Generally, the NNF recruits were in their midtwenties to midthirties. Idealistic individuals and a few couples. People with passion and the ability to give up what they were doing for something lofty to believe in.

And they all believed in Lucas Burke, with one exception.

Katie Kessler, dressed like most others in jeans and a short sleeve t-shirt, sat along a wall for ten minutes, filling out a questionnaire. The first lie she wrote was her name. Katie Novick. Novick was her mother's maiden name. Her second was an address. She listed a post office box she used to have in Cambridge, Massachusetts. As for references, she listed two friends from school. She'd call them after to back her story. Then came job history. Instead of indicating she was a Senior Lawyer at the United States Supreme Court, she indicated she had taken law classes at Harvard and had had a job in a now closed Boston law firm. Both were true as far as she went. She did take classes and the law firm she had worked for dissolved.

Katie Novick put on the committed face of a naïve drifter looking for a cause and a hero. Talking to others along the wall, she felt she was in good company.

She waited another fifteen minutes for a personnel meeting. After the human resources volunteer, only in the job two weeks herself, heard she'd had law experience, she passed Katie along to a supervisor.

"Ah, an aspiring lawyer?" The comment came from a strikingly handsome thirty-seven-year-old man in a sports coat, denim shirt, and jeans who walked in to greet her. He introduced himself before she answered.

"I'm Josh Collins."

"Hi Mr. Collins. I'm Katie Novick."

"Josh, please."

"Nice to meet you, Josh."

"Law, right? We sure need you."

"Actually, law classes. I'm planning on getting back to it. Probably need some inspiration."

"Well, you heard Lucas. You'll sure have it here. And who knows, maybe you'll help write a new constitution!"

"Wow," she said enthusiastically. "I hadn't even thought of that."

"You realize John Hancock wasn't even a lawyer."

"I didn't know that." The lying was coming easier. "But you must have a legal team here and in Washington?"

It was her first attempt to probe.

"Sure, but there's a great deal we have to bring down to ground level so our supporters understand. Besides, it saves money."

"I get that."

"So, you're ready to join up?"

This was more than she expected. *Yes*, she thought. But she wondered at what cost. She played it carefully.

"Well yes, but—"

"No but's. You start right now. You'll be working with me."

Uh oh. That cost.

Collins had a medium-sized office with two other volunteers. He offered her coffee, and they sat across from one another at his Ikea desk. She learned that he was an economics professor on sabbatical from the university, a faithful believer in the movement; single, and—based on where his eyes were drawn—already interested in her.

He was handsome and constantly smiling. For her part, Katie remained polite and warm. And she wasn't wearing her engagement ring. She also hadn't worn it enough outside to leave a tan mark. As far as Collins was concerned, she was the new girl, and she was available.

"Okay, so here's where we'll start Katie. We're on the ballot for upcoming special elections."

"Referendums?" she asked, knowing the answer already.

"Very good. In California, Vermont, New Hampshire, and of course, Montana."

He handed her a stack of files.

"Read through these. Get up to speed. They'll keep you busy through the day."

"Thanks. Would you like a paper or a summary?"

"Naw. We'll talk it through. Just get familiar with the arguments."

She looked for a place to sit.

"Ah, where?"

"The bullpen. Come on. I'll introduce you around."

She was grateful not to be in the same office with him.

• • •

"How's it going?" Roarke asked, reaching Katie at the hotel. It was his third phone call of the day. She had ignored the first two.

"The hotel is basic. Affordable. But I found an Airbnb to move into."

"I meant how are you doing?"

"Everything's okay."

"They bought your cover?" Roarke noted.

"It's not like that," Katie replied.

Another lie. This one to Scott. She grimaced.

"All right. I've gotta ask. And I love you."

"Me too you."

"Am I hovering?" he asked.

"Like a drone. Which, by the way, you're not sending overhead to watch me, right?"

"No, but I could."

"Don't even consider it, mister."

Their conversation continued for another five minutes covering the apartment she'd move into, the food, and the variety of people she already met. There was no mention of the economics professor.

• • •

What Katie was doing for Burke's movement was what she had been doing for the court, but from the opposite side. Her assignments were clear:

How can we fight the Supreme Court?

What are the winnable arguments?

What are the fundamental arguments our legal team can use?

And there was another question, Josh Collins, the campaign's financial expert asked, "What can we fundraise off?"

It was a small operation, and in less than twenty-four hours, Katie Kessler made it close to the inner circle. Partly because they needed sharp, mature people. And largely due to her apparent self-confidence.

Her access to Collins gave her a chance to sit in a meeting with Lucas Burke. He was toned down without an audience, but every bit as personable and charismatic. Burke impressed her as being completely authentic. Not an actor portraying a part, but a political rebel who was true to his beliefs.

"So, Katie, what do you think of our little movement?" Burke asked.

"Not so little. A phenomenon," she said truthfully.

"To the core. And we're going to shake the system," he added.

"You already are."

"But can we win?"

Katie thought carefully. *Could they win?* She didn't believe so. But the followers lived for the chance.

"Yes, Ms. Novick?" another voice asked from behind her. Colder. More calculating than Burke's. "Can we win?"

Katie turned to the speaker. "I'm sorry..."

"Of course. We haven't met. I'm Clay Lindstrom. I work with Lucas."

Burke laughed. "He's understating things. Clay runs the show. It's safe to say he's the architect of our success."

"And so, to the question again, Ms. Novick. Can we win?"

Katie cleared her throat. *Was he probing me? Does he know?*

"It depends on what you mean by winning, Mr. Lindstrom?" Katie answered. "Local and state referendums? Perhaps. Maybe not immediately, but eventually. The court of public opinion? In some regions. The Supreme Court? I think you'll need Washington's best to argue the point."

Lindstrom smiled. Not a friendly smile.

"A perfect response for someone who has had *some* law classes."

He's baiting me, she thought.

"Three battles, Mr. Lindstrom. Three different strategies. Do you want the answer that pleases you or the honest answer?"

Lindstrom addressed Collins. "Well, Josh, you were right. She's got the goods."

To Katie he said, "And I want answers that get us positive results."

Katie gave him direct eye contact.

"Well, Mr. Lindstrom. It's ultimately a political game. It's going to take time, patience, and money."

"There are always game changers, Ms. Novick," he said with a laugh.

She had no idea what that meant. She looked worried.

"I've scared you."

Clay Lindstrom extended his hand and smiled. It looked sincere.

"You'll have to forgive me. Even Lucas says I come on too strong."

It wasn't an apology, and she recognized it, but she shook his hand anyway. She had to.

"Good to meet you, Mr. Lindstrom."

"Welcome to our grand experiment. We need smart young people like you to succeed."

"And I have a lot to learn," she replied. She meant every word, but not the way Lindstrom or Collins would have known. Or as least she hoped they wouldn't know.

"How long will we have you?"

Katie looked at Josh.

"Katie will be working with me, Clay. I'm hoping she'll grow with the organization."

Lindstrom bore down on Katie. "Is that your intention?"

Katie answered his expression and his question with the same seriousness.

"I believe that change is occurring in the country at ever-increasing speed, Mr. Lindstrom. Regional differences have long divided the United States. Mr. Burke's message is resounding. It's a populace message that won't be popular everywhere. I suppose that's the challenge. And I've always been up for a challenge."

Clay Lindstrom continued to study her. He pursed his lips, nodded ever so slightly, then stopped to study the new recruit. The moment grew uncomfortable. Not what Josh Collins wanted. Sensing the awkwardness, he said, "Clay, I really feel Katie's going to be a great asset. She's got what it takes, and she believes in us."

Lindstrom relaxed his stare and smiled. "Let's hope so, Josh."

Katie gave as perfect a smile as possible in return.

• • •

Scott Roarke's last call of the day caught Katie in her new apartment.

"Good day?"

"Absolutely," she said with all the enthusiasm possible.

Katie had to work on her acting.

CHAPTER 51

MISSOULA, MT
ONE WEEK LATER

Katie had successfully deflected Josh's dinner invitations three times by working late. But by the fourth time, she felt she had to accept. *Anyway*, she thought, *it might help glean information.*

"Finally, a yes. Thank you," Josh said. "You work too hard. So tonight it's just fun."

This was not what she wanted, but she said, "Great."

After work she especially chose an outfit that wouldn't appear provocative. Black slacks, a simple blouse and flats.

Josh picked her up at her apartment and drove her to The Pearl Cafe, one of the city's fine dining restaurants.

"Oh no, no, no," Katie declared when they walked in. "Too nice." She also thought to herself, *too romantic.* "And expensive."

"Come on."

"Only if we go dutch."

"No way. I've been asking all week. This is on me. But I get to learn more about you. Deal?!"

"Deal," she softly replied, wishing she had declined a fourth time.

A young hostess led them to a corner table. Katie quickly settled on an inexpensive pinot noir, promising herself she'd make the one drink last through dinner.

Josh had a dirty martini. *Not a good sign.*

Before the drinks came, Josh gave her a primer on the menu. "I know we're nowhere near the ocean, but the oysters are really good. Served with Prosecco Mignnonette and Balsamic Pearls."

"As in the Pearl Cafe?" she asked thinking, *Definitely not the oysters.*

"Don't know. Maybe."

She read the menu and saw the Charcuterie plate, which she immediately proposed they share.

"Okay," he said. "And for the main course are you a steak or fish person? Or a vegetarian. There's a mushroom crepe."

"Alaska's closer to Montana than Massachusetts. I'll go for the Alaskan Halibut."

"And the Tenderloin for me."

Their drinks arrived, and Katie immediately made a toast to Lucas Burke, rather than having Collins take the lead.

It didn't help. He added, "Who brought us together."

"Well, yes he did," Katie replied taking the first small sip.

He asked about her Airbnb. She said it was tiny, emphasizing she had picked a place with a single bed and only a kitchenette. "Simple, but it's working out fine."

Josh owned a small house. She failed to follow up on any description. Particularly the bedroom.

When their appetizers came Josh reached across the table and patted her hand. It was a gesture just short of a caress. He sensed her tense.

"You don't have to be nervous. I promise I won't bite."

Katie smiled.

"I'm sorry. I am a bit nervous."

She launched into an account that would be, for the purposes of the conversation, only part of the full story.

"I had a relationship that started at the office where I was working in Boston. My boss got wind of it. Complications. I ultimately had to leave."

The story was true to the extent that she stated. But there was a great deal more. Her relationship was with Roarke. The complications involved an international conspiracy and murder. She had to leave in a hurry.

"And another where work also confused things. Too close quarters and too much at stake."

Again, true, but only up to a point. The specifics remained unsaid over dinner.

"When?" Collins asked.

"Not so long ago that it still doesn't affect me."

He studied her expression and offered a sympathetic smile.

"I understand," he said. "But you have to know, you're very different than other women who have come through here. There's something beyond the surface adoration for Lucas. Deeper. I suppose that's what's appealing to me."

He withdrew his hand.

"So, I'll be good, but hopeful. How's that? We'll see how things go."

Katie forced a smile.

"On an entirely different subject, I still get the sense you don't like Clay a whole helluva lot. You're avoiding him."

She laughed. "Was it that obvious?

"To me, yes, but no worries. He basically focuses on Lucas morning, noon, and night. Immediate issues, long-range planning, speeches, and travel. Keeping the machine going."

"Suppose so," Katie replied.

"And we'd be nowhere without him. He comes on strong to most everyone. Don't take it personally."

But Katie Kessler did.

"I had a college teacher who liked to quote Maya Angelou. 'When someone shows you who they are, believe them the first time.'"

"That's harsh."

"I'm not always subtle."

Katie suddenly realized she had gone too far. She recoiled and audibly sucked in air.

"Oh, I appreciate that he has to be tough. It takes a lot to change the way things have been for so long."

She was hating the subterfuge. But she couldn't tell Josh the truth. Instead, she smiled and offered another lie.

"We'll see how things go," she repeated.

WASHINGTON, D.C.
THE SAME TIME

Roarke tried a different approach. He connected five of his red dots covering states to form what looked like a peaked roof. At the top, Boise, Idaho, extending west to Sacramento and ending at Rohnert Park, California. To the east, the line went down and over to Grand Junction and Montrose, Colorado.

He stepped back. *All right,* he thought. *Now what?*

Roarke kept the north/south vertical line cutting through the East Coast cities. He stood back.

Nothing.

After another hour of nothings, he left the White House dialing Katie's phone. The call would only show up as an unknown number.

No answer.

MISSOULA, MT
THE SAME TIME

"Hey, you need to get that?" Josh asked, noting her phone vibrating on the table.

She looked at the display. She recognized the number. Scott's. Then lied.

"Nope. Probably just another robo call."

She pretended to block it on the phone's settings.

"I get them all the time, too. Hate them," he said.

They returned to small talk, off any romantic track, which allowed Katie to enjoy his company and the dinner. The food was tasty, and they laughed through stories about growing up, best and worst teachers, places they'd visited.

She actually thought that he could make it in D.C. working for the Office for Management and Budget. But of course, she couldn't mention that or the fact that she could probably help make it happen.

Katie had no real agenda, but a few questions she wanted to explore.

"How did you come to believe in Lucas?"

"Roundabout," Collins answered. "I was working as a legislative aide in Sacramento. Mostly getting discouraged."

"I never asked. Republican or Democrat?"

"Democrat, more progressive than most. I thought California was actually too big to manage. You know it's the world's fifth largest economy and full of divisive politics."

"Yup," she said, encouraging him to continue.

"After a bunch of years, I quit and hooked up with the Calexit movement, thinking it might just have a chance. But when the news broke that an American with deep ties to Russia was actually behind the movement, it fell apart. At least for a while. So then, I started looking into Oregon, Vermont, and other states where the issue was also being considered. I wrote a few Op Eds that ran in some papers, and I got a call from Clay. He asked me where a movement could take hold and where it couldn't."

"Like…?"

"Well, Texas? Won't happen there. It all comes down to what will be defensible in federal court."

Katie nodded, knowing full well he was right.

"And Oregon and Vermont? What are the chances given the laws there?"

"Let's say, more likely. The only sure thing is that it comes down to money. These battles aren't cheap, and, win or lose, they take a long time."

"So you took a job."

"Yes. There are ups and downs. But it got my juices flowing," he admitted.

"Lindstrom has the funds?" Katie asked.

"So far. Angel sources. He always says, 'Don't worry.' Of course we do, but he hasn't missed a payroll yet. Which, by the way, I'd like to get you on."

"I'm okay right now," Kessler said. There was no way she could accept money. Besides, her Social Security number and passport could give her away.

"Let's see if I pass the Lindstrom test, first," she said. It's just been a little over a week."

"Okay," Collins replied. "But I'm impressed."

Katie returned to the question of money. "So Lindstrom has his own Koch brothers?" referring to the conservative financiers.

"Someone's out there. I don't know who. Since we're not a true political party, but an organization, we haven't had to file any disclosures."

"I suppose that's good."

"It worries me a little considering I'm signing checks. But the lawyers say we're okay."

"What about Lindstrom?" she asked. "He's different than Burke. Aloof. Cold. Distant."

Collins laughed. "You've got to see him on the road. He'll whisper something in Lucas's ear, enough for him to make a point, and then Lucas will turn it into the best damned impromptu speech. He's amazing! Together they're amazing."

Katie flashed on a congressman named Teddy Lodge and felt a cold shiver.

WASHINGTON, D.C.
THE SAME TIME

Roarke walked to his Georgetown apartment on the 2500 block of Q Street. A summer breeze refreshed him but didn't take his mind off his maps. On one hand, he believed the assassin wouldn't leave any visible clues. But *someone planning might. Someone not as smart as a skilled assassin. Someone not thinking.*

Then he dismissed the notion. He was over-thinking. Too much staring at a map. He needed to get into the field.

Bessolo, he said to himself. He'd call the FBI agent in the morning.

MISSOULA, MT
THE SAME TIME

"What's Lindstrom's story?" Katie asked as she swirled her wine. She'd broken her own rule. She was midway through her second glass.

"Too much work," Collins replied. "I'd much rather get to know you better."

"In time," she said brightly. "I'm curious." She paused realizing she needed to provide a reason. "Like you said. He's amazing. I mean, look where you all were a year ago."

"Almost nowhere," he replied.

"And now, you're front page news. Soon Lucas will be on *Meet the Press.*'"

"We're hoping."

"It'll happen. Hell, Lindstrom will make it happen."

"See, you're coming around," Collins smiled.

She wasn't. Katie was just exploring.

"What's his background?"

"An Army brat. Always moving. Mother from Toole County, right along the Canadian border. Might be some oil money there. I'm not sure. Father a colonel or something with assignments around the world," Collins recounted. "From what I heard, Clay was a bit rebellious. A handful as a teenager. His family sent him to some East Coast prep schools. That didn't work out. So they shipped him off to school in Switzerland."

"God, he must have hated that."

"Whatever you do, don't ask. He generally doesn't like to talk about his background. He says it takes away from Lucas and the whole movement."

"Well, that makes sense," Katie said. "College?"

"Right here. The state university. That's where he met up with Lucas. He managed his run for class president his senior year."

She leaned forward and whispered, "This sounds like a political relationship that actually could take them to the White House."

"Whoa. That's not on the table. They've made it clear the movement isn't about them. Anyway, that would disenfranchise Lucas's followers."

"I don't know," she argued. "He's very convincing. If one approach to America doesn't work, maybe another would."

Josh Collins stiffened. "All right. Really, that's enough work. You're treading on dangerous territory."

"Don't tread on me?" she asked. "That was a revolutionary battle cry. A flag with a rising rattlesnake coiled and ready to strike."

"We are a movement ready to move," he countered. "For freedom from Washington."

Collins paused and cocked his head. "Are you having freshman doubts?" he wondered.

Katie knew she had definitely pushed too much. She smiled and reached across the table to pat his hand.

"Sorry. It's the wine speaking. Should have stopped earlier."

Now she stopped and gave a more honest response.

"No, that's not it. I've gotten so deep into the legal arguments I guess I needed to understand the passion behind it all."

He squeezed her hand. "Well, I get that. And I have to tell you, you're making yourself very valuable."

"Really," Katie said

"Really. I mean it. Lucas even asked how you'd do on the road meeting with state caucuses. And that would get you a paying job."

"One step at a time."

With that she took another sip, wondering why she had gotten herself into this mess. And that wouldn't be the last of it tonight. She'd need to make excuses after dinner. More personal ones.

CHAPTER 52

THE NEXT DAY

"I'm planning on another trip. Some old-fashioned hoofing around Europe," Vinnie D'Angelo cryptically said on his phone call with Roarke. "Feel like tagging along? We always seem to turn it into an experience."

The open cell wasn't the platform to go into details. Neither had to. They'd known and worked with each other long enough. Shorthand worked.

"Sneakers or dress shoes?"

"I'd say more the sneaker variety."

Code for Roarke. Quiet surveillance and maybe some running. He replied with, "Hey, less to pack."

"Pack what you need," the CIA operative said. "I know this great pasta place. Why don't we meet up there, say dinner tomorrow?"

Roarke knew the location. *That fast?* he thought.

He could book an overnight commercial flight from Dulles. However, once again given the circumstances, which he considered extreme, he'd hitch a military transport out of Joint Base Andrews to Naples. No frills. Fewer questions. Better than traveling as a tourist.

. . .

"I'm going on the road," Roarke told Katie after making his travel arrangements from his office.

"Not here!" she automatically said.

"Nope. A little further away."

"Can you hold a sec?" she asked. Katie had taken the call in her office, but now walked out to get away from the Burke staff, and Josh Collins in particular.

"Sorry, had to step out," she continued a half-minute later. "They're giving me more responsibility, and I want to learn as much as possible before I pull out."

Roarke winced. The term *pull out* carried a familiar espionage ring.

"I don't like the way that sounds, honey."

"It's okay."

It's okay was different than *I'm okay.* Katie was not good at dodges, and Roarke picked up on the distinction.

"What's going on?"

She looked around. Volunteers and staffers were still coming to work. She gave them polite nods and forced smiles.

"Can't really talk now."

"Are you in trouble?"

"No. Honest. I just forgot what it's like to look available."

"I didn't realize you were going to do that." Roarke said with disappointment.

"Fewer questions."

Roarke realized that was precisely his thinking about traveling with D'Angelo. "Right, but more lies."

"Like *your* job!" It was her quick jab.

"Katie, please." This wasn't the way he wanted their conversation to go. Especially when he was heading out of the country.

A long silence followed. The longest they'd ever had on a phone call. Then Katie asked a follow-up to the beginning of their conversation.

"So where are you heading?"

Roarke sighed. "Can't really say."

"See, Scott! I'm not the only one! Gotta go. Call me from wherever."

Katie hung up, wishing she hadn't.

Roarke immediately dialed back. When she didn't answer he left a message.

"I'm sorry. I'm really sorry." Then he did what he wasn't supposed to do, but figured it was better to tell her than not. He said where he was going.

Ten minutes later Katie listened to the message and cried. Josh Collins noticed and walked to her desk in the bullpen.

"What's the matter?" he asked with real concern. He touched her hand again.

She breathed deeply and looked up at her boss.

"Come on, what's the matter, Katie," he said compassionately.

"Sorry. That relationship I mentioned. It threw me off."

This time it was the truth.

. . .

Roarke had four hours before he needed to show up for his flight out of Joint Base Andrews. The best he could do was an Air Force KC 10 Extender that would be aloft for a scheduled mid-air refueling west of Gibraltar. Even the president's call couldn't shake loose a quicker, more direct route. But he'd never seen a KC 10, the stripped-down military version of the DC 10, extend the boom to refuel an F/A18. At least it would be interesting. In the meantime, he arranged to meet Bessolo at his FBI offices.

The FBI agent opened with, "Stranger in a strange land?"

It was a typical welcome for Roarke.

"You know, Bessolo, I get along just fine with other folks in the bureau." Roarke had one more point to add. "And your boss." He smiled. "So why not thaw out a little."

"This is as warm as I get. Ask my wife."

"You're not married," Roarke laughed.

"Oh yeah, right. Well, if I were, she'd say the same thing."

Bessolo and Roarke had actually come to a good working relationship, but the edge kept them competitive, and that competitiveness helped them both.

"Got anything for me?" Roarke asked.

"Backtracking a few things our friend left behind."

"Oh?" Roarke was intrigued.

"An Apollo toolbox made exclusively for Walmart," Bessolo replied.

"Sloppy suddenly, or he is sending us down a rabbit hole?"

"Don't know. I'd like to think he had to get out in a hurry, but we're checking it out store-by-store, CCTV-by-CCTV. We're looking."

CHAPTER 53

MISSOULA, MT

Katie got Browning's approval for another week off from the court, though the chief justice wasn't thrilled. She needed the time to figure out Clay Lindstrom. From what she'd already gathered, he was a master manipulator and a control freak. He liked to keep Lucas Burke close to the vest and others further away. If he wasn't running Burke for office, then what was the real play. *There had to be a play*, she thought. *Time to find out.*

"Excuse me, Mr. Lindstrom," Katie said, knocking on his door and simultaneously opening it.

Lindstrom was watching CNN, twirling a pencil in his hands.

"Go away. I'm thinking," he barked.

"I'm sorry." She went for a line she thought she could sell in. Something to get him to talk. "I need some advice?"

He looked frustrated but waved her in.

Katie held in her arms case history files on secessions. Her research at the court and some flip side understanding from the Burke camp probably made her one of the most up-to-date people in the country on the subject. She was ready to use it to her advantage. She placed them on his desk, taking the seat opposite him.

"Thank you, Mr. Lindstrom."

"So what do you want?" He turned down the sound on CNN.

She reached for an answer. Something. Anything. Fast.

"Well, as I see it, important deadlines are coming up. Can you help with clarity on the larger plan?"

Lindstrom stiffened. He stopped twirling the pencil and leaned in.

"What do you mean, larger plan?"

"Larger political plan. Lucas isn't running for office, but without a doubt he could be great. People are asking. It only seems natural. We have a wonderful movement, but we will be stalled out by local and state legislators, courts, Congress, and ultimately the Supreme Court."

She put her argument forward in that order but felt herself wince when she noted the Supreme Court. He caught the look.

"Something wrong, Ms. Novick?" he asked.

"Sorry. Nothing. Well, something," she said recovering. She decided to let out the fishing line like she used to at Sebago Lake in Maine when she went fishing as a kid with her father.

"The press loves Lucas. He's a natural. At rallies, in person one-on-one, on TV and radio. And you're a great manager. He'd make a great candidate. The country could use Lucas Burke."

Lindstrom relaxed, but only a little. He began twirling his pencil again.

"You came in asking for advice. I haven't heard what advice you want."

"I probably phrased it poorly."

"Then phrase it better."

Lindstrom was showing real annoyance.

Katie put on a confident face and started again. "Is there something bigger I'm not seeing?" Without hesitating she added, "If so, what more can I do?"

Instead of Lindstrom getting upset more, he smiled. She recognized it as an insincere smile; merely a face he put on.

"Oh no, Katie."

He hadn't called her Katie before. It was patronizing and worrisome.

Lindstrom continued. "We're a movement and a resource to states and regional constituencies. A fresh new idea to encourage other fresh new faces to come forward. To change the way things are. Lucas would surely make a great leader. But that's not where we're going."

She decided to press further.

"But you're building such tremendous interest in Lucas, why not run him? If we can't deliver one way, we can deliver another. A transformed America." She lowered her voice. "There's so much Lucas and you can accomplish, especially with…"

She let the fishing line out more.

"…the fear sweeping the country."

Lindstrom sharply interrupted.

"I think that's enough, Ms. Novick."

Katie was abundantly aware that he abandoned the momentary informality.

"I have work to do," he continued. He twirled his pencil faster. "And I recommend you stick to your own knitting."

Lindstrom stood; a signal for her to leave.

"I think that covers the advice you sought."

"Absolutely, Mr. Lindstrom. Thank you."

As she prepared to leave, she noticed a map of the United States on the wall adjacent to the door. She stopped and looked at it, noting dozens of flags on toothpicks stuck in various locations.

"Those are places where Lucas has delivered speeches. We're going to double it in the next month," Lindstrom said eyeing her interest.

"It sure is impressive."

Katie nodded. Like a child in a museum reaching out to touch a painting, she passed her hand across the Rand McNally Map.

"You have to be very proud."

Lindstrom ignored the comment.

As she felt the map, she was aware of holes where other tacks had been. They were spread throughout the country but weren't represented by flags.

"Ms. Novick."

Katie stared at the map.

"Ms. Novick!" Lindstrom implored. "Back to work."

"Yes, of course."

Katie slowly withdrew her hand and returned to her desk. She nonchalantly glanced around the bullpen. Her office mates, mostly young and enthusiastic, were talking to one another, laughing, or on the phone. A few were into their second and third cups of coffee. Katie smiled to anyone who gave her eye contact. She considered them all good people. Dedicated and hoping to foster real change.

Back to work, she thought calling up Lindstrom's order. "Okay, back to work," she said under her breath.

Katie clicked on a news report on Burke's forays into New Hampshire. She began reading, but her mind soon drifted elsewhere.

CHAPTER 54

MISSOULA, MT
THAT EVENING

Most of the staff had left for the night, including Josh Collins and Clay Lindstrom. Only two volunteers remained. One was Katie.

She spun her Office Depot chair around and looked at Lindstrom's locked office door. It had called out to her for hours.

Over the next thirty minutes she busied herself at the copy machine, printing articles, and filing research. Nothing suspicious. Everything normal. But it was all busy work. Katie was waiting for her last office mate to leave.

"Gonna call it a night?" she asked Josie Corcoran, a peppy twenty-two-year-old volunteer from Kentucky.

"I wish, but no," the young woman replied. "Pulling quotes for Lucas. He's got speeches in Colorado coming up, and he wants authentic westward ho pioneer stories. You?"

"Legal stuff," Katie replied.

She was actually thinking the opposite. *Illegal stuff.* Katie wanted to get into Lindstrom's office. Nearly an hour later she decided to take the chance.

Katie removed a credit card from her wallet, gathered some papers, tucked them under her left arm, and walked as authoritatively as possible to Clay Lindstrom's office.

Glancing over her shoulder and using her body to block what she was doing, she slid her MasterCard between the doorframe and the door, hoping she'd be able to jimmy the lock the way hers had been done at her Beacon Hill apartment years ago until she installed a dead bolt.

It worked. The interior door lock had a simple mechanism.

Damn girl, she said to herself. Opening it, she looked back, ready with an excuse if Josie called out. She didn't.

Katie entered. *Now what?* She turned the lights on, acting as if she belonged and the door had not been locked. *Act normal. Look like you belong.* Better than slinking about using her cell phone as a flashlight.

Inside, she looked around. *First Lindstrom's desk.* She crossed the room, spread out the papers she'd brought in, as if organizing was her true purpose. Next, she sat and began opening drawers. The center, then the three on the right side and the three on the left.

It was her first illegal search ever. She was actually grateful she came up with nothing. The drawers were empty, which in itself, seemed odd, but not evidence of any wrongdoing.

She rose, gathered the papers and walked back to the door. Katie stopped. The map caught her attention; the map that had been nagging her all day.

She looked it at from four feet, two feet, and closer. Scanning from coast to coast. Then north to south. An ordinary map. Multicolored by state. Capitals and major cities included. Rivers, mountain ranges, and lakes. Without realizing, she reached out and felt the paper. It was full of tiny bumps, the kind of indentations left by pins or tacks.

Katie shrugged. She dismissed it as likely locations where Burke had had speaking engagements. Nothing meaningful.

She turned to leave, disappointed that her search hadn't turned up anything. As she took a step, she noticed she was rubbing her right thumb and forefinger together.

It was the tactile cue that got to her. She stopped, spun around and was drawn to the map again. Drawn to touch the minute holes.

She ran her fingers over the surface, gliding slowly up and down the East Coast, then further west and south. Katie took a step closer. Soon she was using two hands as if they could see something her eyes couldn't.

The pin pricks. The holes in the map.

Something, she thought. "*But—?*" she whispered aloud. The answer eluded her.

Katie had the presence of mind to take her cellphone out of her back pocket to snap a few pictures; wide and tighter. She was about to get even closer shots when Josie yelled from the bullpen, "Hey you, how about wrapping up in there and going out for a drink?"

Katie nervously tucked her camera in her pocket, turned off Lindstrom's overhead light, and left making sure the door was locked.

"Sounds great to me," Katie replied as if she had done nothing wrong.

CHAPTER 55

Katie sipped an acceptable Manhattan at the local Outback Steakhouse. Josie worked on her second Bulleit with two rocks. The ninety proof Kentucky Bourbon loosened her tongue, while Katie took her time with her drink.

"Yeah, Lindstrom's tough to crack. Like he always has his guard up and his radar on. I guess it takes a man like him, but personally, I don't like him," Josie admitted. Katie laughed. "Let's just say he's slow to warm to."

"As if anyone can warm up frigid?"

Josie brushed her brown bangs and tossed her head back. Then she returned to her drink.

"There is that," Katie replied.

"Oh my God, let me tell you about my first day," Josie continued. Her speech was beginning to slur. "I got so scared I was ready to walk out. It wasn't until I met Lucas that I felt everything would be okay. But still…"

"What happened?"

"This woman from Georgia. She's gone now. How she even stayed the day, I don't know. But she was gone within the week."

"What happened?" Katie asked again.

"All she did was take a couple of pictures of Lindstrom and posted them on Instagram. When he found out, he went positively ballistic. 'No pictures of me. Ever! No posts! We're here for Lucas!' Swear to God, he was screaming. I thought he was going to rip the cell out of her hands. Then he calmed down as if nothing happened."

Katie recalled her own experience with Lindstrom. But she engaged Josie further.

"All that over a photo?"

"Exactly," Josie replied. "Lucas overheard, and he apologized for Lindstrom."

"And Lindstrom. Did he ever apologize?"

"Clay Lindstrom? No way."

"So why was he so concerned about a photo? Katie asked. "Hell, it's not as if he's unknown."

"Maybe so, but he hates it. He says it takes away from Lucas. He's just a control freak. I guess that's what it takes," the volunteer added.

All of this gave Katie more concern. She had to be careful.

They finished their drinks, and Katie signaled for the check.

"My treat," she offered warmly.

Katie Kessler had learned a good deal. Josie Corcoran, nothing.

The check came, and Katie opened her wallet to take out her credit card. It wasn't in the usual sleeve. She checked the billfold portion. Only assorted receipts. She looked in other slots. Then she dug into her purse, hoping it could have fallen in.

Josie crinkled her brow. "Something wrong?"

Katie continued to search.

"Hey, if you're short, I can—" Josie began.

"Just looking…" Katie didn't finish the sentence aloud. But she began to panic.

Oh God! I left it in his office.

3:15 A.M. MT

"Where are you?" Katie asked. "I've been trying to reach you for hours."

"In a rental car, hun. Driving the countryside."

The country was Italy. The countryside, the Amalfi Coast.

"Wish I were with you now," she admitted.

Roarke sensed trouble. *Or was it fear?*

"What's the matter?"

"I got myself into a situation."

Roarke was driving with a Bluetooth earpiece in his ear. She explained what she'd done.

"Why for God's sake…?"

"Because I was stupid. Because…I don't know. I had a feeling."

Roarke resisted raising his voice, but he was upset.

"Jesus, you're an officer of the court." He took a breath and tried not to upset her more than she was. "What were you thinking?"

"I wanted to get a better handle on Lindstrom. Something's off. I've watched you get that feeling and—"

"And I'm trained."

"It's just that when I was wrapping up talking with him, I started thinking he was hiding something. And then there's this map of his."

"Map? What map?" Roarke asked.

"A map of the U.S. Like yours. With little flags for where Burke's gone to."

"So?"

"So I don't know. I was acting on a feeling. So I broke into—"

Roarke immediately interrupted. "Watch what you say."

"Right."

"And that's where you think you dropped it."

It was her credit card.

Katie sighed. "What should I do?"

Roarke regretted letting Katie go. Not that he really could have prevented her. But she had no experience going undercover. And that's precisely what she had done. But this wasn't the time to lecture her. She was nervous. More than that, she was frightened.

"Do you have any idea where it might be?"

She pictured it in her hand jimmying the lock, and walking in. "Oh shit! On his desk"

"Okay, not the best of places, but here's what you go with—you realized you lost it when you tried to use it at the bar. You figured you dropped it in the office."

He thought for a moment.

"Any cleaning crew at night that would have picked it up?"

"Not tonight. They come Fridays."

"Did you have your purse with you when you talked to him? Were you holding a jacket? Your wallet?"

"No, only folders."

"Then here's what you go with. You were beginning to order something online at your desk, right?"

"But—"

"Listen to me," he continued while driving the curves. "You were ordering something online. You pulled your card out, it was stuck in the materials you brought in." Roarke slowly and declaratively created a scenario for Katie to practice.

"Yes," she said repeating key elements. "I must have stuck my card in the file by mistake, carried it in, where it fell out."

"It happens," Roarke said.

Katie felt she could sell it if she spoke calmly, with eye contact and a smile.

Roarke sensed that she had calmed down.

"But, shouldn't I just go in earlier and try to find it before—"

"No!" Roarke said fearing it could compound the problem. "Stick with the plan. Sell it like you're selling it to a jury. Control, Katie. Control."

"Okay," Katie said.

"Can you do that sweetheart?"

"Yes. Yes, I can."

Suddenly, another realization came to her. She gasped.

"Oh shit!"

"What?" Roarke asked.

"It's worse."

"Why?"

"My name. The card has my real name. I've been using my mom's maiden name. He'll have my real name and can trace me back to the court."

Roarke stopped again. This *was* worse.

CHAPTER 56

THE NEXT MORNING

Katie arrived early. Especially early. She was outside waiting for the office manager to arrive to open up.

"Morning," she cheerfully said.

"Good morning," the office manager, a recent political science major from Berkeley answered. "Early for you."

"Lot's to do."

She had rehearsed what to say and when to casually get to it. How to deal with her credit card loss. And if discovered, how to handle the more difficult issue—her name on the card.

Katie intentionally passed on morning coffee. She was keyed up enough.

Control, she said to herself. *Control.* A mantra. A calming word. But it was going to be hard. Harder than facing her bosses at her Boston law firm nearly two years ago when she dug for information on behalf of Roarke.

"Hey, can you open Clay's door? I think I dropped something in his office last night."

"Wish I could. I don't even have a key. Go figure."

Control.

A few minutes later Josh Collins arrived. She waited until he poured his coffee and settled in for the morning. *He'll have one,* she thought. But he didn't.

"No problem," she said. "It can wait."

"What do you need?"

She decided to go for the truth, as vague as it might be.

"I think I dropped one of my credit cards yesterday. Realized last night when Josie and I were grabbing drinks."

"See. If you'd gone with me, you wouldn't have to worry about paying," he offered.

"Well, it was girl's night out, and when I reached for the check—" she replied dodging his latest advance.

"Next time, though."

"Next time."

"Clay will be in soon. He's already called me twice. In the meantime, I'm glad you're in early. You can join me for a call with our NHexit caucus. It starts in five."

"But…" She wanted to see Lindstrom as soon as he arrived.

"But what?"

"But I'm not prepared," she said.

"Katie, I don't think I've ever worked with anyone more prepared. You'll be fine."

Ten minutes into the call, Katie heard a few staffers say hello to Lindstrom. She straightened in her seat and turned slightly to watch him walk past the bullpen.

Control, she thought again.

Hours earlier, Katie had practiced what to say in front of her bathroom mirror. She repeated it silently in her Uber ride to the office. She determined she'd remain matter of fact with no panic in her voice. He couldn't read any panic. She couldn't let him see anything but relief that her credit card was in his office.

Control

The call wrapped up just shy of thirty minutes. She gathered her notepad and walked out. Clay Lindstrom caught her at the entrance to his office.

"Ms. Novick?"

"Yes," Katie replied with a smile.

"I was just coming to see you."

He held out her MasterCard. "I assume this is yours?"

Lindstrom backed a few feet into his office with the credit card, forcing her to follow.

"Oh my God," she exclaimed breathlessly. "Thank you." She delivered her well-practiced line. "I guess I dropped it yesterday when I came in with all my files. Must have been under everything and—"

"Is that so?" Lindstrom asked.

"Drove me crazy last night. I realized it when Josie and I—"

"Who's Katie Kessler?" Lindstrom interrupted, reading the name on the card.

Shit!

She abandoned her prepared script.

"Actually me. I'm Novick and Kessler. Both," she laughed lightly.

Control was suddenly harder.

"How so? I'd like to know who's working for me and I don't like surprises."

So far he hadn't accused her of breaking in. *I can handle this*, she thought.

"It's Novick now," she said confidently. Used to be Kessler. Well, for a short time."

"Marriage?"

"If you can call it that," she replied thinking, *he said it, I didn't*. "A mistake. The card's left over."

"So now it's Novick?"

"Well, it's Novick again," she repeated.

Katie did not want him to focus on anyone named Katie Kessler. It would end badly…and likely cost Katie her real job. The Supreme Court.

Get back on track, she thought. "Thank you for finding it. It was driving me crazy all night."

Lindstrom stood and glared. "Ms. Novick, to be perfectly honest, I'm not sure you're the best fit for us. What's more, I don't trust you. I can't put my finger on it. Your attitude. Your questions. Your manner."

"I understand, Mr. Lindstrom."

"No, I don't think you do. Take your card. Take it and goodbye."

"But—" She stopped not wanting to give in too quickly.

"Goodbye."

"Mr. Lindstrom. I'm really sorry."

"Goodbye Ms.—" he studied her one more time, "Novick."

"Sir."

"I won't say it again. Leave. For good."

Katie turned, glanced at the Rand McNally map one last time and without another word, returned to her desk, gathered up her few personal items and left. She barely looked at the utterly confused Josh Collins. She prayed it would all end there.

CHAPTER 57

POSITANO, ITALY

"Hey buddy, welcome."

Vinnie D'Angelo gave Roarke a genuine hug when they met at Chez Black, a beachside restaurant known by tourists for its wonderful Mediterranean fish dishes. Not known by tourists was the fact that members of international intelligences services loved the food there too. Another draw? The Mediterranean Sea docks providing fast in-and-out access.

"Been busy?" Roarke asked as they sat.

"Yes, meeting with old chums. Making new ones and figuring out who might not be."

In that one sentence, Roarke gathered D'Angelo had at least met with Ira Wurlin in Jerusalem, he'd talked to other intelligence agencies, and possibly gotten a lead on the assassin's identity.

"Lots to share, but first let's eat," D'Angelo said.

They relaxed and laughed for two hours. Other patrons came and left. It wasn't until the restaurant had cleared out that D'Angelo got back to the point.

"I have a lead." he said.

Roarke was completed engaged. "Figured."

"But I didn't want to knock on the door alone."

"Back up?"

"Something like that."

"Where?"

"Naples. Sorry, you just came from there. But I'm a sucker for the pasta and clams here."

"No argument from me," Roarke said patting his stomach.

"So this door we're knocking on?" Roarke asked. "A friend?"

"Call it a relationship."

"From what I hear, there are two kinds of Naples *relationships.* 'Father or Godfather,'" Roarke said with emphasis on *Godfather.*

"Well, then, I think you understand completely," D'Angelo acknowledged. "A relationship who likes to make sure things don't get out of hand."

"Have they?"

D'Angelo merely looked at Roarke. The answer was obvious.

"I haven't actually met this particular gentleman, but he's quite well known to a certain individual in Israel who's put us together. And the man we're meeting had family, actual family in New York."

"Had?" Roarke asked. "Past tense *had?*"

"Recently past tense. Mother's nephew. His first cousin. A DA in New York. Manhattan District Attorney Alfonso Apicella. Apparently a good guy. You'd be interested to know he had a heart attack. Or at least what doctors believed was a heart attack. Only thirty-nine. At his funeral, the mayor of New York spoke. Said he was a great man with a great future ahead. A great political future."

Roarke fully got the meaning. "And this family member is not happy," he stated more than asked.

"Not at all. He's been following the news and doesn't quite buy the coroner's findings. Given the circumstances, neither do I."

"We," Roarke chimed in. "Definitely we."

THE NEXT AFTERNOON
NAPLES, ITALY

They didn't really have to knock on a door. It was all arranged by the Israeli Mossad chief. They'd meet Salvatore Apicella at *La Bella Sophia Donita,* one of the more than 5,000 restaurants in Italy thought, assumed, or confirmed as mafia owned.

Gastronomy was a perfect way to feed the machine. Money passed freely, much of it cash. Deliveries came every morning. Trash left every night. *Agromafia,* the business of *restaurants,* reportedly brought in more than thirty billion Euros annually. Even that amount couldn't be accurately calculated for obvious reasons. Moreover, the mafia groups had infiltrated Italy's food business up and down the line from food production to trendy bars to restaurant chains.

Crime bosses used extortion to force farmers to sell at low prices and for competing restaurants to buy high. All in all, it was a great underworld investment. The only thing that tended to cause a problem with city officials was a health complaint from a tourist group. Cutting corners in service often meant that a restaurant manager might not be managing anything at all after the complaint.

Salvatore Apicella greeted D'Angelo with a full body embrace. He knew exactly what the CIA operative did for a living. Roarke figured how and why. The same Mossad chief who put them together.

"Signore Apicella, so good to meet you. Thank you for your time."

"We have things to discuss," the Mafia boss said. "Sit and introduce me to your associate."

Salvatore Apicella was in his early seventies and every bit as formidable as when he was a young street lieutenant for his father. He wore a blue shirt with a white collar and a gold tie sprinkled with blue birds. Over it, a $4,000 blue double-breasted jacket with a light blue pocket square and dark gray pants. His leather shoes were probably twice the cost of his jacket.

He had a full head of hair, stylish Italian glasses, and a look that could kill…and had.

"Signore, this is Scott Roarke. He is with the president's Secret Service agency. There is no one I trust more in the world."

"Then I shall trust him, too." Apicella held out his hand. Roarke politely shook it.

"Thank you, Mr. Apicella." Roarke said, keeping his comments short as D'Angelo recommended. He also felt the grip of a man in charge. It was the same handshake the president gave people he meant to intimidate.

A bottle of deep red wine and an antipasto plate arrived as soon as D'Angelo and Roarke sat.

"We shall drink and talk," the Italian insisted.

He poured three glasses. "It's a *Greco di Tufo* from a grape introduced to us by the Greeks more than two thousand years ago. But in the village of Tufo it improved with the area's volcanic soil.

"*Salud!* To good health, a long life for us all." His voice deepened. "And a shorter one for the murderer of my cousin."

Roarke was just as happy to get right to the business at hand. He sat uncomfortably with his back to the door. From his perspective, it was the worse place to sit anywhere, particularly in a mafia restaurant.

Apicella read his discomfort.

"Relax, Mr. Roarke. You are safe here."

"I try never to completely relax."

"Ha! Spoken like a man prepared to take a bullet for your president!"

D'Angelo took control of the conversation.

"Signore, I appreciate your willingness to discuss your cousin's death. You question the circumstances?"

"Of course. You don't?"

"We're here," the CIA operative responded.

The mafia boss continued. Coldly. "Alfonso was killed. He was killed by the assassin you seek."

"How do you know?" Roarke asked.

D'Angelo shot him a cold look.

"Your country's news, Agent Roarke. Have you not come to the same conclusion?"

"Things have been moving very quickly."

"Then it's time for you to move quicker than the events."

"Do you know who the assassin is?" D'Angelo asked directly.

"If I did, he'd be dead now. So, no. But he has unique skills which narrows the number of candidates. I have a list of five."

D'Angelo expected to be given the list. The Mafioso just patted his jacket breast pocket.

"And in order to read your list, Signore?" D'Angelo asked.

"Perhaps I will come up with something later," Apicella laughed. It wasn't a joke. "If he is on this list, you will be doing us all a favor. I hope that is agreeable."

"I'm not in the position to make deals. I am in the position to listen. You want revenge. We can deliver it."

Salvatore Apicella considered the point.

"Well played."

He reached in and removed a folded piece of paper. Apicella slowly slid it across the table to D'Angelo. The CIA agent waited before touching it to see if there'd be any immediate contingencies.

"It's yours to read Vincent."

D'Angelo opened it, read the names, and passed the handwritten paper to Roarke. He perused it and put it on the table face up.

"I'm familiar with three of the names, Signore Apicella. Each were dead ends. Two others are new."

"Make it easier on yourself," Apicella said. "Kill them both."

WASHINGTON, D.C.
THE SAME TIME

Sam Thornburn checked into the Washington Marriott at Metro Center with a smile for the young woman desk clerk.

"We have you for three nights, Mr. Thornburn?"

"Yes," he said, handing over his credit card.

Three nights at the hotel. The next morning, Thornburn and his moustache would disappear. He'd be reborn as Allen Coppersmith and move into a less public environment, a Georgetown Airbnb. In between, he would refresh his memory of the mass transit system, tour Washington to see if traffic patterns had changed, retrieve supplies from a Bethesda storage unit, and wind his way to 610 F Street, NW.

"Is the room available now? I'd love to get settled."

He'd won the desk clerk over.

"You're in luck," she said. "Sixth floor is ready or if you'd like to wait for a higher floor—?"

"Six will be fine."

In fact, Sam Thornburn, a freelance British writer with a winning smile, was anxious to get in and get out. He had to start exploring multiple exfiltration routes.

NAPLES, ITALY

"This man?" D'Angelo asked. "What can you tell us about him?"

The CIA agent pointed to a name on the list. Petoir Dubois. Possibly French, Dutch, or Belgian.

"Why would you choose him between the two?" the Mafioso asked.

"His training." D'Angelo remembered what Wurlin suspected.

"Ah, yes. Well, a very interesting consideration." Then he added, "Considering…"

"What?" Roarke demanded leaning forward. D'Angelo touched his arm. A signal to lay back.

"Little is known about him. It's only a name. Not likely his own. People call him *Le Fantôme*," Apicella said.

"*Le* what?" Roarke asked.

"*Le Fantôme.* The Phantom."

The name resonated with Roarke, but he couldn't quite place it.

"I've never utilized his services," the Italian admitted, "but his reputation precedes him."

"Former French special forces?" D'Angelo asked. The Mossad chief had dropped the suggestion.

"Who can say? He's *Le Fantôme*," Apicella replied.

Another word suddenly came to Scott Roarke.

"A ghost."

"What?" D'Angelo asked.

"People have described the assassin as a ghost; a phantom. He's there and gone. Invisible even to security cameras. If Petoir Dubois is *Le Fantôme*, then I bet *Le Fantôme* could be our man."

Roarke slammed the palm of his hand on the table. The sound immediately drew the attention of Apicella's two bodyguards who stood only feet away behind him. They automatically drew their guns from shoulder holsters. Without even seeing them, Apicella raised his hand. They returned the weapons and regained their stance.

"You bet?" the mobster asked.

"Yes," Roarke replied. "I'm sure you act on bets, Signore Apicella."

"Of course." Apicella laughed loudly. "When I control the odds."

"Well, tell us more about *Le Fantôme* so we can run the table on him."

WASHINGTON, D.C.
THE SAME TIME

Sam Thornburn wore casual bland clothes: A white cotton shirt, faded jeans, and sneakers from Target. All bought with cash. All to be worn one-time only, then discarded. It was a constant waste of money, but another way he erased his appearance. He was a phantom.

He found the Washington subway system easy to navigate, though the CCTV cameras were everywhere. By ducking and weaving he could get lost in the station crowd, but the stops were often far apart, which would allow police time to converge ahead.

Washington's cabs were easy to hail. He could grab a cab, ride, change, ride again, and disappear. He discarded other rideshare possibilities. Tracking was too easy.

The man temporarily known as Thornburn once again determined that the most effective way to remain invisible was to walk. He meandered through parks, up and down streets, and ultimately to F Street, up toward Sixth Street NW. He smiled as he strolled by the International Spy Museum. Maybe one day he'd go in. His destination was ahead. A beautiful modern building fronted by glass, which provided a warm invitation to the inside and two beautiful theaters, the Landsburg and Sidney Harman Hall.

He didn't pause to admire the building. Just a stop to tie his shoes and glance up.

This was the home of Washington's Shakespeare Theatre Company, a renowned facility that featured works of the Bard, his contemporaries, and today's playwrights influenced by Shakespeare.

Over the years, the theater company had presented some two hundred productions for nearly three million patrons. Thornburn was most interested in one upcoming performance. He wouldn't need a ticket. But he was certain he would add to an unforgettable night.

CHAPTER 58

WASHINGTON, D.C.
THE WHITE HOUSE
THAT NIGHT

"It's been quiet for a few days," the president noted. "What do you take that as?"

"Could mean he's on the move or he's finished," replied FBI Director Mulligan.

"According to Roarke, he's not finished," said Taylor. "Finished has an exclamation point at the end. All we have so far are commas and periods."

Mulligan agreed, as did National Security Advisor Dr. Holt Yates.

Morgan Taylor now turned to his CIA director. "Jack, what about your boy D'Angelo?"

"He's following up some leads."

Evans didn't have enough to raise any hopes.

"Something or nothing?" Taylor pressed.

"Something. A part of something. A thing that could lead to a something."

That was pretty much the same report Roarke gave to the president an hour ago. Something.

Taylor was getting impatient.

"Christ!" Yates exclaimed. "Sounds like fucking Donald Rumsfeld-speak."

"Whoa. Don't dismiss what they're onto so fast. Rumsfeld did say there are known knowns, known unknowns, unknown unknowns," Taylor replied.

"Right," the CIA chief explained, "but there's an actual name for the reasoning. It's called *The Johari Window*. It goes back to the mid-1950s. Two American psychologists developed a theory to help people understand their relationship and connection to problems and problem solving. Joseph Luft and Harrington Ingham. Jo and Hari. *The Johari Window*. Rumsfeld picked it up."

"Hold on a minute."

Taylor went to a bookshelf above a credenza and pulled Rumsfeld's memoir; a book with lessons to follow and those to ignore.

He paged through the book and stopped. "Here." The president cleared his throat and read.

"'Reports that say that something hasn't happened are always interesting to me, because as we know, there are known knowns; there are things we know we know. We also know there are known unknowns; that is to say we know there are some things we do not know. But there are also unknown unknowns—the ones we don't know we don't know. And if one looks throughout the history of our country and other free countries, it is the latter category that tend to be the difficult ones.'"

The president closed the book and returned it to the shelf. Walking back, he continued, more sharply, "Time to get beyond unknown unknowns, gentlemen. Let's hope that *something* leads *somewhere* fast." For emphasis Taylor added, "Before the exclamation point!"

CHAPTER 59

WASHINGTON, D.C.
THE NEXT DAY

The annual event was always a highly-anticipated, headline-making Washington sell-out. This year, it would make more headlines. The man currently known as Thornburn would guarantee it.

In a week, the Shakespeare Theatre Company would present a hallmark legal evening; a mock trial born out of one of the season's plays, *It Can't Happen Here*, originally staged in 1936, a year after the publication of the Sinclair Lewis book it was based on.

The case would try a character in the book and play, a newspaperman, for treason, or more relevant to the news, the crime of publishing, in contemporary terms, *fake news*. The principal character would be prosecuted and defended by teams of prominent Beltway attorneys. Chief Justice Leopold Browning and three other Supreme Court justices would adjudicate. The theater audience would vote to determine guilt or innocence.

The event was conceived in 1994 to explore the connection between classical Shakespearean theatre and contemporary law. Since then it had broadened to include works beyond the Bard. It was staged annually in June before a crowd of tuxes and gowns and always delivered an intellectual, raucous, scathing, and scandalous evening.

Thornburn was still working on details that would significantly alter the program. On day two of his Washington stay, the staff was more than willing to give the reporter with a British accent a behind-the-scenes tour for an article he promised to write for *The London Times*. His morning walk-through of the theatre gave him added confidence about his plan.

THE SUPREME COURT
THE SAME TIME

Katie Kessler had only one option. The right one.

"Good morning, Judge Browning," she began. "I need to tender my resignation."

Browning looked up from his paperwork and over his reading glasses.

"Well, pray tell why, Ms. Kessler," he said without a hint of emotion.

"I made a tremendous professional error, and it may put the court at risk," she said.

Browning extended his hand for her to take the seat opposite his desk.

"Counselor, please sit and choose what you decide to share most carefully."

Katie complied and took a deep breath before continuing.

"During my time off, I volunteered for Lucas Burke in Montana."

The chief justice raised an eyebrow, but not his voice. "Go on."

"I wanted to understand the movement and its positions. Instead, I may have put myself and the court in a compromising one."

For the next five minutes, and without comment from Browning, she explained. Katie concluded with a soulful, "I'm sorry."

Browning kept his eyes on her as he had with hundreds of witnesses he faced in court. He read her expression. She was sorry. But *sorry* was something to try with a parking enforcement officer, not the chief justice of the United States Supreme Court.

"You're quite correct, Ms. Kessler. You *have* put us in a potentially compromising position; one that escapes a parallel. Perhaps you belong in the Secret Service with your fiancé."

It was the one remark she wished he hadn't said.

"So it's your intention to resign."

"Yes, sir," Katie replied. She produced a letter from her purse and passed it across the desk.

He read it and placed it face up.

"Thank you for the opportunity to work with you," Kessler said. She lowered her eyes. "I wish it could have been longer."

She quickly recalled her first meeting with Browning. How she talked her way into his brownstone on the eve of the last presidential Inauguration. And how she gave the scariest, most convincing argument of her short legal life.

Now she wondered if she'd ever practice law again.

Browning removed his glasses and studied his legal aide.

"You are, by far, the most impulsive, impetuous, and foolhardy young lawyer to venture forth in Washington in years. You should be on one of my movie posters—an actor playing a brilliant attorney who has just two hours between getting hired and making a case-winning argument. You understand that the law doesn't really work that way?"

"Yes, sir."

"Impulsive," Browning said again. He re-read Katie's letter. She simply wrote, "I hereby resign my position as an associate attorney at the United States Supreme Court effective immediately."

"To the point," he commented. "From the time I first met you, you've always been that."

Under the circumstances Katie wasn't quite sure it was a compliment.

"Sir, I'll gather my things up now."

Katie Kessler rose, not waiting for a final goodbye.

Browning cleared his throat. A deep, intentional sound. She'd heard it before. It was his way of saying she wasn't excused; that there was more to come.

"One moment."

Browning turned to his computer and typed a short internal message. He read it aloud.

"To the Office of Human Affairs. This email will acknowledge that I have accepted the voluntary and immediate resignation of Katie Kessler, Associate Counsels. Her letter to the office of the Chief Justice will be entered into the record. Sincerely, L. Browning."

The words stung, but she held back her tears.

"There," he said. "That seems to do it."

His hand hovered over the ENTER key. Katie saw that he didn't hit send. Not wishing to see this final act to her professional life, she softly asked, "May I please be excused, sir?"

"Not quite yet."

This caught her off balance.

"Sir?"

"As of this moment, and apparently according to your wishes, I could make you a private citizen."

"Correct," Katie said. But she stopped. Browning was always precise. He said *could*. There was a distinction between *could, would*, and *you are*.

"As you know, not many people reach my office, let alone get invited into my home in the dead of the night. Though over your short career as a lawyer, you seemed to have managed both rather convincingly."

"I suppose I have," she said sheepishly.

"A supposition. That's a place we lawyers often start from, wouldn't you say?"

"Yes, sir. In our search for facts."

"And let's just suppose we never met, and you found your way into my house once again."

She permitted herself a smile.

"Just suppose," he continued. "What might you say if I gave you five minutes?"

"Like the first time we met?"

"I suppose," the chief justice said taking his hand away from the computer keys.

MONTANA
THE SAME TIME

Josh Collins left a fifth message on Katie's cell phone.

"Where are you? I've been texting and calling for two days. Please, call me back. I need to know what happened. Lindstrom can be difficult, but I'm sure I can fix things. Call me. We can get together later."

He had no idea she'd quickly packed up, left, and was sitting with the Chief Justice of the United States Supreme Court.

SUPREME COURT
THE SAME TIME

Thoughts flooded Katie's consciousness, but she didn't know exactly where to begin.

"The clock is ticking, counselor. This is your time to make your defense."

"My defense?"

"Four-and-a-half minutes."

"I don't think I understand…"

Katie summoned her courage. She'd been here before.

"The republic, Justice Browning. There's an organized attempt to divide the republic."

"Tell me something new," he said. "Legal arguments."

"I don't have them. But I have my fear. And my fear is that your life is in danger."

"You and Agent Roarke have suggested as much. What does that have to do with your sojourn?"

He tapped his watch.

Katie felt as if she wasn't the lawyer but a defendant.

"A feeling."

"A feeling. That doesn't sound very legal."

"Maybe not, but I can't discount it."

"Then you better find the way to explain it," he chided.

"Sir, there was a map." She talked nonstop for the next four minutes.

PARIS, FRANCE
THE SAME TIME

D'Angelo's contacts at the French intelligence office came through with information on the name the mafia don provided. He left the meeting at the *Direction général de al sécurité extérieure*, the DGSE, France's external intelligence agency with an address outside of Dinan, Brittany. He was told it was unconfirmed, but not completely dismissed. He should, under no circumstances, approach it alone.

Vinnie D'Angelo wouldn't.

"Up for a drive in the country?" the CIA operative asked Roarke when they met up at a bistro in the *20th arrondissement* close to the DGSE offices.

"Always."

"This one might not be smooth going."

"Hasn't been up to now," Roarke replied. "Sounds like we'll need some supplies."

"Yup."

D'Angelo had a friend. The friend had the weapons they needed.

THE SUPREME COURT
THE SAME TIME

Browning bore down with a serious look.

"Now we're getting somewhere. You're trying to tie this secessionist movement to the assassinations across the country."

Katie raised her right hand as if she was feeling something in the air. Then she clenched her fist. Browning watched with interest as she worked out a thought.

In her mind's eye, she saw two maps. One in Lindstrom's office, captured on her cell phone camera. The other in the basement of the White House. On Roarke's wall.

"Yes! Yes, I am," she declared.

The Supreme Court chief justice didn't immediately respond. Katie took it as a cue that she'd failed. She stood again but froze when he cleared his throat.

"Ms. Kessler," he demanded. "Where the hell do you think you're going?"

SIDNEY HARMAN THEATRE
THE SAME TIME

The man with the false ID wrote notes and took pictures of the venue, all with the approval of the theatre public relations executive. Thornburn asked the relevant questions that a reporter would ask. But he saw things that only a trained spy or terrorist would see. Vulnerabilities. Ways that a diversion would drive people toward more danger than away from it. Escape routes. Opportunities.

The chief justice on a theatrical stage. What could be better?

He relished the thought, the resulting coverage, and the impact on his bank account.

Bravo! he allowed. *Bravo.*

THE SUPREME COURT
MINUTES LATER

"You haven't sent your email, Judge Browning," Katie noted after twenty minutes.

He looked at his computer. "Ah, you're right. I haven't."

The chief justice rubbed his chin, an almost acted gesture.

"No, I haven't," he repeated.

"Perhaps it's time for full disclosure, without violating any confidentialities."

He pressed a key, but it was on the upper right of his keyboard. *Delete.*

"I don't understand," she replied.

"I was informed where you were going."

"Who?" she shot back.

"Confidentialities, counselor."

"Scott!" she said angrily.

"I'm not at liberty to say who told me, but once I learned, I made a call myself."

Katie lowered her eyes. She couldn't imagine.

"To the Marshal's office, Ms. Kessler. I do have some influence with our Supreme Court Police."

"And…"

"No cross-examination. Just listen."

Katie leaned back in her chair.

"Under 40 U.S.C. § 6121, the code from which the Supreme Court Police derives its enforcement authority, you became empowered as a member of the Threat Assessment Unit. As you know, the mission of the Supreme Court Police, a U.S. federal law enforcement agency, is to protect the Supreme Court building, the building occupants, the historic building and grounds, dignitary protection, emergency response, and security."

"You didn't."

"I did."

The chief justice called up an email trail and hit print.

"Ms. Kessler, you went to Montana as a special investigator. And you've come back with information. Your next meeting will be with the Attorney General."

"Holy shit!" Katie exclaimed. She immediately apologized for her language.

"I'd recommend a different term, but the expression of appreciation is duly noted." He paused and unexpectedly added, "So is your concern for me."

CHAPTER 60

DINAN, FRANCE
THAT NIGHT

"Can't really talk, hon," Roarke whispered over his earpiece. "I'm a little busy."

Roarke was looking through eight-thousand-dollar Steiner 8x30 Military LRF 1535nm 226 Binoculars. In his sights, a French farmhouse that appeared asleep, if not empty.

"You told Browning what I was doing?" she asked.

"Not exactly."

"Not exactly what?"

"Not *what*," he said. "*Where* was more like it."

"Scott!"

"Katie, I can't talk now. Really."

D'Angelo let out a snicker from the cover of the bushes where they laid low more than two hundred yards from their objective.

"Well, we're going to. Where are you?" she demanded.

"Honestly darling, this is not a good time. Just tell me you're okay."

"I'm okay. Back home," Katie replied. "And…thank you."

"Thank you."

Roarke smiled. "I love you."

D'Angelo smirked hearing only half the conversation.

"I love you more," she said. "Most."

He pressed his earpiece and ended the call.

"Are you through?" D'Angelo asked.

"Oh, shut the fuck up," Roarke whispered good-naturedly. "Back to work."

Work was surveillance. The surveillance was serious. They'd give it more time before going forward.

. . .

Roarke pegged the Frenchman as an early riser. He also believed their subject was far from the quaint Brittany farmhouse.

He and D'Angelo talked about perimeter risks. Cameras. Listening devices. Booby traps.

An hour before dawn they began to slither forward, talking quietly via their voice-actuated walkie talkies. Thirty minutes later they were on their bellies within fifty yards of the house and twenty feet apart.

"Any threats?" D'Angelo asked.

Roarke scanned the target.

"Paint cans and paint brushes. Right out of the napalm handbook."

He focused the binoculars low, along the foundation.

"You?" Roarke asked.

"Checking for pickle jars."

"Getting hungry?"

"No." D'Angelo laughed. "Just seeing if there's anything a lethal concoction could be poured into. Something found locally and ordinary. Attached to a trip wire."

Roarke used his night vision scope to peer inside the house to check for signs of life and any tipoff of impending death: Gasoline-filled soda bottles, thermoses with glycerin ready to mix with chemical potassium permanganate, a pyrotechnic box on top of the refrigerator with fireworks shells attached to black balls.

"Can't see," Roarke whispered. "Doesn't mean it's clean."

"Agreed."

"Might be more passive," D'Angelo proposed. "A silent alarm and web cams hooked up to his cell phone. Ring-ring to Perth Amboy, New Jersey, or whatever Motel 6 he's in. He types in *fuck you#* and boom. So watch out for any fish-line tripwires."

"With every move," Roarke replied. "Hoping now some old French lady's just asleep inside."

D'Angelo focused his binoculars on a particular point. "Check out the mail slot to the right of the front door. Looks like some delivery has gone on. Magazine or a flier sticking out. We could peek in."

"Or it's wired," Roarke replied.

"If it had been, there'd be the telltale signs of mail carrier leftovers and nothing for that thatched roof to sit on."

"Doesn't make me feel any safer."

"No guts, no glory," D'Angelo replied.

"It's the *no guts* part I don't like."

D'Angelo was not foolhardy. "Cover me. I promise I'll be careful."

"Shit," Roarke said. "If you go and get yourself killed I'll really be upset with you. I don't know anyone else I'd trust to partner up with in a business."

"Only thinking of yourself."

"Hey, just do as you said. Be careful."

Roarke focused his own pair of binoculars on the neighboring grounds. "I'd feel a whole lot better with DGSE robots."

"Trust me. I don't have a death wish. I'll call in the reserves, but first one look."

"Too dangerous," Roarke concluded.

"So was Libya, pal," D'Angelo said.

"And Russia," Roarke added.

"My point exactly. We did okay there. We'll do okay here."

"Promise?"

"Cross my heart," D'Angelo said as he slithered forward on all fours covered with leaves and brush.

Roarke never liked that expression.

• • •

D'Angelo wormed forward. Slowly. If this were the assassin's home, he figured it would be hard-wired inside. But outside? *Motion detectors.* He froze.

Deer, coyotes, rabbits. They could trip them all day long to the point of distraction to the assassin. He'd ignore most warnings from any phone interface, unless… *Multiple hits.*

"Roarke, check for solenoids. IR break beam sensors. PIRs. High corners of the cottage. Trees. Low ground. Crawl level."

D'Angelo was trained to approach a target as a threat. Now one inch at a time.

"Roger that," Roarke said. He trained his binoculars on the likely spots. Nothing immediately came into view. Then the unlikely places, as D'Angelo asked. Low approach to where a trained team would advance.

He took his time, adjusting the focus, examining every possible location.

"Bingo," he whispered. Roarke saw a device. He panned his binoculars to D'Angelo.

"Your four o'clock. Right corner. Bottom of the drain pipe."

D'Angelo turned his head back and to the right.

"Got it."

The *it* looked like a distance sensor that employed an invisible laser source. Especially cheap, under fifteen dollars, and especially effective.

It was popularly called Time of Flight because it detects how long light takes to bounce back to the sensor. Good for determining distance in meters of an object directly in front. Very good. Precise.

D'Angelo had strategically used them himself, hoping he'd never get trapped by one, or likely multiple ones aimed to triangulate, communicate, and cooperatively work with explosives.

If he'd walked forward as a mail carrier or other service providers, the assassin would likely give him a pass. But the trap was set for anyone crawling toward the objective.

"And more," Roarke said calling out directions. "Looks like you're not in the field of view. But close. Back out the same way you came in. This is bigger than both of us."

"No argument there, partner," D'Angelo said. "I owe you."

"Hey, it was your idea."

"Right, but you're the one behind a tree."

Vinnie D'Angelo backed up without turning around. Still slowly and carefully. But blindly.

Four feet from point where he stopped, his right foot touched what he thought was a twig. It didn't give. In fact, it bent.

"Shit," he whispered into his comm line.

"What?" Roarke keyed in.

"Just hit something. Feels like an antenna sticking up. Could be a buried seismic sensor. Missed it going forward. But now…"

"I'm coming over to you," Roarke replied.

"No!" D'Angelo insisted.

"Okay, but don't move. Let me look around."

The CIA agent let out a long breath. If there was one sensor, there would likely be more. They were about the size of a small candle. Cylindrical, an inch or so wide with three or four inches underground.

Applying weight was better than stepping on a mine, but only so long as it wasn't hooked up to other devices.

"I see it," Roarke said. "Looks like a Pathfinder antenna. And another, three feet on your right."

"Yup." D'Angelo took a deep breath. "Question for you."

"Go."

"How much would you say an elk weighs?"

Roarke immediately got the question. He pictured their size. "A guess. Only a guess. Three hundred pounds. Probably more."

"A deer?"

"Adult male 250? Three hundred? A female, less. 125 to 150."

D'Angelo considered his options and calculated the time

He figured a signal was already transmitted to a telephone. The Frenchman's phone.

He weighed 233. Too much for a female deer. Too little for a male. One not to full size? Perhaps.

The weight could be calculated as a deer or a man. Both could move quickly. The deer would be standing high and visible on camera. An operative low to the ground. He was low to the ground.

They already concluded that the house was possibly wired to explode. The question now, the size of the blast field.

"Not looking good, Scotty."

D'Angelo had never called Roarke *Scotty*.

"Recommend you back the hell up."

Roarke trained the glass on D'Angelo. He stared deeply into his eyes from thirty yards. D'Angelo nodded once and gave him a *What the hell* shrug.

Then it happened. A flash from the farmhouse, followed by an overwhelming blast of heat and fire that overtook the grounds. Roarke had a fraction of a second himself, to turn and brace behind and against the three billion-year-old boulder that saved his life.

CHAPTER 61

WASHINGTON, D.C.

The Frenchman returned his cell phone to his pocket and returned to his late dinner at La Chaumière on M Street. He hardly paused between bites of his *Scalopines De Veau a La Française,* and certainly didn't feel any distress. His sensors and cameras had alerted him to an intruder. A human intruder, on the ground within his wireless perimeter. He waited to determine whether the sensor was reacting to a deer grazing. It would have been a waste to blow apart his beloved cottage and kill an animal. A four-footed animal. After all, he wasn't even a hunter. Not that kind at least.

Though the weight was similar, three cameras, one infrared, gave him a perfect, transatlantic view of a man crawling on the ground. A man likely trained to recognize he had made a deadly mistake. His last.

A few minutes after pressing a prompt on his iPhone, his waiter came by and asked, "Is everything to your satisfaction, sir?"

"Completely," the assassin replied. "Absolutely delicious."

"May I bring you our dessert menu? Perhaps the *Mouse au Chocolat* with Tia Maria served in a cookie cup, or profiteroles, a house favorite. Then again fruit or cheese plate?"

The Frenchman considered the offerings but declined. "I'll pass on dessert, Robert, but I would like a nice dessert wine. A *Sauternes.*"

"I have just the thing for you. *Chateau Rieussec, Grand Cru Classé.*"

"Wonderful. I've just given up a house I loved. This will be a drink in its honor."

"Very good, monsieur. In honor of your house."

CHAPTER 62

THE DEMOCRATIC PEOPLE'S REPUBLIC OF KOREA
FOURTEEN YEARS EARLIER

"It's a waiting game," the CIA operations officer warned, Jee Gyuen. "You wait for opportunity. You never rush. If you rush, you die. If you die, you're no good to yourself or your country."

Jee Gyuen's country was the United States. He was the son of immigrant South Korean grandparents. A Korean father and Chinese mother. At home his family spoke Korean. Outside, he was instructed to speak perfect English. Similarly, they taught him Korean traditions and the need to honor them, while assimilating into American life.

Two halves of the same person. Two worlds. Now, two names: Gyuen and his birth name, which he hoped to use again.

As a young boy growing up in Newton, Massachusetts, he learned about how his grandfather, Joon Hwang, suffered in a North Korean prison during the Korean War. He served as a scout and a translator for the U.S. Army 7th Infantry. For all intents and purposes, that qualified him as a spy, which cost him dearly when he was captured. The grandson heard grizzly stories of torture, starvation, freezing cold cells, sleep deprivation, and beatings. Daily beatings. It was worse for Koreans working for Americans than even what many American POWs endured.

Joon Hwang was ultimately freed. Part of a trade for high value military captured by the South. But he never walked the same, talked the same, or laughed the same.

The United States gave Joon Hwang and his family passage and a new life in the States. His father met and married another Korean immigrant. They had a son who developed a strong bond with the elder Joon. Night after night, he listened to his grandfather's war stories and was inspired in a way Joon Hwang never expected or would ever know.

Seven years after his death, the grandson filled out an application with the Central Intelligence Agency. His unique understanding of North Korea history, the Korean language, and Korean traditions sped him through the process. Two years later, he completed intense training, and graduated with a new name and the legend to go with it. Jee Gyuen would be the son of an exiled North Korean family living in China who decided to return to the Democratic People's Republic of Korea. That story required immense planning. There had been an actual Jee Gyuen, but he had died in a motorcycle accident while visiting Australia, a fact covered up by ASIS, the Australia Secret Intelligence Service, in cooperation with the CIA. Six months later, a rebirthed Jee Gyuen returned to Jinan in eastern China where he enrolled at Shandong. Two years later, he moved to North Korea with a personal and professional goal.

"You wait, you live. The long game," the operations officer was told by Langley superiors. "You look for people who believe there's more than what the regime offers. You befriend them. Test them. Mentor them. Most will complain quietly but never take a real step toward engagement. Every once in a while, someone will. But it may take years for them to mature. Both in age and in responsibility. That's the person you want; the person we need you to find. It takes years. The long game."

Now nine years later, Jee Gyuen's original operations officer was the director of the Central Intelligence Agency. Jack Evans thought about his charge every day. He wished he could pull him out of North Korea now, but his assignment was far too important. Jee Gyuen had cultivated a mole inside the North Korean navy. Chin-wah Lee. Under the circumstances, he might very well be America's most valuable asset.

One day, perhaps soon, Evans would have to get them both out.

CHAPTER 63

FORT WAYNE, INDIANA
PRESENT DAY

"We are more than a movement. We are an active force. In twenty-seven states. And now, thanks to you, the good people of Indiana, make that twenty-eight!"

Clay Lindstrom stood at the back of the 3,500-seat auditorium wearing a satisfied look. Lucas Burke was covering all the points without notes, without a teleprompter. Once again, he was proving himself a natural; a valuable player in a complicated game.

Lindstrom strolled down the center aisle and examined the faces. Engaged, enthralled, devoted. He liked what he saw. They reminded him of the looks he'd seen while preparing for this endeavor two years prior. For research, he'd enrolled in self-help guru sessions. There, he saw convention rooms filled with faithful followers who sought an absolute; a directive they could take to heart. He witnessed great showmanship and powerful messaging so effectively communicated that true believers would walk across hot coals to demonstrate their commitment.

Clay Lindstrom had the message. He found his communicator in Lucas Burke.

"I'm thinking," Lucas continued, "that we're at a crossroads. To the left you see a sign that says freeway ahead, speed limit, seventy miles per hour. It's an open road that'll drive you off into the sunset. Not bad. Familiar, comfortable. Perfect for cruise control.

"But to the right," he continued, "another choice. Signs there, too. One indicating a bumpy road with potholes. The speed limit is thirty-five. You strain and see another road sign warning about twists and turns. And the road itself goes uphill. But it looks like the sun is rising over that peak. Rising, not setting."

Lucas had everyone enraptured by his delivery and his story.

"Which road do you take?" he asked rhetorically. "Left or right?"

Everyone remained silent.

"Until recently, I would have gone left. Automatically. Without hesitation. Clear sailing. A nice ride off into the sunset. It looked great. Today? Today, I'm thinking the bumpy road with all the dangers offers more promise. Sure, it's a slow uphill route, but that sun is rising on a new day. Our day, my friends. And once we're at the top, what a view! A view of the future. Free of federal laws. Free of unwanted taxes. Free of foreign wars.

"What's the Indiana motto?" Lucas asked, summoning the growing emotion in the room.

A man yelled from the middle of the auditorium.

"Crossroads of America!"

Lindstrom had timed his walk to the exact row where his paid plant called out the reply. He smiled and scanned the room.

"Absolutely right. The Crossroads of America!"

"What's your name?" Lucas called out.

"Robby Allen," the man yelled back.

"Where you from Robby?"

"Fort Wayne, sir. About ten blocks from here, but ready to go all the way to win with you!"

Lindstrom thought Allen had more than earned his hundred dollars. Now it was time for him to shut up. He wanted to get a cue to Burke to move on, but Burke felt it himself.

"Well, thank you, Robby. Great to have you along."

Burke raised his voice. "And it's great to have all of you here. You've been the crossroads of America all the way back to the eighteen hundreds. The Cumberland Road, now I-40. Railroads that transported people, food, and supplies. The crossroads. Well, here you are again. Now, the crossroads between the past and the future. The continuation of Washington's domination and the beginning of your independence.

"Imagine, the country of Indiana!"

Cheers erupted, and Burke waited.

"A full trading partner with the New Northwest Front and the Southwest Republic."

Applause and cheers. Longer.

"Diplomatic and commercial relationships with The Republic of California. Vermont/New Hampshire."

Even more sustained cheers. A full two minutes.

"They'll all be in business with you. So will a smaller, more manageable, more modern United States."

A round of "Yes! Yes! Yes!" followed. And cheers. And everybody was on their feet yelling and stamping their feet to the rhythm of the chant.

Lindstrom reflected on how far they'd come. Votes on secessions were scheduled in eleven states. More would follow.

The wave of assassinations had accelerated the rate that voters were becoming engaged. Far quicker than Lindstrom had ever considered. He imagined how pleased his old school friend would be.

Of course, Lindstrom also realized that the very question of a state seceding would be bogged down in District, and ultimately, the Supreme Court. But the idea wasn't just to win, though he had a team of Washington attorneys dedicated to keeping lawyers arguing the point in the courts for years. It was to turn up the heat on the ensuing chaos that would further weaken American society. It was the further splintering of a united country, not just by growing gulfs between Republicans and Democrats and conservatives and liberals, but to create the tectonic disruption of trust and faith in the American way of life.

It was working.

Representative officials weren't showing up for their jobs. Worse, many were resigning. On a local level, it was already affecting social services and courts. On a national scale, Lindstrom had watched Morgan Taylor's press conferences with delight. Nothing the president said seemed to matter.

Taylor called for calm on Wall Street. The market wasn't buying it. And the press—large to small—from the *New York Times* to Arizona's *Casa Grande Dispatch*, and cable news channels on either side of the political spectrum were reporting the sentiment of their readers and viewers. If the federal government wasn't able to protect America, then it was time to rely on the states, or reformed regional constituencies.

Disharmony. Disunion. Dissolution. Lindstrom had collaborated on creating a perfect storm and political winds were blowing against the establishment.

A movement and a well-placed assassin. Simple. Elegant. Effective.

Soon, Lindstrom would cash out and travel; money never an issue again. And Burke? Lindstrom smiled to himself and thought he could do whatever the hell he wanted. Run for some real office or hide if he ever figured out what had really happened.

Clay Lindstrom thought of a proverb his friend had taught him in Switzerland. He practiced it in Korean but never really got the pronunciation down. It still resonated in English.

"While the cow is tied up to the tree,

take advantage of the opportunity to cut off its horns."

That's what he was doing. He could hear cheering.

It took another full minute before the crowd quieted. Lindstrom watched as Burke seized the moment again.

"Hey, forget the Crossroads. Become the center of North American enterprise. Secede and succeed," Lucas shouted. "Got it? Secede and succeed. Secede and succeed!"

Lindstrom turned to the stage. He hadn't heard the phrase before. Burke was off script, but with a winning slogan. He heard it again from his political marionette. And he liked it.

"Secede and succeed!"

The crowd picked up the chant.

"Secede and succeed! Secede and succeed!"

Ten minutes of ever-louder "Secede and succeed."

Lindstrom roamed the auditorium and texted his Montana office with instructions to rush order 50,000 pins with the slogan. "I want a blue background, a white star with big red letters: Secede and Succeed."

"Secede and succeed!" It sounded good to Burke. It sounded even better to Lindstrom. And when the Supreme Leader of North Korea saw the broadcast on his satellite downlink of CNN International, it sounded great.

CHAPTER 64

WASHINGTON, D.C.
THE WHITE HOUSE

Morgan Taylor watched as press secretary Joe Poppiti fielded reporters' questions live on TV. Poppiti did the best he could. But his brief answers conveyed the frustration the administration was experiencing.

"The FBI is following every lead."

"No, we don't have evidence of a foreign power behind them."

"Yes, our allies are aware they could be similarly attacked."

"Of course, the president is monitoring Wall Street."

Other responses from the forty-seven-year-old former *Washington Post* political editor had more substance.

"FBI Director Mulligan has told the president that the agency is searching for a lone assassin. To date, each of the arrests are the work of copycats, headline-seekers, or angry, misguided individuals encouraged by what they've seen. Rest assured, they will be prosecuted to the full extent of the law. Meanwhile, the bureau's principal subject is still at large."

Taylor saw Washington gulp. He had misspoken. Misspoken badly.

This answer resulted in a dozen hands shooting straight up. The press secretary picked veteran TV reporter Michele Bailey.

"Joe, the FBI has a principal subject? We haven't heard that before. What can you tell us?"

"To be clear, there is no principal subject. I should say the FBI is always trying to narrow the field. Beyond that, I can't say."

"Can't or won't, Joe?"

"Can't. I don't know. Let me correct that. We don't know."

He didn't. But President Morgan Taylor was about to find out.

"Scott's on the phone for you, Mr. President. From France."

"Thank you, Louise."

"Sir…"

"Yes?" he said to his long-time assistant Louise Swingle, noting some concern.

"He sounds distraught."

"Thank you. Ask Bernsie to join me. But you can put the call through now."

A minute later, Bernie Bernstein approached the president's desk. Taylor gestured for his chief of staff to sit.

Bernsie watched and realized something was terribly wrong. The president shook his head. His eyes teared up.

Finally he responded. "Scott, you're going on speaker. Bernsie's here. Can you please start over?"

Bernsie heard a deep sigh.

"Mr. Bernstein…as I told the president, I'm in France, outside a town in Brittany. Vincent D'Angelo and I were surveilling a target's house…"

Roarke's voice cracked. Bernsie completed the horrible thought in his mind and turned away.

"Oh God," he whispered, sensing what was to come.

"We acted on a tip from the DSGE and another source I can't go into now. The grounds were booby trapped. Vinnie…"

No one spoke. No one could.

"Scott," the president began only after the long pause, "I'm so sorry. I know you two were very close."

"Yes, sir."

Roarke rarely employed *sir* with the president.

"Like brothers. We'd been talking about starting a business together soon."

"I didn't know," Taylor intoned.

"It was just talk…"

Taylor waited a moment. He had real questions to ask but didn't want to rush Roarke.

"Scott, this target. Is he our man?"

"He is."

"I'll need you to provide details to the DNI, Director Evans and Mulligan so we can get him."

"I'll tell them what I know. They can get details from French intelligence. I've got my own work to do. Can Louise get me a flight out of here and arrange for Vinnie?"

"Yes, but Scott, let the bureau do its job now. Just come home."

"With all due respect, this is my job, and I'm going to kill this fucker."

THE SAME TIME

Katie approached the security post at White House West Wing. Her own Supreme Court credentials proved her identity to the Marine sentries, but she was not on the admit list. She noted that four Marines guarded the entrance to this side of the White House, also known as the Executive Office Building. Four meant that the president was present.

"I'm sorry, Ms. Kessler. We haven't been notified about your visit."

"Sorry," she said. "Give me a moment."

Katie backed away, removed her cell phone, and dialed a number by memory. A direct number that few people had. It rang four times.

"Louise, hi, it's Katie Kessler."

"Katie, so good to hear from you."

Louise Swingle was always pleasant. She liked Katie a great deal and hoped that she and Roarke would last.

"What's up?"

"I know Scott's not in…"

No response. Neither a confirmation nor a denial. She couldn't provide any specific information, not even for Katie.

"…but I'm outside the West Wing and need clearance. I have to check something in Scott's office."

"I'll call you back if there's a problem, dear."

"Okay."

The delay was not unexpected to Katie. Louise had a number of calls to make. First to the West Wing Marine post to confirm she was there and alone. Then to Scott to register his approval. Even though Katie had been a special White House attorney, she no longer was. Her old job did not give her the right to enter now.

As Katie shifted her weight from one foot to the other, she felt her phone vibrate as she thought it might.

Roarke sent her a simple text message. A question mark.

She typed quickly and cryptically.

Outside yr work. Thinking about where u put those pins. Love a look?

Katie hoped he'd understand. It took a while. Then a two-letter response:

kk

There was nothing else. No x's and o's. No happy-face sign. No suggestion of where he was or what he'd been doing. She hadn't talked to him since their short conversation the night before. Obviously, this was all she was going to get.

Two minutes later, the Marine guard who had been holding onto her court identification reapproached. He had a pass in his hand that had come through the Oval Office.

"Ms. Kessler, you'll be good to go as soon as we give your things a scan."

"Thank you," she said, thinking more about Scott and what was wrong.

• • •

Roarke's conversation with Louise included permission to open his office for Katie. A member of the Secret Service was present when she got there.

"Good evening, Ms. Kessler. I understand you'd like to go in."

"Yes, Chyna." She knew the agent well. "Thanks."

"Good to see you again. I'll be just outside if you need anything," the thirty-three-year-old slim Secret Service agent said. "Any idea how long you'll need?"

"Not sure. You don't have to hang around."

Chyna Ludwig laughed lightly. She did. She kept the door open to Roarke's spartan basement office, stood at the doorframe, straightened her black two-piece suit, and reported to her supervisor via her wireless.

Katie entered slowly. She had a single-minded objective: To closely examine the map, actually the maps, Scott had been working on.

She entered and flicked on the light. She slowly looked around the room, smiling when she focused on his desk; remembering when they had made love. The rest of the area held memories of political, legal, and personal conversations they'd had over the past eighteen months. Now she felt, as Roarke did, that if there were answers for this new crisis, they would be here.

Katie faced the corner behind and to the side of his standard-issue metal desk. That's where Roarke had taped up ten Classic Edition Rand McNally maps of the United States. Each had red dots in the same spots—locations where public officials had been killed. The difference among them was the way Roarke had drawn lines between the dots.

Some of the lines suggested letters. Others formed geometric shapes. Nothing revealed anything definitive.

But Katie wasn't interested in just looking at the maps. She stepped forward, reached out, and touched the map with her eyes closed.

Now to put herself back in Lindstrom's office, to when she ran her hand across his map. To what she felt. To what she thought.

She started on the upper right, in New England. She found the first dot with her index and middle finger. She slid her hand down finding another dot a few inches down, then another, and two more.

Katie opened her eyes. Roarke had drawn a thin black line connecting each of them. The dots were exactly where she had remembered pinholes in Lindstrom's map.

She did the same on the left side of the map, from the northwest, through part of central California. Then she passed her palm across the southwest, feeling more dots.

Next, Katie opened her cellphone photo app. She'd taken wide shots of Lindstrom's map. But to her eye, they didn't show any detail. Frustrated, she scrolled to the single tight picture she'd gotten off. She expanded the size and panned across the area that covered part of Colorado and South Dakota. "Nothing…nothing…nothing," she whispered. Suddenly Katie stopped. *Something*. It appeared to be a small pin prick in Colorado. Directly through the name Grand Junction. She looked up at Scott's map again. Down to her phone. Then up again. Then she put the photo directly next to Grand Junction, Colorado on the Rand McNally map.

"Christ!" she exclaimed.

The Secret Service agent stepped in and observed Katie standing in front of the wall of maps. "Everything okay?"

"Oh yes!"

"Just checking."

Katie was lost in thought. She needed to calm down.

"I'm going to be a while," she told the agent.

"Not a problem. Anything you need?"

Katie considered the offer. "As a matter of fact—"

She asked for more United States maps.

• • •

While she waited, Katie texted Roarke a simple:

Coming home?

His reply:

Soon. One stop first. Check with LS.

Obviously he couldn't, or wouldn't communicate more. So Katie dialed LS.

"Louise, Katie."

The president's secretary caught the urgency in Kessler's voice. "Working out okay downstairs?"

"Yes, thanks. But where's Scott? I'm worried."

"On the road."

"I know that. Is he okay?" Katie implored.

Swingle hesitated.

"Come on Louise! He just texted me to check with you."

"I'm sorry, I really don't know anything."

"Have you talked to him? Please."

"Yes. Only briefly. He needed to speak with President Taylor." She paused again. "And he sounded different."

"How different?"

Swingle struggled for the right word. After a moment it came to her. "Sad."

CHAPTER 65

PARIS, FRANCE

First, Scott Roarke endured a *Who the hell are you and what the hell were you doing there?* barrage from local cops. Roarke used his lack of French and a real sense of confusion to stall until someone at his level pulled him out. That came three hours into questioning when French Secret Service swooped in to take him to a debriefing in Paris.

Francois LeLouch lifted his eyes from his paperwork when Roarke entered. He was immaculately clothed in a blue tailored Givenchy suit from Jecenko, one of Paris's best men's shops. The sixty-eight-year-old lanky foreign spy had come out of the cold at the end of the Cold War to take an office job at France's equivalent to the CIA. Now decades later, gray and weathered, he headed the DGSE, the General Directorate for External Security. LeLouch was director of France's equivalent of the CIA.

"Mr. Roarke, I'm tremendously sorry for your loss," LeLouch offered. "Director Evans tells me you were very close."

"Yes, like brothers."

LeLouch offered his hand. "Doubly terrible."

"Thank you, Director-General."

LeLouch walked him to one of two chairs facing his desk. Roarke took one, expecting the spy chief to walk around and sit at his desk. He didn't. Instead, he sat next to Roarke; reinforcing his concern.

"You want to know more about the subject," LeLouch said.

"I want to know everything."

"I understand. I will share what I have. I've just reviewed his file. A copy is being transmitted to Director Evans. We don't have a lot. He is, as they say, *Le Fantôme*. We believe his given name is Henri Brouchand. He was killed fighting in Libya during the fall of Gaddafi."

• • •

Le Fantôme worked alone, but he had a network of contacts in France. They weren't employees, but they were enriched by the intelligence they shared. DGSE researcher Padrig Gilardi was one of them, recruited three years earlier over coffee and cash.

The thirty-four-year-old intelligence officer casually slipped out of the three-sided DGSE headquarters in the 20th arrondissement while Roarke and the Director-General spoke. He briskly walked to *Bibliothèque Mortier*, the nearby library, and used one of the computers publicly available to post a message to *a friend* on Facebook. It was an internet friend; the one who paid for the coffee and given him that first envelope. He cryptically communicated news of the meeting currently taking place at the DGSE and the identity of the visitor. He figured it should be worth another five thousand Euros.

• • •

Roarke sat upright.

"Dead?"

"Well, in a matter of speaking," the DGSE chief replied. "He came to us from Special Forces. We needed someone for a complicated assignment. First he had to die. It was arranged. Then he changed the arrangements."

Roarke appeared confused.

"For the sake of a cover?"

"Precisely, Agent Roarke. He had to go completely off the grid. Suffice it to say, Brouchand saw greater opportunity for himself if he was dead. We had to acknowledge his death, and in the process, he reinvented himself as a killer-for-hire using dozens of aliases. The latest one you discovered."

"You created *Le Fantôme*," Roarke declared.

"I'm afraid we did. We trained him. He excelled, and then he went commercial. We only managed to follow him after the fact. After many facts. His kills. He'd strike and disappear. Strike and disappear. We recognized his style, but we've never gotten ahead of him. Over the years, he's become more efficient. More lethal. Always learning. We recently suspected he was busy in America."

"And you didn't share that information," Roarke complained incredulously.

"Suspected. Only suspected. More convinced now that you got lucky and found the farmhouse."

Roarke reacted sharply. "*Lucky?* My friend is dead. A dedicated officer is dead."

LeLouch paused. "*Excusez-moi.* Such a poor choice of words. I'm sorry again."

"Go on," Roarke said.

"His reputation grew, and his price increased."

"So did his bravado if he was willing to live so openly," Roarke observed.

"With obvious care and likely only for a limited time. With investigation we hope to identify other residences."

"Any photographs?"

LeLouch reached for a file on his desk and removed a service picture of Henri Brouchand. He handed it to Roarke.

"How old?"

"Fifteen years."

"Any more?"

"There were. All gone. Apparently his money has also mattered to some people in-house. We're investigating."

"And beyond here?"

"Special forces. Same problem. He's very good."

The DGSE Director-General noted the way Roarke's eyes narrowed.

"I imagine much like you, Agent Roarke."

. . .

With an old photograph in hand and nothing more to accomplish in Paris, Roarke left for his flight home. He studied the picture of Henri Brouchand, *Le Fantôme*.

Tall. Chiseled body. Square chin. Dark, intense eyes. Short black hair. Ears tight in. No visible scars, but the photograph was old. He envisioned an older version of Brouchand and knew that Touch Parsons would be able to extrapolate for him. Using his iPhone scan app, he made a copy, uploaded it and emailed it to the FBI Photo Recognition expert with a simple note.

Plus him 15.

He hit send, certain Parsons would understand.

Le Fantôme was an expert. And now, thanks to the killer's professionalism, Roarke was going back to D.C. feeling empty and alone.

The White House bumped Roarke up to Business Class on his midday flight. It could have been the middle of the night. All the shades were drawn. He put his seat back into full recline and closed his eyes. But Scott Roarke didn't sleep. He thought about the Frenchman's next steps and returned to an overwhelming concern: The line on the map that went through the nation's capital.

He didn't know that Katie Kessler was thinking the same thing.

CHAPTER 66

WASHINGTON, D.C.
KATIE'S APARTMENT
LATE AFTERNOON

Katie met Roarke at the door with a long, heartfelt hug that began with just one word whispered in her ear. "Vinnie." And with that she fully understood.

She led him into her living room where they sat on the couch and cried together. She held him in her arms, stroked his head, and rocked him gently. Little by little he explained what had happened. And his guilt. The sense that he'd failed. Worse. He failed his friend. But as he replayed Vinnie D'Angelo's final moments, his voice changed; his body stiffened. Roarke pulled away and stared ahead with a cold expression. It came from a deep hateful place. Katie had seen it before when she was threatened by an assailant.

Revenge.

ROARKE'S OFFICE
THE NEXT MORNING

The White House kitchen brought Roarke and Katie french toast, bacon, and scrambled eggs. More than either could have eaten had they been hungry. But they weren't. Roarke was eager to get back to his maps. He was convinced it was the way to get to the assassin. Katie had her own agenda. She walked between him and the wall.

"Before you get started, let me show you what I've been working on," she said enthusiastically. "It might make up for you being upset with me for doing such a bonehead thing as going to Montana."

"It might."

"It will. I promise."

She led Roarke to the opposite wall where she'd drawn designs on more than thirty sheets of white copy paper.

"Take a look at these. I got creative."

Most were her representations of the map lines Roarke had made. Some looked like the letters S, T, E, M, O, and I. Others, numbers.

"I thought they were easier to read this way than off the maps."

"Sure, but why."

"Well, I had a *feeling*."

She rubbed her thumb and index finger together, went to one of his maps, and traced her hand across.

Roarke watched her, not understanding.

"The feeling," she said, "was mutual. A map in Montana and yours here."

Katie explained.

Roarke was astounded by the multiple connections his fiancée had made: Simple holes in Clay Lindstrom's map that represented where tacks had been inserted, then removed. Locations that matched up with Roarke's research. Locales where officials had been assassinated. An accidental discovery that in her mind linked the movement with the killer.

Roarke put his hand over hers as she traced the map one more time.

"I felt them, Scott. I took a mental picture of what I'd seen here." Reaching for her phone she added, "Then photos on my cell."

She showed him the pictures, wide and tight, and how the close up shot of Grand Junction revealed a small hole in the map.

"Forward all of them to me. If anyone can pick out more it's Touch Parsons."

As she did, Katie added one more thing. "It was scary, Scott. I was so glad to get out of there."

She almost added, *Alive.*

A MILE AWAY
THE SAME TIME

Le Fantôme sat on the bed in his Georgetown Airbnb. On his lap, a yellow pad with a rough hand drawn schematic; a high view of a large area, sketched with squares and rectangles representing things in the space.

To his right, a pamphlet opened to a photograph of a theater which matched up to his sketch. He compared his drawing to the photo. He was pleased with his work.

The pamphlet was from the Washington, D.C., Shakespeare Company. The picture showed a production on the Harman Theatre stage.

The Frenchman thought for a moment, then made a notation on the sketch. He circled an area at the back of the theatre; then he perused photos of the theater he'd taken on his iPhone; the same cell phone he had used to trigger the explosion at his house.

He scrolled through a number of pictures and stopped on one that showed the control room at the opposite end of the theatre. He made the image bigger and leaned back against the wall. "Maybe," he said quietly. But he had other options to explore at Sidney Harman stage at Washington, D.C.'s Shakespeare Theatre Company.

ROARKE'S OFFICE
THE SAME TIME

"So here's what I did. I focused on any patterns the lines made. Like a Rorschach Test. Kind of depends on how you look at it. What you see into it."

Roarke liked where she was going. She'd even transferred them to 8½ by 11 printer paper, arrayed in six rows across and five down. Easier to view.

"I tried lots of combinations," she explained. "There are probably a lot more when numbers turn into letters, and vice versa. Things combine to make abbreviations. Maybe there's even a math solution."

"Or none at all," Roarke added.

"Or none at all," she repeated. "I'd hoped something would come up positive. But nothing. Even when I tried playing with the first letter of every city to see if it would spell anything. Not much I could do without enough vowels."

Roarke laughed. It was the first he'd laughed in days.

"Like you said. Rorschach. Let's keep looking."

They went through them row by row, sometimes getting close to formulating an opinion, then abandoning it. But in each case that looked good, the line went through Washington. That alone kept Roarke convinced there was a pattern.

"There's more I haven't put up," Katie said when they finished with the wall. "But they don't even seem to represent anything. Just designs."

Roarke gestured, *be my guest.*

She spread out five papers on his desk.

ILT1	QOI	SHI	1111	611
O	OC	__C	OSH	43

Nothing jumped out.

"Thanks for trying, honey," Roarke said. "I should have sent this puzzle over to Langley weeks ago. If I had, Vinnie would still be…"

"You don't know that," she said softly. "But you're probably right. There's nothing here."

Katie wiped her own tears. Roarke nodded knowingly. It was going to take time.

LE FANTÔME'S APARTMENT
THE SAME TIME

The Frenchman methodically ripped up his notes into increasingly smaller pieces and in a series of three toilet flushes, the evidence of the plan he decided on disappeared.

He'd figured out what he wanted to do, how he'd do it, and how he'd escape. If he couldn't come up with an escape, he wouldn't proceed. But he did, and it was elegant.

Other than money, he had no personal stake in the mission. He'd already determined this would be his last target. Considering what happened in France and the follow up message he received, this would do it. One and out.

As the last of the pieces circled the toilet, he thought about the private jet he had already booked out of the United States. The Bahamas, then Jamaica, Mexico City, Havana, Madrid, and ultimately onto a small, completely secure villa in Santorini, Greece. Six identities. Six passports. And then a new, quieter life.

ROARKE'S OFFICE
THE SAME TIME

Roarke leaned across his desk to turn off a lamp. As he did, he glanced at one sheet of paper covered in part by another. More of Katie's work that hadn't made the wall. What caught his eye was a drawing that looked like it was part of a house. A roof.

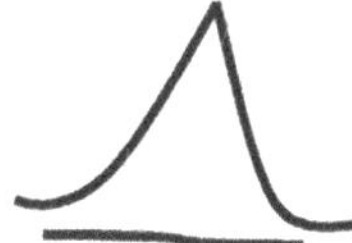

"What's this?" he asked.

"One of my discards. Just scribbles."

The scribbles reminded him of the farmhouse in France. He took a deep breath and was about to walk away, but he moved aside another paper that covered more of the design.

Now it wasn't so much a roof, but a symbol balancing on a circle to the left, and on the right, another drawing that appeared to be a backwards "S" which connected to a small letter "l" or the number "1."

"Katie, do you have the map you drew this from?"

"Sure. On the table at the center of the room. Buried somewhere in there. I'll find it."

She leafed through the stack and extracted the map with the drawing Roarke now held in his hand.

"Here," she said.

Roarke grabbed six thumbtacks and moved a bookcase out of the way. He took the map over to the dry wall and stretched it out. While he held it, Katie pushed the tacks into each of the four corners, and another center top and center bottom. Then he stepped back.

"What do you see?" she asked.

Roarke traced the lines with his fingers.

"Doesn't say anything to me," Katie commented.

He smiled. "You're right. It doesn't. In English."

Roarke stepped back and repeated the thought. "In English." Then he reached for the office phone and punched in a series of numbers, never taking his eyes off the map.

"Louise, it's Scott. I need a favor fast."

Katie watched with heightened interest.

"Find me someone in the building who reads Korean!"

CHAPTER 67

WASHINGTON, D.C.
THE WHITE HOUSE

"Korean," Roarke said. "Korean." His smile grew wider.

"How do you know?" Katie asked.

"My Taekwondo in LA. I picked up some words. Could never write it, but I recognize the characters. These are definitely Korean characters. And depending upon what they say—"

A knock at the door interrupted him.

Roarke crossed the room and opened the door wide. Two people stood at the entrance. The Secret Service agent who had previously accompanied Katie down and a young man who looked like he'd just graduated from college yesterday.

"Agent Roarke?" he said nervously.

"Yes." Roarke flashed a nod to the other agent that all was okay.

"I got a call to come."

"What's your name?"

"Redding. George Redding." He fumbled with the ID he wore on a lanyard.

"What do you do, Mr. Redding?"

"I'm an analyst for State, the Asia division. I was over for a meeting."

"How long have you been with the team?"

"Well, counting today?"

Roarke laughed.

"Counting today."

"Four days, sir."

"And before that?"

Redding looked around the room and noticed Katie for the first time. She smiled but didn't introduce herself.

"I interned at the department. Graduated Georgetown this spring. I'm an FP-06. A roving administrative assistant."

FP-06 was a low level designation in the U.S. Foreign Service, with the *P* standing for *probationary*. If things went well tonight, Redding might move up a few notches.

"Well then, Mr. Redding, welcome to the basement where real things get done."

Roarke indicated that the Secret Service agent could leave.

"Yes, sir. Someone's assistant found me and said—"

"That assistant's name is Louise Swingle. Do you know who she is?"

"No, sir."

"She's the gate keeper. President Morgan Taylor's assistant, Mr. Redding. So right now, you're working for the president, and what you're about to evaluate is absolutely top secret."

Redding gulped hard.

"Do you have security clearance?"

He stumbled over his response. "Sort of."

"We'll work on that later. But from here on out, you're not to talk about this with anyone. Not your girlfriend or boyfriend, mother or father. It doesn't make your memoirs thirty years from now. Am I clear?"

"Yes, sir. Absolutely. Yes."

Redding paused. "Is it okay if I ask who you are?"

Roarke laughed. "Of course. I'm Scott Roarke. Secret Service like the agent who brought you down here. And Katie Kessler is an attorney with the Supreme Court."

"Thank you," he replied with another gulp.

"All right then." Roarke walked the young man to the map on the wall. "Take a look, Mr. Redding. Tell us what you see."

George Redding studied Katie's designs.

"Take your time."

"Thanks, but I have it."

"You have what?"

"The Korean. You needed someone who reads Korean. That's what I do. I'm fluent. This is clearly Korean."

Katie stepped forward excitedly.

"What's it say?"

She put her hand on his shoulder.

"Well it translates into a few words, but they're all relatable."

"They are…?" Roarke prodded.

Redding drew the characters in the air as if to confirm his supposition.

"Do you have a sharpie and paper?"

Katie found a thick black marker on Roarke's desk and a blank sheet paper. She handed it to Redding.

Redding drew the characters with his back to Roarke and Katie. Then he held it up to the left of the map to compare.

"It's pronounced as *suen-gni*."

"Which means?" Roarke asked.

"It can be translated a number of ways. The most specific?"

"Yes."

"*Triumph, win.* To another degree, *overthrow* or *conquest.* Probably the best definition in English would be *victory.*"

Roarke's eyes widened as he let out a long breath.

"Of course, it depends upon the context," Redding said. "Do you know the context?"

Roarke didn't speak. Katie did.

"Yes, he does, Mr. Redding. Yes, he does."

CHAPTER 68

MINNEAPOLIS CONVENTION CENTER
THE SAME TIME

Clay Lindstrom liked everything he saw. Burke's speech, the size of the crowd, even the sales on buttons, hats, and t-shirts at the merchandising tables.

"You can turn up the heat more," Lindstrom had told Burke on the plane ride. "People are afraid. They're losing confidence in the system. You can allay those fears, Lucas. You hold the answer."

Burke ate it up. The fact of the matter was that he'd proven himself far better than Lindstrom had ever hoped. In the last month alone, they'd added eight million signatures to state petitions. Secession was going to be on more ballots in November. And in a week, it was coming to an even earlier vote in Oregon. The first test state. One they could win.

Lindstrom watched his man on the jumbotron screen. Burke stepped back from the microphone on an applause line. He removed his sports coat and draped it across the stool. Walking forward, he loosened his blue and gold striped tie. It brought the reactions Lindstrom intended. Some hoots and whistles. Burke smiled and returned to the microphone.

"So what's it going to be?" he shouted. "The old way or the new way?"

"The new way!" the crowd screamed back.

"What do we want? Regulation or independence?"

"Independence!"

This last line, changed for each city, always worked.

Here it was Minneapolis.

"Washington or Minneapolis?" Burke yelled out.

"Minneapolis!"

"I can't hear you," he said putting his hand to his ear.

"Minneapolis!"

"I can't quite hear you!"

"Minneapolis! Minneapolis! Minneapolis!"

The speech went on for another twenty minutes. High energy moments and quiet moments. At the podium microphone and walking into the audience with his wireless.

Lucas Burke had this audience in the palm of his hands, like the others he'd whipped up. He was leading a movement, but so far with no real personal endgame…until tonight.

Burke relaxed and let the audience cheer more. The reaction continued for another thirty seconds. Then he dramatically raised his hands high, then lowered them. The room fell completely silent. There wasn't even a cough.

Now, Lindstrom thought from the rear of the hall.

Now, Lucas Burke said to himself as he stepped forward. *Time to make it all count.*

"There's been a buzz that I had an important announcement to make tonight!"

"Run for president!" a man shouted some twenty rows back.

Burke smiled.

Another yelled the same thing, and then another and another, until the entire crowd began a precise chant.

"Pres-i-dent! Pres-i-dent! Pres-i-dent!"

Burke showered in the adulation. The reaction was off script and well before the true applause lines. Still, he loved it.

But the moment was beyond what Lindstrom had planned. Burke had to wrest control of the crowd. Lindstrom walked forward, down the center aisle until Burke caught his eye. Then the director of this entire program gave a quick wave of his hand across his neck. The sign to cut it off.

It took a minute of trying. Now Lucas Burke had to adlib his thanks.

"I'm touched. I'm honored," he began. "But we all know what we came here for; what brings us together. It's independence from the central government, from federal standards and regulations, from national taxes that don't pay dividends at home.

"So as wonderful as your endorsement is, I have a better idea. And here's where *I* can really use your help, and *we* can become even stronger *independently*."

Lindstrom was pleased. He retreated to the wall again. Burke was back on track, offering a phrase that was all new. One that he liked. A lot.

We can become stronger independently. The opposition of *we* and *independently* worked. He instantly saw it in billboards, on buttons, in TV ads. *Brilliant!* He thought. *Now for the closer.*

"Want to hear my idea?"

"Yes!" the crowd screamed.

"It's a good one!" he added.

"Yes!" they repeated more enthusiastically.

Fucking idiots, Lindstrom thought. *They haven't even heard it yet.*

Burke hushed everyone and brought his voice down.

"We've built our movement person-by-person, region-by-region."

He pointed to people in the crowd. "With you, and you, and you, and you!"

"And me!" shouted a woman.

"And me!" said another.

Then a chorus of "And me!"

Burke looked truly touched. Lindstrom was ecstatic.

"We have believers in the great Northwest. Washington and Oregon. Throughout California. We'll be on ballots down South and across New England. In the heartland and right here in Minneapolis.

"But we also must realize that separate movements, separatists, still need *a whole* to belong to, as trade partners, as negotiators, as risk sharers, as friends. The United States of America has violated its partnership with the states. But we, as independent nations can do better. We can succeed. We do it by…"

Burke paused for emphasis and complete quiet.

"…forming a new entity, but one that serves the people for real. Out of our independence, we create," his voice peaked, "the United

Separatists of America. A new USA, our USA. The United Separatists of America. Separate nations but part of a coalition, a partnership, a community without a Washington, D.C., but with power in numbers.

"Yes, we will become even stronger independently!" he said shouting into the microphone. "We will become stronger in our new USA!"

Lucas Burke stepped away from the microphone and let the crowd take over for the next five minutes.

CHAPTER 69

THE OVAL OFFICE
THE SAME TIME

Roarke was ready to launch into what he had, but the president held him up.

"Before anything else, my condolences, Scott. I'm sorry about Mr. D'Angelo. I know you were tremendously close."

Roarke lowered his eyes. "Thank you."

"Director Evans and I have already called his wife. There's not much we could actually tell her about what happened. She didn't press."

"She's a remarkable woman," Roarke said. "I've already decided to help look after the kids."

"I expected as much," President Taylor said.

"As soon as this is all over," Roarke added.

"Talk to me."

Roarke unrolled the map he'd brought into the Oval Office and looked for a place to put it.

"Something that might matter with the investigation."

"The killings or the killer?" Morgan Taylor asked.

"One may lead to another."

"Serious?"

"Very."

"Hold for a sec."

The president dialed the FBI Director at home. Simultaneously, he pointed to his desk. Roarke laid out the map.

"Bob, I know it's late, but expect an early morning meeting. There may be a development."

The president looked at Roarke who nodded at the president's use of words.

"Good," Taylor said getting his answer from Bob Mulligan. He hung up and returned to Roarke.

"Mind telling me what I'm looking at?"

"The dots represent locations of assassinations. The lines connect them."

"And?" Taylor asked.

"This was one of almost fifty versions. I was looking for an abbreviation, a word, a code. Anything that might give us a clue. I didn't come up with anything."

"Then what's this?"

"I didn't come up with anything, but Katie did."

"Ms. Kessler? We're crossing a line, Scott. She's works for the court now, not for us."

"Well, there's been a bit of change. She's actually under the jurisdiction of the Supreme Court Police, not the Chief Justice."

"What?"

"It's a long story. For now, let's just say she's cleared to work on the investigation."

"*The* investigation," Taylor responded. "One in particular?"

"Now, specifically, yes. Katie's outside with a junior aide from State. I'd like to bring them in. To help explain."

"It's your show."

The president continued to examine the Rand McNally map of the U.S. while Roarke went to the outer office.

"He's ready," Roarke said waving them in.

"Really?" Redding asked. "The president?"

"Really," Roarke replied.

A moment later, Roarke introduced the very nervous FP-06 to the President of the United States. He was surprised to see Taylor in a pink and white plaid shirt and jeans. They shook hands.

"Welcome, Mr. Redding." He noted the young man's expression;

the sense of awe that most people have upon first seeing the Oval Office and the commander in chief.

"Agent Roarke tells me you're here to help."

"I'll do my best, Mr. President."

Katie had hung back behind Redding.

"Ms. Kessler, always good to see you. I understand you have a new job."

"For the present, sir."

"Hard to keep up with your career," he quipped.

Katie smiled. "Yes, sir, I suppose that's true.

Taylor turned to Roarke. "Well, continue."

"Mr. Redding, you're up." Roarke said in turn. "Let's walk President Taylor through this."

"Yes, sir."

Redding crossed to the map. The president remained to the right of his desk looking at the map at an angle.

"I gather it's the design, son?"

"Not a design, sir. Letters. Or more accurately characters."

"Characters?" the president asked.

"Yes, sir. Characters that are words."

Taylor stepped in front of the map, next to Redding. He cocked his head slightly.

"And these words are in…?"

Redding now produced the version he created. The president looked back and forth between the two.

"Korean, sir. This is clearly Korean. Without a doubt."

President Taylor still didn't understand.

"So you've connected all these dots," Taylor said, "and you've end up with a Korean word."

"The dots mark locations where assassinations occurred," Roarke explained. "The characters spell out intent."

"Or one of your fifty attempts to read something into it," Taylor asked.

"No, sir. It's clear intent."

Roarke nodded to the young State Department employee. Redding cleared his throat realizing that what he had to say had far greater meaning than he understood.

"Victory, sir. The word means *victory* in Korean."

The president straightened and thought about the revelation.

"Young man, I take it you're fluent in Korean."

"Fluent? Yes, I am, sir."

"And is there a difference between South Korean and North Korean?" Taylor asked.

"There are shades of differences," Redding answered. "After the establishment of the Democratic People's Republic of Korea, the two countries took on different policies regarding their common language. The North began to set out small character differences, but in 1964, the regime took it further, establishing some new norms it termed 'A Number of Issues on the Development of the Korean Language.' Changes in linguistic policies continued separating standard Korean from where the north was going. They included rules for spacing and some symbols."

"And the word as it exactly is here?" Taylor stabbed the map.

"Definitely *victory,* or *win.*The other variant, depending upon usage—"

"Yes?"

"It also translates as *conquest.*"

Redding paused, calculating the best way to say what was next.

"Mr. President, I don't know what this is all about, but I recognize it's important. Very important. There's no reason to relate victory, win, or conquest with South Korea on a map of the United States. But North Korea? And to your question, it's the same word in both."

"What does it prove?" the president asked.

"On the surface, arrogance, or a mistake," Roarke argued. "A signature or fingerprints of sorts. Left unintentionally."

"That belong to?" Taylor let the question hang in the air.

Roarke looked at Katie. She took the cue.

"I can explain," she said.

Katie launched into what she had done, which brought them to this moment.

CHAPTER 70

WASHINGTON
NINETY MINUTES LATER

"Why can't you call during normal work day hours?" asked FBI Agent Shannon Davis, a longtime friend of Roarke.

"Normal hours? What are those?" Roarke handily replied.

"Right. I forgot, and you don't sleep either," the career law enforcement officer said. "What do you need?"

"A background check."

"Ask Siri. Ten bucks will get you what you want."

"Hey, don't be a dick," Roarke said. "Besides, I've got a woman on the speaker phone."

"Hello, Shannon," Katie laughed.

"Hello, Katie," Davis replied sheepishly. "Still hanging out with the president's fair-haired boy?"

She smiled as she looked at Roarke. "Forever."

"So I heard. Congratulations. I suppose I owe you an engagement present. So what's the name?"

"Two," Roarke answered. "Clay Lindstrom and Lucas Burke."

Silence.

"Hey, are you there?"

Davis began slowly. "I'm here. You do realize the quicksand you're putting me in?"

"Matter of fact, yes."

"Can't this come through normal channels for just once?"

"It will. In the morning. I want to get a jump on it now."

"Oh Christ," Shannon added. "Is nothing easy with you?"

Katie broke in. "Nothing, Shannon. But believe us. This is damned serious and extremely urgent."

Davis sighed over the phone. "For you, Katie. Not your asshole boyfriend."

"Fiancé," she said correcting him. "Consider this your present."

"Right. So what do you need?"

"Everything," Roarke stated.

"When?"

"Immediately."

"Give me three hours. I'll call you."

"How about we meet you at the bureau in four?" Roarke looked at Katie for agreement. She nodded.

"With coffee and muffins," she added.

"Pistachio. And warm. See you in four," Davis replied, then for good measure he added, "God, I hate you both."

The FBI agent hung up from home and raced out the door. He'd actually do anything to help Scott Roarke at any hour.

* * *

Shannon Davis was one of the bureau's best. A great field agent. A detailed-minded researcher. A go-to mentor for younger agents. And above all else, a dedicated law enforcement officer.

The interesting thing about an investigation, once it becomes an investigation, is that even a third-party investigator can usually determine why the initial question was asked. And when it comes from someone whose radar is up, like Davis, there's inevitably an "Oh shit!" moment.

Davis hit it at hour three, amazed that no one had searched so deeply before and immensely pleased with his own detective skills that he had found it so quickly.

But he didn't stop with his first breakthrough. He searched domestic, ICE, and even on international websites. One "Holy Shit" led to another.

* * *

"Pistachio as promised," Katie said when Davis greeted them in the lobby at the FBI. "And it wasn't easy at 2:30 a.m."

"The price of admission. You're in," he replied good-naturedly.

"Casual Friday?" Roarke joked, seeing Davis in warm-up pants and a sweatshirt.

"Fuck you very much, Agent Roarke."

"Coffee, too," Katie laughed. "Non-fat vanilla latte?"

"Perfect."

They retreated to Davis's office, sipped their coffee, and chomped down their supermarket muffins. Roarke was eager to find out what he'd uncovered. Davis, a lawyer as well as an FBI agent, asked his question first.

"Why do you need this?"

"You scored?" Roarke instantly gathered.

"I explored. But I get to ask the questions now. Why did you want me to dive in?"

Katie replied. "I had an itch I had to scratch. I went to Montana and volunteered for Lindstrom."

"To what?"

Roarke interrupted. "To spy."

"Not to spy, to understand," she corrected. "Inevitably the court will be dealing with Burke's secessionist movement. I figured—"

"Not good," Davis said.

Katie nodded. "Not good," she repeated.

Davis stood to his full six-foot three-inch height, then leaned on his desk with his arms supporting him. Katie expected a lecture. Instead Davis said, "And you had no idea?"

Now she looked confused, but Roarke spoke first.

"About what?" Roarke asked.

Davis straightened and turned to Roarke.

"Oh God, I love knowing more than you!"

"Come on," Roarke said.

"Well, I had to dig a bit."

"That's why I called."

"And you didn't give me squat."

"We gave you names," Katie complained.

"Not who or why, but no matter. Your game. And I see why you handled it that way. It made me discover."

"Discover what?" Roarke asked urgently.

"By any chance did you see the news tonight?"

"No. Why?" Roarke asked.

"Christ and you'd take a bullet for the president, but you don't know when a sword is aimed at the whole country?"

"What, for God's sake?"

"Burke, the same Burke you have me researching, basically just called for the formation of a new USA. The same letters standing for a different entity. United Separatists of America."

"Jesus!" Katie exclaimed. She immediately saw how the court issues would escalate. "I have to call the chief justice!"

"Not yet. You'll want to hear what I came up with."

"On Burke?" Roarke asked.

"As a matter of fact, not really. That doesn't mean there isn't anything there. Hell, I've only been on this for a couple of hours. He looks squeaky clean. High school quarterback, debating champ, president of his class, yadda, yadda, yadda. The perfect Boy Scout. A natural candidate, even though he's not actually running for anything. But when he does, which I suspect he will, he's a cover story for *Boy's Life*."

"Then I don't get it," Roarke said.

"I do," Katie replied. "Lindstrom."

"Correct. Clay Lindstrom's the real character."

"The man behind the man," she added. "Go on."

"College buddy of Burke. Political strategist. More Libertarian than Republican or Democrat. Cold, calculating, shrewd. Actually, more than that. Smart. Smart enough to turn Burke into his personal gravy train."

"That was my impression," Katie noted.

"But would you also say smart enough to have a plan bigger than Burke?"

"Shannon, cut to the chase," Roarke interrupted. "What do you have?"

"An old school tie."

The FBI agent explained.

"We're going back. Before college. Before meeting Burke, Lindstrom was an Army brat who went from school to school. Eventually to one in Europe. Switzerland. An exclusive school that catered to very rich or well-placed families. Many dignitaries, some in foreign service, others in the military, like Lindstrom's father. When it came to the upper echelon, students' names were often changed for the record. But kids talk and things get out."

"And Lindstrom made friends with one of these kids," Roarke concluded.

"Very good friends. Two peas in a pod, you might say. One an American with an attitude, another, an Asian with a heritage."

Roarke's interest piqued. "Asian?"

Shannon Davis pulled up a Krieg-Hegler School transcript, then Lindstrom's passport photo at the time, and a number of travel records.

"Looks a little like him," Katie said.

"It is him. And now the kid he befriended."

Davis's fingers moved over his computer keys. He retrieved the file for a student identified Chul Yeoung-Su.

Roarke and Katie read the name. It didn't mean anything to them.

Next, a photograph of a group of kids at the school's basketball court.

"I haven't found single photographs yet, but there's Lindstrom in the back row and next to him…"

Roarke moved closer to the computer.

"I'll make it bigger for you," Davis said.

He zoomed in on the other student.

Roarke felt a cold shiver go down his spine. The next words came out very slowly.

"Oh my God."

"You recognize him."

Katie hadn't yet. "Who?"

"Look closely," Roarke implored. To Shannon he asked, "And you're sure?"

"Newspaper, magazine articles, books. Positive."

Katie continued to focus on the picture. Then it came to her.

CHAPTER 71

THE WHITE HOUSE
THE SITUATION ROOM

The president called the briefing to order at 0700. Front and center was Roarke and Katie's map. Around the conference table were Taylor's key players: Vice President Jonas Jackson Johnson, Attorney General Eve Goldman, CIA Director Jack Evans, FBI Director Robert Mulligan, Homeland Security Secretary Norman Grigoryan, Secretary of State Bob Huret, National Security Advisor Dr. Holt Yates, Chairman Joint Chiefs General Eddie Pollack, and Chief of Staff Bernie Bernstein. Roarke and Katie were in the back of the room.

"Good morning," the president said. "Help yourself to coffee, juice, and water. Breakfast will be down in thirty minutes. We'll get lunch if we're still down here."

A few poured coffee.

"Some of you are aware of the subject. Others, not. Rest assured, you'll catch up fast."

The president waited a moment for the participants to get settled. Then he turned to Scott.

"Agent Roarke, you have the floor."

As he walked forward, Roarke began explaining how he'd been tracking the assassinations based on news reports and FBI determinations.

"The president tasked me early. From the beginning I had the suspicion that we were dealing with a single, expert, likely military-trained killer. I'm now convinced."

Roarke didn't discuss D'Angelo's death. Those who needed to know already knew. Next, he ran through his site investigations and collaboration with bureau personnel. He finished his preamble standing in front of the map.

"Now to the process. Extremely low tech. It's right behind me."

Roarke stepped aside.

"Actually, this is one of dozens of maps that Ms. Kessler, on loan to us from the Supreme Court, and I developed."

Katie appreciated the inclusion and gave Roarke a smile.

"We placed red dots wherever a killing of interest occurred. We connected those dots to see if a pattern emerged. People like patterns. It's a natural instinct, and it can provide a psychological footprint. Sometimes unintentional. In this case, it might not even be known to the gunman."

Bernsie raised his hand.

"Gunman? You mean the assassin may not even know what he's doing?"

"Precisely, Mr. Bernstein. A tool."

"A pretty deadly one."

"Yes."

"So who is he working for?" FBI Chief Mulligan asked.

"We're jumping ahead, but to your question, someone domestically and someone off-shore," Roarke responded. He motioned for Katie to join him, but she waved him off.

"And you determined that from the design on that map?" Eve Goldman wondered aloud for the room.

"As a matter of fact, yes."

Scott Roarke traced his hands over the characters on the map.

"It's not a design, Madame Attorney General. They're characters. They spell *conquest* or *victory* in Korean.

. . .

"Korean?" the National Security Advisor proclaimed. "Do you realize the supposition you're making from your doodles?"

"Dr. Yates, it's not just assumptions drawn from one map. I'd like to invite Ms. Kessler up to walk you through what she discovered."

"This better be good," Yates said loud enough for the president to hear.

"Trust me, Holt, it is."

Katie had practiced what to say. She did it with authority, taking special care not to reveal too much, not to say anything that might red flag her intentions to the attorney general. She simply explained that her research on the secessionist movements took her to Montana. There, she met Lucas Burke and his principal advisor, Clay Lindstrom. In the course of her time there, she observed that Lindstrom had a map similar to what Agent Roarke had been working on.

"So?" Yates interrupted.

"It had pinholes where the assassinations had occurred."

"Oh, come now, Ms. Kessler," the National Security Advisor continued. "Holes in a map you inadvertently stumbled upon in Montana lead you back to Washington, and from that you conclude—?"

"I didn't conclude anything. I was surprised at what I discovered.

Believing that the lines might connect to something, I shared my surprise with Agent Roarke."

"Your fiancé, as I understand," Yates bellowed as he wrote on his pad.

Katie was startled by the snide comment, but not deterred.

"To be clear, Dr. Yates, he is Secret Service Agent Scott Roarke," she replied with emphasis on *Agent*. "And I am the assistant counsel to the Chief Justice of the United States Supreme Court. Furthermore, I took photographs of Lindstrom's map, turned them over to Agent Roarke, who then forwarded them to the FBI for analysis."

"Yes, of course," Yates continued dismissively. "And with three words that certainly require more definition?" He read from notes he had just made. "*Surprise, might*, and *something*." He put his notes down and addressed her sternly. "Counselor, you're willing to put us on war footing with such vague suppositions? I don't think so."

Kessler never broke her eye contact.

"No one's going to buy this," the National Security Advisor said under his breath. Then louder. "Nobody, Mr. President."

Taylor didn't reply. He anticipated Scott Roarke would. His friend didn't disappoint.

"For the moment, Dr. Yates, consider the Korean characters—"

"Designs, Agent Roarke, designs," Yates argued.

The rebuttal steeled Roarke. "To you, the *designs* might not stand any evidentiary test. But they meet mine. My job is to protect the president of the United States. If this map in any way suggests an assassin may be targeting him or other high value targets, then, Dr. Yates, it gets my full attention. And quite frankly, it should get yours."

Roarke reached in his pocket, removed a thick red Sharpie, took the top off, and turned to the map.

"Especially when one of the lines runs right through Washington, D.C."

He circled the nation's capital. This prompted Eve Goldman to write *FISC* on her notepad. The initials stood for Federal Intelligence Surveillance Court. It was also known by another abbreviation. FISA for the FISA Court, established under the 1978 Foreign Intelligence Act to oversee and act on requests for surveillance warrants against suspected foreign spies operating in the United States

• • •

"Agent Roarke," the vice president asked, "I'm trying to wrap my head around your supposition."

"Yes, Mr. Vice President."

"On a grand scale you're attempting to link the assassinations of public figures to an anti-American political movement concocted by a foreign power based on someone carelessly mapping it out."

"Perhaps carelessly left, but strategically noted without recognizing the meaning himself. Random to him, but intentional to someone above."

"Above him? Above the assassin?"

"To be clear, this is not the assassin's map, but the mapping of the assassin's targets, predetermined along the lines of the Korean characters."

J3 looked confused. Yates snorted. But Eve Goldman looked up over her glasses and offered a prosecutorial question.

"Without any idea who the assassin is or who he could be working for?"

"Actually, Madame Attorney General," Roarke answered formally. "I'm glad you asked. We do have an idea. A very specific idea."

Roarke shared what he'd gathered from Shannon Davis. With names, dates, and places. Eve Goldman circled her notation again.

• • •

"North Korea?" The vice president considered his own question. "Active measures against the United States? Christ, this is well beyond Russian computer hacking or election influence. More like Murder Incorporated."

"Without hard proof," FBI Director Bob Mulligan commented. "Eve? We're going to need—"

"Yes, FISA warrants." The attorney general held up her pad. It had her initial notation, now surrounded by potential arguments to present to the FISA court.

"Enough to get warrants?" the president asked.

"A supposition made only from connecting dots?" Attorney General Eve Goldman rhetorically asked. "I don't know a judge who will sign off on it based on what we have."

"Write it up. Take statements from Agent Roarke and Ms. Kessler," the president instructed. "Perhaps the fact that Ms. Kessler was deputized as a member of the Supreme Court Police will help?"

"What?"

Eve Goldman was surprised and about to comment when Katie stepped forward with a modest, if not high-level explanation.

"It was Chief Justice Browning's idea," she said.

The attorney general settled down. Katie didn't add that her elevated status came after her return, though paperwork suggested otherwise.

CIA Director Evans spoke next. "With or without FISA we can go through every intercept in and out of Pyongyang for the past year."

"Make it so," the president ordered. "And Dr. Yates, you work with Director Mulligan and Attorney General Goldman on the FISA request. We have no idea what's coming down the line."

"Tell us more about the man you suspect is the assassin," Homeland Security Secretary Norman Grigoryan asked Roarke. "And how and why you think he is."

CIA Chief Evans already knew, but Roarke recounted the story for the room. He began strongly.

"We believe he is a former French special forces officer who went off the grid. Acting on a tip, CIA Operative Vincent D'Angelo and I went to a residence in France where a confidential source believed he lived. We determined," Roarke lowered his eyes and struggled with the next few words, "that the intelligence was correct."

Roarke took a moment to compose himself. The group got the meaning.

"The killer is pretty well known in intelligence circles as *Le Fantôme*."

"*Le* what?" General Pollack, Chairman of the Joint Chiefs asked.

"*Le Fantôme*. The Phantom. And he's just that. Invisible. Living in the shadows. He's our man. A foreign spy operating in the United States, who through remote detonation, killed an American CIA agent. That should help your FISA warrant."

CHAPTER 72

THE SITUATION ROOM

There were more dots to connect than just the ones on Roarke's map and everyone knew it.

"If it holds up, it's an absolutely elegant plan," Secretary of State Bob Huret said. "Infect and inflame. Devalue. Degrade. Degenerate. Destabilize. The best of the worst active measures all in one package."

"One more Big D," President Taylor added. "Destroy. Is Pyongyang out to destroy America? Considering Agent Roarke's suspicions—"

"This would qualify as an act of war, Mr. President," Secretary Huret declared. "Are we really prepared to go there?"

"Time for options," Taylor replied side-stepping Huret's question.

General Pollack began to list them, none of them immediately good. Roarke tuned out. He was thinking about where *Le Fantôme* would strike next. As far as he was concerned, it wasn't merely a possibility. It was an inevitability.

The White House? The Capitol? The Supreme Court?

Roarke knew the assassin took special care to avoid high visibility locations with hard to penetrate security. He struck in public when and where victims and their protection, if any, were not paying attention.

So who's the target here?

He'd already proven that the Supreme Court was vulnerable to penetration and the chief justice still took too many chances for a high value target. Then there were the principal leaders in Congress. *The Speaker of the House, the senate majority leader.* He dismissed anyone below that with the reasoning, *Why come to Washington and shoot low? No,* Roarke concluded, *leadership on up, all the way to the vice president and president.*

The president would be the hardest to take down, especially if he limited his travel and quite literally stayed away from White House windows. Likewise for General Johnson. *But Judge Browning, Speaker Patrick, and Senate Majority Leader Tom Pertwie?* He wrote the three names down but came back to the one who worried him the most.

The president was on his feet while listening. He circled to Roarke's chair at the far end and looked over his shoulder just as Roarke tapped his pen on one name.

Roarke whispered. "This is who I'd go after."

Morgan Taylor raised his eyebrow.

"The softest target with the least protection—Chief Justice Leopold Browning."

• • •

"It's insane!" Bernsie said.

"Insanely brilliant," CIA Director Evans said sharply. "Gamed out perfectly. Plant a political enemy within to seed unrest, and at the same time pick off public figures in a way that further undermines the civil authority. An insanely brilliant plot. Likely learned from the Russians or his Chinese friends.All the while, North Korea maintains deniability from a man who remains an enigma."

"A nuclear-tipped enigma," Taylor declared. "What's the latest in his psych workup?"

"I'll have it sent over," the CIA director added. He reached across the table for the phone.

"I don't want to read a report I can't talk to. Give me an expert. Who's your best , Jack?"

"Dr. DeCapo."

"Great. Get him."

"*Her*. A shrink."

"Okay. One hour, in my office."

"Got it." Jack Evans made the call.

Before concluding the meeting, more than two hours after it had begun, Taylor gave assignments to each of his team. The last was to Roarke. "Scott."

He didn't need to say more. The president had seen his note.

"I'm on it, boss."

CHAPTER 73

THE OVAL OFFICE
FIFTY MINUTES LATER

"Dr. DeCapo is here, Mr. President."

"Thank you, Louise," Taylor responded on the intercom line. "Send her in."

Morgan Taylor and CIA Director Jack Evans immediately stood. Dr. Debra DeCapo entered. She was anything but what the president imagined; not the typical CIA employee, in shape or substance. DeCapo was in her mid-to-late sixties, trim, dressed in a perfectly tailored black suit with freshwater pearl accents. She also wasn't the typical $103,639 per year agency clinical psychologist. DeCapo was the best because she didn't exist.

"Dr. DeCapo, nice to meet you," the president said. "I actually knew a DeCapo in the Navy from Portland, Maine. Any relation?"

DeCapo smiled. "I don't think so."

The CIA director laughed. "Actually, DeCapo is an anagram, Mr. President. The letters stand for Deep Clinical Advance Psych Operations. She's outlasted five predecessors and few people know her real name."

"Then DeCapo it is.

Jack Evans handled the introductions to J3, Yates, Huret, Grigoryan, General Pollack, and Bernstein. Taylor was anxious to get moving.

"Please, take a seat." He invited her to sit in a single chair across from him. "It still is Dr.?"

"Yes, with multiple degrees and specialties."

"You know what we're interested in."

"Yes, Director Evans explained."

"A clinical assessment."

"Well, to be accurate, I can't exactly give you that," DeCapo replied.

The president began to react, but she politely held him up.

"Not a clinical assessment because I haven't had him as a patient. Professional, yes. And detailed. So my question, Mr. President, is how detailed do you want to get?"

"I want to know what makes him tick. Better than the last go-round with the previous administration. Tell me his fears and worries. What keeps him up at night? What internal and external pressures he feels? Is he rational, unpredictable, dangerous, or suicidal? We can start there."

DeCapo removed a stack of folders from her Coach briefcase. "May I?" she asked before spreading them out on the coffee table between them.

"Of course."

The president studied the CIA shrink. She arranged the files in an order, but no way suggesting compulsiveness. She sat up straight and smiled.

"Ah, trying to analyze my behavior, Mr. President?" she observed.

"Don't take it personally. It's my job, but from a strategic standpoint, not psychological."

"And mine is to examine the psychology and leave the strategy for others."

"So we're going to get along perfectly, Dr. DeCapo."

"Based on *your* file, I believe we will." She smiled ever so slightly.

"My file?"

"Of course, Mr. President."

Taylor looked to his CIA director and got a shrug back.

"Of course, Dr. DeCapo," Taylor relented.

"Before I get to your questions, a bit of an overview."

"Please."

"There is a means to what we do. What I do."

Morgan Taylor nodded.

"I have not met the man. I don't care to meet the man. But I'm going to give you a very solid profile; what we call a remote psychological assessment using thirty-four normal and maladaptive personality classifications.

"Much as you were just doing," she laughed lightly, "I evaluate. Through video and photographs. I consider body language and facial expressions. I look for nervous ticks, eye movements, stances, and sitting posture. How he shakes hands, how long he holds eye contact, and even the crotch of his pants when he's talking to a woman…or a man.

"I incorporate elements of core characteristics culled from first-person reports. Some our own. Former state department officials, cabinet members. Anyone who's met him. They include sources who know they're talking to us and others who don't. Defector interviews intercepts, and classified intelligence. All designed to create an accurate and current psychological profile."

"I want to know how determined he is to attempt to destabilize the US," the president stated.

"How far he'll go short of conventional warfare."

"If you allow me a few minutes," DeCapo said. ""I'll try to answer, but first, some history."

"Go on."

"In 1939, Swiss psychologist Carl Jung went to Berlin and met Adolf Hitler. Jung reported that Hitler sulked. He never laughed. He projected asexuality and an inability to convey sincerity or human emotion. Jung sensed Hitler's evil came from the deepest, darkest places within and extended to the cult he created. Jung more than sensed it. He felt it.

"The encounter provided a rare opportunity for an expert psychologist to see into a truly dangerous, deranged, deadly, and diabolical individual. A psychopathic leader with an Army, Air Force, Navy and the SS behind him.

"The access to Hitler was unheralded. As political psychologists, we don't get to do that often. Moreover, though we've seen the practice erode recently, there's been a code of ethics that prevents members of the American Psychiatric Association from giving opinions on public figures they have not examined themselves with consent. I'm sure you know the Goldwater Rule, named after a 1964 magazine published a poll with psychiatrists speculating whether Senator Barry Goldwater was fit to be president. Goldwater sued and won."

"I'm aware of changes in the way the Goldwater Rule is seen. But do you have any such restrictions or reservations, Dr. DeCapo?" the president asked.

"I work for you, Mr. President. And nothing gets published under my name."

"Go on."

"So now to specifics. As a youngster, the subject, I prefer to call him that, grew up in an environment where he knew only wealth and power. Where individualism, outside of his own rarified circle, neither existed nor had purpose in the greater society. He was groomed to take over the government, as his father had before him.As such, he was spoiled from the beginning, and he grew into a spoiled-man body. Because of his status, he skipped important life experiences that normally help shape maturity."

Secretary of State Huret, National Security Advisor Yates, and Homeland Security Secretary Grigoryan took notes that related to their own concerns.

"Family forced him to be competitive and impulsive. He attended a private Swiss school under an assumed name where he reportedly cared more about NBA player stats than most of his studies. He was pulled out of the school when his father worried that he was becoming too Westernized."

"Apparently he didn't give up his basketball jones," the vice president noted. He referred to the bizarre friendship with a former NBA star.

Dr. DeCapo smiled, but didn't laugh, having created an assessment on the player as well.

"At twenty-nine, upon his father's death, he was given the keys to the country, at which point he relied on the basic tools he'd been left with. Wealth and power. Wealth giving him the means to continue to threaten, blackmail, and eliminate dissenters. And the power that came with the job: The means and methods to torture and execute. The propaganda machine to keep citizens in line. The weapons to threaten enemies near and far. He's subscribed to the Machiavellian manifesto in its most basic form, with additional pages written by Hitler, Lenin, Stalin, and gruesome new chapters from his own family.

"Imagine living where everyone could be viewed as a potential traitor. Imagine having to question everyone's motives, from within and without, including generals, his extended family, South Korea, the United States, and even China.

"For months after his father's funeral, his handlers worked on his image before allowing him to make official public appearances. And they bulked him up on carbs and gave him a boxy haircut like his iconic grandfather. For added effect, he was outfitted in historic Mao-style suits. The living embodiment of the revered founder.

"But during this makeover period, his face was emblazoned on buildings, billboards, and banners. Propaganda videos were everywhere on television and the intra-web, and he started showing up at military parades and staged war games. The media even showed him developing attack plans against the United States. He became, with apologies to Gilbert and Sullivan, 'The Very Model of a Modern Major-General.'

"Meanwhile to exert his own legitimacy, he had to convince the military that he had the guns, that is to say, the psychological guns to lead. The best way to accomplish that was by rounding up and killing suspected enemies and anyone else he viewed as a threat or whose deaths would serve as a warning," she added. "A son following in his father's and grandfather's footsteps, exhibiting the same deadly determination that had kept the family in control for decades. And soon, he was fully recast as the Supreme Leader, a man no one should dare cross, including close relatives."

"Point taken," Bernsie said.

"But, his brutality tells me that he's as brainwashed as the twenty-four million North Koreans he rules."

"What's he like? Deep inside?" The question was from Vice President Jonas Jackson Johnson, a military man through and through.

DeCapo's expression sharpened.

"As others have discovered, he's paranoid; often isolated with limited options. He's a man-child, and because of that, volatile. He has an Army of a million. Missiles and nukes. Toys in his hands."

"Watch out for the parts that can choke you," J3 commented.

"Mr. Vice President, he's someone we must all take most seriously."

"Believe me, I do, doctor. We all do."

"He's the walking embodiment of the big six constellations of personality disorders," the CIA shrink continued. "Sadistic, antisocial, paranoid, narcissistic, schizoid, and schizotypal."

"Explain," Secretary Yates encouraged.

"A person who has extreme difficulty making or maintaining close relationships."

"That's why he doesn't trust anybody but kisses up to sports heroes?" Yates wondered.

"Very good, Dr. Yates. Yes. He seeks, demands, and requires adoration. Traits that are in keeping with dictators and other narcissists. People in power, with evident personality disorders. But it gets worse," she added. "Compared against others in trade scores—yes, we score disorders, he's as high up Saddam Hussein, Charles Manson, and Jim Jones. The associated mannerisms include preoccupation on an equal basis with both minor and grandiose decisions. Such individuals may be predisposed to having a superior manner and the obsessive belief in their own self-worth above all others.

"Now here's what you should be especially worried about—the same things I warned your predecessors."

Everyone automatically sat forward.

"This man has absolute power and probably billions in Swiss banks. He lives high on the hog, spending hundreds of thousands a month, maybe millions; constantly moving from residence-to-residence. Of course, this feeds into his paranoia. Most of it legitimate. Many so-called loyalists would, if they could, assassinate him."

DeCapo now narrowed her focus from the room in general to Morgan Taylor.

"Mr. President, you cannot project conventional rational behavior onto the subject. For a kid who grew up with video games that go boom, he's playing with the biggest one of all." She paused for emphasis. "And he's playing you and every other president he's been up against for a fool."

"Got that," Taylor declared.

"All of it built upon a cult-like philosophy, in Korean called *The Juche*."

"The what?" Yates asked.

"*The Juche*. It was advanced by his grandfather as a guiding principle of the revolution. It's based on the conceit that *the individual* is the master of his destiny. But in practical terms, the individual is really *everyone* who makes up the *single nation*. All for one. All as one. The ideology is a variation of Marxism-Leninism. Belief in *Juche* ultimately means following the supremacy of the leader who represents the body of the one. It's a very effective way of holding onto power in a totalitarian state. You're either part of the whole or…"

She left the thought linger.

"But there's more critical thought to understand. These are areas of his personality that I've studied and weighed against my own clinical research and a worthwhile baseline that originated in the U.S. Army's *6-22 Leader Development* field manual."

"The Army did a study on him?" General Pollack, the Chairman of the Joint Chiefs asked.

"No, sir. Perhaps I misstated. The baseline is from the manual, not a study on him. But it is relevant. The publication looks at leadership categories and identifiable danger signs," she reached for the right phrasing, "that from both a psychiatric point of view and the vernacular, spot the danger signs that an officer might be losing it."

Pollack nodded his awareness. Bernsie uttered, "Oh shit!"

"Exactly," Dr. DeCapo noted. "The *oh shit* category applies. Think of cracks in the armor. Captain Queeg in *The Caine Mutiny*. The diminished grasp of trust, critical thinking, self-awareness, empathy, and likely most important, discipline and self-control."

"And he scores poorly on all counts?" the president asked.

"F, Mr. President. He fails on all counts. But to understand what he might do, I'd like to go through the analysis a bit more."

"We're here for you, Dr. DeCapo," Taylor said.

She opened a file she'd placed on the table and found a specific extract.

"Staying with the Army Field Manual and the issue of trust, I'll quote, 'Leaders shape the ethical climate of their organization while developing the trust and relationships that enable proper leadership.'"

"Yes, that would go all the way to this office, Dr. DeCapo," the president admitted.

"It most certainly does. However, a leader who lacks trust can still wield power by remaining remote and isolated, by making propagandistic promises and threats, and by eliminating subordinates from the chain of command."

"Ego," J3 said.

"Oh, that's just the beginning, Mr. Vice President," DeCapo said.

"Next, the category of Discipline and Self-Control. The manual states that a leader should demonstrate control over behavior and bring it in line with the needs of the organization. Quote, 'loyalty, duty, respect, selfless service, honor, integrity, and personal courage,' are all essential. The leader must show discipline, and cannot act, and I'll quote again, 'viscerally or angrily when receiving bad news or conflicting information.' But this man is known for impulsive emotional outbursts. He allows his selfish personal agenda, emotions, and his survival instinct to dictate his reactions to threats.

"In psychiatric circles, it's all about filters. To my mind, he lacks them because of legacy. He's had no other role model other than rule by terror and adoration. A dangerous morning cocktail he drinks every day he wakes. As a result, he has little or none of the next category, which is Empathy.

"The Army publication underscores the importance of empathy. You can be sure that though he's a dictator who claims he cares, he lacks empathy. It's not in his DNA. Which leads me to Critical Thinking and Judgment, the area of greatest concern.

"In the truest sense, it's the struggle you, Mr. President, must also face. The internal battle between being a good leader or a bad leader. Decision to decision. Crisis to crisis. Speech to speech."

"Perceptive, Dr. DeCapo."

"It's my job." She continued. "A good leader seeks to obtain the most thorough and accurate understanding possible and anticipates multiple likely consequences to likely courses of action. In the vernacular, if A happens, then what's the appropriate response to A? A bad leader? Well, forget the appropriate response to A. There is, in all likelihood, no way to accurately predict what the response to A would be except perhaps for erratic, unpredictable, defiant behavior. And that's where your real danger lies."

Key words echoed: *Erratic, unpredictable, defiant.* They each suggested terrible outcomes. The group had gathered at the president's request to talk through such scenarios in the past. They'd sent out Red Teams to test defenses against predictable threats. But there was no firm footing here. As a theoretical exercise, they were standing on psychological quicksand. In reality, the possible outcomes were only worse.

"Let's talk through some *What if equations,* if we could, doctor," the president proposed.

DeCapo didn't actually know the precise reason she had been summoned to provide her analysis, but considering the brain trust in the Oval Office, she figured it was incredibly serious. The president's question now made it all the more serious and timely.

"I'll do my best."

"What if he is publicly humiliated? To be more specific, what if I accused him of an act of war?"

The CIA psychologist, visibly reserved up to this moment, shuddered.

"An act of war, sir?"

"Rhetorically on one level, but depending upon the precise words, would he consider it more seriously? More serious than just name calling from the White House in past administrations?"

"Yes, I believe he would. It's far worse than simple sloganeering."

"And if my announcement came with some bite?"

"Bite? An interesting choice of words that requires further definition. A threat of sanctions? More saber rattling in return. Nothing new. However, if your threat included a ticking clock, then…"

"Yes?" Morgan Taylor said drawing out his reply.

"I believe," she locked eyes with the president, "he could preemptively act."

"Could or would?" Bernsie asked.

"It's hard to tell what a petulant child will do. But would, more than could. Even considering recent *rapprochement*, most of all, he believes in himself. *The Juche*. He, among all people, is the master of his destiny. It's his guiding principal, his personal psychosis, and my learned analysis."

She exhaled loudly. "And I'd bet he'd use everything he has to prove it."

The president stood and walked to his desk.

"Thank you, Dr. DeCapo. We've got a great deal to figure out."

There was much to consider, but the president held a high card that only one other in the room knew. The director of the CIA.

CHAPTER 74

YUKTAE-DONG, DEMOCRATIC PEOPLE'S REPUBLIC OF KOREA

Chin-wah Lee kept accurate records of system upgrades. Part of his job. And part of other peoples' jobs were to keep accurate records on Lee.

They constantly watched and wrote reports. Immediate supervisors observed. Closed-circuit cameras recorded, and impatient functionaries made surprise visits. So far, he had no dings to his name. If anything, Chin-wah Lee was considered methodical and loyal. His North Korean superiors were only right on one count.

Lee fully understood what he was doing for the enemy. Cyber intrusion. Malware. Malicious software. A worm. A killer sleeping inside nearly all of the Democratic People's Republic of Korea's submarines. He didn't control the trigger, but Chin-wah Lee surely loaded the bullet in the chamber.

What was the word his handler used? he asked himself. *Exfiltration. Spy craft for escape.*

Jee Gyuen explained exfiltration had to be timed. Not too soon as to alert officials and risk capture. Not too late after…*After what?* He didn't think about it much at first. More as time went by. Now he was certain. *After DoS.* Following Autonomous Denial of Service to internal systems. In other words, ways to disable subs. *Disable. A polite word for so many things.*

Eventually military investigators would trace the malware back to his computer. To him. *How long would it take?*

Chin-wah Lee needed assurances from his handler that his exfiltration was real.

. . .

Teacher/friend. A reason for having dinner and walking down the street together. This was the nature of their public relationship for years.

The malware handoffs always took place in movie theaters. The routine never changed. Gyuen bought popcorn, relatively new to North Korea, to share. He'd surreptitiously drop the small USB drive with the adhesive in the container. Early into the movie Lee would find the drive, put it in his mouth and decline to eat any more.

Now, thanks to their conspiratorial collaboration, more than ninety-five percent of the eastern submarine fleet was infected. Lee would only know if, but not how, it was all activated when he got the order to exfil. He wanted to know when. He was ready now.

Jee Gyuen didn't have an answer, but he reiterated his promise.

"I will get you out."

It was more than a promise to Chin-wah Lee. It was an act in honor of his grandfather.

CHAPTER 75

THE WHITE HOUSE GYM
THE NEXT DAY

Roarke walked into the gym, responding to a call from Louise Swingle. The president was working out on the Sole E25 Elliptical Machine. The second part of his daily thirty-minute workout.

His goal was to trim another fifteen pounds from his midsection and reduce his cholesterol level. He usually did a half-hour to cable news, but tomorrow's news, still to happen, was more pressing than today's. He stepped off the machine to talk. It was as good a place as any.

"Good morning, boss," Roarke said.

"Morning," the president replied. "Sorry to get you up early." It was 0455.

"No problem." But Roarke knew it was.

"Over there," the president pointed to the side. "On top of the towels. There's a file."

Roarke obliged. He opened it. It contained a travel schedule for Lucas Burke and Clay Lindstrom, including media appearances. One of them was coming up in Washington.

"Okay, what do you have in mind?"

"I'm just wondering if it's time to up our visibility at the same time we're undercover."

Roarke read through the material. The D.C. stop on the schedule suddenly made sense.

"A page out of an old playbook?" Roarke asked.

"Exactly."

THE FBI
THE SAME DAY

"Roy," we may have something," Touch Parsons said over the phone.

"It better be good," Bessolo declared.

"It may be."

"Send me what you have."

"Prefer you come on over. Roarke, too."

An hour later, the three men reviewed the FBI photo recognition expert's work at his Quantico office.

"Some background gentlemen. Starting with what we got from Walmart. It was going nowhere as long as the corporate attorneys were involved. Then, when a cousin of the chairman of the board, a state representative, was killed, it suddenly became personal. *Voilà.*

"Amazing what orders from up high can make happen. A thorough search of point of purchase sales of Precision 135 tool boxes over the past six months. They included Canada for good measure. Thousands of sales caught on their CCTV cameras. Most visible, some not, some blurry. Some shots obscured."

"And?" Bessolo anxiously asked.

"Well, it took Roarke's work to show us what we were looking for. He got me a fairly decent early picture from the DGSE."

"The only one they had," Roarke clarified.

"I aged it fifteen years, changed hair color, the hair line, glasses, no glasses; all the variables. Then put it in the mixer," indicating his mainframe computer, "and pressed ENTER."

"And you got a match," Bessolo beamed.

"I got shit."

"But you said—"

"Nothing from the surveillance cameras at the registers," Parsons continued. "But remember I said that some cameras were out, blurry, or obscured?"

"Knowing where the camera was, he would have avoided it or turned away," Roarke concluded.

"Give that man a prize," Parsons joked. "So, in those circumstances, some four hundred, I asked for all the front of the house footage at those stores, from thirty minutes before and thirty minutes after the purchase of the tool box. And that's where it got interesting."

Touch Parsons swiveled in his chair and faced the computer.

"I did say, *voilà*."

"You did," Bessolo replied impatiently.

"I've got two images," Parsons said. One was an aged photo from his own work paired with an enlarged and enhanced screen grab from a Walmart in Ocean Springs, Mississippi.

Bessolo stared incredulously. "I don't know."

Roarke looked back and forth at the facial characteristics in the aged photo. "Could be?"

"Could be," Parsons exclaimed. "Could be? Really?"

Parsons produced more than three hundred markers confirming the exact similarities. But he wasn't finished.

"Wanna see the rest?" the FBI computer wiz asked.

"There's more?" Bessolo wondered.

"From the parking lot, here's his rental car. And that, my friends, leads us to an Avis in Shreveport where he rented the Buick Skylark, but never returned it."

"We'll track the credit card," Bessolo said.

"Already put in for that. Seems the Barclays card went into default, and the name on the account was bogus."

"So we ultimately have nothing," Bessolo added.

"No," Roarke replied. "We have his face."

KATIE'S APARTMENT
THAT NIGHT

"Up for tickling the tiger?" Roarke asked Katie while they were snuggling on the couch watching *Bosch* for the second time on Netflix.

"Always. Which tiger? Jungle or plains?"

"The jungle," Roarke laughed as he stroked her arm. "The media jungle."

Her head was comfortably nestled up into him.

"Umm," she cooed. "Sounds like more than a tickle. Laying a trap?"

"Could be."

Roarke turned the remote volume down and explained what he had in mind. Something he had done before to spook Jeff Newman, Congressman Teddy Lodge's campaign manager, at a presidential debate. That encounter led to important developments in the last presidential election.

When he finished Katie asked, "Is your boss on board?"

"As a matter of fact, he suggested it."

Roarke kissed her on her head, then asked, "So?"

"I don't know," she said. "I get the first part. But really the second?"

"That's what makes it intriguing. First he gets unbalanced, then unhinged. We make him make a mistake."

"The trap."

"If it works, yes. If it doesn't, then we're no worse for the wear. It'll come down to whether or not he gets rattled. Up to now, he's had no reason worry. It's time for a reason."

Katie nodded, but didn't give Roarke an answer. She was already rattled herself.

CHAPTER 76

NBC STUDIOS
WASHINGTON, D.C.
TWO DAYS LATER

Meet the Press. It remains American TV's longest running news program and longest running show overall. Newsmakers of every stripe have paraded through the NBC doors to appear on the weekly series since November 6, 1947. Wannabe presidents, presidents, and former presidents. Spokesmen, spokeswomen, and spokes-liars. Talking heads on network salaries and politicos looking for free publicity. Members of

Congress, the nation's great legal minds, historians, foreign dignitaries, up-and-comers, and those after their fall from grace. They all come. Today was Lucas Burke's day.

Burke was scheduled for the third segment, approximately twenty-two minutes into the live broadcast. The plan was for the host to interview him for up to eight-and-a-half minutes if he was really good. If Burke was really, really good he'd join a panel with other guests on the other side of the mid-show station break. The producers hadn't told Burke that. The NBC host would invite him to stay on the air, an audible call, if they wanted to hold him over.

Burke was nervous. Clay Lindstrom adjusted his gold tie that popped atop his casual black shirt and black sports jacket. Lindstrom intentionally did not outfit him in Washington blues with a red or blue tie. Lucas Burke had to look more youthful and dynamic, active and vigorous, charismatic, yet authoritative. He was the perfect guest on the great national platform. He wasn't running for elected office himself, but he represented an ever-growing constituency.

"Stay on point," Lindstrom reminded Burke. "Take a beat before answering anything. Don't lose eye contact as you listen. Depending on the question, nod, smile, or tip your head in thought. Keep your focus as you consider what to say, and begin your answer by leaning forward ever so slightly. Never backward."

"I got it," Burke said.

That wasn't good enough for Lindstrom. He had more.

"Smile when you feel upbeat. Be serious when launching into your agenda. If you have to pivot away from a tough question, and you will, do it gradually, rephrasing the question, and then transition. But restate it in a long way. The audience will forget what was originally asked, and the producers will be telling the anchor through his earpiece to move on.

"The main thing is you can't look rattled or thrown. This is your first appearance. You'll want more. So at the end, a good handshake and thank you across the desk will say a lot."

"I'll be fine," Burke replied. "Relax. You worry too much."

Just the opposite, Lindstrom thought as Burke was called into makeup. *He didn't worry enough.*

. . .

The studio was smaller than Burke envisioned. Bright, colorful, but smaller.

A stage manager, wearing all black from a t-shirt to jeans, socks, and sneakers, asked him for a voice check. Burke knew how. Normal speaking voice.

"One, two, three, four. One, two, three. This is Lucas Burke, and I'm—"

"We're good," the career stage manager said. Tom Ryder had been with the show for years. He treated everyone equally. He had his own political bias and opinions, but always kept them to himself. The major league guests knew him by name. Sometimes he'd give the anchor a heads-up about a guest, like *Nervous, hiding something, drinking.* For Burke it was just a thumbs-up from behind the first-timer.

Now the host organized his script, though he worked off a teleprompter. He had questions on his desk.

"Mr. Burke, nice to meet you."

"And you in return. Excited to be here."

"And I'm grateful you are able to join us. You've got quite a movement going, which we'll talk about, but I'd love to expand beyond secessionism into your view of the entire political landscape."

"I'm not a candidate."

"Which makes your perspective all the more interesting."

"Ten seconds," the stage manager called out.

"We'll get into it," the *Meet the Press* anchor said. He cleared his throat and addressed the camera.

The last three seconds to air were delivered just with Ryder showing three, then two fingers, and one followed by a sweep of his hand forward under the camera lens.

"We're back, and joining me is a voice heard more locally and regionally, and increasingly cross-country on late-night radio talk shows. He's the titular, if not self-anointed leader of the secessionist movement that's gaining energy and attention. Montana native, businessman, and I suppose politician, though he says he's not running for office, Lucas Burke."

Lindstrom watched from off camera. He had been told to stay in the Green Room, but he wanted to be on the floor. He was not happy with the innuendo in the introduction. *Another thing to try to check and approve in the future*, he thought.

"Welcome to *Meet the Press*, Mr. Burke."

"Lucas, please. And it's an honor to be here."

Lindstrom smiled. *Good, nothing threw him.*

"Let's start with a simple question. Who's Lucas Burke?"

Burke did as he was told. He smiled, even nodded, and waited to respond.

"I'm an everyday Montana guy, with some cowboy independence in me. I'm single, but not single-minded. I have opinions, but I'm not opinionated. I'm all about issues, not labels. So all my voting has been outside of party affiliation. Big government, small government? All of that kind of bumper sticker talk never gets to the heart of the matter I believe in."

Lindstrom sensed the pivot coming.

"I'm concerned about how we've become bitter enemies with one another right here at home. Republican vs. Democrat. Conservative vs. Liberal. Alt Right vs. Progressive. It's led to a toxic environment and the widening gulf between us points to the fundamental differences that un-unite the United States."

Perfect, stay on track. Lindstrom was pleased with the way it was going.

"Studies, some from Pew Research Center, note that each side has 'very unfavorable' views of the opposition. Partisan enmity grows by the year. We'd probably have to go back to the Civil War to see a time with more disunity.

"But there are people in the middle. Actually, people stuck in the middle. The independents. Truth be told," he said in a folksy way, "they outnumber members of either party, but they don't have the platform, the voice, or the power to be heard. If they lean toward any of the two competing parties, they do so because of the damage they feel the other political party has done."

Now bring it back around, Lindstrom willed.

"So back to your question, who am I?" Burke asked rhetorically. "I'm a believer in a political reality that we would do better in a new USA.

Call it the United Separatists of America. United in the fundamental principles that bring us together: Freedom, faith, free speech. Equal rights and civil rights. Voting privileges for all. But separate in the areas that will never bring us together: Regional self-governance, gun ownership, trade, top-down regulations. We are actually multiple countries. Am I advocating a Civil War? No. Though that's part of the propaganda against our movement. The Civil War was a terrible chapter in our shared history. However, it brought about freedom. That's what I seek. What we seek. A peaceful civil separation sought by millions where we will all be Americans. Some with the United States of America. Others with the United Separatists of America. Independent nations working together in a coalition. Friends, brothers, sisters, and allies."

"Beautifully said," a deep voice intoned over Lindstrom's shoulder.

Lindstrom nodded without looking for the source.

"Your words or his?" the voice asked.

Lindstrom turned and missed the next comment in Burke's run.

"Excuse me?"

"I'm sorry, we should keep watching."

"Do I know you?"

"No. No you don't, Mr. Lindstrom."

Lindstrom snorted and returned to the interview, glancing back and forth from the live set to a monitor with a close up of the host.

"No matter how you frame it, Mr. Burke, you are advocating the dissolution of the republic," the host stated. "Correct?"

Burke answered the question with a question. A typical sidestep. "Aren't we already divided? Polarized by region, faith, and politics?"

"Yes, but—"

"It's always been unwieldy. Americans from one state impugn citizens of another. The Northeast and California feel they're carrying the burden of some Southern states. And they are. Southern and Northwest states have tremendous philosophical differences with other distinct parts of the country. And they do. We're already separated by our differences. And there are no deeply rooted social norms keeping us together. Yes, we have the flag and pride in the republic, but those are feelings. Beyond that, we are already divided."

The man behind Lindstrom leaned in. "Working well, wouldn't you say? Especially with key political figures dropping dead."

This time Lindstrom spun around and got right into the man's face. "Whoever you are, shut the fuck up, or I'll get security."

Scott Roarke laughed at the warning.

Lindstrom's comment was off-mic enough not to get picked up. But the stage manager heard it and gave Lindstrom a commanding look to keep quiet.

Roarke backed away whispering, "Okay. Enjoy the show. I am."

Clay Lindstrom fumed. He tried to concentrate on Burke's answers but now couldn't. His early thought rushed back. *Worry.* And now with reason. He looked back. The man was gone.

Good, he whispered. But he couldn't dismiss the comments as idle chat from a dissident. The man revealed himself as an enemy. His statements were designed to provoke. They did.

Lindstrom forced himself to return to the business at hand, Lucas Burke's debut on the national political stage. He listened to a sound bite sure to go viral.

"No, I'm not seeking to lead any nations that will emerge in our new USA. But I am proud to lead the movement that gets us there."

Clay Lindstrom pressed his lips together. His useful idiot was hitting all the talking points. Perfectly. From the side of the stage, he looked around to see how everyone else was reacting. That's when he saw someone who troubled him even more than the stranger over his shoulder.

Across the studio, under a door with an illuminated "On Air" sign was a woman; a woman he instantly recognized from Montana. She caught his eye contact and smiled. Then Katie Kessler turned on her heels and also left.

CHAPTER 77

MISSOULA, MT
BURKE HEADQUARTERS
TWO DAYS LATER

"Then who the fuck is she?" Lindstrom demanded.

Josh Collins felt like he was on trial. Clay Lindstrom had been grilling him and everyone else for an hour. Burke remained silent in the background. Josie Corcoran was in tears.

"I don't know," Collins said for the third time. "She just walked in, like most of the volunteers."

"And nobody vetted her?"

Silence was Lindstrom's answer.

"Well, let me tell you," Lindstrom shouted. "We've been penetrated."

"Calm down, Clay." Collins objected to the usage, the tone, and the vitriol.

"I will not calm down. This woman showed up at the studio. She was there to rattle me."

"Maybe that's where she works now," Collins proposed in defense of Katie. "Did you ask?"

"Yes, the fuck I asked. She doesn't. And she wasn't alone. There was a guy who also tried to rattle me."

Lindstrom suddenly stopped his rant. His expression dropped.

"What?" Lucas Burke asked.

Lindstrom looked around the room in thought. Then he focused on the map on the wall near the door. He could see the woman asking about it. Touching it.

"Out! Everyone out! Now!"

Josie Corcoran was the first to follow the order. But she went further than instructed. Through the offices and out the front door. Josh Collins cleared everyone else from Lindstrom's immediate wrath and instructed them to return to work. Lucas Burke remained behind.

"You care to explain what just happened?" Burke asked.

"No," Lindstrom declared. "Not at all."

Burke left. He tried to give a pep talk to the staff, which failed.

Meanwhile, Lindstrom went online, which was exactly what the FBI eyes and ears hoped he would do.

CHAPTER 78

THE WHITE HOUSE CABINET ROOM
THREE DAYS LATER

"We've got some activity, Mr. President. Nothing to take to a Grand Jury," Attorney General Goldman reported. "Could just be normal travel plans. Then again…"

Goldman explained what the wiretaps had produced.

"Smoking guns?"

"Let's just say wispy," FBI Director Mulligan added. "But we're monitoring. Microphones inside will help."

"And?" Taylor asked.

"Tonight."

"Make it so," the president said. Then he dismissed the attorney general and bureau chief. Eight others remained waiting to deal with what came next: military options.

"Let's hear it, gentlemen. Old plans in mothballs. New ideas on the drawing board. Anything you have that's in the incubator. Effective and proportional."

The president paused. "All on a what if basis. Understood?"

Taylor's question elicited nods from everyone. Around the table, Vice President Johnson, Secretary of State Bob Huret, National Security Advisor Yates, Director of National Intelligence Evans, Homeland Secretary Grigoryan, Chairman of the Joint Chiefs General Eddie Pollack, Defense Secretary Boyd Miller, and Bernie Bernstein. Eight voices at the table and one decision maker.

"Considering we've got no diplomatic playbook to follow, I want everyone to weigh in. We have established patterns for how to respond to normal nations. North Korea is not normal. So, who wants to lead off?"

"I've got good news and bad news," Holt Yates said, weighing in first. "The good news is we have operational war plans against North Korea. *Oplan 5015.*"

"Prefer not to term that good news, Dr. Holt."

"Of course, Mr. President. Sorry for the reference." He cleared his voice. "*Oplan 5015* covers limited war scenarios from small-to-big including 'decapitation raids' that target North Korean leaders, to preemptive strikes on strategic military and civilian targets."

"And is the bad news that it could lead to all-out war?" Bernsie asked.

"It comes with complications," the national security advisor offered.

"Right," the chief of staff said under his breath.

"Updates on their nuclear capability?"

"I'll take that," the defense secretary stated. "They've succeeded in miniaturizing a nuclear warhead and placing it on a ballistic missile. They're further along with their targeting capabilities than their tests would suggest. Many of their failures are bluffs created for us. They don't want us to think they have the range to threaten mainland U.S."

General Eddie Pollack cut in. "May I speak to that point?"

"That's what we're here for," Morgan Taylor replied.

"Boyd Miller and I have been looking at this like it's three-dimensional chess. With perfect intelligence, we could take out North Korea's command structure with strategic strikes. We could target its offensive capabilities, and with a massive surprise attack, limit its retaliatory ability. But, and with no disrespect to Director Evans, we do not have perfect intelligence."

Jack Evans acknowledged the statement with a tap of his pen on his pad.

"We still also lack a real understanding of what North Korea still has hidden in their nuclear arsenal. From number of nukes to the true depth of their delivery systems. Surely, Pyongyang is powerless to prevent us from targeting everything, but whatever we do will assuredly bring a response that will obliterate our 28,000 troops in South Korea and Japan, tens of thousands of American students, tourists, and business people, let alone up to one million or more of Seoul's ten million."

Pollack continued, "In addition to their million-man army, they have a modernized multiple rocket launch system with extended range. And without getting into the weeds, tens of thousands of self-propelled guns and some thousand ballistic missiles, from Scud Hwasongs, to their Taepodongs and Nodongs."

"Their reliability is well under seventy percent," the CIA chief noted.

"True, Director Evans," Pollack replied, "but the panic and massive civilian casualties stack the percentage in their favor. In addition, they have a cache of chemical and biological agents and a very capable submarine fleet."

The president sat up when he heard that last point. He traded quick eye contact with CIA Director Evans.

"And let's just say, we hit them, they hit us, and we hit them back harder. What next?" Pollack asked. He answered the question himself. "They launch their nukes. And then, God help us all."

The warning had been declared many times before and by many administrations. But it didn't lessen the impact now.

"We can't win a war with them without becoming the worst mass murderer in the history of the world," Pollack concluded.

"And we won't," Taylor said rising in his chair. "North Korea's decision to hide their nuclear arsenal and launch capabilities was itself a threatening act. We know it and they know we know it. Defensive and potentially offensive. But we will not launch a first strike."

"So basically, we're damned if we do, damned if we don't," Yates said despairingly. "Assuming you can prove responsibility, if *you* do nothing, then *he* will believe he can do more. "

The president was aware that his national security advisor had intentionally substituted *you* for *we* in his response.

"And without being held accountable Mr. President, he *will* do more."

"I did not say *we* won't act, Dr. Yates," Taylor responded sharply.

"Correct. But come back in an unequal, lesser manner, then he'll declare victory. His standing among his people and his hold over his military will grow exponentially. Meanwhile, there's your own image to consider."

"I'm not concerned."

"You should be, Mr. President. Anything short of visible retaliation will contribute to your personal problem."

"And that is?"

"Public frustration with you and your administration. Us," the national security advisor continued. "Inaction. Inaction can be marketed as cowardice by the opposition. People need an enemy, and they need a president who has the will to punish that enemy."

The president suddenly stood. In a calm, but unquestionably presidential voice he said, "Gentlemen, we'll take two minutes and return with clearer heads."

During the break J3, Pollack, and Miller conducted a sidebar. Evans and Huret broke off for a conversation. Bernstein tried to make small talk with Yates. The president considered whether his national security advisor was the right choice for the long haul.

* * *

"Stiffer economic sanctions?" the vice president proposed when they reconvened.

"I've got a thousand reasons why it won't work and maybe only one way it could," Secretary of State Huret said. "We could finally exclude all their transnational accounts from passing through our U.S. banks. Exclude one hundred percent of their hard currency."

"North Korea's money goes through our banks?" Bernsie asked. "How the hell does that happen?"

"Because we haven't completely prevented it," Huret explained. "Sanctions have focused on weapons sales, oil, and the acquisition of missile and nuclear technology. We often turn the other cheek when it comes to channeling money through the Swift Money Transfer Messaging Network. And when there's real pressure to enforce harsher banking regulations, the big banks make a few strategic calls to some high-level politicos. You know what happens next."

"Banking calls in their chits from key members of Congress," Bernsie guessed.

"Precisely," Bob Huret acknowledged.

"So who's got something else?"

"We haven't talked about an internet strike," Vice President Jonas Jackson Johnson stated.

"It won't work," the national security advisor quickly argued.

"Why not?"

"The North Korean internet is not an internet, it's an *intra-net,*" Holt Yates explained. "It's completely closed off, available only to select officials and elites. North Korea as a whole only has access to the internal info containing state-approved sites. It's called *Kwangmyong,* and it's the tightest online censorship system in the world. The bottom line, they've got us by the short hairs."

Jack Evans jumped back into the conversation. "Dr. Holt's right. We tried to disable, no that's too nice a word, we tried to sabotage North Korea's nuclear weapons program by planting a computer virus. In the past, we'd been successful against Iran's centrifuges. My predecessors hoped it would have worked on Pyongyang. They tried. The NSA modified the virus to activate when it hit Korean-language settings. Trouble is, it didn't work."

"At all?" Bernsie asked.

"Not even slightly. Their *intra-net* is a pretty good way to prevent a cyber-nine-eleven. Of course, as we know, this doesn't mean they can't hit us successfully. The division that's done that before, and surely can again, is Bureau One Twenty-One. They've got some eighteen hundred hackers, top of their class at school, doing the Supreme Leader's bidding."

"Christ, they're impenetrable." Bernsie stated.

The CIA chief looked down, and then to the president without immediately responding. The chief of staff caught the look.

"What?"

Evans cleared his throat and continued. "A mainland cyber attack will fail and likely bring a counter strike in larger measure."

"What about on-ground sabotage," Joint Chiefs Chairman Pollack proposed.

"Spies?" Evans asked.

"Yes."

"Basically it's the toughest country in the world to infiltrate. The elites don't interact with anyone they don't know, and they're not open to inviting newbies. In fact, they're more likely to execute people they don't know than talk to them. So we're reliant on intel that comes from overhead and defectors. And they're not banging down our doors."

"What about turning North Koreans into double agents?" Pollack responded.

"Takes years," Evans noted. "I don't feel comfortable going into that any deeper. So the bottom line is that we're pretty blind on the ground."

"What about China?" Homeland Security Secretary Norman Grigoryan offered. "Bring them into the problem, have them help with the solution."

"That strategy failed in the past," the president noted. "Besides, we'd be giving away any element of surprise."

The room fell silent again. Morgan Taylor saw blank expressions. Finally, Bernsie spoke up.

"Come on. We have the world's most powerful armed forces and intelligence apparatus, and all I'm hearing is that we're out of gas. I get it that no one can predict how the leadership will behave from one day to the next. But we have to start somewhere. For God's sake, he's launched a two-prong attack, killing representatives and fomenting insurrection!"

"We don't know that!" Yates repeated.

An argument broke out. Shouting. Some swearing. Yates at the center of it. Taylor calmed it down after a minute with a direct order.

"Enough! Everyone's wound tighter than an eight-day clock. I want to hear educated options from my best experts, not junior varsity quibbling. Am I clear?"

"Yes, Mr. President." The group said as one.

"Do we get anything from cell phones, Jack?" Taylor asked.

"Little. It's like the internet. Pyongyang and the rest of the country is hermetically sealed. Cell phones exist but are generally restricted to the capital. There are more than one-million devices, but we glean little. Our best intelligence comes from satellites rather than scooping up internet and phone chatter. Even when we get information, we have to evaluate its accuracy. North Korea is masterful at deception. We thought we had targeted a nuclear facility at one point through phone chatter, but it turned out to be nothing more than a large hole in the ground. The things we see are the things they want us to see. They know we're watching."

"Which is why I go back to China," Grigoryan said. "They could fix this in a day. It's in their best interest."

"You'd think," Bob Huret said, "but no. The last thing Beijing wants is a unified democratic Korea. A democratic neighbor is more of a threat to them than the North's missiles are to us. And our sanctions aren't going to bring them to their knees."

"So there's really nothing we can do?" Bernie Bernstein came to believe.

"Not exactly," President Morgan Taylor said. "There is one possibility we haven't discussed."

"We can agree that every visible move will result in the end game where missiles fly," the president concluded.

"Yes, something like that," Bernsie replied.

"Every *visible* move," Taylor said again with quiet emphasis.

He glanced at his CIA chief, who understood exactly what he meant.

"Yes, sir," affirmed Jack Evans. "Every *visible* move."

With that, the president called for a break and a change of venue.

CHAPTER 79

AN HOUR LATER

I need to see you

Roarke read the text from his Pentagon buddy, CPT Penny Walker, to which he responded

When

Soonest

Ninety minutes later he was in the lobby at the Pentagon. Walker met him with outstretched arms. She began with condolences.

"I'm so sorry. We'll all miss Vinnie."

"Yes."

She hugged Roarke, gently patting his back.

"The country lost a great man. You lost even more."

She felt Roarke nod.

"…a best friend."

She stood on her toes to whisper in his ear. "Got something that should help."

Roarke slowly pulled back and looked into Penny's eyes. They were filled with tears, which she wiped away. She straightened her uniform, regained her composure, and said more formally, "Come with me."

Walker waited to explain more until they were in her second floor office. As she closed the door she said, "Okay. Strictly off the books, Scott?"

"Two old friends just getting together," he said.

She crossed to her computer. Roarke followed and peered over her shoulders. She typed in her passcode, an especially long string of letters and numbers. Then she opened a file with a picture.

"Recognize him?"

"It's him. Different, but it's him."

"Touch shared his age-forward work with me," she explained. "Then I got to thinking."

"You always thought creatively," Roarke said bending down.

"Damn straight. And I still do. Made Touch a very happy man."

She turned and kissed Roarke on the cheek.

"This is new. Looks like an airport," he said.

"It is. Savannah."

"When? How'd you get this?"

"You're not my only ex, Roarke. I've got a friend at Fort Meade."

Fort Meade. Fort George G. Meade. A Maryland Army base named for a Civil War General who served as commander of the Army of the Potomac. The facility houses the United States Army Field Band, the Defense Courier Service, the Defense Information Systems Agency, and much of the United States government's most secretive spy apparatus—the NSA.

More than 20,000 people worked for the NSA at Fort Meade. One had access to a great number of files.

"Who?"

"Ah, I don't share lovers' names, dear boy. But I do share intelligence under special circumstances. Your *Fantôme* arrived six days ago. Delta flight in. He rented a Hertz compact, cream colored, and traveled north."

CPT Walker cycled through a series of photographs: Airport arrivals, curbside, the rental agency, CCTV cameras along I-95 North, even a McDonald's.

"Christ almighty, the NSA collects all of this?" Roarke asked.

"Can't hear you," she quipped. "But I understand it requires a few more algorithms than most people can input."

She smiled broadly.

"And I'm not most people."

Roarke was stuck by one thing in particular that Penny said.

"I-95 North? He's here, isn't he?"

"Yes," CPT Walker said. She brought up another photograph.

THE WHITE HOUSE

President Taylor moved the meeting to the Situation Room and added fifty-six-year-old Admiral Jim Drivas, Director of the National Security Agency and forty-nine-year-old Admiral Walter Conn, Chief of Naval Operations. Both war tested. Both formidable men who could speak truth to power. They took seats to the right of Jack Evans.

"Jim, Walter, thank you for joining us," the president said. "We'll be getting to you soon. First, Jack, where are we on *Edison*?"

"We're very close, Mr. President."

Knowledge of the operational plan code named *Edison* had been limited to the president, CIA Chief Jack Evans, and a handful of high-ranking U.S. military and civilian intelligence officers, including General Eddie Pollack and the two new additions to the briefing. It was time to reveal *Edison* to the other stakeholders in the room.

Those out of the loop traded looks. Evans waited for the president's go-ahead to explain. He got it.

"Go ahead, Jack."

The CIA chief worked without notes, but he was completely prepared.

"*Edison* is an ongoing operation in North Korea involving deep cover operatives and one primary asset. Its purpose is to…"

Evans stopped short.

"It's all right, Jack, proceed."

"…deliver a punishing blow to the Democratic People's Republic of Korea."

CIA Director Jack Evans went into detail. It took five minutes. When finished he asked for questions. Hands shot up.

"Can you place a percentage on success?" J3 asked.

"There are multiple moving parts. A great deal depends on our Indian partner and technology working. But we have high confidence."

"How high?" Holt Yates asked. It was a sharp question from someone visibly upset that he had been out of the loop.

"We're currently looking at eighty-five percent."

"Does that mean that eighty-five percent will have one hundred percent success rate, or we only predict eighty-five percent across the board," Holt demanded. "There's a difference."

"Dr. Holt, it's dependent on the tech side. How effectively signals will be received."

"May I take that?" Admiral Drivas asked.

Evans agreed.

"It's a three-phase process. We determine the desired outcome, we send the appropriate trigger via low frequency VHF transmission, and shut the fuck up."

The curt response quieted the national security advisor.

Taylor had the next question. "Do we have positions on the targets?"

"We're constantly tracking them," Admiral Conn responded.

"Then it's a matter of planting the seed."

"Yes sir. In success, the enemy will believe there's been a catastrophic failure with no way to prove otherwise, though in time, they may suspect."

"To be clear, *no way to prove otherwise* means?" the former Navy attack pilot now president of the United States asked.

"Exactly what it sounds like, sir. Fifty to seventy North Korean submarines will disappear."

No one asked for further definition.

THE PENTAGON

"We had him in numerous locales in D.C., then nothing," Walker explained.

"I know this building." Roarke pointed to the wall in the background. The CCTV camera caught him just before he walked inside. "It's a theater. Sidney something on F Street. Why the hell would he go to a theater?"

Walker was ahead of his question, already doing a Google search.

"Sidney Harman Hall. Home of the Washington Shakespeare Theatre."

"Schedule. Go to the schedule." Roarke said urgently.

"On it."

The home page covered upcoming classic Shakespeare plays and original productions by emerging playwrights. Nothing that seemed like it would draw the assassin.

"These haven't opened yet," he noted. "What's up now?"

She reduced the size of the display on her screen so they could see more of the home page.

There were acting classes and art installations. Penny was about to click through another page when a photograph of men and women dressed in judge robes caught Roarke's eye.

"That!"

Penny clicked on the link.

Join us as fiction and history meet on the stage. As treason gets its day in court. As a panel of justices hear arguments based on Sinclair Lewis's classic novel and the subsequent play, 'It Can't Happen Here.' You're the jury in a case presided over by U.S. Supreme Court Justice Leopold Browning. It's our annual Shakespeare Festival Mock Trial!

The Army officer read the date.

"Scott, this is—"

"I see."

Roarke was simultaneously on his cell and out the door.

THE WHITE HOUSE SITUATION ROOM
THE SAME TIME

"This mission must remain a secret," demanded President Morgan Taylor. "Forever. Does anyone need a clearer explanation?"

Bernsie looked around the room. He spoke for the group. "No, sir."

"The circle stays tighter than D Day. Forever means never. Exposed, we risk a war. Possibly nuclear. We will be branded war criminals. Kept absolutely under wraps, we will deal a punishing blow. We will send a message he and his generals will understand but can never publicly respond to. It will suggest failure on the part of his navy. In the process, we will eliminate a key element of his offensive capability. This will undoubtedly lead to the immediate execution of many subordinates. And it's completely off the books. Deniable. Clean.

"No interviews. No memoirs. Nothing that suggests the existence, nature, and execution. Ever. Never. Forever. I'll ask again."

This time, the president polled everyone individually for their oath of silence.

"*Edison?*" Bernsie asked. "What's the name refer to?"

"A reference," Taylor answered. "*Edison?* It's all about plugging in."

CHAPTER 80

THE PENTAGON

"Come on, answer!" Roarke said as he ran down the hall. But Katie didn't pick up. He left a quick message. "Katie, when you get this, drop everything. Call me immediately!" He texted the same thing.

Outside, Roarke sprinted to the first Army pool car in line. "I need your car!"

He flashed his ID. The driver gave it a cursory glance and ignored it. He wouldn't take any orders from a civilian.

"Down the line, asshole. I'm waiting for a general."

"Corporal. One more time," Roarke declared. "You drive me, or I take your car and you'll be getting a phone call that will end your future prospects."

"Yeah? Who?"

"Your commander."

"I'm waiting for my commander," the driver arrogantly replied.

"Not him, Corporal…" Roarke looked at his name on his uniform. "…Warren. Your commander's commander."

"He's at the top."

"No, he isn't."

"Then who?"

"The Commander-in-Chief!"

Corporal Warren sat up in the seat of his Lincoln Navigator. "May I see your ID again, sir."

"At a stop light if I say stop. Right now, you work for me. Drive or out. Either way I'm going."

The young Southern enlisted man smiled; actually excited. "Yes, sir. At your disposal."

Roarke sat shotgun and announced their destination. Warren floored the gas.

As they tore off, a very confused general stepped out of the Pentagon and yelled at his driver, who had slammed the pedal so hard that it left a cloud of dust.

* * *

Roarke hit a speed dial number on his phone. "You're about to hear nothing," Roarke told the driver, "absolutely nothing. You got that soldier?"

"I don't understand."

"You will."

Roarke quickly connected to Louise Swingle.

"Get the boss, Louise. Urgent."

"He's—"

"Interrupt him!"

"Just a moment," the president's secretary said.

While he waited, the corporal's cell phone rang.

"Yes, sir, general," Warren said, "I understand, sir, but—"

Roarke heard Warren's general screaming a string of profanities.

"Give me the phone. What's his name?"

Warren blanched. "Hyams, sir."

"Okay, Hyams," Roarke confirmed taking the phone. "General Hyams, don't talk. Just listen. Short and sweet. I've commandeered your driver and your vehicle."

"Who the fuck is this!" he demanded.

"You can claim it later depending upon the state it's in. The address is easy. Sixteen hundred Pennsylvania Avenue."

With that, Roarke hung up and went back to his phone.

Corporal John Warren smiled inwardly.

"Fast or faster, sir?"

"Faster, corporal. A lot faster."

Twenty seconds later, Roarke was connected to the Oval Office.

"Boss, I know where he is."

Roarke explained.

"I'm on the way from the Pentagon. Passed GW Parkway and just now crossing the Fourteenth Street Bridge. I'll need backup. But not until I say."

"We'll get everyone out first," Taylor said.

"No, not yet," Roarke said. "We have a chance. I want—"

"I know you do, but…"

Katie beeped in.

"Hold for a sec. Katie's calling." He switched over.

"Katie," Roarke began urgently. "Where are you?"

"An event with Browning."

She realized she had mentioned it only in a general sense.

"At the Shakespeare Theatre on F?"

"Yes," she said relieved. "Any chance you can break away?"

"I'm on the way."

"Good," she said. "I'll save you a seat."

"Listen to me very carefully. Is Browning there yet?"

Katie suddenly sensed the importance.

"I… I don't know. I can check. You know him. He travels under his own steam, but—"

"Check!"

"Scott, what's wrong?"

"It's going down tonight."

"Going down?"

"The guy who killed Vinnie. He's scouted the theater. We have proof."

"Oh God!" she exclaimed.

"What can I do?"

"I'm on with the president. We're figuring it out. Just locate Browning and secure the room."

"Okay."

"Don't say anything to create panic. Nothing!"

"Okay," she repeated.

"Call me back."

"When will you be here?"

They were on Maine now, however Roarke saw that traffic was backed up on Seventeenth. He tapped Warren on the shoulder and pointed.

"What?"

Roarke was insistent. He kept pointing.

Warren obeyed. He steered right, drove onto the Washington Mall, and hit his horn hard. Pedestrians jumped. The corporal blasted the car horn again and again.

"Twelve minutes. Be careful!" Roarke exclaimed.

He switched back to the president.

"Sorry, sir. Katie's at the theater. She's checking on Browning."

"We're doing the same," the president said. "Damn that man! Refusing security! All right, Scott. How do you know all this?"

"Captain Walker. She's been busy. And we're certain."

"How certain?"

"Completely," Roarke replied. "Absolutely no doubt. CCTV confirmation. Photographs of him scouting. Tonight's too perfect. He's there."

"We have to evacuate," President Taylor continued.

"Not yet. Katie will keep the chief justice and the others isolated."

Roarke looked at his watch. Ten minutes before the event was supposed to begin. The same ten to get to the venue.

"Please. The audience is filling in. I don't want to lose our chance."

Taylor hesitated. "The judges are safe?"

"I'll find out soon. I'll call you."

"Backup is on the way."

"Hold them at the door. They have no idea who they're looking for. I do. Give me time!"

Roarke hung up and slumped back into his seat.

"I know," Corporal Warren said. "Faster. Trust me. I can shave time."

He honked more as he steered onto an open section of Seventeenth.

CHAPTER 81

THE SHAKESPEARE THEATRE COMPANY
F STREET
THE SAME TIME

Katie thought fast. *Get Browning and the others to a secure place. Keep them there. Lock the door.*

She flashed her full access lanyard to a house security guard. The attendant flagged her through. Katie ran up the escalator, brushing past the late arrivals, reciting a constant chorus of "Excuse me's." Exiting, she stopped and realized she had no idea where she was going.

"Hey," she asked another officer who was young and likely moonlighting. "Is there a place for the VIPs? A waiting room?"

"A what?"

She held up her ID. "Where the judges are?"

"I really don't know, ma'am.

"It's miss." *Definitely moonlighting.*

"Who would?"

"You'll have to ask down the hall." Moonlighter pointed to a grownup in a dark blue double-breasted suit, tan pants, and a power tie on a white shirt with a blue color. He had a short, stylish beard. Katie figured he was an executive of some sort.

She ran.

Another "Excuse me," as she began, then, "You work here?"

"You might say that."

She held up her SCOTUS ID.

"I'm with the Chief Justice. I have to find him. Immediately. Some VIP room probably."

"The Green Room. But he's out now. All the participants were taken down to the stage."

Not good.

"How do I get there?"

He re-read Katie's identification.

"I'll take you, Ms. Kessler. I'm Brooke Stuart, the general manager."

He offered his hand. She shook it, but added, "Mr. Stuart, we may have a security issue."

"Should I—"

"Just get me to the stage. They can't go on."

That's when they heard the announcer's introduction over the public address system.

"Ladies and Gentlemen, welcome to the Shakespeare Theatre Company's Bard Association Annual Mock Trial."

* * *

The chief justice stood in the wings wearing his black robe and his game face.

"One more touch, Mr. Chief Justice," said the middle-aged makeup artist now working on Browning. Wearing plastic gloves, he applied a light powder.

"Is all of this necessary?"

"Oh, your honor, you want the camera to like you," the makeup artist said effusively. Like everyone else backstage, he wore all black; from t-shirt to tight pants, shoes and socks. He only stood out because of his long black hair pulled into a knot in back.

"That's enough," Browning said showing his discomfort. He'd gone through full makeup a few minutes earlier with another makeup artist. "No one's going to be as close to me as you are."

"C-SPAN, Justice Browning."

"All right. All right."

But he wasn't all right. Browning hated it, and he didn't hide his discomfort.

The announcer was now reminding the audience to silence electronic devices and not take photographs.

"We're finished," Browning said. "No more."

"Just one more dab." He stepped back to admire his final application. "There. Perfect."

Now, a young female stage manager wearing a headset came to the chief justice's side.

"He's all yours," the makeup artist added as he faded away.

"Almost ready for you, sir,"

"You'll tell me what to do?"

"Of course. We just wait and listen for your cue."

The announcer continued reading his script.

"We begin tonight with the STC Chair and Trustee of the Bard Association, Michael Blowen."

Blowen took the cue from another of three stage managers working backstage. The sixty-five-year-old corporate executive bounded onto the side in a black pin-stripe suit and white shirt and walked center stage with a welcoming smile.

"Thank you and welcome," he told the full house of 775. "Tonight's mock trial is based on Sinclair Lewis's prophetic nineteen thirty-five novel, *It Can't Happen Here.*"

Many in the audience knew the book. Relevant political news in recent years had made it an Amazon best seller.

"Of course, we're talking fiction," the trustee said.

It was written as a laugh line, but Blowen swallowed his words.

"Yet, the arguments you will hear may ring especially true, and at the conclusion of this evening's arguments, you will be asked to serve as jury and vote on devices at your seats. Affirm the charge of treason against newspaper man Doremus Jessup, or free the character from the book. It will be your choice. Guilt or innocence. But first, join me in welcoming tonight's participants."

"Now?" Browning asked the stage manager.

"Almost."

The off-camera announcer continued. "First, Supreme Court Marshal Wendy Heller."

Another stage manager assigned to the stage-left participants sent the marshal out. She crossed the stage and stood behind a desk adjacent to where the court judges would sit.

"Next, please welcome tonight's prosecution team. Representing the government, Corey Adams and Kaitlyn Stanley from the law firm Tiberio, Osterwald, O'Brien and Mull.

The lawyers, all in their early forties and on the partner track, took their positions behind a red table that faced the still empty justice seats. They carried law books and yellow pads, and politely acknowledged the audience's applause.

"And now, counsel representing the defendant, Titus Freeman and Joyce Michaels from the law firm Styles, Sullivan, and Westfall.

The duo entered and stood behind their red table next to the opposing team.

Browning watched from the wings.

"You're up next, sir," the stage manager warned. "Ten seconds."

The chief justice puffed out his chest.

"And of course, it's time to meet the esteemed members of the Supreme Court," the announcer declared. "Presiding over the arguments, the Honorable Chief Justice Leopold Browning."

The stage manager tapped his shoulder. "Now." Browning entered.

"…and also adjudicating, from the United States Supreme Court, Justices Frances Barliatta, Margaret Moore, Russell T. Jones, and Raymond Chen."

Over the audience's applause the Supreme Court Marshal loudly intoned, "All Rise!"

Browning took the center seat, stage right, flanked left by Barliatta and Moore and to his right, the two men.

As the applause subsided, the marshal proclaimed, "Oye, oye, oye. The Supreme Court is now in session. Please be seated."

The stage manager was relieved everyone hit the correct marks. The makeup artist checked a backstage monitor. He was pleased with his work, too. The audience was ready for the opening statements.

That's when Katie arrived backstage.

"You are about to participate in a dramatic court event," Blowen continued. "The trial of newspaper owner Doremus Jessup. The charges are treason against the government of the United States, treason by advocating the overthrow of President Berzilius Windrip."

The president of the board of trustees explained that neither Jessup nor Windrip existed in real life. They were creations of Sinclair Lewis, written with a semi-satirical hand.

The book presented the startling scenario of a Machiavellian politician who runs for president on a platform of fear and hate and subsequently defeats Franklin Delano Roosevelt. Upon the election, he vows to bring sweeping social reforms and traditional values, all with patriotic fervor. But instead, he asserts totalitarian control over the government, the people, the military, and all aspects of society. The ultimate impact of Sinclair Lewis's award-winning work was his vision. He foresaw the rise of Adolf Hitler and things to come.

Taking up a grassroots battle against President Windrip was Vermont journalist Jessup. In the course of the plot, he was arrested and sent to a concentration camp.

"The court case, as presented today, will be between Jessup's defense attorneys and the government prosecutors seeking a conviction. It will all be based on testimony culled from the book and actual case history."

Browning appeared a little nervous to the crowd, or at least uncomfortable in the surroundings and the stage lights.

"The Supreme Court will begin with the government's opening arguments." With that Blowen stepped off stage.

The chief justice patted perspiration with a handkerchief and took a sip of water from the glass on the table in front of him.

"Thank you," Corey Adams said as he rose. "My co-counsel and I will present conclusive evidence that…"

. . .

The last few minutes gave Roarke time to think. About strategy. About weapons. About how to take his adversary down. About the danger he was putting everyone in by not evacuating.

Roarke unfolded pictures of *Le Fantôme* to study the details. He'd already committed them to memory, but there was always something more to see.

Warren caught a glimpse of the man's face as Roarke examined the printouts.

"That's your man?" he asked.

Roarke ignored the question.

"Just drive, corporal."

"Yes, sir."

Roarke examined the pictures again. One photo, then another. Then back to the first. Comparing them. All he saw were a killer's cold eyes opened wide to threats around him.

Roarke finally had to look up and ahead. The fast maneuvering was beginning to make him nauseous, which he couldn't afford. He did so just in time as they swerved back fast from one lane to another, around slower cars, and ultimately onto a sidewalk passing a UPS truck. They had a clear path to Seventh until all traffic stopped.

"Shit!"

The corporal slammed the breaks.

Warren scanned his rearview mirrors. He had no wiggle room. No way to back up. He was boxed in on the left and right.

"I'm sorry, sir. Three more blocks. Maybe if—"

There was no *maybe*. Roarke dug in his pants pocket for his Bluetooth earpiece. He placed it in his left ear, turned it on, and opened the door.

"Corporal, you're free to go."

Roarke removed a Secret Service business card from his wallet and quickly wrote on it.

"If Hyams gives you trouble, you use this. It's your get out of jail card."

With that, Roarke opened the door and ran.

Warren looked at the card. It had a phone number and three words.

Boss, help him

To the Army corporal it seemed as if Roarke didn't know if he'd make it out himself.

. . .

"Where are you?" Katie frantically asked.

"Two blocks away."

"Hurry. They're on stage now.

"What should I do?"

"Nothing. I'll meet you."

CHAPTER 82

WASHINGTON, D.C.
FBI BUILDING

"Christ Almighty!" FBI Director Mulligan said at the end of the call from the White House. His complicated day just became more complicated.

The FISA court had approved the NSA's warrants, and Mulligan also received separate approval to wiretap all Burke campaign office phones, as well as Burke's and Lindstrom's home and cell phones. Other surveillance devices would be installed surreptitiously over the next few days. Meanwhile, airline travel records were being sucked up in the government search.

But now, more trouble. Immediate trouble. He'd soon get photographs to work with and an even more pressing problem. A real-time threat.

Mulligan had put a team of fifty on the first problem, including Duane "Touch" Parsons, who would be running his FERET programs against U.S. Immigration and Customs Enforcement records looking for any international travel the Burke team may have done over the last two years.

The FBI chief targeted the past two years for immediate review. Though many international conspiracies could incubate over far longer, Mulligan put Burke/Lindstrom on a compressed time period.

But now the focus was on Sidney Harman Hall. He called his Number One Field operative, Roy Bessolo, and explained the situation.

"This has Roarke written all over it," Bessolo replied.

"You got that right," the FBI director confirmed.

"POTUS says Roarke wants a chance to nail him."

"Hell," Bessolo barked, "I might end up liking the guy after all."

Bessolo checked his watch. He calculated the route. Quickest way this time of night was north on Tenth for two blocks, right on F for three. Running.

"On my way. My guys will follow."

Bessolo was out the door. He yelled down the hall. "Shik!"

"Yeah!" agent Dave Shikiar replied from his office twenty feet away.

"Grab the team. 610 F NW. Now! And hoof it!"

With that, Bessolo was down the stairwell; faster than waiting for the elevator.

. . .

Roarke and Bessolo simultaneously converged at the theater's main entrance. They were both panting from their sprints.

"Talk to me," Bessolo didn't need a lot of information.

"Subject is here. Target is Browning," Roarke replied.

"Picked a hell of a good place."

"Tell me about it."

Roarke noted that Bessolo was alone.

"The cavalry?"

"On the way," the FBI agent said. He uncharacteristically asked, "What do you need from me?"

Roarke handed Bessolo the photographs. "Cover the entrances and exits. Hidden places. But I don't know the layout."

"No, but I can get it," Bessolo stated.

"Good. I'd prefer capture, but I wouldn't be upset—" Roarke stopped short.

"Got it."

Roarke nodded thanks. Bessolo made a call and followed Roarke in. Both flashed their identifications. Bessolo held back to coordinate with his people. Roarke asked an usher for directions to the stage. A half minute later he was at the entrance to the hall. He cracked open the door and stepped to the side of a young usher.

Roarke scanned the theater. Audience lights were down, the event had started. On the left, a table with five chairs. Browning was in the middle seat flanked by other judges. Center stage, another table with a Supreme Court marshal, likely unarmed tonight. Next to her, a small round table displaying the traditional Scales of Justice atop red velvet that matched the theater curtain backdrop. Further right, facing the justices across the stage, two other tables, each with two people.

"How do I get backstage?"

"Ticket?"

He produced his ID again.

The George Washington University coed didn't understand. "But your ticket?"

"Secret Service, Miss."

Damn. He needed to get closer, unobserved.

He focused on angles and points of origin for a clear shot. From the audience perspective, right to left would be best. He looked up. His immediate view was blocked by balcony seating. He had no idea what was above and beyond that. Lower seating also offered dead-on angles.

He saw all of this in ten seconds.

"What's your name?" Roarke asked the young usher, a petite brunette with a southern accent.

"Lucy Brillhart."

"Okay, Lucy Brillhart, I really need your help, and we have to be very quiet. Take me backstage." He pointed to the left side where the judges would be. "The quickest way."

The history major, hoping to watch a historic debate, now wondered whether she would be involved in making some herself.

"Out and around," she said excitedly.

As they rounded a corner, Roarke saw Bessolo deploying his team. The FBI agent pointed up to where he'd be going. Roarke nodded and followed the student.

. . .

"Here," Lucy said quietly opening the stage door. "Anything else?"

"Thanks. No." He had a second thought. "Stick around but hang back in case I need you."

"May I ask…?"

"Just stay back."

Most of the backstage production team stood or sat on folding chairs and listened. For all but a few, their work was done, and they could enjoy the evening. Only the hair stylist and makeup artists needed their supplies out for touchup during intermission.

Katie had ended up on the side behind the attorneys. She watched Browning and sensed that he was struggling with his words. So far she didn't see Roarke

. . .

Roarke peered out from the wings. Directly in front sat the five justices, sitting behind a flimsy plywood desk that would never stop a bullet. Beyond lay the packed theater, the lighting grid above, and the projection booth at the far end.

The house lights were down; the audience was in the dark. An obvious advantage for *Le Fantôme*. Roarke counted the rows of orchestra seats. Eleven. Beyond them, a slightly elevated tier, then another divided in three quadrants. Above that, the mezzanine in another three sections. Each offered clear cross-shots to Chief Justice Leopold Browning.

Turning back behind the set he spotted Katie standing some fifty feet away. The quickest way to get to her was to cross the stage. That was out. They had eye contact, and he motioned for her to walk around.

Roarke looked out into the audience again, scanning right, left, and up toward the projection booth and control room.

"Sorry, Scott," she said joining him. "Couldn't hold them. They'd already left for the stage."

"Okay," Roarke replied. He kept surveying the crowd while weighing the president's request. *Get the chief justice out. Evacuate.* But he still wanted a chance at the assassin.

Now Roarke focused on the control booth at the far end of the hall. It offered a straight shot but would have required killing the crew. That had not happened. He saw a full team working in the booth and now Roy Bessolo.

Roarke next evaluated the lighting grid. It was harder to see with lights shining onto the stage. He was certain one of Bessolo's team would check it out completely.

Then he stepped away from the curtain again and surveyed backstage more completely. Nothing had changed from before. He walked to the other side where Katie had been to check the view from there. From that side he rescanned the theater. *Percentages,* he thought. *Not just percentages, experience.*

Roarke ruled out a low percentage shot with no way to quickly escape. Also, the assassin never revealed himself to be a mass murderer.

So Roarke concluded there'd be no bomb. It had to come from a distance. *No,* he thought. *A short distance. End of the aisle seats.* That's what he'd choose.

Roarke moved the curtain ever so much to see up the line better. He was now slightly behind the attorneys' desks, in the dark.

A short shot. Concealed handgun.

But from where?

From the perspective of the stage, a right hand shot from a left end aisle seat? Left hand from the right side as he looked out. For handgun accuracy sake, he focused on the front eleven orchestra section rows.

CHAPTER 83

WASHINGTON, D.C.
SIDNEY HARMAN HALL
THE SAME TIME

The lawyers argued their cases on stage. Roarke tuned them out, literally trying to hear the assassin's thoughts.

He rated the chances of spotting his man at less than fifty-fifty. He needed to increase the percentages.

Roarke stepped back from the wings and speed dialed Duane Parsons.

"Touch, Roarke here," he whispered. "You've got all the images?"

"Yup," the FBI photo rec expert replied. "Working on ID'ing more."

"Is he left or right-handed?"

"Come on, Roarke, I'm good, but with only still photographs?"

"I need it!"

"When?" Parsons asked.

"Now. Left or right, Touch."

"Jesus, Roarke."

"Touch, now," he implored as he withdrew his Legion Gray 9mm Sig Sauer P229 from his shoulder holster.

. . .

On stage, Browning listened intently as if he were weighing an actual court proceeding, but he appeared to be uncomfortable, touching his tongue and mouth, and scratching. First his face, then his hands.

Kate saw his motions and wondered, *Stage fright?* She looked at a TV monitor with the C-SPAN feed. He was sweating. Then she thought again. Leopold Browning wasn't afraid of anything, and she'd never seen him sweat. Even a day in the Supreme Court building when the air conditioning was down.

. . .

Roarke scanned right to left. Up and down the aisles. He searched for a man, or a man dressed as a woman. Someone young or someone old. White, black, Hispanic. *Le Fantôme* was a chameleon. He could be any of them.

Roarke heard Touch Parsons through his earpiece. He responded with a whispered, "Yes."

"Right-handed, Roarke." Parsons said.

"Are you positive?"

"Fuck you. You asked me. I'm telling you. Obvious from the pictures. Which hand he reaches to open a door. Right. The side of his body that's puffed out enough to hold a gun holster. Left. Oh, and one more thing. Something else I discovered. If you ever get to say hello, try this name on for size. Martín."

"Martin?" Roarke replied.

"No. French." Parsons pronounced it slowly. "Can't guarantee it one hundred percent, but you know me with percentages. Now get the bastard!"

Scott Roarke hung up before *bastard*. He concentrated his search on the audience section immediately in front of him. The shooter would have his right hand free along the aisle. But Roarke couldn't see from where he was standing. He needed to get into the aisle beyond the first few rows, along the right side of the audience.

Shit.

He looked around. Lucy was there, almost anticipating his request.

"Side door?"

"This way," she said.

She led him to a door at roughly mid-orchestra. Roarke waved her back. Four rows ahead he saw a man fidgeting. He had his program rolled up in his right hand. Like a tube to hide a barrel. Roarke stepped forward cautiously. He wanted to avoid causing a commotion, but he wanted something more, and he was willing to ignore the problem he'd cause.

Another step.

The man in the aisle seat was now just two rows away. He had his program up.

Another step.

Then the man lowered the program and leaned over to the woman sitting next to him. He whispered something, and they laughed. He unraveled the program just as Roarke was behind him, equally relieved and disappointed.

Katie intercepted Roarke in the aisle.

"Scott, it's Browning. I think he's sick."

Roarke looked up and across to the stage.

"He's not paying attention. He's having trouble breathing. It looks like—"

Roarke caught a pained expression on Browning just as the chief justice turned away from the audience, vomited, and fell forward.

CHAPTER 84

Roarke charged up the aisle and onto the stage. The other participants stood. The audience gasped.

"Doctor! We need a doctor." Roarke shouted. "Doctor and an ambulance." Katie was immediately at his side.

No fewer than twenty physicians came forward. The first, a young woman who appeared to be Indian or Pakistani, checked Browning's breathing. It was labored; the pulse, weak and irregular; his skin, clammy.

"What's that?" Roarke asked, pointing at the deep scratches on Browning's face.

The doctor examined them, instantly shouting, "Don't touch him!"

Roarke withdrew his hand and Katie picked up on the doctor's command.

"He started scratching right after he went out."

"I saw that too," a second, older physician interrupted. He offered a fast diagnosis. "Heart attack."

"I don't think so," the first doctor argued. "The symptoms…"

"Yes?" replied the senior physician judgmentally.

Roarke now noticed Browning's hands. They were caked with his makeup.

"There's makeup all over his hands," he exclaimed. "From scratching?"

The younger doctor examined Browning's hands, without touching them. Then his face.

"Yes," she said.

Roarke drifted backstage. He did a quick inventory. Everyone from minutes earlier was there. Everyone except—

Across the stage he saw a man in black run toward the backstage exit. He carried a shoulder bag. *The makeup artist with the ponytail!* Stats raced through Roarke's mind. *About the right height, right build, right age.*

"You! Stop!" he shouted.

The man ignored him. Lucy, the young usher, heard Roarke's command and tried to block the man. The assassin slammed her to the ground.

Bessolo barged in from the near side, "Talk to me, Roarke!"

"The makeup guy!" Roarke yelled as he began to run. "

Without another word, Scott Roarke ran to the door. Lucy was rising to her knees.

"Are you—?"

"Okay. Yes," she said.

Her nose was bleeding badly, but she appeared otherwise alright.

"I tried to stop him."

Lucy definitely made some history today.

. . .

Sixth Street, NW. Two ways. Evening traffic. He needed a car. Fast. A fast car fast.

The assassin looked toward the oncoming traffic. A Lincoln. A Mazda. A Toyota. *No,* he thought. Then a *BMW.*

Le Fantôme, stood in front of the oncoming mineral gray metallic 330e iPerformance sedan. His gun out and ready.

The driver hit her brakes, stopping inches from him. The near collision had her heart racing. But the assassin's gun made it abundantly obvious what he wanted.

With a string of "No, don't hurt me, please don't hurt me," she got out of the car. Not fast enough for the killer. He grabbed the woman fashionably dressed for a formal dinner and threw her down. Other cars had to stop. One nearly ran over her.

It would slow up traffic, which he needed.

The Frenchman closed the car door, put the high-performance vehicle in gear, and accelerated at the sight of a figure darting out of the theater stage door.

. . .

"In pursuit," Roarke said over his open phone. He was on with Bessolo who was assisting the doctors. "In a dark gray B'mer heading west."

Roarke ran onto the street, saw the downed woman and the traffic stopped around her. "Civilian down."

"Be right there," the FBI agent said. "Stay put, we'll get him."

Roarke heard the order and ignored it.

He was already on the second car in the line, a Mercedes C300 Coup. Fast and furious. Up to sixty mph in under six seconds.

"Secret Service. Out!" he demanded.

"What? No! I'm with the German embassy."

Shit, Roarke thought. Approaching the vehicle from the side, he hadn't seen the diplomatic plates.

"Sir, I'm taking your car now! Out!"

He produced his ID. If that didn't work, it would be his Sig Sauer.

The ID worked, but there would be excuses to make later.

Roarke took off. He avoided the woman and the crowd, steered onto the sidewalk, and back onto Sixth. He had two blocks to make up.

CHAPTER 85

WASHINGTON, D.C.
THE SITUATION ROOM
THE SAME TIME

"Okay, let's hear it."

Morgan Taylor invited fact, opinion, and debate. Everyone had agreed the conversation would never go further than the room.

The Situation Room was no bigger than a living room. It was where ideas were born and participants saw enemies die in real time. Bin Laden and American Special Forces. The bad and the good. Where Lyndon Johnson went nightly for ever-worsening Vietnam War news. Where George H. Bush visited every morning at 0500 during the Gulf War. Where Bill Clinton said he'd end up if his phone rang at 2:00 a.m. Where George W. Bush went for updates every day for weeks after 9/11.

Phones were checked before entering. And the ticket for entry was given out only at the highest White House level.

Disposable information trafficked through the White House via memos, reports, and endless meetings. But the most important data with eyes-only designation flowed into the "Sit Room."

Today would be one of those sessions.

"Everything you've got. When you're finished, we'll all leave and nothing will be said of this meeting again, with the exception that the mission, if improved, is carried out. "

Once again, he addressed everyone from the vice president to the newest addition to the conversation, Attorney General Eve Goldman.

"Thank you. Now, let's begin."

THE SAME TIME

The Indian doctor, first to hop on stage at Sidney Harman Hall, took charge. She also took extreme care not to touch Browning. She stayed with Browning and waited for the paramedics to arrive.

Katie had the presence of mind to grab plastic gloves for the doctor from one of the legitimate makeup artists. The doctor put them on and now felt confident handling Browning.

"You," she said addressing Kessler, "Make sure the paramedics are all gloved."

"Absolutely."

THE SITUATION ROOM
THE SAME TIME

Morgan Taylor held a blank yellow notepad.

"General Pollack, the floor's yours."

"Thank you, sir. I'll lead with baseline information so everyone has the same footing."

He looked to the president for affirmation. He got it.

"First, a primer of the Korean People's Army Navy. For lack of a better word, our target. The navy is a separate branch of the KPA, headquartered in Pyongyang. It has two separate fleets. East Sea and Yellow Sea, with distinct combatant groups. The Yellow Sea Fleet is comprised of six squadrons, approximately three hundred vessels. They're headquartered in Namp'o with ports in Pipa-got and Sago, and lesser bases in Tasari and Ch'o-do. Meanwhile, the East Sea Fleet has ten squadrons, seven hundred vessels, and is headquartered in Toegjo-dong, with satellite bases at Najin, Wonsan, and others closer to the DMZ.

"Not that long ago it was a sixty-thousand-force brown water navy, principally charged with coastal defense. Then things changed. That thing was money. Money plowed into submarine operations. That's what we're looking at today. Submarine bases along both coasts. And specifically one that I prefer not to identify."

No one objected.

"North Korea builds small and medium-sized submarines and runs a fleet of older Chinese and Russian-made vessels. Most are the Romeo-class, out-dated and slow, but still capable of screwing with shipping lanes. They can attack surface ships, lay mines, and deploy commandos.

"The fleet's major problem is that they're only of 'reasonable quality.' That means they spend less time at sea than what would be considered normal for submarines. More time in port for upgrades and repair. That said, the North's forces, by sheer number, outclass and outnumber the South's anti-submarine warfare capability. An imbalance in undersea power."

Pollack went into detail about the number of diesel electric submarines, from Whiskey-class vessels supplied by the old Soviet Union, to more than seventy Romeo-class subs from China.

Their submerged speeds varied from thirteen knots down to four. Crew sizes ranged from fifty-four to twenty. The weapons' complement included missiles, torpedoes, and sea mines.

"They represent a real danger, but," he said lowering his voice, "we have the means to disable them."

The vice president beat the chief of staff to a question. A single-word question.

"Disable?"

Pollack deferred to the president before answering.

"We'll get to that, J3," Taylor replied. "For now, let's stay on background."

"If I may, I'd like to turn the briefing over to Admirals Drivas and Conn," General Pollack stated.

They were the designated tag team.

"Thank you," Drivas said. The NSA director had a PowerPoint presentation prepared. He opened the first slide with the wireless remote.

"This is North Korea's Sinpo-class ballistic missile submarine. An SSBN. Its design is based on Russian models. They're built in North Korea, and the KPA is adding more to the fleet yearly. Its nickname is 'The Whale.' Their introduction represents a deadly step forward into the regime's fighting capability."

The picture looked impressive, especially against photographs of North Korea's older sub fleet.

"It has a range of fifteen hundred nautical miles, two launch tubes, and ever-improving down range effectiveness. The Sinpo-class takes

Pyongyang to the next level in submarine warfare. And we consider North Korea firing a ballistic missile, possibly nuclear, from one of these new subs as a credible top line threat.

"Admiral Conn?" The chief of Naval Operations took the pass.

"We've monitored test launches that have gone hundreds of miles toward Japan and set distance records east. I don't need to remind anyone that *east* is Hawaii and further east is the U.S. mainland.

"Every year North Korea adds to its submarine fleet. Right now they're outnumbering our Pacific sub force nearly two-to-one. While our force is better equipped, better trained, with better ships, numbers talk."

"I'll say," National Security Advisor Yates complained.

Admiral Conn went through five other slides detailing risk assessments to South Korea and Japan. He concluded with a ghostly reminder—successive slides of a sunken ship, a 1,200-ton gunboat raised by winches, and pictures of a torpedo drive shaft.

"In 2010, a North Korean submarine torpedo sank a South Korean naval ship, the *Cheonan*. Forty-eight souls died. Of course, North Korea denied the report, but a dive team recovered parts of the torpedo. It had lettering that matched North Korea's design. Proof that North Korea has little fear of aggressively deploying its submarine fleet."

Admiral Drivas switched on the last slide. A photograph of bodies in the sunken ship's hull.

The Situation Room fell silent.

"Jack?" the president called on his CIA director.

Jack Evans stood.

"I'm going to tell you part of a story," he began.

Individuals knew parts. Mulligan had more. The FBI's photo recognition work and the death of CIA agent Vinnie D'Angelo. And thanks to a discovery by the FBI, a story that started in Europe.

"Two boys meet at a private school in Switzerland," he explained. "They develop a friendship that turns into a long-term relationship. And they bond over a ludicrous fantasy. As they move through life, they realize they can turn their fantasy into a reality. They stay connected and make things happen. One friend grows up and becomes the puppet master of a sweeping separatist movement in the United States. The other grows up to become dictator of the Democratic People's Republic of Korea. Together, they execute their childhood plan to destabilize America."

Mulligan's short speech sucked the oxygen right out of the room.

"Mother of God," Attorney General Goldman said.

Secretary of State Bob Huret was more blunt. "Holy shit!"

. . .

The paramedic team rolled the chief justice through the elephant doors at the back of the theater and into the ambulance. The Indian doctor argued with the Supreme Court Police sergeant who wanted her removed. She found an ally in Katie Kessler.

"No room," the officer replied.

"She comes with us," Katie declared. "Get your own ride!"

THE SITUATION ROOM

The phone rang.

"Yes, Louise," the president said.

He listened.

He added a thank you and hung up.

"I'm sorry," Taylor said to the room. "We're going to have to cut this short. We'll reconvene as soon as possible."

The group stood without questioning. They all knew the president would hold anyone back who would be necessary.

Bernsie gave the president a look. Taylor held both palms out. A signal to stay. And to the vice president and CIA chief he said, "J3, Jack, hang for a bit?"

Everyone else was excused. To the three who remained, Taylor stated, "Justice Browning is on his way to GW in critical condition. Likely poisoned."

Bernsie gasped. Jonas Jackson Johnson bowed his head.

"And there's more," Taylor continued. "Roarke is chasing down our killer."

. . .

The ambulance raced through Washington streets in a 2.2 mile, nine-minute high-speed race from F Street NW to Sixth.

"He's in a coma," Dr. Avantika Gupta said. She assisted the paramedics with an IV drip.

"You said poison. What kind?"

"Not sure. And we won't have many options. But I've seen the symptoms. This looks like aconite poisoning."

She told one of the two onboard paramedics to call ahead. She wanted a stomach tube prepared, twenty milliliters of Tincture of Digitalis, a list of other stimulants, and diluted brandy.

"Brandy for you, doctor?" the paramedic asked.

"Up his rectum if he can't retain the stimulants."

"How do you know all this?" Katie wondered.

"The hard way. Two boys from the country. My internship in Delhi. Aconite is one of the most powerful poisons ever discovered. It's the active ingredient of the plant, but especially deadly if extracted from the root. Easily absorbed through skin contact. One-fiftieth of a grain can kill a sparrow in seconds. One-tenth grain, a rabbit in five minutes. Your judge undoubtedly had been exposed to much more."

"The makeup," Katie said mostly to herself.

"What?"

"The makeup artist is an assassin."

Dr. Gupta gave a quick nod, then returned to her training. She focused on the patient and suddenly yelled to the driver, "Faster. We're losing him."

CHAPTER 86

WASHINGTON, D.C.

The Frenchman saw the snarled traffic ahead. He hung a quick right, went one block to Seventh and then left. But traffic looked no better there. He was approaching the Capital One Arena, home of the D.C. hockey and basketball franchises. No game this evening, but bar and restaurant nightlife immediately made this a bad choice. Slowing down was not an option. Straddling traffic on either side of the road was. Doing so caught the eye of a Metro cop freelancing as a pub bouncer. He made the mistake of trying to stop the BMW himself.

Roarke watched the man go down. "On Seventh," he shouted to Bessolo while downshifting his Mercedes. "Man down." He gave more specifics while swerving around pedestrians himself and blaring his horn.

"I'll call it in," Bessolo replied. "Got some good news."

"What?" Roarke honked more, working his way back onto the right side of Seventh.

"The woman he knocked down says her phone is still in the car. We'll track it."

"Do it!"

Meanwhile, Roarke was intent on catching up with the killer, now a block ahead.

• • •

F Street takes a half jog left past the Spy Museum. The Frenchman followed the flow, weaving around slow-moving cars, passing the National Portrait Gallery, and taking a sudden sharp left onto Tenth.

Though he didn't know it, he was now driving between two locations where assassin John Wilkes Booth had accomplished his goal: Ford's Theatre on one side and the house where President Abraham Lincoln died on the other.

On the straightaway down Tenth, he checked his rearview mirror and caught a quick glimpse of the Mercedes cutting the distance between them. He added another ten mph to his flight and nearly collided with an SUV. His horn and the screeching tires sent a dozen people diving for cover and no fewer than three men in suits reaching for their cell phones.

Another glance into the mirror. He saw that the Mercedes made its own sweep around the SUV, which settled in front of a barrier, and avoided the pedestrians.

No, he realized. *Not pedestrians.* He should have paid better attention. *FBI Agents.* He had committed the best routes to memory, but not all the landmarks. A tactical error. The Frenchman brought the chase right past FBI Headquarters. Tenth and Pennsylvania Avenue. Plus, he was only blocks from the White House. He looked at the dashboard GPS and came up with an idea. A quick right on Constitution.

CHAPTER 87

Working with the approved FISA and FBI warrants, Burke and Lindstrom's phones were now bugged and their computer searches traced.

Agent Beth Thomas was on the ground in Missoula tracking and listening from a rented office across the street from Burke headquarters. She phoned Washington.

"Subject's booked a 7:30 p.m. SkyWest flight out of Missoula to Salt Lake. It's actually a Delta Connection. Then to Atlanta and Mexico City. Give me the word and we can pick him up at the airport."

"No," replied the FBI director. "We'll get him at the gate in Atlanta. Just as he's prepared to leave the U.S. Book yourself on his flights. Keep him in sight. How long is his layover in Salt Lake?"

Thomas checked. "Two-hours, forty-nine minutes."

"And when does it leave?"

"Under two hours."

"Go! I'll hook you up with an agent there!"

* * *

Lindstrom left the office without talking to anyone. He took an Uber to the stunned look of Lucas Burke.

* * *

Beth Thomas hung up, grabbed her always-packed rolling suitcase and had a colleague drive her to the airport while another stayed to watch the office.

CHAPTER 88

WASHINGTON, D.C.

Roarke figured their two cars were fairly matched. He was also certain that if his phantom had a prescribed escape plan he might be off it. That could be good. Things had already gone awry. And things would get harder for him. Police. Helicopters. Spike strips. Road closures. Washington was one of the worst cities in the country to be in a car chase.

"Tracking him now," Bessolo said on the phone line Roarke forgot was open. "We're working on accessing his car computer, too. That's harder."

"Call the phone. Connect me!" Roarke declared as he made the turn onto Constitution.

"If we do that he'll toss the phone. We could lose him."

"Goddamnit, Bessolo, I'm looking right at him! Just do it!"

• • •

Constitution was surprisingly open for a Saturday night, but the assassin decided the worst place to be would be adjacent to the White House lawn. So he had another turn coming up. A sharp left. And a decision.

He slowed.

The Mercedes behind him moved up.

The Frenchman tapped his brakes.

His tail got closer.

"Come on," he said calmly. "Time to look into your eyes."

The Mercedes closed in. Fifty feet, forty, thirty, then twenty. Suddenly his pursuer swerved out from behind and pressed ahead, running parallel and to the left of him as they approached the next intersection.

The assassin peered over to the Mercedes driver. He recognized the face. He'd seen him on his remote cameras crawling on the grounds of his French farmhouse. The second agent. The one who survived.

He shot him a cruel smile. It drew the man's attention as planned. Now he turned into the Mercedes. A brush more than a bump. But the driver reacted instinctively, swerving left up and over the curb and onto the Mall. He came to a sudden stop inches before hitting a Magnolia tree.

Now the Frenchman sped up and made a wide left onto Twelfth. That's when he hit a couple crossing the street.

• • •

"Fuck me!" Roarke exclaimed.

Roarke looked over his left shoulder, then his right. Clear. He put the car in reverse, waited for an oncoming car on Constitution to pass, backed up, and resumed the pursuit.

A left onto Twelfth. And a traffic jam.

Roarke slowed. Two people were down. Traffic was stopped around them. Twelfth Street was now blocked.

He had two possibilities. Across the Mall lawn or the tunnel.

"Bessolo. Still there?"

"Yes. Dialing for you."

"He ran over people at Constitution and Twelfth. Southbound Twelfth is jammed. Any tunnel construction in the tunnel under the Mall?"

The FBI Agent yelled out to his team.

"Tunnel under the Mall at Twelfth? Construction?"

Roarke couldn't wait for the answer. He floored the Mercedes and blasted his horn.

Tunnel.

• • •

The assassin hit ninety above ground. Roarke ran a dangerous eighty in the tunnel. Each honking furiously, veering around slower cars. Each with a heavy foot on the gas ready to push faster.

In the tunnel, cars hugged the walls as Roarke jammed past. On Twelfth, the Frenchman drove cars off the road with sharp, unexpected swerves.

Roarke was aware of Bessolo saying something in his ear. But the Secret Service agent didn't process it. Driving required all his attention.

Five more cars to pass. Five more near collisions. Hell to pay down the line. Nothing compared to what would happen if he didn't catch his man.

On the street, another right turn. Independence Avenue and a long straight shot. Time to open up.

. . .

Options. The Frenchman ran through the possibilities. Routes he'd memorized. Exfil routes. First he needed more room. He figured that soon they might be able to track his car through onboard computers and disable it. But that would take more time. He still had a window. Maybe five, maybe ten minutes. That's when a cell phone rang on the passenger seat. *Zut!* he mouthed in his native language. *Le téléphone de la femme. Damn!*

He reached for it, first thinking to toss it out the window, but he automatically pressed answer and held it to his ear with his left hand. At the same time, he checked his rearview mirror. No one behind him.

"Yes?" He paused and instinctively knew it was his pursuer. "You!"

"Yes," Roarke replied in an unmistakably deadly tone. "And Martín," he said using the name Touch Parsons had given him, "you're a dead man."

. . .

Roarke roared out of the tunnel, careened right onto Independence, and stepped on the gas.

. . .

The Frenchman clenched the steering wheel, channeling his outrage. No one had uttered his actual name for years. Now there was more to do than merely escape. The Americans knew his identity.

"Who are you?" he asked.

"Roarke."

"Well, Roarke. See me in hell!"

"I'll see you well before then!" Roarke declared.

Martín threw the phone out the window.

CHAPTER 89

MISSOULA INTERNATIONAL AIRPORT
THE SAME TIME

Beth Thomas arrived and caught sight of Lindstrom at the TSA post. The guards knew him from all his travel. He cleared security quickly. Thomas had more trouble. Her gun. Despite her ID, it took time. Time she didn't have.

While trying to convince a supervisor she caught Lindstrom observing her.

Damn! He made me, she thought.

"Can we speed this up?" she demanded.

Finally, a supervisor approved her passage. *But finding Lindstrom?* She ran to the Salt Lake City flight gate. The doors were closed. She asked the airline attendant to check and see if Clay Lindstrom had boarded. Her FBI identification made the unwilling woman more than cooperative.

"No, Agent Thomas. He didn't. And the flight's closed now."

Thomas called the bureau and was automatically connected with her assigned colleague Shannon Davis. She explained what happened.

"See if he's booked another flight."

"On it," he said. She heard his fingers fly over the keys to access new reservations.

Thomas spotted the bank of monitors listing departing flights. It was peak travel time. There were numerous departing planes.

"Make it fast! Bunch of flights leaving soon."

Thomas was visibly frustrated. No more time to waste. She began walking until she came to a split. Two spurs. *Left or right?* she asked herself. Then aloud, "Shannon, talk to me."

"Hold on," Davis said from twenty-three hundred miles away.

"I can't hold! Come on Davis, give me something!" she said sounding every bit like her boss, Roy Bessolo. "Where the hell is he?"

"I'm working on it, Beth. Just stay put."

Thomas ignored the request. She chose left.

The Missoula terminal served state airports and other locations.

It was considered an International Airport because of connections to Canada. That's what she feared. She stopped at another screen. More options than she first saw. An Alaska flight to Seattle in fifty minutes and Frontier to Denver sooner. Then she heard the boarding announcement for an Alaska departure to Calgary International.

"Shit!" she said.

"What?"

"Check if he's on the 7:10 to Calgary."

"Instead of?"

"Anything else! It's 6:55!"

Beth Thomas didn't wait for an answer. She bet he was on that flight. But if she was truly seen by Lindstrom, she couldn't continue the pursuit. *Damn,* she thought. She wanted to make the arrest herself.

She arrived at the gate but hung back. Boarding was nearly complete on the nonstop and the perfect way out of the country. From Calgary, Lindstrom could go anywhere or get lost in the Canadian woods.

"Beth, you there?"

"Yes," she replied over her Bluetooth earpiece.

"Booked to Calgary."

"Shit. I think he ID'd me at security. Unless I take him now."

Davis continued. "He's also booked and paid for a Denver flight leaving in ten."

Damn. Wild goose chase, she thought.

"Which has he checked into?"

"Stand by."

CHAPTER 90

WASHINGTON, D.C.
THE SAME TIME

The Frenchman opened up on westbound Independence. The BMW had power under the hood, but not a lot of time on the clock.

He accelerated from thirty to eighty along the long block between Twelfth and Fourteenth that housed the Department of Agriculture, pushed it to ninety-five as he passed the United States Holocaust Memorial Museum. But without warning he had to slam his brakes. A row of sightseeing buses had slowed at the curve that began to encircle the Washington Monument to the right. He barely avoided slamming into one bus, scraped a second, and burned off all his speed.

He honked, maneuvered around four more buses and pressed ahead. But the seconds he lost were seconds the Mercedes gained.

• • •

Roarke ran over the phone Martín had thrown out. But he was still on with Bessolo.

"On Independence." Roarke said. And then, "Jesus Christ!"

"What?"

"Nearly took out a bus. Christ he's fearless. Catching up."

"We're working on closing the bridges."

Roarke considered what he'd do.

"My bet is he'll hug the river and look for a place to duck back in."

"Doing it anyway," Bessolo declared.

Roarke rounded the curve at the Washington Monument, another reverse curve at the end of Seventeenth Street, then a straightaway adjacent to a line of trees that obstructed any view of the Lincoln Memorial Reflecting Pool. To the left, the Jefferson Memorial and the Martin Luther King, Jr. Memorial and West Potomac Park.

So far, Martín declined turning down any of the side routes. An indication he didn't want hostages.

Roarke reasoned the next critical choke points would be as Independence converged with Ohio Drive, the Arlington Bridge, and Lincoln Memorial traffic before emptying into Rock Creek and Potomac.

Roarke was ten car lengths back. Not good enough to do anything.

• • •

Martín swore in French and English. The American was still on him and, driven by revenge, was a far greater threat than any Capitol Police.

He gave no room to anyone merging from the left. And none circling off the bridge and entering on the right. He took the sharp turn to get on Rock Creek at forty-five and nearly lost control. Sheer shock made others stop on the approach.

* * *

"Damnit!" The blind curve gave Roarke no warning of the trouble ahead. He had to hit his brakes hard. Not hard enough. He rammed a Nissan. The Nissan slammed a Toyota. Then he got rear ended himself. The collision wasn't hard enough to deploy his airbag, but he was boxed in.

Scott Roarke instantly opened his door, ran to the first car in line that had been virtually run off the road by Martín. A Chevy Impala.

Again, he showed his ID and gave a sharp, unmistakable order.

"Out! Secret Service. I'm taking your car."

He heard one long Midwest question. "Butwhatwhy?"

Tourists. A rental.

"Now!"

They fumbled with their doors. And out. Roarke jumped in and gunned the new car. It delivered more pickup than he anticipated.

* * *

The Potomac was on Martín's left. Virginia beyond it. But it offered him no escape route. The city remained his best option. He raced along Rock Creek, beyond Pass Peters Point, under the Kennedy Center terrace, past the Watergate Hotel and condos. The parkway was surprisingly open for the hour. That gave him renewed confidence. That and the fact that he thought he'd left Roarke behind.

* * *

Roarke spotted him about two hundred yards ahead as he tore through the intersection of Virginia Avenue and Rock Creek. Good news, Martín didn't know he had another vehicle. The bad news, he was going as fast as possible, but not making enough progress until…

Driving slowed as they both headed up the hill running parallel to the actual creek. Roarke thought that the Frenchman intentionally took the chase down more than a few notches to avoid police. Especially if he thought he wasn't being pursued.

Roarke eased up as well. He'd closed the distance to under fifty yards when Martín exited onto Waterside Drive.

. . .

For a moment the assassin considered ditching the car and running into the woods to the left. That moment came and went. Not part of the plan he was currently mapping in his head.

He checked the rearview mirror. No Mercedes. No police. Just a sedan.

The traffic light ahead was just changing from green. Martín slowed, took in a deep breath, and checked the mirror again. Light was dropping fast now, but there was enough to see inside the car coming up on him.

"Damn!"

He hit the gas ignoring the red light and clipped the back end of a Mini Cooper crossing the intersection. The impact spun around the smaller car. Martín straightened out. The chase was on again.

. . .

The road race moved into city streets. A hard, high-speed right turn onto Massachusetts Avenue, followed by an immediate left, through another light, and onto Belmont. Martín bounded across a sidewalk, crashing through trashcans, knocking a biker off, and back onto Belmont for a block.

Security was tight in the neighborhood. Roarke knew it. The Frenchman didn't.

Ambassador residences and embassies. Capitol Police and foreign officers. Men and women with guns.

"Bessolo!" Roarke shouted into the phone.

"I'm here. On Belmont. Might have him." "On my way. In a copter now."

There were any number of places to land, but without permission, it would be hard.

"Stay up. I'm in an Impala. Light blue."

The assassin suddenly stopped fifty feet short of a construction barricade.

"Roadblock past the intersection."

"Where'd you say you were?"

"Belmont and," Roarke checked the GPS, "on Tracy. Perfect!"

It wasn't.

. . .

The assassin started backing up, ignoring the fact that he was on a collision course with Roarke's car. But twenty feet before hitting him, he simultaneously broke, shifted, spun, and threw the BMW into drive. He passed Roarke who commenced a far slower three-point turn.

Now a right up Tracy and speed bumps which the Frenchman all but ignored, taking them at fifty.

Roarke followed a painful half-minute behind.

Another turn. This time a left onto Kalorama, with more speed bumps and bends. Past five and ten million-dollar homes, a hotel, and foreign security officers who all made radio calls as one car and then a second sped past.

. . .

Martín had some thirty city maps memorized. D.C. Metro was one he concentrated on now as he made a right on Connecticut off Kalorama and darted around the slower moving uphill traffic. Connecticut crested, and then it was downhill to his destination.

. . .

Roarke bounced as the Impala took the hill. Without a seat belt on, he hit his head on the roof. Sparks flew as the back bumper scrapped the pavement.

At fifty mph, he passed the Hilton Hotel, known by locals as the

Hinkley Hilton. The Secret Service had a real lesson in presidential protection that day in 1981 when Reagan was shot. With the chief justice poisoned, Roarke feared today was almost as bad. He didn't even know if Browning was alive.

The thought evaporated as he saw the Frenchman two blocks ahead. Two blocks that he couldn't make up as traffic cut his speed in half. Dupont Circle. More streets converging. More cars. More pedestrians.

* * *

The killer honked. Five fast and insistent blasts. It wasn't enough to get the car in front to move out of the way. So he bumped him hard, creating another fast acting accident scene. Martín pulled hard left, which put him in the wrong lane to drive the circle to the right around Dupont Circle. But there was another, quicker way.

Barely slowing, the assassin plowed up the curb. Another blast of the horn. Couples dove out of the way on the northwest side of the park. A musician lost his guitar under a tire, wine bottles broke, and dogs were yanked hard by their owners. He missed everyone, which was pure luck.

Martín darted around park benches, circumvented the fountain, took out a city trash can, and emerged with Nineteenth Street straight ahead.

* * *

The Frenchman cleared the way. Roarke followed. Right through Dupont Circle. His right hand hitting the horn, except when he needed both hands on the wheel. On the other side of the park, a multiple crash scene. One car upended, gas spilling out, and passersby trying to help a driver out. Two other cars were in a tangled mess.

Roarke weaved through the mess and stopped short of the corner of Nineteenth. The BMW, with the driver's door open, was thirty feet ahead.

Roarke exited the Impala, drew his weapon, and approached the BMW wide and from the left. That's when he heard a shot and screams.

. . .

Martín fired a second time in the air.

"Down! Now!"

Those who turned to the first shot saw a man running toward them. On the second, they hit the ground.

Creating his own shock and awe, Martín had a clear path to the Dupont Circle Metro stop escalators.

CHAPTER 91

MISSOULA INTERNATIONAL AIRPORT

FBI agent Beth Thomas got confirmation from Shannon Davis. Lindstrom had booked the Calgary flight on the run. She waited for him at the gate. The flight loaded. He never arrived. That's when she realized her mistake.

Thomas ran back to where the original commuter flight was taking off. The gate was closed, the flight had left.

A ticket agent was closing the computer down for the night.

"That Denver flight?"

"Sorry, miss. You're too late."

"FBI!" she said sharply. Her badge and ID underscore the exclamation point. "Did a Clay Lindstrom board?"

"Really?" the ground-based agent responded, somewhat exasperated and ready to go home.

"Really and for that matter, if he is on, don't let that plane take off!"

The urgency defeated the attendant's exasperation.

"Okay, okay. I'll check."

But Thomas's answer was visible out the window. The SkyWest flight lifted off.

The agent typed and mistyped.

"Sorry it's taking so long," she said covering her own nervousness. "Rindstrom with an R."

"No L! L! Lindstrom!" She spelled it.

"Okay, yes. Mr. Lindstrom boarded at the last minute."

"How long is before it lands?"

The fifty-something-year-old agent, flustered, checked flight time.

"Ninety minutes. But there's a weather delay in Salt Lake City. Expected twenty minutes late."

Thomas was dialing on the end of the word *late*. She called Washington requesting back up in Denver and to have the bureau secure a private carrier—immediately. Northstar Jets came through. The airline assured that their French built Falcon 50EX would be gassed and ready for takeoff in thirty minutes. Top cruising speed, nearly twice the commuter flight, just under Mach 1. Beth Thomas ran to their terminal.

CHAPTER 92

Martín didn't look back. Roarke only looked forward. The Frenchman had thirty steps on him by the time he came to the Metro station.

Martín ran down the escalator, pushing people aside to get by faster and produce obstacles for Roarke. He shoved a woman down; she knocked an elderly man; the old man fell on a child. Martín leapt over the kid and bumped off a teenager with a backpack and regained his footing.

The down escalator was on the right. Roarke quickly saw the chaos. To the left, a pair of escalators going up. But they were crowded with slow moving commuters leaving the Dupont Circle Station.

There was an immediate alternative. Roarke jumped up onto the metal housing between the down escalator and the first up escalator. He slid on his back with his legs outstretched. Midway, his feet slammed into a raised barrier intended to prevent the very thing he was doing. Roarke put both hands to his left and vaulted off the barrier onto the up escalator. Now he ran down the up side, pushing people aside. As he neared the bottom, he spotted Martín running full speed toward the station turnstiles.

In one fluid move the Frenchman fired a shot in the air. Plaster splattered and provided the desired effect. Pedestrians scattered. Martín then took an incredible no-hands leap over the turnstile.

Parkour, Roarke thought. *Parcours du combattant.* Vaulting, jumping and rolling, running and climbing. It all made a fast man faster. A strong man stronger. A dangerous man more dangerous.

Now on firm ground himself, Roarke sprinted toward the same turnstile, vaulted off his right foot, and thought he'd made it. He didn't. His left foot caught the far side and he went down hard on his shoulder. The pain didn't bother him. It was the time he'd lost…again. More seconds. More distance. And Martín obviously planned to get away on the next subway out.

Which way? Outbound toward Shaddy Grove or back, deeper into D.C.?

He didn't see which ramp Martín took. But the stunned look on commuters' faces told him. Inbound.

The Frenchman tore past more people on the incline toward the subway platform. He made the wrong choice. This side had just off-loaded. He needed the opposite track where people were waiting for the Red Line to arrive.

He looked left and right down the tracks. No lights. No wind from an oncoming train.

"Martín, stop!"

The order came from the top of the ramp. Martín looked around. The pursuer was running.

Roarke saw the Frenchman raise his gun.

"Down!" he yelled to the people near him.

As he ducked, Martín fired, just missing Roarke. But the bullet sent shards of tile and plaster flying, striking five people.

Roarke hopped over the waist-high railing. He landed hard, sending another bolt of pain through his body to his shoulder. Again, he ignored it.

By now, Martín was crossing the tracks, carefully stepping over the power rails. With little more than a two-step run, he launched sideways onto the opposite platform.

Roarke stood, calculating the risk of firing, but he couldn't. Martín had grabbed a woman and held her as a shield. The Frenchman was about to take a shot at Roarke, but the woman bravely kicked him in his leg with her two-inch heels. It threw off his aim. Furious, he hit her hard with the side of his gun, threw her to the ground, and ran further down the platform.

Now Roarke checked for subways. Still clear. He jumped off the inbound platform and crossed the tracks as Martín had done moments before.

Commuters ran wildly away from the man being chased and the man in pursuit. One young boy fell off the platform. His father leaned over. The boy reached for his hand. The father yanked him up.

The woman who'd been hit by Martín was bleeding. Two people helped her, and then ran with the fleeing crowd. However, Roarke yelled for everyone to stay down. Some did. Some didn't. Now he had a shot.

Martín heard the "stay down" order. He spun around a woman in a powered wheelchair, ducked behind her, and pushed her toward the track. A man ran forward to stop her, but Martín put a bullet in his leg. The woman barely stopped herself before going over the edge.

Roarke lost his shot. But in the moment, he used the onrushing crowd as his own diversion.

The Frenchman scanned for Roarke. He'd disappeared. Or hidden behind people. Or jumped onto the rails.

Roarke moved silently, controlling his breathing, calculating the distance and when to reappear.

Martín swore. The display on the Metro station digital screen indicated the next train was still two minutes out. Two minutes. No place to hide. It was all timing and luck. He'd missed one train and the other…

Fight or flight?

The assassin didn't have to make the decision.

Roarke sprung up from the rails just behind him and laid a tackle at calf level sending Martín to the ground.

The assassin rolled to his left, away from the edge, keeping his gun-holding right hand extended. Roarke, on his knees, had his 9mm in his hand. But both used their free left hands to block the opposing guns. A standoff until Martín head-butted Roarke hard. The impact sent Roarke backward. Martín followed up with a sharp punch to Roarke's ribs. Then another. And a third. He swept his right arm wide, knocking Roarke's gun out of his hand, then a fast elbow jab aimed at Roarke's head.

Roarke dodged the incoming elbow. Martín's elbow slammed on the ground with a crunch. He didn't break it, but he felt a sharp radiating pain.

Roarke leaned in, jerked Martín's gun upward, and inserted his finger on top of the killer's. Now either man could pull the trigger.

The gun swung around, toward Martín, then toward Roarke. Muscle against muscle. Each man fighting for position. It hovered between them until Roarke anchored his right foot and pushed his whole body up, jerking Martín's hand and raising the gun to his right ear.

He fired, more by accident than intention. The sound blasted both their eardrums. The only thing either heard was loud ringing.

Roarke brought his foot up and kicked the gun from the assassin's hand. It fell below. But in the process, he lost his balance. And his advantage. Martín was younger, taller, with greater agility. An advantage he employed.

Martín spun around with a right high kick to Roarke's head. Roarke deflected it, but the second sweep from his left foot connected to his stomach. Roarke doubled over. The assassin grabbed Roarke's head, and while bending, flipped Roarke over.

Roarke turned the motion into a somersault. He regained his footing and delivered a solid right punch to Martín's head. Mirroring the Frenchman's move, he used his momentum to wind up and come back with a roundhouse kick to the stomach, followed by a right-handed upper cut to the head. Martín staggered back.

Three feet separated them, enough for Martín to suck in a breath, brace, and return a right hook to Roarke's chin, then a second, and third. This forced Roarke back against the wall. Roarke reached for Martín's throat. A move he quickly realized was a mistake.

The Frenchman brought his arms up between Roarke's and quickly spread them apart, deflecting the threat. Then he swung his arm around Roarke's head and used his body to bring him over his shoulder and again onto the ground.

Martín stepped in for a heel kick to the head. Roarke rolled right, but his head was still an easy target. In one swift motion, Martín landed his heel on Roarke's ear.

Dazed, Roarke closed his body tight, arms in, legs up, as Martín punched Roarke's calf and thigh. First soft places causing immediate pain, and then hard bone that could do more damage.

Roarke backpedaled on all fours, an old athletic exercise that worked. But Martín was still too close. He launched a fast, powerful disabling right punch toward Roarke's crotch, but missed. His fist hit the ground hard.

Through the continuous ringing in their ears, they didn't hear the announcement of the subway, now a minute away. But they could feel the wind coming toward them, pushed by the oncoming subway. Both men looked in the direction of the train.

Roarke rose up just as Martín lunged. The Frenchman pinned Roarke to the subway wall and delivered three fast blows to his ribs. Using the wall for stability, Roarke pushed back, swung up his hands, blocked the fourth punch and countered with a left hook to the jaw.

Roarke followed up with an axe kick, but Martín saw it coming and dodged. He backed up toward the edge of the platform near where he'd dropped his gun.

The gun could end it. Martín saw it first. He bent down to pick it up just as Roarke's foot came up under his gut.

Now Roarke's turn to recover the pistol. Only inches to go, but Martín grabbed his leg. Roarke went down and Martín delivered another series of punishing side jabs into Roarke's aching ribs, followed by an elbow down and into his shoulder. Roarke tightened again and sent his curled right knuckles up into Martín's throat. Not enough for a larynx-smashing cut, but immediately hurtful.

Now, feeling an advantage, Roarke pulled the killer in, cupped his left foot around Martín's right leg and swung the assassin over his thigh. His back took the brunt of the fall.

The wind increased, and the ground-level warning red lights began flashing. What they couldn't hear, they saw and felt. The wind seemed to energize the killer.

Martín rolled over, vaulted up, and attacked wildly. First a quick jab to the face. Another round house kick to the stomach. And as Roarke doubled over, a left upper cut to the chin.

Roarke struggled. He looked beyond Martín to the lights of the oncoming train. Maybe twenty seconds before it arrived. He used two of those seconds to come back with his own sharp kick to Martín's kidneys as the Frenchman turned to pick up the gun again. Then a set of four follow-up jabs. Martín staggered. Roarke delivered two more sharp knuckle-bearing punches that looked like it might do him in.

It didn't. Martín blocked a third hit and answered with an elbow to Roarke's head and a punch to his stomach that sent the Secret Service agent off balance, over the edge and onto the tracks.

The wind was stronger. The sound now louder than the ringing.

Roarke mustered all his strength, grabbed for a familiar shape on the ground, and climbed back up on the platform only to see that Martín had recovered his weapon.

Anticipating the shot, Roarke dodged left. The bullet barely missed him.

The Red Line subway pulled into the Metro station. Martín ran alongside ready to jump in once the doors opened. The train stopped. Martín looked back, spotted Roarke's profile and fired again. This time a true shot. The 9mm bullet tore through Roarke's left shoulder. But Roarke's right hand held what he had found on the tracks. His own pistol.

Roarke aimed for the largest target. The full front-facing body. Martín took the shot in the stomach, but it didn't stop him.

The train doors opened.

Martín brought his gun up again. Roarke beat him. The second bullet hit the former French special forces operative in the lungs. He began coughing up blood.

"That's from Vinnie D'Angelo."

He fired a third time hitting the assassin squarely in the heart.

"That's from me."

Martín fell backward into the open subway car. He was dead before hitting the ground.

CHAPTER 93

Beth Thomas touched down ahead of the commuter flight. Under FBI authorization, the FAA cleared the Northstar Jet to SkyWest arrivals. She disembarked and met two members of the Denver bureau who accompanied her through a ground level door up to the gate.

"He won't be armed," Thomas explained. "But I want to take him quietly. He's made me. So I'll stand to the side and point him out. Approach him quietly. I don't want to see someone's cell phone video on CNN tonight."

"Got it," replied one of the two agents, intentionally dressed casually. The second agent agreed.

Twelve minutes later, the fifty-seat twin engine CJR-200 taxied up to the gate. The agents took their places. Considering Lindstrom was one of the last to board, Thomas expected he'd be one of the last to disembark. This was good. She was right.

Lindstrom walked off the flight ahead of only ten others. Thomas stood against a wall some twenty feet away. She gave a casual nod to the two regional agents to identify the subject. The agents registered the signal and began to fall in behind Lindstrom. But too closely. Too loudly. Lindstrom sensed danger.

He didn't run. But it certainly wasn't a walk. He increased his pace to catch up with other departing passengers.

Damn! Beth Thomas thought. She motioned for her team to slow down and back off. Then she swept wide, keeping Lindstrom in view.

A minute passed. Then another. He continued to walk to the exit. Lindstrom eased in line with the other passengers; then pushed ahead. He glanced back. No one was on him.

Relaxing, Lindstrom shook his head, exhaled deeply, and confidently turned toward the sliding exit doors just steps away. A woman blocked his path.

"Mr. Lindstrom. So good to see you."

The woman from the Missoula airport.

"Let's walk out together and not make a scene."

Beth Thomas pulled her black blazer aside. Her FBI badge lay on a lanyard. Her standard issue handgun was inches away.

WASHINGTON, D.C.
TWENTY MINUTES LATER

FBI Director Mulligan took the call at his desk.

"Suspect's in custody," Beth Thomas said. She didn't identify Lindstrom by name. "We're heading in."

"Good job."

"He wants his attorney."

"Of course he does. Get the name. We'll do some research. But first things first. You lead the un-Mirandized *Dirty Team*. After we get somewhere a *Clean Team* can read him his rights. He'll get his lawyer and proper attention. Unless, of course…" Mulligan stopped short and thought about another scenario that didn't involve lawyers.

"He wants to know what we're holding him for."

"Ask him if he's a citizen of the United States."

Thomas turned around and lowered her phone.

"My boss wants to know if you're a citizen of the United States."

"Of course I am. I know my rights."

Thomas returned to the call. "He said—"

"I heard," Bob Mulligan said. "Then tell him treason."

• • •

"Mr. President, we're holding Clay Lindstrom, and we're about to take Lucas Burke in for questioning," Director Mulligan explained. "Before the night's out, we'll have all his computers, cell phones, and files. But we're trying to do it in such a way as not to draw the press in. Our cover is a massive computer virus."

"What's the chance he'll cough up anything?"

"Can't say. But we'll make sure that he knows the alternative."

"And charging him?"

"Well here's the problem. Treason. But the bar for actual proof is high. Collaborating testimony will help. Had Martín lived…"

Taylor had no argument with Roarke's actions.

"Well, he didn't. What about Burke? Involved, too?"

"Don't know if he was a dupe or a co-conspirator. Computers may tell us more. The best of all worlds, we get a confession."

The president saw nothing but problems.

"Get it," Taylor said.

. . .

That night Clay Lindstrom had a terrible traffic accident. Possibly fatal. At least that was the news report that circulated on the air and the worry that spread through the office. No one could get any real information. That's because Lindstrom was alive and well, somewhere off the grid with no idea of the terrible crash he'd allegedly been in.

CHAPTER 94

UNDISCLOSED SAFE HOUSE
THE NEXT MORNING

"Ready?" FBI Director Robert Mulligan asked his companions.

"Ready," they responded verbally and with subtle affirmation.

"Let's do it."

The FBI safe house, more of a tricked-out mansion, was down a private county road, twenty-six miles outside of Salt Lake City. The perimeter was patrolled at three hundred yards and again at one hundred yards. Where agents weren't, cameras and motion detectors were. It would take a well-planned tactical mission to penetrate the property, let alone access the compound.

The Washington team entered. Mulligan handed over his standard issue automatic before being led beyond the foyer. The others didn't carry weapons, but nonetheless they were checked by an agent. Two other agents accompanied them to a study, or a room that looked like a study or a library. But a mirrored wall meant that observers were watching and multiple video and recording devices picked up every movement and word.

The group entered. Clay Lindstrom, wearing jeans, a t-shirt, athletic socks, and sneakers, paced. Given the manner in which he was being held, without legal counsel yet, with 24/7 supervision in a secure facility, he considered he was getting first class treatment. At least for now. It could also mean he'd soon be taken to the wood chipper to become mulch.

The library opened and closed. Robert Mulligan walked in. He recognized the FBI chief immediately. *More questions. More denials.*

"Mr. Lindstrom, I'm—"

"Yes, I know. I want a lawyer."

"You're under protective custody, Mr. Lindstrom."

"Now it's protective custody? Last night I was being charged with treason. So protection from who?"

"Well, that will be part of our discussion. But first…" Mulligan gave a thumbs-up to the mirror. The door opened. Attorney General Eve Goldman joined Mulligan.

"Mr. Lindstrom, Attorney General Goldman."

"Well, it appears the discussion is about to move to a very high level," he said with confidence. "Hello, Ms. Goldman. What do I owe the honor?" Lindstrom thought *deal.* "Director Mulligan tells me I'm under protective custody."

"For the moment," she said coldly.

Moment? Lindstrom didn't like the word. And he suddenly didn't like her. "Like I said, I want my lawyer."

"Well, let's talk. Then you can decide," Mulligan replied.

He gave another thumbs-up to the mirror. The door opened again, and the third government representative entered. Lindstrom gasped.

"I believe you've met," Mulligan said.

"Ms. Novick," Lindstrom said.

"Actually, it's Kessler."

"Apparently people aren't who they say they are," replied the shocked Lindstrom.

"Oh, that's precisely the nature of our discussion," Mulligan added.

"I'm not comfortable with Ms. Kessler being here."

"She's present on behalf of her employer," the attorney general replied.

"And who would that be?"

"The chief justice of the United States Supreme Court. Leopold

Browning. Currently at George Washington University Hospital in critical condition," Goldman continued. "Another part of our discussion."

Lindstrom sat down. The wood chipper suddenly seemed more likely.

MISSOULA
ONE WEEK LATER

The FBI's computer forensics team supported Lucas Burke's innocence, though he had no idea why he was being questioned. Repeatedly. The FBI also interviewed other staff members including Josh Collins.

There were questions back and forth about Lindstrom. Probing questions from the FBI and curious questions from Lucas and the staff about Lindstrom's condition.

"Touch and go," they were told.

No one seemed overly sad. Their allegiance was to Lucas Burke. But without Lindstrom, the organization would be in jeopardy.

Over the next week, volunteers un-volunteered. Paid employees stopped getting paid. Lucas Burke called the remaining staff together, thanked everyone, and locked the door.

CHAPTER 95

WASHINGTON, D.C.
THE JUSTICE DEPARTMENT HOLDING ROOM
ONE WEEK LATER

The United States Justice Department granted Clay Lindstrom a special distinction. Few subjects ever meet directly with the nation's attorney general. But few had ever risen to his level of notoriety; an American who willingly conspired with a foreign power against the United States of America.

Eve Goldman read the charges enumerated under U.S. Code 18 §
2381–90: Treason, rebellion, insurrection, seditious conspiracy, advocating the overthrow of government, and recruiting for service against
the United States.

She then read his full confession.

"Any changes, Mr. Lindstrom?" the attorney general asked.

"None."

She slid a pen and the paper across the table in a heavily guarded
conference room at the Justice Department.

"Initial and date the bottom of every page and sign your name to
the last."

Clay Lindstrom took the pen. Before signing he looked at everyone in the room and slowly nodded defeat. To Attorney General Eve
Goldman. To Vice President Jonas Jackson Johnson. To CIA Director
Jack Evans. To FBI Director Bob Mulligan. And sensing someone was
watching through a one-way mirror, he tipped his head again.

He initialed three pages of his confession but stopped on the fourth
page. The signature page.

"There's nothing you can do in retribution," he declared. "You can't
punish them. You won't start a war with North Korea over this."

"You don't need to be concerned about what the United States of
America can or cannot do, Mr. Lindstrom," Attorney General Goldman declared. "Sign the document. You will be protected for the rest
of your natural days. But to the rest of the world, you're already dead
and buried."

Clay Lindstrom would live out his days in isolation. Prisoner Y, in
a prison without fellow prisoners. A man without a name or a country.
He traded the death sentence for information. He gave up the identity of a friend he met in private school. And he gave up the purpose:
"Undermine the United States. Support a shadow government. Assassinate Americans."

His exact words in the admission, "We met at school in Switzerland. We bonded. We came up with an idea. He had money, unlimited
money. We conspired. We waited. We planned. And I damn well nearly
pulled it all off. But don't think it's over."

Lindstrom was brought to his feet by guards on either side. "One
last question?" he asked.

"The very last," Goldman replied.

"How'd you figure it out?" Lindstrom asked.

"We're bigger than you."

"Come on. It was that woman. The one you planted in the office?"

"Don't take it personally, Mr. Lindstrom, but in one respect, it came down to just a feeling." He didn't explain more about Kessler's seeing and touching his map or her cell phone pictures, which had revealed and confirmed more under Touch Parsons's expert examination. Marking the map was Lindstrom's ultimate mistake, which he didn't know he'd even made. It was also the Supreme Leader's most supreme blunder.

As guards walked him to the door, Lindstrom stopped and turned to face the one-way mirror. Not knowing who was on the other side, but certain it was someone even more important than those in the room, he shouted, "You'll never be able talk about it either. You'll never be able to do anything about it. Unsolved murders. That's the only story you'll have to tell. The press will finish the job we started."

Morgan Taylor turned his back on Clay Lindstrom and left the observation room. He had a decision to make.

CHAPTER 96

THE WHITE HOUSE
THE GAME ROOM THAT NIGHT
TWO DAYS LATER
2300 HOURS

"Mr. Speaker," the president said as he came off shooting the Number Four ball into the corner pocket of his White House pool table.

"Mr. President." Duke Patrick saw Bernie Bernstein nursing a Scotch in a high-back leather chair. He acknowledged him with an impolitic hello. "And to what do I owe this unexpected honor at this advanced hour?" he added, failing to hide sarcasm

"A conversation, Duke. I've asked Bernsie to stick around. Consider him my leash."

Duke Patrick didn't like the reference. But then again, he didn't like Morgan Taylor.

"The chief of staff is always welcome."

Morgan Taylor aimed for the Number Five ball, connected, banked it off the opposite side, and nailed the shot, center pocket. As he walked around the table, he invited Patrick to sit. It had the ring of an order.

"Ah, but I'm acting like a bad host. Scotch?"

Patrick nodded.

The president put his cue stick down and poured a drink, two fingers high.

"Neat, correct?"

"Yes."

Patrick accepted without a toast. Taylor picked up the cue stick again and surveyed the table.

"Let's talk about the presidency."

Duke Patrick tipped his drink toward Taylor without comment.

"Actually, it's how I go about filling the position."

The Speaker braced himself with a large gulp for another Morgan Taylor lecture.

The president examined his next shot. "Six ball. Far corner."

"Gamesmanship, Morgan?" His use of the president's first name was meant to put Taylor down.

"In a moment." Taylor smiled broadly.

The cue ball connected dead on, and now the six was off the table.

"Sorry, sometimes the straight approach is the hardest," Taylor said with a slight laugh.

Patrick did not laugh.

"So with that in mind, I'll do my best with you."

Patrick stood sharply.

"Please, Mr. Speaker. This is important." The president paused. "Very. Take a seat. You'll want to hear me out."

Duke Patrick sat and raised his glass again.

"Despite our previous conversations, we both know you still have your eyes on this job. And you've gone so far as to discuss such plans with the vice president."

"Hold on!" Patrick interrupted

"You hold on, Mr. Speaker. You'll have an opportunity to talk, if you so wish when I'm through, but right now you'll listen."

Patrick settled down again.

"Thank you." Taylor chalked the pool stick as he continued. "Personally, I have a four-part approach to this job. It's fairly easy to remember. In case you ever need it, consider it a hand-me-down. Me to you. Important ideas I learned from my predecessors.

"Four considerations to keep in mind as president. First, no matter what trouble comes your way, your job is to pump the brakes. Slow things down. Give yourself, and everyone else, time to think. You can make a bad situation worse by acting hastily. At the end of the day you can always use the hammer, but that's after you've considered all the ramifications. And even then there are times to double-pump those brakes. Evaluate what's best for the country, not what's just best politically, and definitely not what's best for the president. That's the difference between running for president and being president. And that's just Number One."

Taylor didn't invite conversation. He moved on.

"Number Two. You realize that whatever reaches the president is complex enough that it hasn't been able to be solved down the line. Chances are, it's so complex that it will require a complex solution."

Taylor eyed his next shot but didn't take it.

"There's an inertia to the things that make it up the decision tree. By the time they hit the Oval Office, they're bigger than life. Or they're life and death. If you try to simplify the problem, you will fail. And because of that, people could or will die. Presidents who have mistaken complex issues for simple ones fail. So, you know what good presidents do, Duke?"

"Enlighten me."

"You pump the brakes again and again, which leads me to Number Three. You invite, no it's more than that, you put smart people in the room with you. People who will fundamentally disagree with you. As much as possible."

The president nodded to Bernie Bernstein, who waved back.

"You listen to them. And you disagree with most of them. You have to come to the realization that these fuckers may be smarter than you.

If they've earned their way into the administration, they've earned their way into the discussion. That doesn't mean you just give up and do what they say. You pump those brakes some more and think about the impact of the decision that you will have to make. Then you send them back to think about the same thing. More. Harder.

"Presidents make great decisions under great pressure," Taylor noted. "Kennedy: The Cuban Missile Crisis. Nixon: opening China. Obama: taking down Bin Laden. But presidents also make horrible decisions. You know their names, their record, their tweets, and their decisions."

Patrick finished his drink.

"One more lesson. One more Scotch."

While Bernsie poured a refill, Morgan Taylor sank the Seven Ball, an easy three-foot shot.

"Number Four. The press should never have a place in the decision tree. Never. The president leads. The press reports. You don't follow the press. The press follows you. And you never react to what the political opposition is feeding the press."

Now Morgan Taylor stood over Duke Patrick. It was not the first time he took the pose. The president vowed it would be the last.

"You're the political opposition, Duke. You're putting bait out for me, and I'm not going to take it."

Patrick looked away.

"But I digress. And I misstated something."

"What's that?" Duke Patrick said, hoping he'd soon be gone.

"There are actually five points I want to make. Quite related. Number Five is don't take the bait. Only a sociopath or a narcissist takes the bait. Or a weak president who values image over responsibility. And you, Mr. Speaker, have taken the bait from a foreign government."

Duke Patrick blanched. "Excuse me?"

Morgan Taylor ignored the question, turned, and sized up the table. He pointed to the pocket opposite him. With a quick hard shot, he sent the cue ball dead on to the Eight Ball. It angled off the two bumpers and rolled fast into the pocket directly in front of Patrick.

The Speaker of the House winced. *That's gamesmanship*, the president thought.

"Now, would you like to know how that happened?" the president asked.

. . .

Morgan Taylor explained the depth of the conspiracy and how Patrick's own efforts to undermine the administration would have played into the plan. And how any attempt to turn the Twenty-Fifth Amendment into a tool to unseat the president would have sped up North Korea's efforts to cripple America from the inside out.

As the Speaker listened, he realized he had come perilously close to the edge. Moreover, it was President Morgan Taylor who, with the conversation this night, saved him from falling to his political ruin.

"You could have let me fuck myself," Patrick said in a moment of uncharacteristic contrition. "You would have squashed me if it went public."

"Of course," Taylor said. "But there are things more important than our political differences."

Patrick, rarely, if ever self-effacing, lowered his head. "The country."

"Precisely, Mr. Speaker. The country. We both know you want to be president. You've gone so far as to try to turn my vice president."

Patrick took in a deep breath.

"You think I didn't know? That J3 wouldn't tell me?"

No admission would help the Speaker.

"My better judgment is to not trust you. Not now. Not ever. But circumstances have gotten ahead of better judgment. Right now, I need you. Depending upon information we're gathering, we may very well have to retaliate against a foreign government that you, seemingly unwittingly, have a connection with. Not to be indelicate, Mr. Speaker, you've been a useful idiot."

"Awfully harsh."

"Not my words. Lenin's. A fool to be manipulated."

"What do you need?" Patrick said, feeling utterly defeated.

"Your cooperation and your silence. We may need to take action. If we do, it cannot come to light. You deserve to know as Speaker of the House. For the sake of the country, you will never speak a word of it."

"Of what?"

"To be determined."

"How will I know it's done?"

"If and when I tell you."

"What about the House and Senate leadership, the intelligence committees, the foreign affairs committees? They'll need to be briefed."

The president's eyes narrowed to steely slits. "If and when, Congressman."

Patrick had never seen the look.

"Do you know what I mean when I say, 'keep a lid on this,' Mr. Speaker?"

"I do."

"Convince me right now!"

Taylor towered over Patrick. The Speaker felt he was a wounded animal about to be devoured by a more powerful creature in the food chain. A predator he had completely misjudged. He looked to Bernsie to pull the leash. He didn't. Duke Patrick could only get out of this himself.

"Mr. President, I pledge my support to you and the nation. You can count on me for bringing House committees in line." For good measure he added, "If and when. And I will work with Senate leadership. You alone will decide who knows what and when."

Taylor did not give any ground.

"Not good enough, Duke."

"I'm sorry, I don't understand."

"I want a letter that memorializes what you've done. An admission. Your attempt to coerce General Johnson."

"That's blackmail!"

"I prefer to call it an 'understanding,'" the president said with authority. "It stays in my desk for as long as I'm president and gets locked in a vault in my library thereafter. That is, as long as you keep up your end of the bargain. Step out of line, and you're dead on a national level. Actively and forever. You do your job in the House and who knows, you may one day earn your way to the Oval Office legitimately."

Duke Patrick slumped in his seat, sitting lower than he'd ever sat before.

"So, Mr. Speaker, do we have a deal?"

Patrick nodded. "I'll send it over later today."

"Actually…" The president cued his chief of staff who handed Patrick a White House folder with a blank sheet of paper inside. "…No better time than the present."

With that, the president gave him a pen. He added, "And there will be no other time. Only now."

Duke Patrick sucked in a long breath and sighed.

"Oh, when you're through, keep the pen," Morgan Taylor said. "The *president* has hundreds of them."

CHAPTER 97

THE DEMOCRATIC PEOPLE'S REPUBLIC OF KOREA
THREE DAYS LATER

"I have one other thing I need you to do. It will be even more dangerous, but it is absolutely essential."

Chin-wah Lee felt he had been playing Russian roulette for years. Now Jee Gyuen made it sound like every chamber had a bullet.

"What?" the North Korean traitor whispered as he dug into his box of movie popcorn.

Gyuen slipped a note into Lee's hand. Lee didn't rush to read it. When he did, he sighed deeply. *A bullet in every chamber aimed at his temple.*

He lowered his eyes and shook his head.

"It will be the last thing I ask," Gyuen said.

Now everything became clear to Chin-wah Lee. All of the malware he'd installed in North Korea's submarines. All of the chances he took.

"I promise," Gyuen added. "Nothing after this except waiting for the right time to get you out."

Chin-wah Lee, former student, close friend, now an enemy of his country ignored the movie on screen.

A bullet in every chamber, he thought again.

The long game, Gyuen remembered.

Lee finally agreed. He crumpled the note, mixed it with a handful of popcorn, and ate it.

The name and impact of the movie on screen wasn't lost to him. A recent government release. *Our Political Instructor.*

CHAPTER 98

THE SITUATION ROOM
TEN DAYS LATER

"Mr. President," Bernsie stated only seconds into the meeting. "Are you absolutely certain this is the best course of action?"

"No," Taylor replied. "…And yes."

The chief of staff had been in the loop on Lindstrom's arrest and confession and had heard the briefing on *Operation Edison*.

"They're a nuclear power on a short fuse!" Bernsie declared. "With ICBM capability. It's a step toward war."

"There will be no war. There will be no announcement. Nothing to cheer. No headlines here, or likely even there. Pyongyang may never acknowledge the event. But they may suspect. Better they do."

The president drew in a deep breath.

"The regime attacked us under the radar. We'll respond even deeper. General Pollack, you're up."

Joint Chiefs Chairman Pollack stood next to a forty-two-inch video monitor and moved through a series of satellite images. He described new seawalls and T-head and L-shaped piers at Nopyong-ni and Sinpo South shipyards. North Korean submarines slipping into docks at night. Flat-bed trucks driving up to new buildings, harbor adjacent. Buildings, with sea entry, 738 feet long. Long enough to house attack subs.

Satellite pictures showed heavy-lift cranes just outside the structures, off-loading large crates. Crates, Pollack noted, that were transported into the buildings. Crates that measured slightly bigger than ballistic missiles. Crates determined by American intelligence with one hundred percent certainty to contain ballistic missiles.

"What North Korea can't reach with land-launched missiles, they can with their submarine fleet. The enemy is more prepared than ever."

Pollack employed "enemy" with unquestionable emphasis. He continued, "And they have already attacked the homeland."

Homeland Secretary Grigoryan nodded in agreement.

"Our mission is to remove that threat. We have the means."

Attorney General Goldman, sitting midway down the table opposite the monitors cleared her throat. It drew the president's attention.

"Eve? A thought?"

"A concern, Mr. President." She took a sip of water from a White House-embossed glass at her fingertips.

"Do you plan on proceeding under the terms of the War Powers Act, which requires consent of Congress? The law requires you to do so within forty-eight hours of sending U.S. forces into action abroad."

"Due to the fact that we will not be sending U.S. forces into action, I have decided not to notify the leadership or seek approval under the War Powers Act."

"And what about notifying the Congressional leadership, Mr. President?"

"I will inform the Speaker of the House. Rest assured, he won't be a problem."

Bernsie nearly choked on the comment.

"He understands the highly secretive nature of this mission," Taylor continued. "He has personally assured me that it will remain out of the political arena."

Taylor did not say how or why he extracted that assurance from Duke Patrick.

"No U.S. forces will fire a shot in any traditional sense, though actual shots have been fired against us. Our means will be strictly covert."

Eve Goldman nodded. She'd asked the question she needed to ask and had gotten a definitive answer. The former federal prosecutor, Harvard law school professor, and now the nation's highest legal mind swallowed hard wondering what the definition of war really was any more.

"There will be fallout," the chairman of the Joint Chiefs said as he clicked on the next slide, a picture North Korean dictator flanked by his military command. "He fears his generals probably more than us. The enemy within. If they view him as weak, they'll end the dynasty with a bullet. And if that happens, we don't know what the next Pyongyang regime will look like. We don't have enough intelligence to know. On the other hand, our mission will likely lead to some cleaning house. Relatives. Generals. Civilians. It won't be pretty."

The euphemism wasn't lost on anyone. General Pollack switched off the photograph. A White House logo returned to the screen.

Taylor scanned the room for reaction. He saw clenched mouths. Straight lines across everyone's lips. No smiles. No frowns. They were in.

"Thank you, General Pollack."

The president was now ready to tee up the mission, long-under Jack Evans's direction and conducted in collaboration with the Defense Intelligence Agency and Navy Intelligence.

"Director Evans, you may continue."

"Thank you, Mr. President." The CIA director stood. "I have no visual aids. This is absolutely SCI."

Everyone knew what the term meant. *Sensitive Compartmented Information.* The press had an unofficial term for the classification: Above Top Secret.

"In five days, concluding by day eight, most of the firepower held within the submarine fleet of the Democratic People's Republic of Korea will cease to exist."

Evans kept it completely clinical. He went on to explain the deep cover operative and his recruit in North Korea. No names. He reviewed the planning and the strategy, the dangers of exposure, and the need to get the assets out at the appropriate time. Success depended upon secrecy. But the risks were great.

"Can they figure it out?" Bernsie asked. "From what I know, computers leave digital footprints."

"They do. But onboard these will appear as false orders from command. And they may never be discovered after the fact."

"You mean erased?"

"Lost, Mr. Bernstein. There will be no evidence of malware implanted at the source, short of recovery. And recovery will take a long time and be expensive. And the virus, once activated, will do its job."

The job was completely understood.

"How will they be activated?" Bernsie asked.

"Fraudulently."

"What the hell does that mean?"

"You don't want to know, Bernsie," the president said. "Believe me, you don't want to know."

CHAPTER 99

SOMEWHERE IN THE PACIFIC OCEAN
NINE DAYS LATER

"New orders, captain."

CDR Nat Segaloff had expected them. Maybe not today. But they had been on his mind for five years. The last month with greater urgency. Ever since the secretive briefing at Point Loma Submarine Base in San Diego, California.

"I'll take them in my quarters."

Segaloff, an eighteen-year veteran with three years commanding a nuclear-powered Los Angeles Class fast-attack submarine, opened his laptop, keyed in a day-specific password and three other letter/number string-outs only he knew. Any of them inputted wrong would have crashed the program. He did it correctly.

Next, he typed in the message as transmitted from USAPACFLT. Decoded, it was as expected. A mission he and his chief communications officer had prepared for. *Edison.*

He copied the new course direction, rendezvous times, and another set of numbers. Radio frequencies. The *USS Chicago* was the designated messenger once North Korea's fleet was told to surface.

INDIAN NAVY RADIO BASE
NEAR PUDUR VILLAGE
TELANGANA, INDIA
FIVE DAYS LATER

Rear Admiral Arun Sinh Rawat greeted the Americans, two uniformed and one plain-clothed, at the newly completed navy radio facility in India's Damagundam Reserve Forest.

"I'm sure you gentlemen would like to freshen up," Sinh Rawat said to the three travelers from Washington. "We have three hours before our scheduled transmission."

The lead American gave his watch a quick glance. "Two hours, fifty-three minutes, admiral. Let's run through the procedure. We're fine. We had a break before we left New Delhi."

It had been a needed break. Showers and a warm meal in a private hangar. Needed after the thirty-seven-hour flight on the Navy's C-20D Gulfstream. The one-stop Emirates flight from Dulles to Hyderabad would have been quicker, by fourteen hours, but too public. Instead, they flew from Joint Base Andrews to Naval Air Station North Island in San Diego, onto Joint Base Pearl Harbor, Hickham, with another refueling stop at Naval Air Facility, Miswawa, Japan. The next long leg to New Delhi took thirteen hours and two more stops. The final hop to Rajiv Hyderabad International Airport in Shamshabad was just under two hours.

Sinh Rawat, a distinguished Navy admiral, stood eye level to the square-jawed Drivas. But he felt inches shorter in stature and experience. They'd never met before, but the personal visit by Admiral Jim Drivas, who also served as Director of the National Security Agency, made this all the more important and secretive. Drivas was accompanied by an equally impressive colleague, Admiral Walter Conn, the Chief of Naval Operations. A third man, an NSA agent, wearing a black sports jacket, black pull-over shirt, and black pants remained nameless. But today, the contents in his attaché case made him the most important member of the team.

Admiral Sinh Rawat escorted the Americans through the sprawling facility carved out of 2,900 acres of the humid Indian forest. They walked briskly. The hallways had been cleared. The orders were that no one except IT officers with the highest-level security clearance would have access to the guests during the upcoming test.

Except it wasn't a test.

For a time, India was only the third country known to have such a radio facility. The site transmitted signals on Extremely Low Frequency radio frequencies, abbreviated as ELF. Russia had its transmission base station. The United States had operated its own from 1989 to 2004 but abandoned them in the response to local Wisconsin and Michigan opposition where transmitters were housed. But there was a fourth.

The particulars of the frequencies and the reach of their signals required miles of antenna, sophisticated technology, and extreme secrecy. Their purpose was to reach submarines on patrol and underwater on the seventy-six Hz band. On the negative side, there were fears of debilitating effects on locales.

Normally, submarines need to trail a large retractable buoyant antenna or surface to receive radio transmissions. But such antennas on conning towers when submariners come up to periscope depth risked detection. ELF was developed because the emissions are able to penetrate through several hundred feet of salt water, which normally absorbs most RF radiation. ELF technology also provided a solution to radio disruption from electromagnetic pulses from high-level nuclear blasts. The original system design allowed submariners to receive small but critical messages even in the event of a nuclear exchange.

A sub's radio room equipped with an ELF receiver is constantly listening for a base message. However, because of the physics of Extremely Low Frequency, transmission is slow and short. Typically a brief command order.

American submarines were equipped to receive ELF. So were Russian and now Indian subs. But another country was developing its own ELF system as their patrols explored well beyond home waters.

The Democratic People's Republic of Korea had an experimental home base, and its ballistic missile submarines were tuned in.

In exactly two hours and fifty minutes, the North Korean submarine fleet would receive an order sent through the Indian Navy ELF transmitters from a drive currently inside the attaché case carried by a CIA operative. Specific day codes and North Korean fleet Satellite Communications (SATCOM) high frequencies had been smuggled out of a submarine base by a deep cover mole. The specific frequencies best suited to reach the submarines change with time of day and ionospheric propagation, but the information was considered completely reliable. Drivas hoped to meet the CIA operative someday. Chin-wah Lee.

SOMEWHERE IN THE PACIFIC OCEAN
THE SAME TIME

"Dive, make your depth six fife feet," CDR Segaloff said calmly.

"Depth six fife feet. Dive. Aye," came the acknowledgement.

Segaloff looked at his watch, then the map. After the depth correction, another order.

"Steer course two four-fife. Bearing ze-ro ze-ro tree."

The orders were understood and repeated.

"Speed ze-ro nin-er knots."

Segaloff made four more adjustments in the next two hours and forty-five minutes. Then he gave the order to bring the *USS Chicago* to periscope depth and to slow to three knots.

If everything proceeded according to mission schedule, the sub would receive a short, encrypted radio blast from an orbiting satellite in precisely six minutes.

The bridge crew acted with precision. Counting seconds, consulting the clock. It felt more vital than a drill. That sense of urgency kept everyone on alert; sharp, ready for the next order, whatever it might be.

INDIAN NAVY RADIO BASE
THREE MINUTES LATER

"System is a go, sir," reported the Indian IT Officer. "Online." The young lieutenant's job today was to make certain the American's drive talked to the Indian ELF computer. It did. Their three tests earlier confirmed it. But now they were very close to execution.

"Thank you," Admiral Arun Sinh Rawat replied calmly. He turned to the system administrator, charged with maintaining the applications. His job today, to make certain there would be no backups of the data once released. It would go out in the ether and never exist again.

"Commander, are we clear on system protocol?"

"Yes, sir. Confirmed as ordered."

Next, Sinh Rawat addressed the network administrator whose head was buried in his computer monitor. "Mr. Mukherji, how are we looking?"

"Ready for the command, sir."

The NSA chief and chief of Naval Operations stood back. The CIA operative, still unnamed, double-checked everything himself. He gave Admiral Drivas a nod.

5,451 NAUTICAL MILES AWAY
THE SAME TIME

CDR Nat Segaloff didn't question his orders, but that didn't mean he would sleep well. Not tonight. Maybe not ever again. In all his years, he had never fired a missile or a torpedo other than during controlled exercises. He'd patrolled the Earth's oceans in loyal service of the United States. He had served with distinction and honor. He would do so again today but with private regrets.

INDIAN NAVY RADIO BASE
THREE MINUTES LATER

"Sixty seconds," the IT officer stated.

"Sixty seconds," repeated the system administrator. "Systems good."

"Sixty seconds," confirmed the network administrator.

And for the next fifty-five seconds the control room in the middle of an Indian forest reserve was stone cold silent

Then, a countdown as if it were the launch of a rocket. But it wasn't. The network administer started in monotone at ten. He stopped at one, but there really wasn't anything physical to do. The command had been programmed into the ELF computers. At the speed of light, it traveled through one hundred sixty-five miles of underground cables, then a fourteen mile long antenna strung up on hundreds of forty-foot poles across dozens of miles of cleared Indian forest.

Because of the nature of Extremely Low Frequency transmissions and the size of the radio facility, the signal traveled around the globe. But it was intended for specific radio receivers tuned to a specific frequency; receivers that were onboard the North Korean submarine fleet on patrol and submerged.

주문을받을 표면

ABOARD FORTY-THREE SUBMARINES
OF THE KOREAN PEOPLE'S NAVY
THE SAME TIME

There had been ELF test transmissions in the recent past. All from North Korea's own new facility. There was no reason to believe this message would be any different. In any case, they couldn't request confirmation while submerged. And once decrypted, it was not to be questioned. Every vessel followed the command:

Surface to receive orders

CHAPTER 100

PACIFIC OCEAN
ABOARD THE *USS CHICAGO*

Segaloff had two more years before retirement. After today, he wondered whether he'd make it.

"Cassie, one minute."

Segaloff had already brought the *Chicago* to periscope depth for the HF antenna to break the surface. He estimated that considering the low power transmission coupled with solar flux and geomagnetic activity, most of NK's submarine fleet in the Northwest Pacific would receive the burst. If necessary, the commander suspected that the NSA had the ability to hack into Pyongyang's limited SATCOM network and broadcast a backup high frequency command to the remainder of the attack fleet. The percentage would increase, but he'd never know. Even more to the point, he didn't want to. The responsibility he'd been briefed on and about to carry out would weigh on him the rest of his life.

"One minute, sir," replied LT Cassie Donohue. Donohue was an expert in communications, SOund NAvigation and Ranging (SONAR), and onboard weapons systems. Everything found its way through her computers including a special program, brought onboard by people who made her nervous. It had been locked in the commander's safe until today. Until an hour ago when she loaded it.

All she had to do was hit ENTER. But ten seconds before it was time, CDR Segaloff reached over her shoulder and whispered, "Stand down, Cassie. I'll do this."

With a steady hand, Segaloff pressed the computer key and accepted responsibility for the action. It sent a transmission to all the Korean People's Navy submarines that had surfaced. No actual words in the burst; nothing to be decoded by a technician. But the computers recognized the code. It instantly burrowed into the malware embedded by Chin-wah Lee. And then all hell broke loose submarine-by-submarine.

. . .

North Korea's ballistic submarine fleet dove. Not by any captain's commands, but by the malware that triggered and blocked all counter orders. Some subs angled nearly straight down. Others at obtuse angles. All suffered a combination of failing life support systems, torpedo breeches, and treacherous openings into the pressure hull forced by an unseen hand. The dying was horrible, but fast; beyond the limits of human perception. All told, the Democratic People's Republic of Korea lost more than 1,950 souls. Submarines from the East and West Sea. The entire attack fleet. All twenty-two Chinese Romeo-class subs, seven regime-built Romeos, three former Soviet Whiskey class vessels, and eighteen smaller Sinpo and Sang-O class submarines.

The full extent of the catastrophic loss wasn't known to Pyongyang for days. Not until submarine commanders failed to surface to report in or receive new operating instructions. Not until the first subs due for maintenance failed to arrive.

North Korea's silent service launch capability all but evaporated. And with no one else to blame, the Supreme Leader quickly charged his Navy admirals with incompetence. Investigators began investigating. Eighteen were rounded up and drowned. Another twelve lined up to be obliterated with anti-aircraft guns.

It was an enormous tragedy the dictator couldn't publicize or politicize. Nine days later, China quietly reported to Pyongyang about an unspecified HF radio burst it had monitored on an NK satellite frequency. Nothing pointed to any foreign players and even the Chinese had failed to hear and therefore DFed (Direction Find) the burst from the *Chicago*.

Ultimately, North Korea announced the tragic loss of one submarine. The Supreme Leader praised the heroism of the crew as they tried to bring their ship to the surface; all invented to serve propagandistic purposes. He proclaimed there'd soon be a movie dramatizing their bravery. All heroes to the Democratic People's Republic of Korea. And then he moved on, or tried to.

But there was another loss he felt more personally than the thousands who obediently followed him. His old private school friend from Switzerland; the one who had been in such a great position to wreak true havoc on America, was dead.

All in all, things had not gone well in the Supreme Leader of North Korea's twisted geo-political world. He tore a map of the United States off his wall. A map that looked very much like one in Scott Roarke's White House office.

CHAPTER 101

THE DEMOCRATIC PEOPLE'S REPUBLIC OF KOREA
TWO WEEKS LATER

Jee Gyuen received a coded communiqué. A handoff from his own contact in Pyongyang. A street vender.

Time to go. He disagreed. Still too soon to pull out Chin-wah Lee. And without Lee, he wasn't ready to leave.

Lee nervously reported that government secret police were investigating. Some for a few days; others who kept returning. All appeared worried about their own well-being and desperate to come up with something.

"They won't find anything," Gyuen told Chin-wah Lee as they walked off to dinner one night. He tried to be his reassuringly best.

"But they can still call me in. Question. Torture me."

Lee's nervousness could give him away. But Jee Gyuen wanted more time. Again the long game. Always the long game.

"Soon," I promise.

"You promised me before," Lee said.

"I have. And my promise stands."

The rest of the evening they did what they normally did. They went to a movie. While watching the 2005 comedy, *Comrade Supreme Leader Goes Flying*, Gyuen tried to figure things out. Indeed, America owed Lee a great debt of gratitude, let alone safe passage out of the country. America also owed him a life to enjoy and access to his promised Fidelity Investments that had done quite well, especially the international mutual funds. But most of all, Jee Gyuen owed him.

"One month, maybe two. If you leave too quickly, they will make assumptions. Assumptions become connections. Connections become facts. We have to wait."

Chin-wah Lee shivered.

"They'll figure it out," he said during a particularly noisy moment in a film.

"You have to trust me," Gyuen said, wanting to escape every bit as much as Lee. "You first. Then me." Gyuen had already worked out a trip to China where he would get lost in the system. "And someday we'll even get together and have a beer in the open. Free."

Lee settled into his theater seat. *One month, or two?* He would have to make it.

"Request a transfer," Gyuen whispered. "Start looking depressed. Say you're worried about your friends."

"They've only acknowledged one sub."

"But worry can be real. Show that you're worried. It's human. Even here," Gyuen whispered. "Begin making little mistakes. Not many. Not big ones. The kind that people make when they're preoccupied. Apologize. Promise to improve. But cry. Cry for the loss of the country. Soon, they'll respond. You'll get a new assignment. You'll tell me goodbye. Completely understandable."

"And then?"

"And then you will leave a note, and overcome with grief, you will commit suicide by jumping off a cliff into the sea. Poetic justice." Gyuen patted Lee's leg. "An honorable death. Your body will not be found. But, you have to trust me."

Chin-wah Lee had for years. Now he would just have to trust his old mentor, his spymaster, a bit longer. *One month, maybe two.* And for the first time, he wondered if Jee Gyuen was even his real name.

EPILOGUE

HAMILTON, BERMUDA

THANKSGIVING

Scott Roarke and Katie Kessler walked down to the ocean from the Echo Beach Resort Hotel. A needed vacation. A needed romantic vacation. He paced himself. The doctors at Walter Reed National Medical Center told him to take it slowly. He was lucky to be alive. The president went a step further. He ordered Roarke to take time to fully recover. But at the end of the day, every day, no one really told Scott Roarke what to do until now.

His financée had a say. A deciding vote. "Bermuda!"

"We have two weeks, Agent Roarke," she said. "Two weeks to ourselves."

Roarke wanted it, too. But then he had wanted to start a business with Vinnie D'Angelo. Hopes and wishes were in short supply. His love for Katie Kessler was the exception.

CAMBRIDGE, MA
THE SAME TIME

The young immigrant walked into the bar at Grendel's Den in Harvard Square. He had a new name and a new identity. It was early afternoon. Too early for most patrons to begin drinking. He took a seat in the middle of the bar and ordered a soda. He was still getting used to name brands.

"What kind?" the bartender asked.

"A Coca-Cola?"

"Coming up."

He was aware of someone sitting next to him. He automatically shifted, turning away. Old habits from a repressive society.

"Give our friend a Sam Adams," the man said slapping down a twenty. "It's time he experiences a true Boston beer."

The man formerly known as Chin-wah Lee swiveled on his bar stool. His hair was longer and his jeans and turtle neck truly Western. The man next to him offered his hand.

"Really, I think you'll like it. I'm Harry Hwang. Nice to meet you."

The North Korean escapee smiled. A sly, relieved smile. He instantly recognized the patron and teared up.

"Harry Hwang?" he replied to his old teacher, friend, and handler in somewhat halting English.

"That's it. Hwang. A proud family name. And you? What's yours?"

"Tom. Tom Wah. It's Korean," he proudly exclaimed. "I'll take that beer. And I'll tell you what, Harry. This time, it's my treat," he said wiping his eyes. He could afford it, too. His portfolio was doing very well. But then, Harry Hwang knew that.

ACKNOWLEDGMENTS

With this fourth book in my Executive Series, I want to thank wonderful family, friends and colleagues who helped me again, and new experts who provided critical research. Of course, on a personal level there's Sasha, Zach, and Jake Grossman, Tory Sparkman, and my wife, Helene Seifer. At Diversion Books, my thanks go out to Keith Wallman, Editor in Chief, who I can count as a wonderful new friend; Scott Waxman, Diversion CEO and Founder; and the entire Diversion Books creative team that contributed to the design and publication of *Executive Force*.

For expert research in military command, hardware, and armaments I turned again to my lifelong friend and decorated Army veteran Bruce Coons. Special thanks also go to the United States Navy Public Affairs Office and my direct contact, CDR Sarah Self-Kyler, Public Affairs Officer, U.S. Submarine Force and her colleagues who provided additional editorial advice as I navigated tricky naval scenes.

Thanks, as well, to attorney Jim Harris for reviewing the Constitutional issues, Sandi Goldfarb for her ongoing editorial and marketing assistance, and authors Joseph Finder, Kimberley Howe, WG Griffiths, Brad Meltzer, and fellow members of the International Thriller Writers Association. Also, sincere thanks to Emerson College history professor Michael Brown, a former colleague and forever friend, as well as Vin DiBona, Michael O'Rourke and RJ Haines who continue to make producing television shows fulfilling. And I can't forget Stan and Debbie Deutsch, Leslie and Adam Lobel, Janis and Chuck Barquist, Jeffrey and Louise Davis, Michael Andreas, Julie Fleischer, Peter and Wendy Lewis, Peter and Barbara Schwartz, Debra and Mark Masuoka, Fred Putman, Mitch Freedman and Tom Trent—all for their endless support.

THE EXECUTIVE SERIES

BY GARY GROSSMAN

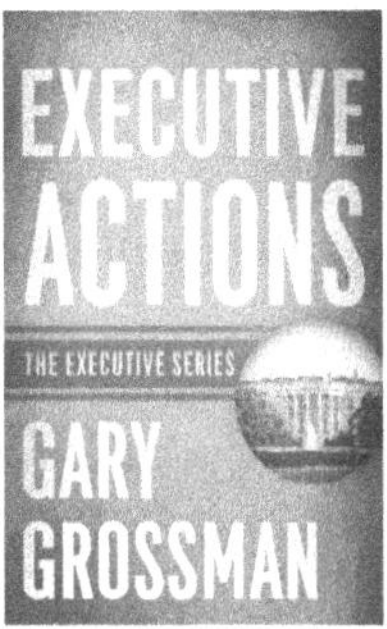

In *Executive Actions*, an assassin takes aim at a Presidential candidate during a primary stump speech in upstate New York. From the very first page, the heart-stopping thriller culls events from today's headlines, intersecting with a scenario that's shockingly real: An insidious plot hatched in the old days of the Soviet Union continues to grow to fruition in the hands of a power hungry, revengeful Middle East despot. At its core, a sleeper is awakened to take a prominent role in American life

"*Executive Actions* is a masterpiece of suspense; powerfully written and filled with wildly imaginative twists. Get ready to lose yourself in a hell of a story."

—Michael Palmer, *New York Times* best-selling author

"A sprawling, captivating political thriller, filled with meticulously researched details and riveting characters. You won't be able to put it down."

—Bruce Feirstein, James Bond screenwriter,
New York Times best-selling author

Executive Treason, Grossman's follow-up to *Executive Actions,* explodes with surprises from the Oval Office to the cockpit of Air Force One, right to Middle America and the broadcast studios of an immensely powerful national talk radio host with devious political motives of his own. With a subplot rooted in American history and a crossover to the power of hate radio, *Executive Treason* delivers "political reality" too possible to ignore.

"Executive Treason is intricate, taut, and completely mesmerizing, A virtuoso tale. Highly recommended!"

—Dale Brown, *New York Times* best-selling author

"More chilling than science fiction. Gary Grossman shows how the media itself can become a weapon of mass destruction. You'll never listen to talk radio again without a shiver going down your spine."

—Gary Goldman, Screenwriter *Total Recall, Next, Navy Seals,* Executive Producer, *Minority Report*

Executive Command, the third book in Grossman's acclaimed Executive series, uncovers a terrorist plot that targets America's most vital and vulnerable natural resource—water. With hundreds of thousands of water systems unprotected, the country is at risk every day. The masterful characters woven through *Executive Actions* and *Executive Treason* meet again with explosive results, worthy of actual front page attention. It's a sharp warning of what could happen now.

"*Executive Command* mixes terrorists, politics, drug gangs, and technology in nonstop action! So real it's scary!"

—Larry Bond, *New York Times* best-selling author

"Moving at break-neck speed and nothing short of sensational. Grossman is a master storyteller who sets you up and delivers. *Executive Command* is not just a great book, it's a riveting experience!"

—W.G. Griffiths, international best-selling author

GARY GROSSMAN's first novel, *Executive Actions*, quickly propelled him into the world of geo-political thrillers. *Executive Treason* and *Executive Command*, further tapped Grossman's experience as a journalist, newspaper columnist, documentary television producer, reporter, media historian, and playwright. His bestselling *Executive* trilogy was followed by *Old Earth*, a geological thriller that spans all time, and *Red Hotel*, a gripping novel co-written with international hotel executive Ed Fuller that delves into the threat of new Russian expansionism. Grossman's work has garnered international praise, taking top book honors at festivals in the U.S. and Europe.

Grossman has written for the *Boston Globe*, and *Boston Herald American*, and contributed to the *New York Times*. He covered presidential campaigns for WBZ-TV in Boston, and has produced more than 10,000 television series and specials for NBC News, CNN, NBC, ABC, CBS, FOX, and thirty-five cable networks.

He is a multiple Emmy Award winning producer. He served as chair of the Government Affairs Committee for the Caucus for Television, Producers, Writers and Directors, and is a member of the International Thriller Writers Association and Military Writers Society of America. He is a trustee at Emerson College and serves on the Boston University Metropolitan College Advisory Board. Grossman has taught at Emerson College, Boston University, USC, and currently Loyola Marymount University. He is a contributing editor to *Media Ethics Magazine*.

Contact Gary Grossman

Website: www.garygrossman.com Twitter: @garygrossman1